Public Enemies

ANN AGUIRRE

FEIWEL AND FRIENDS

NEW YORK

A FEIWEL AND FRIENDS BOOK
An Imprint of Macmillan

PUBLIC ENEMIES. Copyright © 2015 by Ann Aguirre. All rights
reserved. Printed in the United States of America by R. R.
Donnelley & Sons Company, Harrisonburg, Virginia. For
information, address Feiwel and Friends, 175 Fifth Avenue,
New York, N.Y. 10010.

Feiwel and Friends books may be purchased for business or
promotional use. For information on bulk purchases, please contact
the Macmillan Corporate and Premium Sales Department at (800)
221-7945 x5442 or by e-mail at specialmarkets@macmillan.com.

Library of Congress Cataloging-in-Publication Data Available

ISBN: 978-1-250-02466-4 (hardcover) / 978-1-250-08691-4 (ebook) /
978-1-250-07420-1 (international edition)

Book design by Ashley Halsey

Feiwel and Friends logo designed by Filomena Tuosto

First Edition: 2015

10 9 8 7 6 5 4 3 2 1

macteenbooks.com

For the warriors, fighting
for truth, equality, or freedom.

To quote Winston Churchill,
"We shall never surrender."

DARKNESS
IN PARADISE

Six days before Christmas, two thugs snatched me off the side-walk and shoved me into a black panel van.

I would've been terrified if I hadn't been expecting . . . something. Not necessarily a kidnapping, but I'd known there would be a countermove at some point. My main question came from wondering if this was Wedderburn showing me who was boss, the opposition, which meant either Dwyer or Fell, or more mysterious yet—the Harbinger. As I speculated in silence, the iron-faced, concrete-jawed goons gave no sign who'd sent them.

Boston sped by with me pressing a cheek to the window, leaving an imprint on the foggy glass. My heart hammered despite my best efforts to stay calm and my breath came in tiny gulps. *I'm so in over my head.* This time, my boyfriend couldn't rescue me; there would be no more of Kian popping in when I needed him because he was no longer bound to the immortal game—no more access to cool powers—and I'd burned my last favor in cutting him loose.

Eventually, the van parked in a questionable neighborhood not far from the docks. I glanced between the two men up front. One African-American, the other Nordic looking, they were of similar size and shape, roughly six four, with shoulders that seemed five feet wide. Their demeanor and military haircuts made me think they had law enforcement or Special Forces backgrounds, and the coldness in their eyes assured me there was no point in asking for either answers or mercy.

"Get out of the vehicle, miss." The gravelly command came from the driver. As he glanced over his shoulder to face me in the shadowy interior, his dark eyes seemed, at first, to have no pupils, just like the creepy children that followed the bag man around. I couldn't think about that thing without a shudder of revulsion—and the horrifying certainty that it had my mother's head. A chill swept over me.

"Not until you tell me who I'm visiting."

"I could make you," the other one said quietly. "But that would be . . . unpleasant." A faint accent made me think he was German.

The driver shrugged as he climbed out and opened the back doors, secured from the outside. "Eh. She'll find out soon enough, no?" To me, he added, "The Harbinger requests the pleasure of your company." His faux-courtesy didn't escape me, but since I'd gotten the information I asked for, I hopped down under my own steam.

Could be worse. But I was supposed to meet Kian ten minutes ago.

It wouldn't take long for him to realize something had gone hideously wrong. I just hoped he had more sense than to alarm my dad. This wasn't something he could help with, so it was better for him to stay in the lab as he had since my mom's passing, oblivious to the world.

And to me, I thought.

2

The pang as the driver slammed the van door behind me felt more like a chest quake. My cardiac cavity echoed, just a bone cage holding my heart hostage. Intellectually, I knew I couldn't have predicted all possible outcomes . . . and I only ever had three favors. Most of the Teflon crew was dead, and I still didn't know if it had been Wedderburn or the opposition. While I'd managed to protect my best friend, Vi, I didn't realize my mom might be targeted until it was too late. Her death still haunted me. Emotionally, I was all raw meat and rivers of remorse.

The building in front of me seemed like a warehouse, pretty rundown too. Red brick had faded to a rusty orange and at least half the windows were broken or boarded up. Inhaling deeply, I marked the smell of salt water, damp, rotting wood, and a hint of old fish. A newspaper blew across the alley, only to get bogged down in a puddle formed by the broken pavement. It seemed like a major independent player in the immortal game could afford a better hideout, but maybe that was the whole point—misdirection or something. The driver beckoned while the German dude unchained heavy-duty steel doors. They were the newest part of the building, kind of odd.

"Anyone could crawl through one of those broken windows," I pointed out.

Blond Giant offered a scary smile. "That's the whole point."

I thought that was all I'd get, but the driver explained, "The doors are a warning. If people choose not to heed it, then they are, of course, welcome to come inside and play."

"With the Harbinger." I didn't imagine that ended well for random vandals and trespassers but I had problems of my own. "Why does he want to see me?"

The doors banged open as the chains fell away. "Go and find out."

Inside, it was dark in contrast to the relative brightness of a winter day. Shivering, I pulled up the collar of my red coat and took a single step into the overwhelming gloom. The doors slammed shut behind me, and as I heard the men fastening the chains, it was all I could do to keep from screaming for help like a damsel tied to the train tracks. There was no stopping the tremors that worked over me, leaving my legs unsteady.

"Edie Kramer." The whisper echoed all around me, making my skin crawl.

The shadows were so deep and dark, it couldn't be natural. Some ambient light should've filtered in, however dirty the windows, but this cold, damp space felt like an open grave, as if in the next step, I'd tumble six feet down and someone would begin shoveling loose dirt onto my terrified, upturned face. My breathing became audible, the frightened rasp of a child finding that the light switch doesn't work and there is *most definitely* someone else in the room.

"Yes," I managed to say.

I slowed to near immobility, feeling my way forward with outstretched fingertips. This was every haunted house I ever went in, only without the surety that nobody would hurt me and that whatever ghastly thing I touched wouldn't be real. My hearing sharpened, overcompensating for lack of vision. Something skittered on the floor. I froze as tiny feet ran over my Converse.

Just one. A rat, probably.

"I can see you perfectly." It was a light voice, teasing even, and the smile I heard in it made this predicament feel even worse. "Can't you find me?"

4

"Possibly," I said. "If you keep talking."

"I could guide you. If you trust me."

A startled laugh escaped me. "No. But thanks."

"You'd deny me a spot of entertainment?"

"Unless you find *this* to be the most fun ever, then yeah. Definitely."

"Fine then."

The flare of light made me squint, bringing the room into stinging focus. I shaded my eyes because the sudden shift didn't make it any easier for another minute or two. But soon, I could make out the premises, such as they were. The warehouse looked like a rave was held in 1999 and then nobody cleaned afterward. For all I knew, that might be true, as there was a judicious mix of filth, litter, animal scat, and dangling cobwebs. *This is pretty much the perfect place to dispose of a body.* Briefly I considered going out one of those broken windows, but I suspected if the Harbinger was this scary in a playful mood, I didn't want to test him.

Speaking of which, I still didn't see my host. "Where are you?" *Maybe he's invisible like the Cheshire Cat.*

"Chin up, dearling."

In reflex, I tilted my head back and spotted a dark figure perched like a bird of prey on the catwalk above. Something in the angles of his knees and elbows reminded me that this creature wasn't human. The Harbinger hammered the point home by taking a running leap and he didn't plummet so much as dance downward, as if stepping on unseen stones that broke his fall. He landed lightly and swept a theatrical bow, garbed in half a thrift shop, including tailcoat, top hat, black feathered vest, satin trousers, and antique gun boots, to say nothing of the gloriously ornate watch chain affixed not to a

5

timepiece, but a long-necked ceramic cat. Black hair tumbled to his waist, silver strands worked through like starlight.

For some reason, I found it difficult to focus on his face, and it left an afterburn in my mind's eye—a chaotic impression of unearthly beauty married to harrowing despair—scars in the earth full of uncut rubies and holocaust pits with wildflowers rioting along the edges. His eyes twinkled like summer lightning, but I couldn't hold his gaze. Being this close to him made me want to take a step back, as if breathing too close to him might electrocute me.

Damn. And Kian sought this creature out, bargained with it. For me. I have to be brave.

Feeling like Alice in Horrorland, I produced an unsteady curtsy, though I really needed a pinafore to pull it off. "Nice to meet you." I suspected the Harbinger knew I felt exactly the opposite, but there was no etiquette guide for an occasion like this one.

"So you're worth dying for, hm?" He circled me in slow, stalking steps, leaning in to sniff at me as if I possessed some exotic aroma.

"I hope it doesn't come to that," I answered, before I could think better of it.

He stilled, head cocking like a bird. "You don't want my protection? And here I've done such a thorough job of keeping nasty things away. Or did you think you'd defeated the mirror creatures on your own . . . through the magnificent advent of a towel?"

Shit. I *had* wondered if that was really enough, but when they didn't come after me again, I thought I must've stumbled on the solution.

"Thank you for keeping me safe," I said around a fear-flavored lump in my throat. "It's not that I don't appreciate it."

"But . . . ? I can taste the question and I'm in a good mood. Because of you, I shall most certainly feast. And soon."

What does that even mean?

"Does Kian *have* to die?" It was the stuff of fairy tales. He'd bargained away his last chip, his very life, to protect me. In doing so, he'd offered a gift I didn't want, couldn't exchange, and could never repay.

"You could take his place in the compact." The Harbinger made a smacking noise, uncomfortably between an air kiss and *you look delicious.* "Or you could trick someone else, I suppose. But I suspect your very prickly scruples wouldn't permit that."

Pain flickered to life, a constant heat in my stomach. "No."

"I find that fascinating."

"Do you?"

"Most creatures feel nothing so strongly as the need for self-preservation. Yet humanity occasionally produces bright sparks, capable of sacrifice."

"Is that why you wanted to see me?" I hadn't moved, and the Harbinger wasn't done circling. He put me in mind of a shark. I'd heard that if a shark ever stopped swimming, it would die. This being radiated the same hungry intensity, the same predatory drive.

"Partly. I wonder . . . if you would beg for your beloved's life."

"Would it do any good?" I asked.

"Dearling, no. I have to eat, don't I?"

Revulsion flooded upward, nearly choking me. "You mean—"

"I won't be charbroiling him, but life is energy, and there's no one to light candles or whisper my name in supplication. So what else am I to do?" Though his tone was blithe, I had the sense that he minded the latter more than he let on.

7

"They used to?"

"Once. But I was never popular," he admitted. "And this suits me. The trickster is better as a broker, I think."

"You don't play the game?" I thought I recalled Kian telling me that much.

"Only when I make the rules, which change according to my whim. The others take it all *so* seriously. Too much competition can be as tedious as too little, you know. Far more amusing to frolic on the fringes, ruining other people's schemes for the pure pleasure of it."

"I'd like you a hundred percent more if you told me you've made Wedderburn's life worse."

A laugh rang out, dizzying me, for it echoed in the warehouse, carrying with it a mad music and the flutter of a thousand beating wings. When I spun about, the Harbinger and I were alone, standing in a spotlight; I couldn't remember if the brightness fell that way before, but now I had the sense of standing on a stage before an invisible audience.

"All the time, pretty one. I complicate his plots and abet the sun god, then turn about as soon as the wind changes."

"I'm starting to understand why Kian approached you."

The Harbinger's tone turned serious like the ringing of a bell. "The only rule I respect comes from such agreements. So I've brought you here to suggest you enjoy the time you've got left with your darling. Don't waste energy seeking after a crack in the wall."

"Don't people usually do that when they're worried about someone finding a loophole?"

"*People,*" he said gently. "Little one, this is me being kind. Your beloved will not attempt to renege but I fear for *your* prospects if you interfere."

"But aren't you supposed to protect me, no matter what?"

The mad laughter came again, starting an avalanche of pain in my head. A trickle came from my nose, and I tasted copper in my throat. My vision flickered with black spots, the lights brightening until it felt as if my retinas were melting.

"Even from yourself? You do hold me in high esteem. I think . . . I like you, Edie Kramer. In the end, such a small thing may be enough to save you." His tone turned musing. "Or perhaps it'll ruin you entirely."

Entirely echoed inside my skull as I passed out. When I woke, the two henchmen were depositing me on the curb near my apartment building. You'd think two giants manhandling a girl in broad daylight would alarm somebody, but no one seemed overly concerned. I'd learned the hard way, however, that monsters could put on a normal face, making the horrific appear ordinary. So possibly to passersby, I looked like a rolled-up rug.

"Do you ever get used to him?" I asked them hoarsely.

The German ignored me, but the driver's dark eyes flickered toward me. Then he gave a minute shake of his head before hopping into the van and merging into traffic. Belatedly I checked my belongings: backpack, cell phone, yes, everything, check. As expected, I had five messages from Kian, wondering why I wasn't at the mall, since we'd planned to meet for some last-minute Christmas shopping.

Sorry, I texted. I'm on the way. Something came up.

Are you okay? Kian's response was immediate. He worried *so* much now that he couldn't get to me instantly if shit went down. But to my mind, it made things a little more . . . normal between us, when my life was so many shades of colossally screwed up. There was no way for me to be sure if I was still a catalyst or if I'd end up indentured in a few months, come graduation day. But that didn't scare me as much as the prospect of losing Kian.

He's terminal, my brain pointed out. *Four months to live.*

Fighting back a wave of anticipated grief, I ran for the subway. It was too early for the train to be full of commuters, but there were always students and people who defied description. I sat next to a railing to minimize contact and got off at the stop nearest the shopping center. Running kept me fit, so I wasn't too out of breath when I raced to meet Kian, who was still waiting outside, though I was over an hour late. His hands were icy, his cheeks red with cold, and his beautiful lips had taken on a distinctly blue tinge.

"Why didn't you dodge into a coffee shop?"

"I was afraid I'd miss you."

"Like I wouldn't text you if I didn't find you right away."

"I was concerned about you," he admitted, pulling me into his arms. "And they frown on nervous pacing in most cafés."

"Yeah, true. Are you ready to go in?"

"Not until you tell me why you were so late. I can tell something happened." He cupped my arms through my coat, staring down into my face with a laser-focused concern I'd never talk my way around.

"Don't I get a hello kiss first?" I tried.

His smile could've powered a nearby electrical substation. "Sure. But don't think I'll forget the question."

So much for that plan.

Yet I still wrapped my arms around his neck. He pulled me close, letting me snuggle into the open front of his down jacket. Each time Kian lowered his head, each time his lashes drifted shut, I tried to memorize everything about it—how he felt, how he tasted—because time wasn't on our side. Cupping his slightly raspy cheek in my palm, I stroked his jaw as he touched his lips to mine, so cool I shivered, but quickly warming with contact. Without waiting for him, I deepened the kiss, wanting to imprint on him, so that he'd never forget me, not even in a thousand lifetimes, timelines, what-the-hell-ever. For us the odds absolutely sucked. High school relationships usually crashed and burned anyway—without all of the supernatural death cards stacked against us.

"Wow," he breathed, countless moments later. "So. What happened?"

I stifled a sigh. There was no remedy but the truth, though I didn't imagine finding out would make him feel better. He had less power than ever before. "Promise me you won't freak."

"Conversations that start this way are more likely to agitate me, Edie."

"Okay, well." I led him toward the mall entrance, reckoning he was less likely to overreact with lots of people around. Inside, water burbled, tinted by changing lights, blue, yellow, red, back again. "Earlier, two guys shanghaied me, and . . . took me to the Harbinger."

Kian's look could've frozen the fountain into a skating pond.

HOLIDAY
HAUNTED

"What did he want? You didn't sign anything, did you? Even a verbal agreement—"

"No. I think he just wanted to get a look at me." *And to warn me that it was pointless to try and save you.* But I didn't say the second thing out loud.

"Were you scared?" Kian threaded his fingers through mine, leading me into the deceptive safety of a throng of Christmas shoppers.

Old women in knit twinsets mingled with younger people in designer labels. A few people already had on Christmas sweaters and sweatshirts, inviting us to deck the halls and share joy to the world. In my current mood I was more likely to win the Ebenezer award.

"These days I pretty much always am," I admitted quietly.

"I'm sorry. If there was anything else I could do—"

"Stop. You already did enough. Too much, in fact. I wish you cared half so much about saving yourself."

Changing the subject, he ignored that. "Have you decided about Vi's invitation?"

My best friend wanted my dad and me to visit for the holidays, but I didn't think he could handle being immersed in a happy family. Our wound had barely scabbed over, and we'd both start hemorrhaging if we had to watch Vi's mom bustle around the kitchen, fussing over our recent bereavement. On the other hand, the idea of spending Christmas in our eternally beige sublet apartment depressed the hell out of me.

"We're definitely not going."

This year, there was no Christmas tree, no decorations or preparation for what used to be a happy occasion. My mom always went overboard with the lights, making it so the tree could practically give you a seizure. I understood why my dad was hiding, submerging himself in work, but his behavior left me alone. Some days I wanted to scream at him, *You're not the only one who lost her.*

I miss you, Mom. Tears were always on tap, burning at the back of my eyes. It had been over a month, but there was always this wasteland in my head, just a blink away, and suddenly I was mentally in the cemetery, watching mourners drop flowers atop her casket. Trembling, I ran a hand through my hair, wondering if Kian could tell how much this hurt. Other than my great-aunt Edith, who was ancient when she died, I'd never lost anyone before. My private guilt only made this feel worse.

"I have an idea, if you're interested."

The fact that he never stopped trying to make things better helped . . . a little. "What?"

"We could convince your dad to get out of the city for a couple of days."

"And go where? Most places will be booked."

Kian sighed. "True. I'm not used to limitations like reservations."

Despite my mood, I couldn't restrain a laugh. "You worked for Wedderburn too long."

"Definitely."

"It wasn't a bad plan," I said, mostly to cheer him up. "But my dad wouldn't have gone for it anyway."

It would be a minor miracle if he didn't get up and go to work on Christmas, as if it were any other day. Since he did most of the cooking, I'd probably make a cheese sandwich and call it good. But Kian seemed troubled by the prospects of a bleak holiday, and maybe he had a point since it was our first together, and it might be our last too. That possibility made me clutch his hand tighter, prompting him to take a second look at me.

"Are you sure the Harbinger didn't do anything to you?"

To be honest, I couldn't be positive since I'd passed out near the tail end of the encounter. There was no way I was admitting that, however. "I was just trying to figure out what we can do to make the holidays better for my dad."

Kian paused outside a store but I didn't think he was seeing the mannequins garbed in white gowns with silver tinsel and lights decorating the display window like a winter wonderland. "Sometimes you just have to be patient."

"Well, I can't bring him back magically. But . . ." One possibility occurred to me. "We could decorate. And cook."

"As I recall, my efforts didn't impress you at Thanksgiving."

"Then you're in charge of the lights. You'll need to get them out of storage at the old place, though. Will that bother you?"

A flicker of his green eyes said the answer was yes, but Kian squared his shoulders. "Not a problem. After we're done shopping, I'll drop you off, pick them up, and swing by later."

"Cool. We should split up now." At his frown, I added, "How am I supposed to get you a present if you're right here the whole time?"

"You don't have to—"

"Don't tell me how to Christmas." I cocked a brow, silently daring him to keep talking.

"Fine. Is an hour long enough?"

"It should be." I already knew what I was getting.

Fifty-five minutes later, I headed back to the fountain with a couple of colorfully wrapped packages. Kian hadn't arrived yet, so I perched on the marble lip, absently counting the pennies at the bottom. None of them had been there long enough to turn, offering a constant coppery shimmer beneath the silver ripple of the water. The muted susurration of other shoppers provided a counterpoint to the rise and fall of the jets, orchestrated with a light show. As I stared, a shadow fell across the water, as if somebody were standing behind me. But when I turned, I saw no one.

A chill swept over me.

I got out my cell phone. Surveying the scene as if I were about to take a picture reassured me. Nothing weird showed up as I panned across. Nothing sinister here, right? There was an animatronic Santa across the way, waving in a merry, if robotic, fashion, from his prefab North Pole village. Beside him, they'd posted a sign indicating that you could meet a flesh-and-blood Saint Nick on the opposite side of the mall.

Still, I wasn't at ease when I turned back to the fountain. This time I caught a sliver of movement in my peripheral vision, and I remembered the Harbinger mentioning the mirror monsters. The reflective properties could be similar under the right conditions—did that mean the creatures could travel through water as well? It wasn't deep here, and I could *see* the specks in the concrete on the bottom.

There's nothing here.

"Ready?" Kian asked, startling me. I juggled my phone, and he caught it in a neat midair snatch. "Wow, you're jumpy."

"Yeah." I managed a smile. "Let's get out of here."

He lifted a small bag that looked like it might contain jewelry. "I'm done anyway."

"Oooh. You want to tease me, huh? Well, this one's yours." I showed him the box I'd had wrapped earlier.

"It's been a while," he said quietly.

"For what?"

"Since anyone thought of me at Christmas."

"What about your aunt and uncle?" I asked, before thinking better of it.

"She handled everything, and I always got regifted. Stuff they got the year before and nobody really wanted." His level tone belied how much it must've stung.

I thought of him at thirteen, his father and sister gone, his mother broken. His aunt should've made him feel welcome and loved, but instead, she saw him as a burden and treated him accordingly. Remembering his polyester nightmare of a dress shirt—presumably his best since he'd worn it on picture day—made me want to hug him, right here, right now.

So I did.

Though he seemed surprised, his arms went around me too, and he settled his chin on top of my head. "Hey. It's not a big deal."

"Maybe not to you."

He shifted so that his arm was around my shoulders, and with his other one, he took my bag. "You think there's anywhere we can buy a tree this late?"

"I'm sure we can get a fake one."

"Is that okay with you?"

I nodded. "My mom and dad always went together on December first to pick out a real one. So artificial is probably better."

Kian drove around for almost an hour until we found a six-foot assembly-required tree at a discount store. The box was damaged but all the parts were there. He crammed it into the back of the Mustang, and a surge of warmth quivered through me. *I have to save you,* I thought. *No matter what the Harbinger says. No matter what it takes.*

"I'll help you carry the tree," he offered, oblivious to my silent plans.

"Okay, thanks."

Unsurprisingly, the apartment was quiet and empty when I let us in. The night before last, my dad didn't even come home to sleep. I'd always known they were great partners, but until she was gone, I didn't realize how much my parents completed each other. Without my mom, my father was like a partial equation, a chemical reaction devoid of the catalyst that activated it.

"I need your key, Edie."

"Right." Swallowing a quiet ache, I dug it out for him.

"Be back in a bit."

As soon as the door shut behind him, I sliced open the Christmas tree carton and fell backward in a prickle of fake pine, augmented by aluminum and plastic. *There's no way this isn't a hot mess when I'm done.* Once I got started, however, the tree snapped together easily. It was butt ugly—with immense gaps between the branches. I fanned out the greenery as best I could, and by the time Kian came back, I had it looking . . . adequate. Not a high accolade, but maybe lights and tinsel would help. We were quiet as we decorated, decking out the tree while I remembered how it was when my mom was around. There should be carols blasting while the scent of my dad's Christmas cookies wafted through the apartment.

"Do you think your father will mind the influx of holiday spirit?"

"I doubt he'll even notice," I said, sadness washing over me.

"He'll snap out of it."

The retort popped out before I could stop it. "Did your mom?"

When Kian stilled, the glittery tinsel draped over his palms like treacherous pieces of silver, I felt like ten kinds of crap. He didn't look at me as he answered, "Not so far. The cycle's unbroken. She started a new rehab program not long ago."

"I'm sorry, I shouldn't have said that."

"You're hurting. I get it."

"No, it's not okay. Don't make excuses for me."

"All right. But I'm not sorry you mentioned her . . . because I was wondering if you'd go see her with me this week."

"Really?"

"Yeah, on Christmas Eve. It seems like I should try to patch things up." He left unspoken the reason behind that decision, but I knew.

Yet I couldn't refuse. "Sure. What time?"

"I'll pick you up at four thirty. Visiting hours are pretty limited, five to six on Wednesday, and then a few hours on Sunday."

"So you can't even spend Christmas with her."

He shook his head as he went back to twining the garland around the tree. I had been right; the charm increased as we added ornaments. Since we usually got a taller tree, we had way too much stuff for a fake one this size, but Kian and I layered it until all the boxes were empty. The result was gaudy, for sure, but definitely cheerful. *This place could use more of that,* I thought, plugging in the lights. They were a mishmash of twinkle lights and standard glowing ones, but the colorful shadows moving on the wall behind comforted me a little.

"This was nice," he said, wrapping an arm around my shoulders. "Just like it's been a while since I got a present bought just for me, I haven't put up a tree in forever."

"Your aunt kept you out of that too?"

He shook his head. "It's not that she locked me in my room. I just didn't feel welcome, so I opted out. And once I started working for the company and got my own place, it seemed pointless to go to so much trouble for one person."

"That's why the suicide rates skyrocket during the holidays." Given the circumstances that linked us inextricably, I didn't know if that was a clever joke or a horrible one.

"Been there, done that."

"At Christmastime?" Startled, I blurted the question.

"Nah."

I cleared my throat, deciding not to discuss this further. "You want something to drink?"

Things felt weird between us because I was so conscious of what he'd paid for my safety. At first, I reveled in the fact that he loved me, then the reality sank in. While it was a touching sacrifice, his devotion was also a weight around my neck. How could I be worth what he'd given up? A lifetime wouldn't be enough to repay him and I only had four and a half months.

"It's okay. I should probably be getting home."

I let out an unsteady breath. "Don't go."

"Why not? I can tell you're uncomfortable lately."

"It's not that I don't l-love you." I stuttered a little over the L-word, not quite used to dropping it into casual conversation. "I just feel—"

"Indebted?" he offered.

"Yeah."

Before he could respond, a knock sounded on the front door. My life had gotten twisted enough that I tensed up each time the unexpected occurred. Kian glanced me, then headed to answer it. He peered through the peephole and stepped back.

"Who is it?"

"I don't see anyone."

"That doesn't bode well," I muttered.

The knock came again, louder and more demanding, but it wasn't like the thing that tried to beat down my front door before. With his eyes, Kian asked silently what I wanted to do about it. Nodding, I took a step back, just in case we needed to run. He opened up just wide enough to take stock of who was lurking on the other side. I glimpsed a slim figure in a red uniform, very tailored, with gold braid on the sides. The person seemed to be dressed to deliver a singing telegram, but no burst of song was forthcoming as I stepped forward to get a better look.

At first glance, this was a normal person, but then I registered the unnatural pallor and the too-sharp nails, more like talons than human nails filed to a point. The creature smiled, accenting its angular features, and the longer I looked, the more the features shifted, becoming a triangular blob with nostrils cut into pasty flesh at a bizarre angle. Its lidless eyes flickered once, twice, not blinking, but vanishing and reappearing, almost like an afterthought. A shiver rolled through me.

"What is it?" I asked, unmoving.

Your invitation, madam.

I heard it but not in words because the thin slash of its vestigial mouth never moved. Cold crept toward my feet like an invisible fog as the thing produced an ivory vellum card. Kian snatched it away before the messenger got any closer. A snakelike tongue flickered out through its lip-slit; the thing no longer looked even remotely human, more evidence of the illusions the immortals could summon at will.

Or maybe this is the lie, I thought, *so it can feed on your fear.*

It bowed at the waist, giving the impression of jointed, entomic movement and then it rushed away, moving as if it had more than two legs. I slammed the door closed, more revolted than I could articulate, as Kian skimmed the summons. His eyes widened, then he read:

"The Harbinger demands your presence at the Feast of Fools, fancy dress required. RSVP unnecessary, as you are not permitted to decline."

"When is it?" I stared at the expensive stationery, embossed with what must be real gold.

"January first."

"What does that mean, 'fancy dress'? Like evening gowns and tuxedos?"

"Given what I know of the Harbinger, it's probably costumes." He flipped the invite over and nodded. "Masquerade procession begins promptly at midnight."

"Wait, so the party starts that late?"

"No matter what this card says, we don't have to go."

Chewing my lip, I admitted, "I feel like that would be a bad idea."

"What?"

"Pissing off our benefactor. He doesn't strike me as . . . steady."

"You want to go, then?" He seemed surprised.

"That's the wrong word. More that I'm willing to put in an appearance. The whole mandatory attendance thing is unnerving."

"Then I guess our New Year's plans are set, huh?" Kian produced a wry smile.

Cocking my head, I teased, "Did you want to do something more romantic?"

"Avoiding death while being surrounded by monsters should be memorable anyway."

"There's that," I admitted. "I'm glad you'll be there with me."

"Not sure how much help I'll be, if the shit hits the fan." He didn't seem pleased about his current situation, being cut off from Wedderburn's power. "Okay, I'm really going."

"Are we good?" I put my hand out and he took it, pressing it against his heart.

"Better than. I know it'll take some time to understand."

"I do. It's just . . . I hate that you put me above yourself. I know you feel guilty about the time you spent watching instead of helping. But your hands were tied. If *I* get it, you should too."

He let out a sigh. "Edie . . ."

"What?"

"It's not that easy. I can't just get over the fact that I stalked you."

Frustration made me want to shake him. I stepped closer, gazing up into his eyes. "It seems like you feel so guilty that you didn't die back then, you're determined to do it now, no matter how *I* feel."

22

"Let's not think about that right now. Okay?" He leaned down and I met him halfway for the sweetness of a kiss that made my heart ache.

"Fine," I breathed.

His lips always made me not care so much about things I knew were important and worth arguing about. *Stupid hormones.* Kian dropped another kiss, this one on my nose. Then he said, "Lock the door behind me."

"Got it."

There was just no telling what might be lurking in the dark.

GHOST OF CHRISTMAS PAST

spent the next four days trying to fill the hole my mom left. And failing.

Nothing I did made my dad rouse from his perpetual, absent fog. He gave me a tired smile over the Christmas decorations and thanked me prematurely for the present I'd wrapped and tucked under the branches. *It could be a rotten egg.* But somehow I doubted he'd react, even if he opened the box to find one. He'd just look through me and mumble something, before going to his room to hide, to count the minutes before he could return to the lab.

The one time I'd mentioned how much he was gone lately, he'd snapped, "I'm trying to carry on our work, Edith. Can't you understand that?"

What *I* understood was that he'd checked out. I was raised, right? No need for further parental supervision. They'd gone on red alert after I started dating, but at this point, I suspected my dad wouldn't even notice if I moved in with Kian. But I couldn't get really mad over how Dad was handling his grief when guilt played a constant drum solo against the inside of my skull. If I'd been a little smarter, more prepared, more cautious, I'd have saved her.

Or . . . if I'd turned down the deal, which I'd known was too good to be true, I'd be words on a headstone by now, poetry about the beauty of my soul, probably. And my mom would still be around. Yet I didn't let myself think that way for long. Suicide wasn't an option for me anymore. If I quit, it would mean that everyone else died for nothing.

Four p.m., Christmas Eve. And my dad still wasn't home.

Normally, we'd be baking cookies right now. My mom had stopped setting them out for Santa years ago, but the tradition remained. My dad wouldn't be buying the ingredients this year, though, and I knew better than to bother him about it.

As promised, Kian arrived at four thirty, dressed in well-cut trousers and a button-up shirt. His leather jacket might not be the warmest choice but he was even more gorgeous than usual. He'd clearly made an effort since he didn't see his mom that often. I followed him out to his car, pretending I wasn't nervous. I'd rarely been to hospitals—only to visit my great aunt and Brittany—and I'd never known anybody in rehab.

"Don't worry," he said, apparently reading my expression.

"What if I say something stupid? Or insensitive."

"She'll get over it. What's that?" He pointed at the wrapped package in my hands.

"It seemed wrong to show up empty-handed, especially the day before Christmas, so I went out yesterday and got her a little something."

"What?"

"A pair of slippers. I checked online to see what's allowed in most programs."

His green eyes kindled with a warmth that tightened my stomach, every time. "That's amazing, thank you." Patting his inner jacket pocket, he added, "I got her a watch, for basically the same reason."

He led the way out to his Mustang and opened the door for me. I hopped in, restraining my anxiety. This was about as far from normal as any meet-the-parents scenario could be. Somewhere between the facility and my apartment, Kian touched my knee, telling me silently that it would be fine. Weirdly, my tension dissolved. Given his penchant for trouble, he shouldn't be able to reassure me like that, but my nervous system was gullible, apparently.

It was snowing slightly when we pulled into the parking lot. I didn't know what I expected, but this place was fairly nondescript, a historic building that had obviously been renovated. A brass plaque on the front read SHERBROOK HOUSE. Yeah, even the name wouldn't tell you what they did here. Kian opened the door and stepped into a tasteful reception area. Behind, there was a bank of elevators.

"I'm here to see my mother," he told the woman behind the desk. "Riley? I should be on the list."

She checked her records, then handed us guest passes, which we clipped on. "Go up to the fifth floor and check in. The floor attendant will show you to the common room."

Nodding, I thanked her and went with Kian, who was fidgeting, tugging at his shirt collar as we waited for the elevator. He offered a sheepish smile when he laced our fingers together.

"Hypocritical, I know."

"Has it been a while?"

He nodded. "We talk on the phone sometimes. But she mostly calls when she needs to get into a new program."

"And so here we are," I said as the doors opened.

He was quiet in the elevator, and as I watched, his shoulders squared. I could practically see him bracing for some kind of damage, and I tensed in sympathy. My free hand tightened so the nails bit into my palm. It couldn't be easy to watch someone you loved fail, time and again. Dashed hope must cut him up inside, until he was afraid to believe anymore.

"You okay?" I asked.

"When I see her number, I'm never sure if it's her," he said quietly. "Sometimes it's neighbors, friends wanting me to know she's strung out. And . . . I'm always afraid when the phone rings in the middle of the night. It's like . . . I don't even expect her to get better anymore, and I'm waiting to hear she's finally checked out."

"Oh, man." I wished I could think of something better to say. He'd never opened up quite this much before, and his words made me think he must feel like he'd already lost her, along with the rest of his family. "You miss her."

His throat worked. "Yeah. I really do."

I held him for a few seconds, until the elevator doors opened. By the time we stepped out, he was calm and collected, striding toward the check-in desk. We signed the visitor log, showed our passes, and then let the lady inspect our gifts. She seemed relieved that we weren't trying to give Mrs. Riley contraband. With the details sorted, she ushered us into the lounge, where a few people were already sitting with their visitors. All of the inpatients had on pajamas or some version of comfy clothes, like sweats.

27

Since I didn't know how Mrs. Riley looked, I waited for Kian to head toward her. First thing I noticed, she was painfully thin with big, haunted eyes; he'd gotten the green irises from her. Her hair was dull, badly dyed an inky black that made her skin look even more sallow. Her cheekbones were pronounced, as was her chin, and her mouth was pale and chapped, raw even, as if she'd been biting at her lips. Without makeup, she looked older than I expected, deep circles beneath her eyes. Her hands were knobby, raw knuckled, with cuticles ragged from nervous picking. She reminded me of a bird, all hollow bones and ruffled feathers.

He bent and kissed her cheek. "Merry Christmas, Mom."

God, it hurt more than I expected, hearing him say it out loud. Even if he rarely saw her, she was alive, and there was a chance she'd beat the odds this time, astonish him with an awesome recovery. An ache tightened my throat.

"You get more handsome every time I see you," she said with what looked like a fond, if tired, smile. "Do you have a stylist or something?"

"I got your genes," he said, which obviously pleased her, based on how she beamed.

Then Mrs. Riley turned to me. "Who's this?"

"I'm Edie Kramer. Nice to meet you."

For clarity, I presumed, Kian added, "My girlfriend."

"Finally." Her eyes took on a teasing light. "You were such a late bloomer. I'm so glad you're here, Edie. Now you can level with me about how Kian's really doing. He's *so* evasive, especially about his job."

Since that was the last thing I could do, I managed a crooked smile. "Actually, he's taking time off to focus on school."

Kian was scowling at me, as if to say, *Why the hell did you tell her that?* I ignored him.

"Are you okay on money?" she asked, visibly anxious.

Oh, crap. I forgot he pays for her treatments.

"I'm fine," he said. "I've got a good amount in savings and I'm looking for part-time work, something that leaves me more time to study."

And doesn't come with a lifetime servitude clause.

"Oh, that's good." Relief relaxed her shoulders. "You always were so frugal. Remember how you'd lend money to your sister when she burned through her allowance? You had a ledger and everything. Such a little loan shark."

He shifted, seeming not to know how to respond. During the relatively short time I'd known him, he'd never mentioned his sister. I had the sense it was an unhealed wound, a loss he couldn't process. Quietly I reached for his hand under the table and his fingers clutched mine as if I were a rope that kept him from falling off a cliff.

"We brought presents," I cut in, mostly to change the subject.

"Did you?" Mrs. Riley seemed honestly delighted. "How sweet! And you're so pretty too. I have a good feeling about you."

Despite a rocky few years, her demeanor showed glimpses of the grace she must've exuded when she was still a socialite. I could picture her in better clothes with hair and makeup done just so, wearing a designer dress and holding a flute of expensive champagne while gossiping with moneyed guests. In fact, she could still fit in among the Blackbriar parents. I figured a bunch of them had been to rehab.

"Thanks." Producing the gift, I offered it to her with a smile.

She wasted no time in tearing into her package and she appeared pleased with the lavender slippers I'd bought, just simple ballet-style ones but since I'd never met the woman, I had no idea of her tastes. I'd gotten a medium, hoping for the best. She pulled off the somewhat worn ones she had on and slipped into them right away. Wriggling her toes, she beamed at me.

"With socks on, they fit beautifully. Thank you, Edie."

I took that to mean they were a little big, but she was nice enough not to complain. "You're welcome."

Then she unwrapped Kian's present. She had tears in her eyes when he fastened the dainty bracelet watch on her wrist. Leaning forward, she pressed a trembling hand to his cheek, and I had to look away. *My chest hurts.* For multiple reasons, this was turning out to be a lot harder than I anticipated.

The hour passed quickly, though. Too soon, the other visitors packed up, giving hugs and saying Merry Christmas for the last time. Mrs. Riley wasn't allowed a cell phone, so we couldn't offer to call her tomorrow. She hugged me, which startled me, but I went with it.

The woman held on a little longer than was comfortable, whispering, "You'll take care of him for me, won't you?"

I'm trying. I imagined facing this broken woman to tell her she'd lost her son—the only person she had left in the world—and every muscle in my body locked in denial. *No way. She's barely coping as it is. For her that would be the end.*

"Okay," I said.

Kian gave us a weird look as I hurried past, alarmed in every possible way. I knew him; there was no way he'd bring up such a convoluted issue with her. So she'd just get blindsided in four and a half months or whatever. I steadied my breathing.

That won't happen. I'll figure something out.

"You ready?" Kian asked, once he finished saying good-bye.

"Yeah."

There was a line downstairs to turn in the passes and reclaim our IDs. I didn't say anything until after we got in the car and had been driving for a while. Kian broke the silence first, letting out a long sigh.

"She looks pretty fragile, huh?"

I nodded.

"For the last eight years, I've felt like I'm the parent. And I'm tired. But . . ."

"You can't give up. I love that about you." Though I didn't say so, I wished he had that kind of determination when it came to his own self-preservation.

He smiled, reaching for my hand. The snow had accumulated a little while we were inside, dusting the trees and sidewalks. Passing cars had the wipers on and the street was dark with melting snowflakes. I put on the radio, wondering if I'd ever feel better. Between my mom, the dead Teflon crew, and the sword of Damocles hanging over Kian's head, fear felt like a permanent fixture, needles constantly digging into my spine.

Half an hour later, he pulled up in front of my building. "What time should I come over tomorrow?"

"Noon?"

"Sounds good. I'll see you then."

I didn't invite him inside because I saw my dad shuffling up the sidewalk toward us. He wasn't dressed for the weather, wearing only an old tweed jacket my mother had begged him to throw away years ago. His shirt had stains on the front, and it looked as if he hadn't shaved in at least a week. His beard was more gray than brown, something I never noticed before.

Kian kissed me quickly, then I climbed out of the car. He waited until I went in before pulling away. Dad followed a couple of minutes later. I hugged him and was alarmed to feel how skinny he'd already gotten. He'd always leaned more toward reedy than Mom or me, but I could tell he hadn't been eating during work hours. Shit, it was all I could do to make him have dinner after he got home.

"What did you have for lunch?" I asked.

He made a vague gesture that was supposed to reassure me. "One of the grad students brought me a sandwich. I'm fine."

That doesn't mean you ate it.

"You're not. Promise me you won't go to work tomorrow."

At first he gave me a blank look, edged in frustration. "Why—*oh.*"

"It's Christmas Day. Kian's coming. And I need you to help, or all the groceries I bought a few days ago will be ruined."

He exhaled slowly, and it was like watching a light come on in his head. "Right. I guess I'm not doing very well, huh?"

Finally. I was afraid the fog would never lift.

"I want you to be present when you're here. I still need you." Since I wasn't used to saying stuff like that, it was hard, and the words came out choky.

"Okay." Awkwardly, Dad reached for me, offering a one-armed hug. "I promise. We just need some time to figure out how the pieces fit now."

Badly, I thought. *You only see me half the time.*

Still, I was relieved he'd be around tomorrow. Maybe, if we tried really hard, we could coax a smile out of him. The new apartment came with a TV and I could hook up my laptop for a holiday movie marathon. Given his status as a classic-movie nerd, Kian probably adored *It's a Wonderful Life* and *Miracle on 34th Street*. I'd seen both—didn't love them—but I was willing to sit through them if Kian and Dad wanted to.

I chilled with my dad while he paged through a scientific journal. But an hour later, he murmured, "We should get some sleep, if we're making a feast tomorrow."

It was eight o'clock.

But I couldn't *force* him to talk to me. Maybe the progress I'd made was as much as I could hope for so soon. Tired, I trudged down the hall to wash my face and brush my teeth. My room was still devoid of personality, most of my things still boxed up in the closet. This didn't feel like somewhere I actually lived, more that I was killing time.

When I popped my laptop open, I had a message from Vi waiting. She was still online, so I pinged her for a chat. As usual, her room was a mess and beyond her closed door, I could hear her mom yelling at Vi's brother. Then her dad rumbled something while she made an OMG face.

"Sorry about that."

"It's okay. I envy you the noise, actually."

"Oh. Yeah, I bet." She changed the subject swiftly, probably guessing I didn't want to go farther down that road. "Did you get my package?"

"Not yet."

"Crap. It's probably hung up in the Christmas mail rush."

"Thanks for thinking of me. I forgot to send you anything." *Yeah, I'm definitely winning the cruddy friend award this year.*

"I didn't expect you to. Merry Christmas, Edie."

"Thanks. Give my best to your family."

"Oh, if your invitation still stands, I'm talking to my parents about coming to see you. Maybe for a few days during spring break?"

Since I'd mentioned that a while ago, long before the supernatural shit hit the fan, it was probably a terrible idea for all the reasons. But she seemed so bright and hopeful that I couldn't say no. Maybe her parents would do that for me. I'd used a favor to protect her, so Wedderburn should honor the deal.

"I'd love to see you," I said honestly. "I miss you."

"Me too."

Just then I heard Vi's mom yell, "Are you coming down to wrap presents or not?"

Visibly exasperated, she shouted back, "Give me a minute!"

"It's fine. Go do family stuff."

"Sorry. We all have to wrap junk for the relatives. Grandparents, cousins, nieces, whatever. God, it's such a pain."

Vi might think so, but if it went away, if her house got quiet, I bet she'd feel differently. "Say hi to everyone for me."

"No problem." With that, she signed off.

There was no word from Ryu, but it hadn't been long enough since we talked for me to worry about him. That left me sitting in my room, wishing Kian could pop in secretly like he used to. But some things couldn't be undone.

In my darkest moments, I wondered if it would've been better for everyone if I'd stuck with the original plan . . . and jumped off the bridge.

MONSTER'S BALL

Christmas wasn't bad.

With my dad checked in, we made enough food for the three of us and it wasn't depressing or lame like Thanksgiving. There was ham, mashed potatoes, and green beans—not a feast—but better than the frozen junk we'd been eating since my mom's funeral. Afterward, we exchanged gifts. I was astonished my father remembered to buy me anything, even a bookstore gift card. He seemed to like the blue scarf I got him.

Kian offered me a small box. I'd guessed right when I speculated he'd gone for jewelry. Excitement flooded through me as I peeled away the shiny paper, revealing a delicate silver chain threading through the center of an infinity symbol. Instinctively I curled my right hand, fighting the urge to check whether the sigil on my inner wrist was hidden. Casting a glance at my dad, I was reassured to see that he was a reading a magazine. I had mixed feelings about the gift, considering what it represented.

He could probably tell that because he leaned forward to

explain, "That's not supposed to represent interminable servitude. I could talk geometry and calculus, add in topology and Möbius transformations, then move on to fractals and the Koch snowflake, but in reality, it's much simpler. It just means 'endless.' And that's us, Edie. So this necklace, it's how I feel about you."

I let out a little sigh, not exasperation, but more like the sweetness was escaping from my body in tiny gulps. He was doing this so the mark on my wrist wouldn't feel like a brand anymore. Instead, I could look at it and think of Kian rather than his former masters.

"Thank you," I whispered.

"Want me to put it on you?"

"Absolutely."

He stood up and I shifted enough for him to reach, lifting my hair so it didn't get tangled in the clasp. The chain was the perfect length, settling into the hollow at the base of my throat. For a few seconds, he just gazed down at me with the look that said he'd be kissing me if my dad wasn't sitting here reading *Scientific American*. In response I touched his hand.

"My present probably won't seem as cool by comparison."

"If you picked it out for me, I'm sure I'll love it."

With an eager expression, he tore the wrapping like a little kid to reveal the Alfred Hitchcock box set I'd gotten, five classic films. He'd probably seen them but based on my covert observation of his DVD collection, he didn't own them. I knew he loved *Notorious*, so maybe he liked *Spellbound* too. Nervous, I waited for his reaction.

"This is great," he said softly.

"Why don't you play one of them?" Dad suggested without glancing up.

Yeah, maybe suspense would be a better move than a holiday

flick we'd all seen ten times. I got the right cable and hooked up my laptop to the TV, then Kian chose the movie. *Spellbound*, probably because of Ingrid Bergman. We settled on the couch together to watch. After a while, my dad put down his magazine, drawn in despite himself.

Once the movie ended, I asked, "Can I go out on New Year's Eve?"

"With Kian?" Dad asked.

"Yeah."

"Then it's fine."

My mom would've demanded to know where we were going, at what time we'd be home, and when she was around, Dad would've been right there with her. But he'd abdicated since then, trusting Kian to the point that it worried *me*. Not that there was anything to fear, but still. Fathers were supposed to be fearsome and protective, right?

"I'll take good care of her," Kian promised.

That rallied my dad enough to add, "No drinking."

"I promise." Considering that we were going to a party hosted by the Harbinger, getting shit-faced might be the last mistake I ever made.

Soon after, Kian collected his movies and headed home, freeing my dad to retire. I stayed up late reading, which set the tone for the rest of my break. Probably I should be studying, but school had lost its urgency. If I retained my status as a catalyst, Wedderburn would make sure I got into the right college to stay on the path. If I'd already lost, then I wouldn't have the freedom to do as I pleased anyway. Consequently, I felt pretty zen about *my* future. Other people, like Kian and my dad, however, might worry me to death.

The rest of the week was pretty chill. I did a little assigned reading, scrawled some homework, chatted with Vi, and answered an e-mail from Ryu, who'd gone to Sacramento for the break to see his grandparents. The time difference from East Coast to West was better than Boston to Tokyo, so we did a video chat too. At some point since I last saw him, he'd had the blond tips trimmed off, so he looked less J-Pop and more straight-edge handsome.

"How's your friend?"

"Hanging in there." Which was truer than he knew.

The convo didn't last long because it was getting late here, and I had the Feast of the Fools the next day. I still didn't have a costume and I doubted going as a mad scientist like I had at Cameron's party would cut it. After disconnecting with Ryu, I fiddled around online, looking for DIY ideas. I couldn't decide if it would be better to go nondescript or to pick something monstrous. Maybe the immortals would think I was one of them?

In the end, I decided on silent movie actress. A trip to the thrift store the next day hooked me up with a flapper dress, and I did my makeup so I looked pale and otherworldly, which also gave me an inhuman vibe. I used black on my lips and eyes, dark gray on the lids, then I put on a floppy velvet hat and draped a bunch of long beads around my neck. My shoes were plain flats because it made sense to be cautious when going into a situation like this.

My dad was reading in the living room when I came out. "It's a costume party?"

"Yeah." I waited for him to ask something else.

"Make sure you're home before one."

That was much later than he'd have allowed before. But I told myself it was a special exception for New Year's Eve. *It doesn't mean anything bad.*

Kian arrived just before nine. My nerves had escalated to mountainous proportions, as all the horrific possibilities raced through my head. I'd messaged Kian about my costume earlier, so he had on a black suit and tie with a white shirt. Quickly I did his face to match mine; people might take us for a couple of ghosts instead of what I had in mind, but that might even be better.

"Ready?" he asked.

Not really.

But my dad would think it was bizarre if I didn't want to go to the party I'd requested permission to attend. So I nodded, we said bye, and headed for the Mustang. In the car Kian got his phone out, tapping GPS for a clue how to find the address. Leaning close, I saw it was outside the city. *Worrisome.* Chickening out wasn't an option, though.

Attendance is mandatory.

Negotiating city traffic on New Year's Eve took a while, so I was tense by the time we cleared Boston. The route map seemed to be taking us along the coast. We drove for nearly an hour when the GPS lady warned us we were getting close to our destination. Which turned out to be a creepy-as-hell pile of stones with jagged rocks and an angry ocean instead of a pretty beach. There weren't many cars, something that shouldn't have surprised me, because most of the guests wouldn't require transportation. Most could terror-travel—through sewers or mirrors or electrical lines—and were probably already lurking inside.

"Awesome," I said aloud, gazing at the Gothic architecture.

If some eccentric tycoon set out to build a terrifying house, he couldn't have achieved his goal better. From the mullioned windows to the flying buttresses and gargoyles perched on the roof's edge, the place radiated ominous. The lawn was overgrown, bordered by hedges so wild that they encroached on the view. Ivy ran amok on one side of the foundation, digging in its roots so the stones would crumble sooner or later. I breathed in, conscious of damp and salt and something else, sharp and wild, nothing I'd ever smelled.

"This is *so* his style," Kian said.

"That's not very reassuring."

With a faint smile, he took my hand. *Yeah, you're relaxed. You've got nothing to lose, you already bargained it away.* I wanted to yell at him— to ask him how he thought his mother would take the bad news. Now that I'd met her, I felt even worse.

"Come on."

When we approached the door, it opened in the kind of spooky-squeaky slow motion from haunted houses, but when I checked, there were no wires or sensors I could see. Inside, it felt ten degrees colder, and it was chilly enough to snow outdoors. I huddled deeper into my coat as my breath misted white. The ornate marble floor was chipped, the pattern obscured by years of neglect. Here and there, tiles were broken, as if from great impact, and ominous stains discolored the lighter squares. This place only needed the classic warning sign: ABANDON ALL HOPE, YE WHO ENTER HERE.

"This party sucks," I muttered. "Where's the evil butler to take our jackets?"

"You'd freeze without it."

"True." I didn't hear any music, but really, what did I know about the Feast of Fools? An Internet search had only uncovered a bunch of stuff about the Catholic Church. And that definitely didn't apply here.

Kian navigated the warren of hallways as if he'd been here before. We passed shadow-drenched parlors that were sinister in their silence, especially when I registered the flickers of movement within. My heart kicked into overdrive as we rushed past. Sometimes I shut my eyes against the sensation of something standing directly behind me: scrape of unseen claws on my jacket; brushing chill on my cheek. I shuddered as Kian quickened his step.

"This is just the gauntlet. We'll be there soon."

"Sounds like you're a pro."

"Wedderburn's sent me before when he didn't feel like putting in an appearance."

"Kind of like his emissary?"

He nodded, tightening his hold on me. "Don't let go, okay?"

"Are you kidding? Let me guess, in this scenario, *we're* the fools they're feasting on."

He ignored my nervous wisecrack. "Seriously, Edie. Not even if you think I'm on your other side. You might feel someone take your hand, it might even look like me, but *don't* let it lead you away."

I swallowed hard. "I promise."

By the time we got to the heavy double doors, I'd probably put bruises on Kian's fingers, but he didn't seem to mind. "This is the ballroom. I can't even *begin* to explain what it's like inside, so it's easier if we just go in and get this over with."

"Confidence, I am now full of it."

In response he kissed my forehead. "Stay close. I've survived two of these, one entirely on my own. So if you stick with me and don't draw attention, you should be fine." With that, he held out a hand. "The invitation. You brought it, right?"

"Yeah, here you go."

While I watched, partly in fear and the rest fascination, he set the vellum against the wood, which rippled like flesh, then a mouth appeared, grotesquely misshapen, and the thing devoured our card. Only when every morsel was gone did the doors pop open. As requested, I was Kian's shadow as we slipped inside. It scared the crap out of me when the whatever-that-was made a . . . digestive sort of noise as it shut.

"Did we just get *eaten*?" I whispered.

"It's one of the Harbinger's parlor tricks."

"Then I'd hate to see a real application of his power."

I was trying to be funny, but Kian nodded. "You really would."

At first the ballroom was too dim for me to get a sense of what I was seeing. My eyes tried to adjust to the darkness but a blinding strobe flooded the room at random intervals, leaving me purblind. Audio tried to compensate but the room was full of echoes and reverb, disorienting me further, so I could only parse the scene in staccato flashes, imprinted in an inverted color spectrum, so I felt like I'd fallen into negative space.

That went on for what felt forever. It got hard to breathe for the panic tightening my chest, and I held on to Kian as hard as I could. Thin cool fingertips trailed over my other hand, but I knew it wasn't him. I jerked away and strained to see exactly what was touching me. The creature twirled away in a flutter of inky hair, ragged clothes, and the shine of too bright eyes, like a cat in the dark.

"What was that?"

"Harmless. Mostly." That didn't really answer the question.

But before I could press the point, the shadows dispersed to normal levels and the strobe stopped. I blinked, repeatedly, adapting to the candlelight. It was hard to tell what was costume and what was reality, though even if something seemed human, it probably wasn't. The strong smell I'd noticed outside intensified; it reminded me of a deep, dark wood, dense with trees and ancient things, unknowable but earthy too. It also held the essence of a storm—lightning splitting the sky, ozone, dirt, and decay—wrapped around a desiccated bone.

Then the Harbinger appeared before us, defying gravity in a slow drift to a dais I hadn't noticed. This time, he was dressed as a mad harlequin, complete with belled hat and pointy shoes. His hair hung in multiple braids, each adorned with some crazy icon. The cat statue had vanished, and in its place, he carried a carved walking stick topped with a dog head.

I pressed closer to Kian, who was watching the show. He wrapped an arm around me in response but he never looked away from our benefactor. A show of respect, maybe. I followed his example and waited to see what would happen next.

"All of my esteemed guests have now arrived," the Harbinger said. "Which means the entertainment can proceed." That prompted a wave of applause, and like any good showman, our host paused to permit the revelry. He went on, "There stands among us one who is willing to die for love."

Hysterical laughter echoed throughout the room, gaining volume until it assaulted my eardrums in maniacal crescendo. Four creatures slunk toward us, until it was all I could do not to slap them away. I'd been told not to draw attention to myself, and starting a fight would definitely qualify. My eyes couldn't decide what they looked like—sometimes they were arachnid and other times they were feathered head to toe like avian demons. There was probably some awful story to explain their creation, but I was more concerned with keeping them from touching me.

I'd learned my lesson with the thin man.

The Harbinger continued the show, once the derision subsided. "I think we can all agree that such a one must be honored tonight, for there *is* no greater fool than that."

"Crown the king!" came the thunderous response.

What the hell. I remembered something, but so many hands were already pulling at Kian, tugging him away from me and toward the dais. The chant gained ground, coming in hisses and moans, ecstatic screams and hoarse croaks. Kian tried to fight the mob's will, but our hold broke and then there was only the endless tide of monsters surrounding me.

I went up on tiptoes to watch him being shoved upward until he was standing at the Harbinger's side. He clapped Kian on the shoulder. "Tonight, you are king and I, your fool." To the audience, he added, "Behold your liege, the Lord of Misrule."

Four pairs of hands settled on my shoulders, keeping me from moving toward the stage. I tried to shake them off, but the more I struggled, the less it seemed worth it. My mind went strange, fuzzy and indistinct. The scent of cut flowers filled my head and I relaxed. Suddenly, this seemed like the best party I'd ever attended.

"Kian is really hot," I told one of the shadows nearby.

It drew me close with a whisper I didn't catch. *Seems really important. I should—*

"What would you have me do, sire?" The Harbinger broke the spell, and something slithered away from me with a frustrated snarl.

But I was shaky as hell, like I'd gone days without eating, and my mouth was dry as a bone. When I touched my lips with trembling fingertips, they felt like leather. *How long have I been here?*

"I led the procession, like you wanted," Kian said. *What? I don't remember that at all.* "Now I need to find Edie."

"Ah, yes. Your beloved queen. Go to her, then. I'm certain sure she's unharmed."

I suspected his definition and mine were much different. The crowd gave way, letting me meet Kian halfway. He wrapped his arms around me, and I smelled blood on him. His shirt was stained dark with it, and his beautiful face bore streaks of grime. When he lifted a hand to touch my cheek, I saw that his knuckles were scraped raw.

Damn. I didn't even know what to ask.

He beat me to it, swearing viciously. "Something fed on you."

I stared up at him, confused. "Are you sure?"

Reflexively I flinched when he touched a sore spot on my neck. "Yeah. Right here."

That was when I realized I wasn't wearing my coat . . . or the dress I had on before. But sadly, starting with that lost time, my Feast of Fools troubles had only just begun.

DEATH MATCHES ARE NOT PARTY GAMES

A smoothly sinister voice spoke from behind me. "Introduce us."

Kian kept his arm around me as we turned. I still hadn't recovered from realizing I couldn't remember what happened; it was too soon for another complication, but from Kian's expression, I didn't have a choice. The person who'd addressed us, well, he was radiant. There was simply no other word. Garbed in shades of bronze and gold, he should've looked tawdry, gaudy even, but instead he radiated an aura of majesty. I fidgeted, as if I were staring into the sun.

Unlike the Harbinger, I had no problem focusing on these princely features. Everything about him was beautiful, perfectly sculpted. Hollywood would instantly plaster his face all over billboards and make him model underwear, if they ever saw him. But this creature also radiated an uncomfortable heat. Sweat broke out on my forehead and beneath my armpits the longer he looked at me without speaking.

Finally Kian said, "This is Edie."

I wasn't sure if that was the best move, but unless they were asking for your head on a stick, maybe it was best to be polite? Somehow I managed a sickly smile. It made my cheeks feel swollen and my lips felt like they might crack. My throat was so dry I could hardly swallow.

"You need to take better care of her." So far the creature hadn't addressed me.

I was mesmerized by the inhuman spikes of hair that somehow looked more like precious metal. Even his eyes were golden. As if reading my mind, he swiveled his head in my direction, reminiscent of a hunting hawk. The intensity of that stare rocked me back a step.

"She's protected," Kian replied.

A graceful gesture, indicating disbelief. "And you trust her to that one?"

I followed his gaze to the Harbinger, spinning madly across the room, for no reason I could discern. It did seem like a bad bargain, but if there had been anyone more powerful, who wasn't also part of the game, Kian would've approached him instead. Sparks of light prickled in my field of vision, giving the creature before me an odd ambient glow.

"Do you know who I am?" His voice sounded strange.

"Dwyer." I rasped out my best guess. "Formerly known by many names, most of whom were sun gods."

The resultant smile was blinding. "I see why you treasure her," he said to Kian. When he turned to me again, his face fell like sunset, darkening, threaded with orange and scarlet, bright notes amid the shadows. "Mark me. I will destroy you." He might've been commenting on the weather. There was no malice, no hostility, and that made it worse.

Anything I said would sound like bravado because I had no idea what his weaknesses might be. He had so much power, and I felt like a flea in comparison. Once human belief created such a creature, I understood why they'd worshipped him. Even knowing the truth of his origin, I was barely resisting the urge to take a knee.

So I just murmured, "I understand that we're on opposing teams."

"Do you think you're a player?" Dwyer asked, obviously amused.

No. I'm just trying not to be played.

Kian saved me then. "She needs a drink. I'm sure you understand."

With that, he swept us away from whatever bad intentions the sun god had. I didn't see Wedderburn anywhere, but I recognized one of his minions in the crowd. The peeling white face and the smeared red mouth, along with the frizzy hair, could belong only to the terrifying clown-thing that had been called to execute Kian a few weeks back. I pulled on his arm.

"Is that—"

"Buzzkill," Kian supplied. "Works for Wedderburn, one of his trusted mercenaries."

"I can't even imagine how it gets paid."

"Better if you don't."

The bruise on my neck throbbed, as if reacting to the implicit threat. From across the room, the monster's eyes met mine, yellow sclera with red veins prominent throughout, and it lifted a gloved hand to blow me a kiss. *Yeah, Wedderburn wants me to know he's still watching.*

As promised, Kian found me a bottle of plain water, and it hurt to swallow. I downed all of it so fast my stomach sloshed afterward. I leaned my head on his shoulder, miserable as I'd been since we put my mother in the ground. Yet both symbols on my wrists were quiet, so this must be part of the plan. I *hated* that I had supernatural guidance systems imprinted on my skin.

"Better?" he asked.

"A little. How long have we been here?"

"I'm not sure. But probably not as long as you think."

"More of the Harbinger's tricks?" I tugged at my clothes, only to notice that they'd shifted back at some point. So . . . was I wrong before? *Am I wearing the same dress?* The constant unreality might wreck my brain.

"Mostly. I think."

The Harbinger stopped his bizarre frolicking to clap his hands, and the sound rang out like thunder, much louder than anyone else could achieve with two palms. "We have one final diversion before the feast is ended. Shall I show you?"

Like before, the mob practically destroyed the ballroom with enthusiasm. By then, numbness had taken me over; I could only exist in a state of abject terror for so long. Along with everyone else, I watched as two giant amorphous moth-beasts dragged someone up onto the dais. At first glance, I thought it was a girl but when the person rolled over, I realized it was a boy, probably fourteen or so, and small for his age. Definitely human, unless this was the best illusion ever. His terror was palpable, and it made the immortals nearby stir with avid anticipation.

"*Delicious,*" something with sharp teeth hissed.

The boy came up onto his knees, resting delicate hands on the floor before him in a posture of defeat so abject that I took a step forward. Bruises ringed his throat and his wrists, and what he had on could barely be called clothes; the shirt was torn in three places

49

and the pants had frayed until they hit his knees, revealing filthy calves and feet that were sliced up as if he was routinely forced to walk across broken glass. On his right hand, two of the fingers were bent at unnatural angles, either broken now, or they had been, then they healed badly afterward.

"Kian . . . ," I whispered. "I don't like where this is going."

"This one has a most impressive survival instinct," the Harbinger said, indicating the cowering boy with a flourish. "He's been my favorite pet for some time. But his luck might run out today. Shall we find out?"

The audience rumbled in agreement, and the room changed. I had no explanation for it, but suddenly it seemed as if we'd moved from the ballroom entirely. We were standing outside an arena now with a blood-stained pit below. Bones littered the floor of it, along with broken weapons. Snarls came from the sublevel, enough to chill my blood.

"Time for a bit of fun," the Harbinger said.

Before I knew what I planned to do, I broke away from Kian. He reached for me but I wasn't stopping. I'd been passive for too long, waiting and hoping that things would get better. It was time for me to fight, even if I didn't know how. Yeah, there might be fallout, but the Harbinger *had* to protect me, right? Even if I interfered with his grisly show.

Scared didn't cover how I felt just then. *This is a death match, a gladiator fight, and you've never even played Mortal Kombat. You don't know shit about knives or swords or whatever. You're probably going to lose. Horribly.*

But I wouldn't be able to live with myself if I stood by and watched.

When I climbed up on the stage, the Harbinger was a statue, lightning eyes flashing astonishment and displeasure. But he held still and waited for me to play my card. Maybe Dwyer was right, and I'd end up broken if I participated in their game. I only knew that I was sick and tired of being moved on the board.

"He's pretty beat up," I said. "So let me go instead."

Kian immediately protested, but the crowd drowned out his yelling. If I knew him, he was volunteering to fight in *my* place. The Harbinger, however, appeared to be considering my offer with a narrowed gaze. On the floor, the boy cowered, staring up at me with bewildered incomprehension. I wondered where he'd come from, how long he'd been an immortal's plaything. That torture might've left him unable to function, yet I wasn't sorry that I'd stepped forward. It felt like the first clean, brave thing I'd done in ages.

After a moment of consideration, the Harbinger turned the question over to the mob. "Let the audience decide. Who will fight to close the feast?" He pulled the boy to his feet, shoving him toward the edge of the dais. "Show your support."

The crowd responded with a modest round of jeers.

I didn't wait to be dragged forward. Stepping up, I tried to look bold and daring instead of terrified out of my mind. Raising both arms, I struck a champion pose. This was so far outside my comfort zone that it had a different zip code. But my swagger seemed to be working. In response, the monsters hooted and screamed for me; clearly, I'd won this popularity contest.

The Harbinger quieted everyone with a gesture, then he turned to me. I couldn't look directly at him but he had to be beyond pissed. He didn't strike me as the kind who enjoyed being thwarted when he was staging a show.

"You'll fight in his place. Your wish is granted," he intoned, loud enough for the whole arena to hear. Softer, he added, "'Ware that you don't regret your altruism."

I had a moment to be glad I was wearing flats before the two giant moth-things each grabbed one of my arms and flew me toward the pit. My head was still spinning from the suddenness when they let go, about six feet from the bottom. I hit the ground hard; I tried to tuck and roll like in the movies, but I ended up hurting my shoulder. And the snarling intensified, along with a wet, slavering sound.

The creature that slunk out of the shadows had the wings of a bat, a goat's head, and the rest of its body appeared to be serpentine with vestigial limbs that ended in razor-sharp claws. It was roughly three times my mass, and I was already calculating all the ways it could kill me when a black bag dropped at my feet with a clang. My mom would be horrified that I'd gotten myself into such a mess. *There's no excuse for violence, Edie. It's always better to talk things out logically.* Somehow I didn't think this monster would be interested in chatting.

It snuffled through gaping nostrils as I edged toward the sack. Best guess, these were weapons or tools I could use. Even the Harbinger wouldn't expect a human to fight barehanded. Would he? My hands trembled as I lunged, then scrambled back. I was struggling to unfasten the ties when the creature charged. Breathless, I spun to the side. Blindly I reached into the pack and pulled out . . . a heavy stick. On closer inspection, I realized I was holding a spiked flail, a weapon I recognized from playing D&D with my parents in junior high. It was also much heavier than pen-and-paper adventures had led me to expect.

Part of me wondered if this was an elaborate illusion. In role-playing games, if you disbelieved a spell and made your saving throw, the danger disappeared. So I tried that first as the monster turned, clumsily, for another go. *I don't believe you exist. You're not real.* But the thing didn't fade; it ran at me and the claws that raked over my back as I dodged felt pretty damn real. So did the blood trickling down my spine. I'd never known pain quite like the hot stripes etched across my back; even the work Kian had done on me didn't compare.

The claws must be poisoned. As that thought occurred to me, the monster lashed out with its tail, sweeping me at the knees. I bounced forward, my weapon clattering beside me. Pure instinct drove me to roll again and again, until I was far enough to get to my feet. The spikes on the heavy metal ball sparked on the rocks. From above, I hadn't noticed any particular geographic features but there were niches in the stone that let me play a terrifying game of hide-and-seek. I found a crevice too narrow for the monster to follow, slid sideways, and ran all the way to the back.

Judicious maneuvering let me wriggle around to face the beast, now mindlessly slamming at the stones. More terrifying, the wall gave way in small avalanches each time it swung its tail. It tore at the channel with its claws while I weighed how badly I was screwed. Fear made it hard for me to think straight; I had no combat abilities to speak of and I'd dropped the sack that might have something helpful besides the flail. Since I could barely lift the thing, it was hard for me to picture doing any damage with it.

Above, I heard the audience booing my careful, chicken-shit tactics. They wanted blood. Shivering, I factored the rate of excavation against the estimated distance the monster needed to travel.

Math affirmed that if I just crouched here against the wall, I'd die five minutes from now, give or take a few seconds.

I have to make a move.

In retreating here, I'd thought only of momentary safety, nothing about strategy that might let me defeat the thing. Did monsters like this die? It was probably created by our stories, which meant there *might* be gryphons, hydras, and unicorns running around somewhere too. I didn't recognize this thing from the legends I knew, which sucked because stories might've built in an Achilles' heel, like how unicorns could be tamed by virgins. Obviously purity had no impact on this demon's desire to rend my flesh and gnaw my bones.

Four and a half minutes left. Do something.

But sheer fright had my brain on lockdown, so I could only think of how the time was ticking away. More of the stone barrier between me and it sheared away; it lashed out with its claws, slicing the air no more than five feet away. Two or three more solid hits and—

"Get the bag." That eerie whisper belonged to the Harbinger, but he was nowhere nearby. I shouldn't be surprised that he could throw his voice since he had all kinds of other illusions at his command. Yet if I could figure out how to get past the thing, I'd already be doing it.

A flash of light to my left drew my eye. Peering closer, I saw divots in the rock that could be used by a desperate girl as handholds. Holy shit, I was so limiting the way I considered my escape routes. I was focused on 2-D, only forward and back. *But I can totally go up.* My skirt wasn't long enough to hinder my movements, so I twisted around in the niche and set my feet in the outcropping. For a few seconds, I feared that my upper body strength wouldn't let me do this—while the monster smashed ever closer—but I strained with all my strength and went up a couple of feet. Two more, and two again, until I was out of its reach.

Fifteen feet up, I found the tiniest of ledges, imperceptible in the gloom. Like a tightrope walker I crept around the edge of the pit, searching for the bag. It took the beast a little longer to realize I wasn't trapped anymore, then it snarled with rage. The ground trembled as it wheeled. The thing sniffed the air in my direction, suggesting it couldn't see too well. *There's the bag.* But now I was up too high to reach it easily. Climbing down would be too slow.

I have to jump. Before it spots me.

Crouching, I dropped. Somehow I held on to the flail, but the impact hurt my ankles and I fell over when one of them twisted with a painful crack. *Broken?* I had no idea; I hadn't been the type of kid to play outside and injure myself. But now I couldn't even run, and my back was still bleeding. I grabbed the bag and used the handle of my weapon to shove to my feet. With frantic hands, I dug through, finding blades and bottles, but I had no idea what item held the key to stopping this creature.

Just before the beast trampled me, the whisper came again, exasperated. "Red vial."

It was dark enough that it took me critical seconds to figure out which one that was. Distracted, I took another talon slash, this one across my shoulder. The pain made me drop my weapon. Now that I was bleeding in two places, the monster's sounds grew . . . voracious. Long skeins of drool drizzled from the goat's jaws, and when it opened its mouth to bite, the thing had fangs, not the flat teeth of an herbivore. I had no idea what I was supposed to do with the red vial, but there was no time to think. Impulse made me chuck the glass into the open maw lunging at me. My aim wasn't good enough to make a basket at normal distance but since it was on top of me, the vial skimmed right into its mouth.

Reflex made it bite down. I stumbled away as it growled and spat slivers of glass. A few seconds later, it tumbled forward and hit the ground. And with a distinct edge, the Harbinger proclaimed me the winner. When the moth-men came for me, I almost passed out from the pain in my back and shoulder. Somehow I held on until they set me on the edge of the pit. Then the pain flourished into three-point agony. My ankle would barely hold my weight, but against the odds, I was standing in the ballroom again.

"We must have a serious chat," the Harbinger said, clamping my arm with steely fingers.

Kian shoved to the front of the crowd pressing around us and pulled me away. "Another time. We're done here."

The intended victim was still cowering; he stared up at me as I quietly offered a hand. But I didn't have the strength to pull him up. Kian saw what I was trying to do while the monsters around us got increasingly restless, probably sensing the Harbinger's discontent, and he hauled the kid to his feet.

Then he knelt, his voice more commanding than I'd ever heard. "Get on."

Before the rioting started, we ran for our lives.

THESE BOOTS WERE MADE FOR RUNNING

Even with me on his back, Kian ran like all the devils in hell were chasing us. I clung to his shoulders and tried not to think about what would happen if they caught us. The halls were still dark and ominous with pounding footfalls echoing behind us along with the grunts and moans of excited beasts. This might just be getting them more worked up but we had to get out of here. The Harbinger needed to cool down before I saw him again, presuming that was even possible. *I might be on his shit list for all time now. He did say this kid is his favorite pet.*

Despite his injuries, the boy kept up with Kian, his breath coming in gasps that sounded like sobs. Otherwise he was eerily mute as he ran.

Each step carried us closer to the front doors, but the scrape of claws was getting closer. I didn't dare ask what would happen if they caught us. Something snagged my hair but Kian pressed forward and I stifled a cry as a hank tore free. My scalp stung but we didn't stop, racing out into the crisp air toward the car. Somehow, it was still dark, lending credibility to Kian's claim that we hadn't been in-side as long as I thought. He rounded the Mustang and set me down gently, then turned to the boy panting beside us.

"Get in back."

Evidently he understood, though he still hadn't spoken a word. He hopped in and Kian helped me into the passenger seat. A tide of monsters rushed down the drive toward us, and I pictured them literally tearing the car apart as Kian slid over the hood and bounced into the driver's side. As he started the car, something with fangs and claws slammed the window. It shattered instantly, spraying me with powdery glass. He slammed the car into gear and executed a rapid 180, tires spitting gravel. We ran over a howling beast with a *bang-thump* and then we were racing down the private drive toward the road.

Kian cut me a worried look. "You're hurt. And it's freezing in here. Just hang tight, Edie. I'll get you to a hospital."

While I wanted to refuse, that would be stupid. My ankle needed to be x-rayed, and I wasn't sure how bad the claw marks were. My head was feeling woozy, and the affected areas had gone numb, which couldn't be normal. The doctor would probably be stymied about my wounds, which we might pass off as an animal attack, but what about the toxins in my bloodstream? Yet I couldn't go with-out care.

Shivering, I nodded. "What time is it?"

"Half past two."

Crap, I was definitely out past curfew. Yet I suspected my dad was sound asleep, none the wiser. "Seriously? But . . ."

"I know, it felt like days." He glanced over his shoulder at the kid huddled in back. "What's your name? Where do you live?"

Silence.

Maybe he found Kian intimidating, so I tried. "I'm Edie. And you are . . . ?"

"He called me Aaron." The whisper was so faint I barely heard it.

"But that's not your name?" I asked.

Another pause. "I don't remember. You don't have to drive so fast. If the Harbinger didn't mean for us to escape, we wouldn't have."

The kid made a good point. "So the chase—"

"Was for show," Kian cut in.

"I didn't think he'd ever let me go," the boy said softly. "He said I was supposed to live and die for his amusement."

A shiver rolled over me. The casual cruelty reminded me what sort of creature was in charge of protecting me—and I'd be insane to rely on him again as I had tonight. But I didn't regret helping this kid get away. I just had no idea what we were supposed to do with him now. *Surely his family's reported him missing?*

"You need to see a doctor too. I think your fingers are broken." My words came out slurred, likely a result of the poison in my bloodstream.

Kian sped up, glancing at me worriedly. "Hang in there."

Fifteen minutes later, he found a small hospital in some small town up the coast from Boston. The place was tiny compared with the hospital where I'd visited Brittany, but there were also fewer people running around. Since it was the middle of the night on New Year's, they were busy with drunken accidents, and our situation didn't seem as weird as it might have otherwise.

We waited for almost forty-five minutes, and it was getting hard for me to breathe by the time they escorted us back. They tried to take the boy back on his own, but he clung to Kian's hand like he'd

59

never let go. In the end, the nurse let us wait for the ER doctor on the same bed. He asked a few questions about what we'd been doing tonight, and I let Kian do the talking. He told a fairly convincing story about a New Year party gone wrong and an angry guard dog. Afterward, they tended my wounds and checked my ankle, sprained, not broken, then they set the kid's fingers and put medicine on his cuts and bruises. The staff asked where Aaron's parents were, but Kian said he was his brother and opted for private pay.

"Did something else happen?" the doctor asked, troubled enough by my respiration to check again.

"I might've been stung by something," I wheezed.

His concern sharpened. "Are you allergic?"

"I don't—" But I couldn't finish the sentence; a vise tightened around my rib cage, compressing my lungs. My head throbbed from lack of oxygen, and everything went dark and smoky. In a few seconds, I'd be out.

"Anaphylactic shock," someone yelled.

The medical team responded, running around and doing things to fix it. An oxygen mask went over my nose and something sharp pricked my arm. I was feeling better in five minutes or so, enough to sit up. Kian looked near death himself; he stumbled toward me and drew me into his arms, ignoring the people trying to work around us.

"Don't ever scare me like that again."

"It wasn't on purpose," I mumbled.

They kept us for another hour but when it became apparent we had no other weird or mysterious symptoms, the doctor decided our injuries weren't serious enough to keep us overnight, so they cleared us out to make room. The boy flitted behind Kian and me, floating from the pain pills they'd given him. Kian's story sounded dodgy to me, but none of our wounds were the kind that always required reporting, like gunshots. They asked a few pointed questions about Aaron's injuries, but Kian lied well enough to allay suspicion.

Aaron hopped in the back without being asked and I fell into the passenger seat. As Kian started the car, the kid asked, "What are you going to do with me?"

"Huh?" My pain meds were pretty good too.

But Kian had evidently been expecting this question. "Do you want us to drop you off at the police station? They can probably find your parents."

A tiny hitch of breath revealed how horrible Aaron thought that idea was. "If you want to get rid of me, it's okay."

I understood his fear. Who knew how long he'd been with the Harbinger? He couldn't remember anything else, nothing about his life before. So right now, we were the only familiarity in a weird-ass world.

Hesitant, I suggested, "Maybe we could let him recover first?"

Though I felt bad for his family, they'd already been missing him so long. Two more days wouldn't matter in the grand scheme, would it? I'd feel better if we weren't dragging him to the station while he cowered and wept.

"Baby steps," Kian agreed. "Okay, new plan. You can crash at my place until you're feeling better. When you're up to it, we'll see about finding your family."

Long silence.

When I checked on him, Aaron was smiling. He finally whispered, "Thanks."

It was almost seven in the morning when Kian dropped me off at my place. He wanted to walk me in and apologize to my dad, but I aimed a pointed look at the pale, frightened kid in his backseat. "Right now, he's your priority. Get him home, clean him up. Feed him something decent." Another problem occurred to me. "Do you have anything to eat besides cup noodles?"

A guilty look. "I'll buy some stuff."

"You see my point. Look after Aaron, okay? I can handle my dad."

"If you're sure." He dropped a quick kiss on my mouth, and I limped into the apartment to face the music.

Except there was no reckoning. The living room was empty, no worried father pacing, waiting to yell at me. Nothing stopped me from heading to my room at gimp speed or taking a long shower. At seven thirty in the morning, I ate a bowl of cereal and went to bed. I slept until past one in the afternoon, and my dad didn't wake me. When I got up, I checked my ankle—still swollen and bruised—then rewrapped the elastic bandage.

He'd left a note on the fridge, at least, telling me he'd gone to the lab. How surprising. There was nothing to keep me here, so I decided to do a little grocery shopping and limp over to Kian's place. Maybe that wasn't the smartest move, but I couldn't sit here by myself. School would be starting in four days, and we needed to figure something out for Aaron by then. He looked like he should be a freshman but I had no idea if he could even read. The kid likely needed years of counseling and help reintegrating into society.

I texted Kian when I was nearly there and he ran out with no coat, wearing a ferocious scowl, to grab the grocery bags. "Are you trying to injure yourself permanently?"

"It's just a sprain. I have it wrapped, don't worry." I wasn't about to admit how much it actually hurt from walking around on it.

"Get inside and put your foot up. If you move again today, you'll be sorry." His cranky face made me want to kiss him even more. I'd rarely seen Kian mad at me. Under normal circumstances, he was overly patient and understanding, like I could do no wrong because of the way we met . . . and the fact that he didn't help me when he felt he should've. No matter the consequences.

"Fine," I muttered, suppressing a secret grin.

Inside the apartment, Aaron was perched on the couch, staring at the TV. He offered a shy smile, seeming even younger and smaller in Kian's clothes; the T-shirt and sweats swam on him. His hair was blond—I didn't realize that last night—attesting to how filthy he'd been, and he had blue eyes, pale and startling, like a slice of winter sky. His skin suggested he hadn't hit puberty yet. *God, his poor family.*

"Hi, Edie." He lifted a slender hand in greeting but didn't get up.

"How are you feeling?"

"Better. It's nice to be clean. And I like being unshackled." My breath caught at the casual horror implicit in that statement. "But . . . Kian says I can do whatever I want."

"Obviously," I said.

A puzzled look flashed across his small face. "But . . . you saved me. That means I belong to you."

Oh, shit. I shared a look with Kian, who was telling me with his eyes how messed up this boy was. "Uh, no. You're a person, not a possession."

"If you don't protect me, who will?" It was a desperate, heartbroken question.

Aaron's eyes filled with tears that spilled down his pale cheeks, and he made no effort to hide or suppress them. His demeanor was so defenseless and childlike, almost like he was eight years old, that I found it hard to watch. *Maybe that's how old he was when they took him and now he's frozen.* It could also be a survival mechanism, if the Harbinger took pity on captives who wept without restraint or shame. Seeing the kid's expression, I definitely had the impulse to hug him and promise to take care of him.

"Your family," Kian said.

"The Harbinger said he found me thrown away in the street, and if anyone wanted me, I wouldn't have ended up with him."

Ouch. But I wasn't sure I trusted a self-styled god of mischief. For all I knew, he might've yanked Aaron out of a warm bed. "What if he was lying?"

His eyes opened wide, as if he'd never considered such a thing. "He's a god."

"So he claims," Kian muttered.

"You said it could wait until I feel better." That was a crafty deflection and would probably result in Aaron living here indefinitely but I didn't have the heart to argue.

This was probably a bad, irresponsible move, but if Kian had someone else to look after, he wouldn't be able to focus as much attention on me. Which meant, in turn, that I could work on figuring out how to save him from the deal with the Harbinger without him noticing. There would definitely be drama if he realized what I was up to.

Sorry, Aaron and family.

I told myself I was just respecting the kid's wishes, letting him have a respite before the next life-shaking change, but my motives weren't selfless. Kian sighed and sat down on the other end of the couch, patting the spot beside him. It was a weird way to spend New Year's, but we watched TV together and late in the day, Kian made burgers from the supplies I'd brought. Though I went home past nine, my dad still wasn't around. Briefly I considered going back to Kian's apartment but that would be the same as giving up on my dad entirely.

The next morning, I got up early enough to see him before he left for the lab and I made him eat some eggs and toast. He flashed me a wan smile before heading out, leaving me to clean up the breakfast mess. *He didn't notice the fact that I'm limping. He didn't ask why I was late the other night.* Hurt welled up like blood from a deep wound. *He can't help it. He's just not coping very well. I'm sure he'll do better in time.*

But I had no idea how I could save both Kian and my dad. The threats were completely different, but in my heart, I knew the danger was real. *I'm going to lose one of them.* That felt like an inevitable result, cause and effect. Whatever choices I made would ripple outward, and then there would be consequences.

For the moment, however, I had to recover before I could do either of them any good. It irked me but I had to rest until school started. So I sat around my beige apartment for the next few days, chatting with Vi online, and resting my ankle. When school started back, I didn't want to be helpless. I got regular messages from Kian, updating me on Aaron's situation. So far he hadn't been able to talk him into going to the police. In fact, the kid apparently acted like he thought they'd put him in a cage or something.

Davina texted me on Sunday. You okay? Have a good break?

With a wry smile, I answered, You wouldn't believe me if I told you.

Try me. Looking forward to hearing all the implausible deets.

I also got a message from Jen. I'm back. See you tomorrow.

Staring at my phone, I wondered if that was supposed to sound ominous. I recalled what Allison had said . . . and my private conversation with Jen about psychic vampires. But I had no idea who the liar was. Jen *might* be trustworthy and there was no doubt Allison could be malicious. She seemed to thrive on creating that kind of conflict; she might even feed on it. Which would explain her presence in a high school, as teenagers were so prone to drama. I wasn't ready to burn my bridges with Jen, so I sent back:

Glad you're home.

Sighing, I fell back on my bed with a groan.

I should probably get up and cook something, but right now, life felt overwhelming, just too many problems without solutions. If my phone hadn't buzzed, I might've lain there until I fell asleep. But the text made me sit up and take notice.

Come out. I'll be there in five.

Kian *never* came across like that, so I got dressed in a hurry and brushed my hair. Not exactly high style but it sounded like we had trouble. I half suspected Aaron had turned into a monster and tried to kill him or something but he seemed to be uninjured when the Mustang pulled up. The kid was in the backseat, surprising me.

"What's going on?" I demanded.

In reply, Kian sealed up the car using the gel that supposedly guaranteed privacy for a limited time. I wondered how safe it was with Aaron listening. He might be working for the Harbinger, but Kian didn't seem worried and they'd spent more time together. I guessed if Aaron was reporting back, Kian would've caught him by now. Anyway, maybe I was just being paranoid. The Harbinger probably had more esoteric methods of spying on us.

He started the car without answering, slicing into traffic in an urgent twist of the steering wheel. A glance back at Aaron provided no clues. The boy was oddly impassive, all sweetness and innocence, like he was just happy to be included. He smiled at me when I turned. His bruises had faded a little, shifting from black and blue to green, still shocking against his clear skin.

"How are you feeling?" I asked the kid, giving up on a straight answer from Kian.

"Better. I'm eating three times a day and sleeping in a bed." The fact that he thought those things were worth mentioning made me *so* sad.

Kian spoke then. "Raoul called. We're on the way to meet him."

I CONFESS,
I DO NOT TRUST
YOU

"Raoul." It seemed best to make sure we were on the same page, but I wasn't sure how much context I should give aloud.

"My mentor," Kian confirmed.

Right. The one who stole an artifact and is currently AWOL from the game. That meant we were taking a big risk in meeting him, as countless immortals would be paying attention to our every move. Trepidation made me sweat, though the car heater wasn't fully warmed up yet. But I knew how Kian felt about Raoul, and that when the older guy split, it felt like he'd lost his only friend. So he had to be dying to see him.

"Don't think I'm unwilling, but . . . why am *I* going? It seems like additional risk."

"We've taken precautions." That was all he said.

I didn't realize my muscles were clenched until my shoulders started aching. I took a breath, willing myself to relax. Kian seemed to pick up on my mood and he moved his hand from the gearshift to touch my knee briefly.

"Trust me, okay? I'll make sure nothing happens to you."

"I'm not worried about *me*," I muttered.

If shit went horrifically wrong, I had no doubt that Kian would throw himself under the bus to save me. In fact, that was my worst fear.

Aaron craned his neck as we parked. Kian ran around to open my door. I didn't dally on purpose, demanding chivalry, more that I was weighing risks and trying to come up with a potential defensive strategy, should this go pear-shaped. Once I was on the sidewalk, Aaron hopped out and I saw that Kian must've taken him shopping, as he had on khaki pants that fit, new running shoes, a blue quilted jacket, and a gray beanie. Actually, he was a really cute boy, which made me think that was why the Harbinger stole him.

Horrible thought.

Kian led the way, his head on swivel, as we rushed down the sidewalk. We made a couple of turns, and he kept checking behind us the whole way. As for me, I peered like a weirdo into shop windows, searching for stray reflections. I went sharp with anxiety when a stray movement flickered in my peripheral vision. When I wheeled, I saw nothing; that didn't mean we were alone. Or safe. I didn't say anything since I had no proof it was anything but my imagination; I resolved to stay alert in case things escalated.

I followed Kian into an imposing cathedral with giant stained-glass windows angling scintillated shadows across the richly polished wood floor. Each panel seemed to be telling a story; there were angels and mythic figures, but theological fables weren't my strong point. In fact, I couldn't remember being in a church before. The nave smelled of candle wax as we moved deeper into the building, cold because it wasn't time for services. Likewise, the candles at the front were unlit, and I didn't see anyone waiting for us.

"Give me a moment," Kian said.

Without saying anything else, he went into the confessional and a light went on for me. *I bet Raoul's waiting on the other side.* It might be a crime to pretend to be a priest, but a human's religious practices would probably be the last thing any supernatural cared about, unless he was being worshipped. And somebody like the Harbinger would probably sense it if I started lighting candles in his honor, seriously giving praise. Suddenly, it occurred to me to wonder about deities like the Christian God, along with Allah and the Buddha.

So many people believe in them . . . that means they're probably real.

That stunning realization held me motionless until Aaron nudged me. I turned. "Huh?"

"What do you think he's doing?"

"Didn't he tell you?"

The boy shook his head. "His phone rang, he talked for a while, and got really upset. Then he told me to get dressed."

It seemed polite to explain, "I think he's talking to an old friend."

That sated his curiosity and he perched on a pew near the front to wait. On reflection, I decided to copy him, as the casual onlooker might think we'd come inside to pray. *People do that, right?* I'd seen it in movies anyway. It was hard to sit still with curiosity nibbling at my toes, but I kept myself from sneaking up to eavesdrop.

No more than five minutes ticked by before Kian strode toward us. I hopped up, heading for the door, secretly pissed off that I apparently wasn't getting to meet the mysterious Raoul, when he grabbed my arm. "Your turn."

"Really?"

70

Before I could ask, he nudged me toward the confessional. Rather than waste time arguing and increase our risk of getting caught, I went inside. It was a small box with a window to the other side, where I could vaguely make out someone else hovering. The view was obscured for a reason, I figured, so the sinners never got a good look at the priest listening to all of their dirty deeds.

"Edith Kramer?" A rich, deep voice spoke, so inviting that I'd listen to him narrating audio books. He had a faint Spanish accent, just enough to offer a charming embellishment.

"Nice to meet you." Manners were never a bad call, right? *Even if the circumstances are weird.*

"Likewise." He sounded amused. "You must be wondering at the cloak and dagger, hm?"

"A bit. But I understand that you're a wanted man. So you need to be careful." That was probably why he wasn't showing his face.

"You're clever, that'll help."

"With what?"

"I'm sure you've worked this out on your own, but . . . if you keep going the way you have been, you won't survive to repay your favors."

Hearing my chances summed up so bluntly made my ears ring; I went light-headed and my chest tightened until I couldn't breathe. I breathed through the pain. "What do you care? You don't know me."

He must've understood that I was scared because his tone gentled. "While we're not personally acquainted, I'm aware that Kian cares for you very much."

Wow. I tried to imagine them talking about me, long before I met Kian. Pictured him saying sweet things, adorable things, before I changed everything about the way I looked. Considering that, it was hard to hold on to my grievance.

"Well, there's no good way to tell someone they're probably going to die," I choked out.

"A realistic admission."

"But there's no way for me to *win* this game. The deck is stacked against me."

"True, the house always wins, or so they say."

"You must have an idea, though, or you wouldn't be talking to me." I hoped that was true. Otherwise I was beyond screwed.

"Precisely. There are certain skills you must acquire to survive the gauntlet that lies ahead." His knowing tone suggested he'd peeked ahead and he had some idea what was coming.

"Both your safety and Kian's depends on your drive, Edie. Are you willing to work harder than you ever have in your life?"

There was only one answer to that question. "Just tell me what to do."

Raoul laughed quietly. "I shall, next time we meet. This is enough of a start for now."

"Are you back now?" I had questions of my own. "Kian thinks you abandoned him."

"When I was in hiding, I had certain matters to organize. Those preparations are now complete and it's time to move to the next stage."

There was no telling if we could trust him, but since Raoul had pissed off *all* the immortals when he stole that artifact and went off the grid, it seemed unlikely that he could be working for one of them. On the other hand, maybe he could use me as a bargaining piece somehow to get back into Wedderburn's good graces. No, that didn't track since he'd already betrayed him. Dwyer might be interested in making a deal. Pain throbbed in my temples, and I gave up on deciphering Raoul's shadowy loyalties on the spot. All I could do was trust Kian's judgment; we'd talk about this after we left the cathedral.

"Just don't hurt him again, okay?" That seemed like a safe enough request.

"I'll do my best not to," he promised. "Can you say the same?"

I froze. "What are you getting at?"

It was like he could read my private fear—that something terrible would happen to Kian because of me. He felt like he owed me a debt, and like a knight of old, he seemed convinced he could only pay it in blood or personal pain. That was the *last* thing I wanted.

"You won't answer?"

"I'll try to protect him," I whispered.

"Good girl. You have all the influence now. He's not even a pawn, no power from our former master, while he owes everything to one who's not known for mercy." Raoul seemed really familiar with our problems, no need for me to explain.

"I'm aware. And I'm looking for a loophole."

"Excellent. I'll be in touch." The window closed, dismissing me.

"Kian?" I rushed out of the confessional looking for the other two, but I didn't spot them right away.

Then I saw Aaron waving from the front door. Even at this distance, I could tell he seemed agitated, so I quickened my pace, limping quickly down the center aisle toward him. Snow sputtered down, huge flakes that stung as they hit my cheeks. It hadn't been that cold when we went inside, and the sharp temperature drop bothered me.

Does that mean Wedderburn's found us? Does he know about Raoul?

"Hurry," Aaron said, grabbing my hand.

His fingers were cold and thin as he pulled me toward the Mustang idling near the corner in a no-parking zone. Aaron dove into the back and once the seat snapped into place, I slid in front and shut the door. While I was belting in, Kian took off. It felt like we were running from something and my heartbeat reflected that fear as I peered through the back windshield.

"What's happening?"

"Wedderburn."

As if the name summoned him, hail pelted us, freak weather for this time of year and the snow came harder, a sudden blizzard in the middle of the city. I had a thousand questions but with Kian fighting the wheel against the gusts of icy wind, this didn't seem like the time to ask. Since Wedderburn still needed me to repay my favors, he couldn't be trying to kill me, but the gusts definitely seemed to be trying to herd us somewhere.

"Maybe we should pull over?" I suggested.

Aaron was huddled into the hood of his jacket, all big anime eyes and nervously bitten lips. But he didn't protest as Kian snapped a sharp turn, tumbling him toward the other side of the car. That fast, the sun was out, shining brightly on the dry street ahead. A jumble of conflicting thoughts rioted in my head. *Dwyer & Fell's territory, maybe?*

"I'll drop you off at home, Edie. I have some stuff to do." Kian averted his eyes, unwilling to discuss whatever Raoul said to him.

"Can I come to your place? I feel like we need to—"

74

"Some other time. You need to get ready for school tomorrow anyway."

Wow. The straight-up rejection surprised me. But I couldn't beg when I understood what he was doing. I just had to regroup and figure out how to reach him. Raoul had probably told him that—whatever this secret—was crucial to my survival. He'd played more or less the same card with me; I just hadn't known the guy as long, so I wasn't ready to go all in this fast.

"Okay," I said quietly.

It felt crappy getting out of the car but I couldn't think what else to do. Besides, he wasn't wrong. This holiday break, I hadn't spent a ton of time on homework so I had a bunch of reading to catch up on. Still, unease prickled over me as I went inside. It wasn't the emptiness of the apartment; I was used to that. But the rooms had a different smell, nothing I could identify, but I felt as if something had been in here. Like a kid, I searched all the closets and under the bed.

Nothing.

Though all my mental alarms were going off, I got to work, reading my way through the assigned chapters. Then I typed a couple of essays and raced through the problems in my AP Calculus class. Part of me felt like this was a colossal waste of time, as Wedderburn might not even let me *go* to college, if I ended up indentured. But I couldn't live expecting the worst. I'd been in bed for an hour when my dad came in. I listened to him shuffle into the bedroom he slept in alone while guilt rushed in my head in an endless tide.

He didn't knock on my door or pop his head in to check on me. The guilt ripened into a deep, raw ache. *It's like he knows it's my fault . . . and that's why he doesn't want to be around me.* I'd hoped Christmas was a turning point, but it was starting to seem like it was more of a last look from a drowning swimmer. I smothered the bad thoughts and rolled over in bed, careful not to look at the mirror I'd draped with a sheet.

The Harbinger said that doesn't work. If I can believe him.

In the morning, a weird sensation crept over me when I slipped into my uniform, as if I'd outgrown it in a few weeks, not physically but emotionally. To make matters creepier, the trip to school on the train felt surreal too, more so when a cute college guy kept trying to talk to me. At one point, this would've been a moment that came only between the pages of a romantic story. I'd been pretty long enough to realize it came with its own complications, and now I also had to wonder if he worked for an opposing faction, if this random handsome stranger had been sent by Dwyer & Fell to test my loyalty to Kian.

Jesus. Normal teenagers don't have to worry about this kind of crap. But "normal" left the building when I took the deal.

I'd gotten good at ignoring people by fiddling with my phone, but this guy was adorably persistent—in his own opinion, anyway. "Come on, smiles are free. You can't even spare one?"

Any response would encourage him, so I flipped to the next page of the book I was reading on my phone. *Should've put in earbuds.* I didn't look over at him, even when he leaned in, trying to get a peek at what I was doing. It wasn't that he was unattractive; he radiated a Cameron Dean vibe, in fact, which meant I'd never, ever go for him. His attitude suggested he'd never met a girl who wasn't interested.

"Look, Connor, or Hunter, or . . ." I trailed off, sizing him up. "Maybe Logan. I'm sure you're a delightful, privileged asshole but I'm in no mood to experience your charms firsthand. So let's move on to you saying I must be a dyke and call it a day."

"Are you?"

"If it'll shut you up, yes." With that, I got off the train and ran toward school like he might be chasing me.

Usually, I wasn't so confrontational but I was grumpy about Kian blowing me off last night and the fact that my phone hadn't rung even once since then. Before, I had the impression he'd never bail on me—that he was into this relationship even deeper than me—and there was a certain comfort in that. Now the floor was tilting beneath my feet.

Jen and Davina were waiting for me at the front gate, though, so that was a slice of brightness in an otherwise icy, awful day. They reached for me in a joint move, so I guessed Davina had told Jen about my mom. For a few moments I stood in the hug while other students sped by, yammering about their holidays in Tahoe and the islands, tropical and sunny as they likely had been. Comforting to know some things didn't change.

"I'm so sorry," Jen whispered. "I wish I'd been here. You okay?"

Davina had on her cheerleader's uniform, so there must be a game today . . . or maybe she was just wearing it because she could. Finally. "Idiot. Of course she isn't."

"I'm coping." It wasn't like I had a choice. With my dad checked out, one of us had to try to keep life on a normal keel.

"You still with Kian?" Jen asked.

I was kind of impressed she remembered his name but it also jangled my nerves. I just nodded, pulling away with a head tilt toward the main building. "We shouldn't be late on our first day back."

Davina nodded. "Wonder who they got to replace Mr. Love."

"Wait, he's gone?" Jen grabbed my arm. "What happened?"

As we walked, Davina filled her in about all the weirdness that went down, including belly buttons. Jen flashed hers as we walked in the front doors, drawing a whistle from a passing sophomore and a sigh from the teacher who was monitoring the hallway. "No bare midriffs."

"Sorry," she said brightly, tucking in her shirt. "Satisfied?"

I managed a smile. "Yep."

We went our separate ways then. I stopped at my locker and headed to my first class, where I brooded about Kian and what Raoul had said about needing to learn some new skills. *What's he talking about anyway?* My new Lit teacher was neither young nor handsome. They'd apparently pulled some fossil out of retirement, but Mrs. Harrison led a lively discussion, seeming sharp enough that we shouldn't be bored. And she didn't stint on homework, either. There would be no dramatic pining over *this* teacher.

I was a good enough student that I daydreamed through most of my classes, though I had to focus enough not to get killed during PE. Afterward, I lingered in the shower, longer than I should have; I realized my mistake too late.

MESSAGES
FROM BEYOND

Mist whorled in the bathroom, spiraling beneath the hypnotic flicker of a struggling fluorescent bulb. I tightened the towel around me, conscious of how alone I was. The other girls had finished up and headed off to their next classes, leaving me in the locker room. Once, under these exact circumstances, I could've expected a truly heinous prank. Inside me there was still a frightened kid waiting for the torture to resume.

But my problems were broader and deeper now. My skin crawled with the unmistakable certainty that I was no longer alone. I rushed to my locker, half expecting to find my uniform missing or damaged in some ways, but most of the people responsible for that were dead. A chill went down my spine as I struggled into my underwear. Not drying off made it difficult, as did the steam all around me. Visibility was low, and the rows of lockers obscured my vision even more. Still, I got dressed in record time and was shouldering my backpack when the fog parted.

That was the right word too, as it blew to either side, as if driven by a strong wind. Seconds later, I felt that icy touch on my skin; the goose pimples popped up instantly. The mirror was smoky with heat and condensation, so I could just make out the shadowy hint of my own reflection. *God, I hope that's me.* The cold enveloped me on all sides, confirming my suspicion that this wasn't a routine let's-screw-with-Edie scenario. Nothing human could make me react like this. Since I couldn't fight a feeling, I took a step toward the doors, or at least where I thought they were.

A few seconds later, the first letter appeared in a jerky streak on the foggy glass. I. The bottom bled away in tearful drops as my breath came in quiet gasps. Unable to look away, I watched as the rest of the message appeared. AM ALWAYS WITH YOU. My heart was beating so hard it hurt, hammering in my ears. This could be only one person.

"Cameron?" I whispered.

In answer, a chill touch swept over my bare arms. Shivering, I shrugged into my blazer and ran out of the locker room. I had no idea what he meant by that, if it was a threat or reassurance, but I wasn't sticking around to find out. If I had anywhere to hide, I'd probably cower there but home wasn't any safer than school. *It didn't protect my mom.* So while I was pale and shaken, I went to class and pretended I was feeling crappy.

Not much of a stretch, actually.

Later, at lunch, Jen peered at me worriedly as we went through the line in the dining hall. "You look worse than you did this morning."

"That's awesome for my ego," I mumbled.

"Not what I mean."

Davina cut in behind us, earning a couple of dirty looks. She replied with a smile so sweet that the underclassmen probably thought they asked her to do that. "Thanks, guys. I really appreciate you letting me catch up with my friends."

"No problem," a short kid said.

I waited until we'd gotten some food and headed off to a new table. The one the Teflon crew had claimed and graffitied sat empty, and I noticed students giving it a wide berth like it was haunted. Allison headed up a new popular table along with some of Russ's lacrosse buddies and the rest of the cheerleaders; Davina showed no interest in joining them. Apparently she'd only cared about fitting in with that crowd because of Russ.

Who's dead because of me.

My stomach hurt, making it impossible for me to eat the salad and sandwich I'd put on my tray. Quietly I picked at the food, hoping the other two wouldn't notice.

No such luck.

"What happened?" Davina demanded.

Maybe I shouldn't tell them . . . but they already knew most of it anyway. I just hadn't mentioned the immortal game, and guilt flickered through me that I was being more honest with Jen and Davina than Vi. There were justifiable reasons, however, as they were at greater risk due to our proximity, and it wasn't like I could protect them as I had Vi.

With a faint sigh, I summed up Cameron's creepy locker-room visit. By the time I finished, they'd both stopped eating, gazing at me with mute horror. *Yeah, pretty much.*

Davina wrapped both arms around herself and made a face. "Is he with us now?"

"Probably." I couldn't sense him, but that wasn't a foolproof indicator. If science applied to this batshit business, then there had to be an energy cost when he manifested.

"What a perv," Jen said. "That guy doesn't change, even when he's ghosting up the place."

"Huh?" I blinked at her.

"Seriously, Cam chooses to write you a message when you're naked after a PE shower?" She flattened her mouth while lifting her eyes to the ceiling.

For some reason, that made me laugh. "I doubt that's why."

"If you say so. But I have to ask, do you have any sudden urges to make pottery?" She was smirking, so casual that it helped me settle down a little.

"Shut up." *Why is she so cool about all of this?* The question jangled in my head like an unanswered phone. I tried not to show my sudden suspicion. *Dude, you're losing it. Jen's a good friend. You can't let Allison succeed in driving a wedge.*

"If he's . . . gone," Davina whispered, "why is he hanging around?"

"No idea." If I did, I'd release or exorcise him, whatever applied to trapped spirits.

"My grandmother would say it's unfinished business," Jen offered.

"He should've written what the hell he wants, then."

Davina nodded. "Would it kill him to be specific? Wait." She bit her lip as the shitty turn of phrase dawned on her. "Okay, I didn't mean it like that. Sorry, bro." With wide eyes, she glanced around like he might be sitting here with us.

After talking with these two, I felt better, and the rest of the day was less traumatic.

When school let out, Kian was waiting for me past the gates, propped against the stone wall. Today, he had on gray pants and a tailored charcoal wool coat. The wind ruffled his dark hair, and even from this distance, it had a satiny sheen. His beauty was so remarkable that I had to search for flaws every time I saw him. But from the sharp line of his jaw to his kissable mouth, there were none. His skin was smooth and perfect, lightly tinged with gold, and his green eyes shone like gilded jade through a tangle of thick, inky lashes.

Two girls actually paused to snap a picture of him. He frowned, probably because they didn't ask permission. Then they ran off giggling like idiots. The surge of jealousy surprised me; it wasn't that I thought he was *interested* in them. *Kian loves me. Enough to die for me. And he cared,* before. But I was territorial about him, though that wasn't all of it. More that I wanted to protect him, keep idiots from treating him like he was . . . artwork in the public domain.

"That gets old," I guessed.

"I'm sure you're getting the downside by now, too," he said.

"Definitely. There was an asshole on the T this morning . . ." I trailed off as his eyes flashed. Yeah, Kian didn't like hearing about other guys trying their luck.

"I shouldn't let that piss me off."

When he reached for me, I forgot that I was irked over the way he blew me off yesterday, along with everything I wanted to talk about. He drew me close by hooking his hand behind my head and I stretched up to put my arms around his neck. I raised my face for the kiss, prompting the sweetest smile I'd ever seen from him. He kissed me once, softly, so my eyes drifted closed, then his lips brushed my eyelids in turn with such tenderness that the barbs of sweetness pierced my heart.

This is the worst part of love, I thought in silent desperation. *Because now I have so much to lose.*

His mouth came back to mine, and I was starving for him. We kissed until someone cleared his or her throat loudly nearby. Dazed, I turned my head to find Allison standing there. "You think you're untouchable now?"

"What're you talking about?"

"The Harbinger might be looking out for you, but that doesn't mean I can't make your life miserable," she said. "There are a lot of ways to hurt people that don't result in permanent physical harm."

"Don't threaten her," Kian said softly. "I'm not on anybody's leash now, and there's no limit to what I'll do if you mess with Edie again."

"Sexy little guard dog," she mocked, reaching out like she'd pat his cheek.

And he actually slapped her hand away, shocking both of us. Then he tightened his arm around me and steered us toward the car. His Mustang was parked behind all of the black SUVs and town cars, no sign of Aaron. *Does that mean he found his family?*

"Where's the kid?" I asked, as we pulled away.

"My place."

"No luck at the police station?" I expected to hear they still hadn't gone.

To my surprise, he shook his head. "There's nothing on file. Crazy, but he seems to be telling the truth about how there's nobody missing him."

"That's so sad." *Poor kid.*

"Yeah. I feel like we're kind of responsible for him now, you know?"

"We took him away from the Harbinger," I agreed. "And Aaron hasn't exactly astonished me with his street smarts."

"He's got a bad case of Stockholm syndrome. His first day at my place, he asked permission for every damn thing and shadowed me like a puppy."

"You always wanted a little brother, right?" I was trying to find the bright side.

Kian shot me a surprised look, along with a half smile. "Maybe. We won't have as much privacy at my place, though."

"It's fine. I'm sure you can teach him to respect a tie on your bedroom door or whatever. Good practice for college."

He hesitated. "I don't know if I should say this."

"Go for it. You know you want to."

"Will you look after him for me? You know. After."

My faint happiness spun away like broken cobwebs. "This is such bullshit. How long do you plan to pretend everything is okay?"

Like always, my belligerence shut him down. Kian went quiet, focused on driving instead of arguing. But I couldn't let it go.

"Keep this up, we won't even have these last months together. I don't like being shut out."

At that, his green gazed snapped right, practically sparking. "Are you threatening to break up with me because I won't fight with you?" Incredulous tone.

"Maybe."

"How does that even make sense?"

"It makes as much as you promising to die for me and then refusing to talk about it!"

His jaw clenched. "It's done, Edie. Nothing we say can change it."

The rest of the ride was silent to say the least. He dropped me off without another word and, yeah, he was pissed because I didn't even get a kiss on the cheek. I got out with a mumbled thanks and he roared off. I hated myself for bitching at him and issuing half an ultimatum and him for refusing to talk to me about *anything*. Sometimes I thought he still saw me as the dog girl, broken by that one moment and forever fragile, perched on a bridge.

As I turned to head into my apartment, I caught sight of something that chilled my blood. Across the street on the opposite corner, the old man stood with his empty sack, the two dead-eyed children beside him. Their clothes were no longer bloodstained but I knew they could show me whatever they wanted. Before I made a conscious decision, I was running on my bad ankle—into the street against the light. I ignored the shouting drivers and screeching brakes. Somehow I made it to the other side, breathing hard, but they were gone. Only the necrotic stink lingered.

The sun came out, nearly blinding me. I felt no trace of Wedderburn, who'd hired them to execute my mother. Did this mean Dwyer was paying them to torment me now? *Crazy. Sometimes a sunny day is just a sunny day.* Spinning slowly on the sidewalk, I whispered, "Which way, Cameron?"

It was a long shot, but if he didn't hate me—*if* he was an ally— then maybe he could help. I had some crazy idea of tracking down the monsters and getting back my mother's head. I wasn't religious but there were stories about how a butchered body could never rest in peace. If there was an afterlife, I wanted my mom to have the best one ever. Dumb as hell, probably, but this was all I could do after failing to protect her so spectacularly.

A cool breeze drifted along my right arm. "This way?"

No reply was forthcoming but I inhaled a hint of graveyard rot. Yeah, this was the right track. Desperate not to lose them, I pushed into a sprint despite the pain, drawing looks from other people on the sidewalk. I called an apology over my shoulder when I nearly bumped into an old woman. She shot me a glare and mumbled something incoherently cranky as I raced past. Another touch on my forearm, icy damp, and I turned that way. Two or three more jogs, more running, and soon I didn't recognize where I was anymore, and the buildings were looking sketchy, most of them boarded up or obviously abandoned.

"Shit," I said aloud. "How stupid am I?"

I had no proof this was Cameron, and this spirit might be leading me into a trap. Whatever it was, the thing clearly knew I had no ability to be rational when it came to my mom's death. I tried to calm my pounding heart and the roaring in my head that insisted I had to find the bag man *right now* and make him pay. As if my mental call summoned him, he appeared half a block down, flanked by his creepy cohorts. My feet pounded against the sidewalk as I closed the distance between us. I had no plan, just a cascade of endless rage.

But before I reached the old man, the world stutter-skipped, just like it used to when Kian ported me. I stumbled and fell over, scraping my knees on the cobblestones. Wait, what? Dizzily I took stock of the historical feel of the area. *I wasn't here five seconds ago.* Blood trickled down my wounded knee, through my tights, and my ankle was throbbing again.

"What the hell," I muttered.

A single black feather floated down from above.

I tilted my head back to find an enormous black bird perched on the electrical wires above. It watched me with beady eyes, quietly preening its feathers. I blinked and the raven was gone, replaced by a pale-faced Harbinger. Today his eyes were ringed in kohl and his mouth was red, smeared as if he had been kissing someone up until a few seconds ago. Or maybe it was blood. Both ideas were equal measures of terrifying and revolting.

I blinked again and he was on the pavement before me now, not a bird and not man, but the wild smell licked around him like a brushfire.

"You are becoming a problem," he said silkily. "Had I known you would be so much bother, I never would've made the deal."

I stared up at him.

His eyes teemed with possibilities, all silver madness etched into ebony, and he looked so deep into me that I felt his stare gnawing at the back of my skull until it seemed impossible that my brain wouldn't topple out the back and splatter on the cement. Swallowing hard, I couldn't move; he had me pinned like a butterfly in a specimen case.

"I'm sorry," I whispered.

"First you ruin my lovely spectacle, then you abscond with my favorite divertissement and now you're willfully trying to get yourself killed. Have you no mind at all, Edith Kramer?"

I'm normally the smartest person in the room, I tried to say, but my lips burned as if they'd been stitched together. I touched them with trembling fingers but I didn't feel the rough black thread I could picture so readily in my mind's eye. *One of his illusions*, I guessed, but so effective that I literally couldn't speak.

"Rhetorical question," he added, in case I really was an idiot.

I nodded slightly, remaining on my knees.

"You're forcing me to be helpful. Dutiful," he went on, radiating ire. "Faithful. All the most revolting 'fuls.' And you've *no* idea how much I loathe it." He paced around me in a tight circle while I wondered why there were no pedestrians on this oddly archaic street. "So I'll speak one final warning. I cannot be everywhere at once, and if you are so determined to die, why not save your beloved and get on with it?"

The invisible thread unraveled from my mouth, so I could respond. "I wasn't thinking. Just . . . my mother . . . and that monster—"

"Your people created it, dearling." But his gloved hands were surprisingly gentle when he pulled me to my feet. The blood was sticky on my knee, all the way down my shin. The Harbinger cupped both hands around one of mine, somber as a shadow. "Don't act like such an imbecile again. If you get yourself killed, it'll wreck my reputation—to say nothing of wasting your darling boy's sacrifice."

I swallowed hard. "I don't want that."

"Leave the stupidity for actual morons," he finished. "Otherwise it's far too confusing. But . . . I most definitely must punish you. So you don't waste my time again."

FUNERAL
OF THE HEART

The scene skipped, and I stood alone on the street near my apartment.

There was no sign of the Harbinger, but the bag man and his terrifying children were nowhere to be found either. The Harbinger might have saved me, but whatever punishment he had in store was probably worse than simple death. Pain was his purview, after all.

Instead of going home, I headed for the subway. My dad wouldn't be around until late, and I was in no mood to talk to Vi on Skype, pretending to be fine. *I'm tired of lying.* But truth would only freak her out.

Forty minutes later, I walked toward the cemetery where we'd buried my mom. It was a cold afternoon, heavy cloud cover threatening snow. The trees were dark and bare, and the grass was brown. I wove through the gravestones, stepping over tree roots grown up through the ground and tangled like petrified tentacles of some ancient, desiccated beast. A lone statue of a woman stood down the hill, her stone hair pretending to blow in the icy wind. Likewise her gown was swept back from her legs, showing bare feet, bare arms, and a bare face. She was probably supposed to be a Greek maiden or possibly a goddess keeping vigil over a nearby grave, but I had the uncanny sense that her flat eyes were following me as I passed by. Shivering and huddling deeper into my thin school jacket, I glanced back once.

Was her head at that angle before?

I told myself it was and that I needed never to watch the *Doctor Who* angel episodes ever again. But there was something inherently spooky about a graveyard anyway, knowing you were surrounded by acres of the dead. Even in the summer, this wasn't a cheerful place, though it must be prettier. I tried not to step on any plots on my way to my mom's grave, and as I knelt in front of her marker, now engraved with the Einstein quote my dad had chosen, I wished I had thought to bring some flowers. Not that my mother would care, but still. It felt weird showing up empty-handed, impulsive and thoughtless, just like chasing after the bag man. Ignoring how the damp ground soaked through my shredded tights, I bowed my head for a few seconds. In the movies, people didn't seem to feel weird unburdening themselves to dead loved ones, but I checked the area to make sure there was nobody nearby to overhear.

"I've really screwed up," I finally whispered. "You're gone . . . and so is Dad, basically. I don't know what to do. And all I can think about is getting revenge for you when I should be figuring out how to save Kian. I mean, shit, haven't I learned *anything*? Wanting to get back at the assholes at school is what got me in this mess in the first place." My voice broke.

The tears felt unnaturally hot trickling down my cold cheeks, dripping off my chin and onto my jacket. I leaned my forehead against the unyielding headstone to hide my face from anybody passing by. They'd probably guess I was grieving—and while that was true, I also didn't know how to fix any of the enormous problems looming over me. The immortal game cast a long shadow. Nerves drove me to sneak a look at the statue again. This time the angle was the same, but a black bird was perched on top of the woman's head.

Have I seen that one before . . . ? Familiarity warred with foreboding. But all crows pretty much looked the same, so I couldn't be sure. I didn't want to turn into the crazy girl shaking a fist in a cemetery, screaming, *are you following me, bird?* So I pretended there was nothing creepy about its staring.

"If this was an equation, I could solve it. But for Kian, where do I even start?" That was part of the problem, having no insight and no resources.

Unsurprisingly, she didn't answer. At least not out loud. But I heard her sighing. Since I had been listening to her sensible advice since I was a little kid, her voice sounded in my head. *What are you thinking, asking a dead person for help? But since you're here . . . you've been fighting with Kian about his decision, one that can't be changed, I might add. But have you ever once thought about how he must be feeling? You've thought only about yourself, how you'll feel about losing him. Now put yourself in his shoes. He's twenty . . . and he's dying.*

"Oh, shit," I said.

My mom—or my subconscious—was right. He must be scared to death. It wasn't like he made the deal with the Harbinger to be difficult; he honestly thought it was the best way to save me. And all I'd done was argue with him about what a bad move it was. Yet

92

if he hadn't stepped up I might not even be around to give him crap. I hadn't come here to cry, but I did, as quietly as I could manage. By the time I stopped, my hands and feet were numb. It took me a couple of tries to push to my feet and when I turned, one bird had turned into many. Hundreds of them lined the trees, on electrical wires, and the ledges of the mausoleums near the gate. And they were all watching me, all those crows, quietly preening their plumage with a vigilant air.

I took a step toward the exit and they scattered, not disorganized, nervous creatures, but more like an aerial command unit. I'd never seen crows in formation like ducks but these birds were definitely a flock. *Or something worse*, I thought. Pretending I wasn't freaking out, I hurried toward the walls and as if that was their cue, they dove en masse. Suddenly I couldn't see for the fluttering wings and sharp claws lunging for my face. Something nipped at the back of my neck and I had them on my arms and shoulders as I ran. Their talons dug into my biceps, ripping my school shirt, and blood welled up in the shallow scratches.

In blind terror, I tripped over a short gravestone and wrenched my sore ankle again. When I hit the ground, I expected to die from a thousand beaks and claws. But the murder didn't happen; instead the murder of crows flapped away, soaring up and out of the graveyard, leaving me bleeding in the dirt like that was their goal. Sore and bewildered, I got up and staggered toward the iron gates standing open at twilight. As I approached, an old man came around the corner of a tomb with a shovel; he was probably harmless but I couldn't take the risk.

"Miss, what happened? Are you all right?" he called.

I ran. Well, as fast as my ankle would let me.

Two blocks, then three. Finally I had to pause because my leg was throbbing. If I had more cash on me, I'd just call a cab, but somehow I limped the rest of the way to the station, so I could get on the T. Nobody hit on me, likely because I looked kind of nuts, covered in grave dirt and smeared with blood. During the ride, I wished I had a smartphone because it was urgent that I find out what the crows meant. Something had clearly sent them as a warning but I couldn't interpret a bird attack without outside help. I drew more than a few sympathetic glances yet no one tried to get involved in my problems.

Belatedly it occurred to me—more than once I'd seen the Harbinger as a big black bird. And he'd said he would teach me a lesson or something. The birds hadn't hurt me seriously, only scared the crap out of me. Though I needed the Internet to confirm, I highly suspected that this was the trickster version of a spanking. Otherwise, the crows would've pecked my eyes out and eaten my brains through the holes in my skull. And though I'd heard the warning from Raoul, the Harbinger telling me I might make a reckless move that he couldn't protect me from? It was definitely sinking in that I still needed to be careful.

Feeling slightly better, I got off at the stop nearest Kian's apartment and I paused outside his building. It seemed wrong to just knock, knowing he was mad at me, so I texted, I'm outside. Can I come up? A long silence followed, ten minutes, so I sat down on the steps. I couldn't go home without apologizing. Everything else could wait.

Finally, the reply came. If you want.

I limped to his apartment and knocked, my heart thumping like crazy. Kian let me in a minute later. He looked tired and, yeah, still mad. But the anger melted into concern. He reached for me, pulling me into the apartment while he took stock of my dishevelment.

"Edie . . . ?"

"Nothing serious. I need to say this before I explain. Okay?"

"I guess." He sounded none too sure that was a good idea.

"I'm so sorry. If you choose not to tell me something, I have to respect that. It's not my job to second-guess you. And I should never have said that I'll break up with you over this. I care so much about you, Kian, but I'm not very good at showing it. I get mad when I shouldn't even though that's not really what I'm feeling. I guess I just don't know how to admit that I'm freaking out and I don't know what to do. But I promise . . ."

This last part was hard to say, but I choked it out despite stinging eyes and a thick throat. "I'll be with you until the end. And if you're scared too, it's okay. I won't leave, just because it's hard. And . . . yeah, I'll look out for Aaron. After. If it comes to that. I'll live. I'll repay the favors. And I'll be free. That's what you want for me, right?"

He was breathing hard by the time I finished, his green eyes too bright. Kian hugged me to him, so I could feel how hard he was shaking. "I want to be with you," he whispered. "But I can't be. I *thought* I was okay, resigned to the fact that I'd get six months . . . and somebody else gets the rest of your life. That it's more than I deserve anyway. But this is killing me." He rubbed his cheek against the top of my head, drawing in a sharp breath. "Hearing you talk this way . . . I'm so damn scared, Edie."

"I'm sorry. I was trying to make it easier."

"You made it better . . . and worse." He didn't explain but I suspected I understood.

Probably he was glad I wasn't bitching anymore but it couldn't be easier to hear when-you're-gone type of stuff from someone you love. In answer I wrapped my arms around his waist and just held on tight. His hands moved up and down my back as if he were memorizing the feel of me. Five minutes or so later, he stepped back and led me to the bathroom.

"Aaron . . . ?" I asked.

"Asleep." It seemed pretty early for that, but he was probably recovering. Kian flipped down the toilet lid and pointed. "Sit."

Meekly I did. "What—"

"Just let me take care of you, all right? While I do, you can tell me how you ended up looking this way."

Though part of me felt like I should keep it a secret, as he had the business with Raoul, I couldn't apologize and then be all petty two minutes later. So I summarized my afternoon while his mouth flattened. But he didn't yell at me as I half expected.

He kept a level tone. "Do you mean what you said to the Harbinger?"

"No more chasing the bag man," I said.

Without a plan. That silent addendum changed everything. Yet I couldn't just forget about what happened to my mother without feeling even worse. There had to be a way to punish the guilty, even during the immortal game. I might have to make some deals, as Kian had, but I didn't plan to barter away my life. What else did I have of value? Maybe Raoul could guide me. In the confessional, he'd said he would tell me more next time, implying we'd meet again.

"Thank God." Kian interrupted my quiet plot, deftly cleaning my wounds and applying antiseptic. A few Band-Aids patched me up enough to satisfy him, though he studied the scratches on my back long enough to make me wonder if there was something else going on. I shifted and glanced over my shoulder, but the wounds were shallow, normal bird-claw size.

"What are you looking at?"

He touched the bare skin of my shoulder blade lightly, sending a shiver through me. "I just hate that you're hurt. Means I didn't protect you. I got pissed off and—"

"If you didn't, you wouldn't be human," I protested. "And I swear I've learned my lesson, being impulsive doesn't suit me."

"I could stand for you to be a little reckless. With me."

"What did you have in mind?"

In answer, he led me to his bedroom. My nerves prickled with excitement as Kian shut the door. Then he pushed me up against it, kissing me with a thrilling need. Longing sparked through me, compounded by the hovering awareness that I could lose him. Soon he might not be around to touch me at all. Everything Kian, gone, gone to feed the Harbinger. I tangled my fingers in his hair and stopped thinking entirely for a little while.

"I shouldn't push you," he whispered against my lips.

"Mm. I'll let you know if it's a problem."

We were just getting into it with him nudging me onto the bed when the spare bedroom door opened and closed. "Kian?"

Above me, he closed his eyes and groaned. "That kid . . ."

I laughed. "Makeup making out can wait, right?"

"Like I have a choice," he muttered. "He's so needy. I wake up and half the time, he's sleeping across the foot of my bed like a spaniel."

"Yeah, that's weird."

Once Aaron settled down, we went into the living room and I stayed for dinner, telling myself my dad would eat something at the lab. The three of us ordered pizza; Aaron's expression while he devoured it suggested he'd never tasted anything so delicious. While I still didn't trust the kid 100 percent, he struck me as weirdly candid, like there was no way he could keep this up indefinitely with a hidden agenda.

It was ten when I got home. My dad was unlocking the door, but he didn't check the time or ask where I'd been. He gave me a half smile, eyes circled in shadows. His uneven scruff had evolved into an unkempt beard, and I could smell him. He took a step into the apartment and stumbled, either from weariness, lack of food, or maybe even booze.

Damn. This can't continue.

I blocked him from heading straight to his room. "You need a shower. And then we have to talk."

"Not tonight," he mumbled.

"If you ignore me again, I'm calling someone. A grief counselor. Somebody. Because you're not okay. You didn't even notice that I got hurt." I showed him the ACE bandage around my ankle. If he'd been paying attention, he'd have noticed it over my tights. Once, he'd have registered that instantly.

"What happened?" he asked sharply.

"That's not the point. Go shower."

To my shock, he went into the bathroom and the water came on. I closed my eyes for a few seconds, horrified. *We've switched places.* I sat down on the sofa to wait. When he came out, he hadn't shaved but he seemed to be clean. My dad should be mad at me by now; I'd treated him like a dumb kid.

Instead he was still blank, tired. "It's late, Edith. Say what you need to."

"Remember when I asked you to be here for me?" At his blank look I added context. "That was on Christmas. Do you even know what *day* it is? Mom wouldn't want this."

"And *I* don't want to live without her," he burst out.

I froze. "Dad—"

"Don't worry." He forced a smile, the least convincing lip rictus I'd ever seen. "I'm not on the verge of harming myself. I'm sorry if I scared you. Things are actually going well at the lab and I'm absorbed in work, that's all. I thought you were too occupied with Kian and your school friends to notice how busy I am."

That most definitely wasn't true, but I had no evidence to dispute his word. Heart falling, I watched as he got up and trudged to his bedroom. The click told me I had been locked out. Again. Anger warred with worry as I stared at the wood. I walked over and pressed my palm to the door, willing him to get better. *Please, Dad. I can't do this on my own.* If he showed the slightest inclination, I might've even talked to him about my problem with Kian, some kind of theoretical challenge, maybe. *I could've said it was for some kind of gaming campaign. Where diabolical deals would make sense.*

But there was no point wishing for help; Dad was barely treading water. I went into my room, feeling scared and alone, and I couldn't even text Kian without making him feel worse. Sharp pain lanced through my stomach, probably the beginnings of an ulcer. Rubbing my abdomen, I checked e-mail and replied to Ryu and Vi.

And in the morning, I skimmed my phone for the message I'd been waiting for, one from Raoul. He'd sent an address, along with:

4:30pm tomorrow. Come alone in workout gear. Make sure you're not followed.

BADASS
IN TRAINING

The next day I headed out in sweats, a T-shirt, and winter coat, along with my Converse. I got off the subway three blocks from the address Raoul had provided. Maybe I should've messaged Kian, but if his mentor wanted him there, he'd be waiting, right? I stopped in front of an ominous brick building: three stories, most of the windows had been boarded up, and the front doors were chained, while also hung with the sign that read CONDEMNED. There was an older plaque on the side but the lettering was too faded for me to tell what had been here before they shut the place down.

"Seriously?" I mumbled.

"You're right on time," a familiar voice said from behind me.

I whirled and got my first look at Raoul. He was an imposing man in his early fifties, sporting a well-groomed goatee and dark hair with silver at the temples, which crested the back of his neck. Dark eyes studied me, set in a weathered face, and his skin showed a Mediterranean-looking tan. He was handsome, though, and I saw why Kian had compared him to Ramirez from the Highlander series. Though he didn't actually resemble Sean Connery, he gave off the same air of impatient command, like he had something more important he should be doing.

Raoul wore gear similar to mine and he waved me forward, demonstrating how to duck under the chains and slip inside. "Come, I shouldn't be on the street in daylight any longer than absolutely necessary."

"I thought you couldn't be tracked."

"True. But one of the Harbinger's winged spies could spot me and he'd be pleased to sell my whereabouts, wouldn't he?"

Probably.

"What are we doing here?" From the look of the run-down building, it used to be a school.

"Heading for the training facility."

"Excuse me?"

But he didn't answer, leading the way through a warren of dark corridors. The smell suggested nobody had been here in a while, so the bright side was we wouldn't be disturbed. But I was pleasantly surprised when we got to the gym. He'd obviously done some cleaning and it looked like a small dojo with mats and sparring equipment. Some of it, like the bo sticks, I recognized from martial arts movies. There were also poles, kick targets, parallel bars, and a heavy bag.

"You said you were willing to work hard," Raoul said softly. "Now you prove it."

I'd seen countless training montages before; they didn't remotely communicate how hard he worked me for the next two hours. First it was warm-up exercises and then katas. After that, he showed me very basic kicks and punches. I couldn't tell what martial style he was teaching, so when he gave me a chance to catch my breath, I asked.

"This is only a self-defense course," he told me. "You don't have the time to learn an actual style, but there may come a moment when knowing how to dodge or strike may save you. For Kian's sake, you have to know a little something about saving your own life."

Considering how I did against the monster I'd volunteered to fight, I saw his point. "I get it. How often should I come?"

"Four times a week if you can manage it. Depending on how well you take to the lessons, we may work on more advanced training. If we have time."

"You sound like you're expecting something specific and horrible to happen," I said.

He didn't speak, but I saw the reply in his expression. Raoul's dark eyes were somber with acknowledgment. *Yeah, I'm right.* Because the future was fluid and each choice resulted in branching possibilities, he couldn't be sure exactly when the shit would hit the fan, but I could tell he was sure there would be messy splatter sometime soon.

His aspect remained grim. "Don't think about that. Just prepare for it."

"I feel like Sarah Connor in *The Terminator.*" Bad joke, the best I could do.

That roused a reluctant half smile, making me kind of proud of myself. "I'm not surprised Kian's so fond of you. There's a . . . brightness about you. He could use more of that."

"I'm trying." Pain bubbled up as I thought about my dad sleepwalking through life, and my mom, who was gone. The rush nearly took me out at the knees. "It's not always easy."

"No, it never is. And there'll be those that accuse you of being heartless too."

It seemed like he understood what I was going through. I realized I was already talking to him like I did Vi—with no thought about how much older he was. *No wonder Kian bonded with him. He's really good with people.* Or maybe I trusted him instinctively *because* of his relationship with Kian. Whatever the reason, it wasn't like me to connect so fast. I needed to think about what it meant and if I could actually trust him.

"So I'll see you tomorrow?" I chose not to wade any deeper with him until I had some reflecting time.

"Same time, right here. Be ready to sweat."

"I will be," I answered, shrugging into my jacket. "But . . . is there some reason Kian can't know about this? I get the impression he doesn't."

"He wants to protect you. So . . ." Raoul hesitated.

"Just tell me."

"Therefore, I think he'd resist you doing anything that pushes him out of the hero's role. But those ideas are old-fashioned and they result in the chivalrous knight laying down his life."

Actually, that tracked with what I knew of Kian. He'd said as much when I swapped my last favor to protect him and save his life. "Then I'll keep it under wraps. See you tomorrow."

●   ●   ●

In the morning, I let the drama department know I wouldn't be helping with backstage management after all. Since I wasn't irreplaceable, they didn't seem to mind. At lunch I texted Kian to let him know I didn't need a ride. If he came to my school, he'd wonder

103

why I was in a hurry to get home, change, and rush out again. Raoul hadn't mentioned him, so I guessed Kian knew nothing about his mentor's goal of turning me into a badass, one I supported. I was tired of freezing in fear, tired of not knowing how to protect myself. Sure, I might come up against monsters I had no hope of defeating, but it'd be better to die fighting than get mowed down.

The rest of the week, I divided my time: working in the dojo with Raoul, searching in the library for information on how to break a contract, sitting in class or doing homework. By Friday, judging by the tone of the texts, Kian thought I was avoiding him. But it wasn't like that at all; I just didn't have the energy to hang out along with everything else. Once I got used to the intensity of the training sessions, that would probably change.

I hoped.

Because otherwise, we were going to have another big fight. Sighing, I blotted the sweat from my forehead and jogged slowly toward the subway station. The car was packed since it was around seven. All I wanted was to take a shower, put on pajamas, and do some homework. But when I got off the train on my end of town, I saw Kian waiting in front of my building.

His face brightened, until he registered how tired and sweaty I looked. At least I was guessing that was what turned his smile upside down. "Where were you? I've been here for a while."

"My dad's not around to let you in?" Dumb question, it was only seven. It would be a miracle worthy of notifying the pope if he showed up before nine. But it was also a red herring, diverting attention from my activities.

"That's not an answer."

Dammit. Should've known that wouldn't work.

"I was working out. Now that my body's awesome, I'm trying to keep it that way." I kept my tone light, offering him a smile.

"Then why are your knuckles scraped?"

Catching myself before I could glance down, guilty, I shrugged. "Maybe I scratched them on a wall."

His jaw clenched. "Edie. You're a terrible liar. You've been dodging me for days and now you can't even look me in the eye."

Just to prove him wrong, I lifted my face and gazed into his green eyes. "Better?"

"Not really." A sigh escaped him. "Can I come in? It's Friday night, and Aaron's watching movies at my place. I thought we could hang out."

"Sure. Just let me shower. Coming?" I let us into my apartment and went straight to the bathroom to investigate how many bruises I had. Today, Raoul had been teaching me how to fall since I couldn't always avoid getting hit.

My right arm had a hematoma, so did my hip and my left leg. Raoul didn't pull his punches when we sparred, and if I didn't block, I bore the failure on my skin. If I was careful, Kian wouldn't see any of that tonight. I took a quick shower, washed my hair, and looked for clean clothes. Not sweats since I hadn't seen him in a week, but I didn't think we were going out, so it didn't make sense to dress up. It was ridiculous I could still think about stuff like this, considering all of my other problems, but some parts of being a teenage girl didn't yield to larger issues. Eventually I settled on black capri pants and a pretty purple sweater. Kian was perched on the couch when I came out, though his pose communicated his discomfort.

"What's wrong?" I asked.

"Are you really asking me that?"

"Sorry. I'll make sure we spend more time together next week."

"That doesn't explain anything."

"Do you want me to lie to you?"

That startled him into silence. Then he shook his head. "If you can't tell me, say so."

"Okay. Well, it's nothing bad. Just . . . something I'm doing for my own peace of mind. But, no, I can't talk about it, just like you can't share whatever Raoul said to you that day in the church. And I'm not pushing. So it's fine to ask for the same back, right?"

Kian eyed me for a few seconds before nodding with obvious reluctance. "Well played."

"Any news on Aaron?" It seemed like I should change the subject.

"No. But you know what's weird about him?"

"Everything?"

He laughed as I settled on the couch beside him. "Well, yeah. But specifically?"

"You'll have to tell me."

"He didn't know anything about modern technology. Like the TV, computer? He couldn't remember how to use any of it. So I've been teaching him. But he acts like it's magic or something. When I start talking about the science behind it, the beams and rays, his eyes glaze right over."

"Not everyone's as smart as you." Ironic for me to be saying that—Kian loved poetry, but he also understood the hard sciences. In my experience, that was kind of rare.

"You had to be there, I guess. I swear he was like those old comedy sketches when some guy from the Renaissance is plopped in the middle of a modern city."

"That's . . ." I stared at him, unable to believe the idea I was entertaining. "It would explain why nobody's missing him. Right now."

Kian's eyes widened. "'Now' being the key word?"

"Do you think it's possible?"

"That he's missing, not geographically, but chronologically?"

I nodded. "My hypothesis is on the table. Discuss."

"As a theory, it's crazy. But—"

"There's a compelling rightness about it. This might sound incredibly basic but . . . have you asked him what year he was born?"

I got a stare in return, then a slow headshake. "No, it's not the kind of question I'd ask unless this was a movie where somebody's waking up with massive head trauma."

"Do you mind if we do a little fact-finding at your place? I know you had something more romantic in mind tonight, but I'll make it up to you tomorrow."

"Promise?" Kian asked, low.

"Yeah." I kissed him quickly and then put my coat back on.

It wasn't strictly necessary but I also left a note for my dad. *Went to Kian's. Home later. Love you.* The fact was, he probably wouldn't see it until morning, if at all. But my conscience wouldn't let me go about my business as if I lived alone. I loved my dad, no matter what; he was pretty much all the family I had left. Sighing, I pulled a wool beanie on and then headed to the door, where Kian was waiting.

"Ready?" He reached for my hand as we left the apartment building.

It was a cold clear night, city lights sparkling diamond bright all around us, white from the streetlights, red from the stoplights, yellow and orange neon from restaurants across the street, blinking a garish invitation. My breath came out in a wisp of smoke, twirling upward into the night sky until I couldn't see it anymore. I thought of the molecules packing together, reacting to the cold air. Such tiny particles, making up the bigger picture; there was always science at work, even in the simplest process. For some reason, I didn't feel as scared as I did before—maybe because Kian was with me, maybe because I was slowly learning how to fight back. There was no way I'd turn into a ninja overnight, but those hours with Raoul were helping.

That new mental ease also made me realize something and my smile faded. "It's probably not as great as you imagined."

"What?"

Several cars passed before I spoke. "Being with me. You built an ideal from watching me. But up close, I'm awkward, annoying, not smart in a way that's *ever* helpful, plus I get mad over dumb things, and—"

"Hold up."

He stopped walking between my apartment and his, and since we were holding hands, an extra tug twirled me back toward him. Kian caught me by my upper arms, just before I hit his chest. For a long moment, he stared down into my face before curving his palm to my cheek. The heat of his skin came as a small, sweet shock, sending a pleasurable chill through me.

Smiling, Kian ran his thumb over my cheekbone lightly. "You think you're a disappointment?"

"How can I not be?" I couldn't meet his gaze.

Changing how I looked had changed how people treated me but a complete internal shift would take longer. I didn't have the confidence I pretended, even now. Intellectually, I believed that Kian cared about me, but it was hard to accept emotionally—to put my full faith in it. It was hard to trust that his devotion could survive obstacles like the ones we were facing, and in my worst-case scenario, he couldn't stand me when the Harbinger called for payment, and Kian died wondering what the hell he was thinking, chucking his life for me.

"Sometimes you surprise me," he admitted. "But it's never bad. I love getting to know the *real* you because it means I'm part of your life." Then he bent, punctuating the rest of his words with slow, gentle kisses. "I wouldn't change this time with you for a hundred years with anyone else. Now let's go talk to Aaron."

I followed when he tugged on my hand, hardly able to breathe for the ache in my chest. There was no way I deserved Kian, though part of me thought he might actually be some kind of karmic repayment for the shit I went through at Blackbriar. Not that I actually believed in any kind of universal balance. Supernatural forces were definitely at work, but they cared more about winning points and ruining another player's gambits than maintaining equilibrium.

Aaron was watching one of Kian's classic DVDs when we came in. He smiled at me and made room on the couch, all wide-eyed innocence. *Are you punking us, kid?*

I thought hard about it, but in the end I still asked, "What year were you born?"

"1922."

Kian sucked in a breath, sinking onto the love seat opposite. "Are you kidding?"

But the boy's blue eyes were clear as he shook his head. "I've been away a long time. The world is very different now."

Shit. No wonder he didn't want to go to the police station.

"How old were you when . . ." Kian trailed off, probably not knowing how to phrase it.

"Six when he took me," Aaron answered.

We had tons of questions, mostly historical, and Kian sat with his tablet, verifying trivia about what Boston was like back in the day. Considering his age when he was stolen, his right answer ratio seemed about what I'd expect, hovering near 60 percent. But it was really late when we wrapped up, and I'd ignored one text from my dad already.

Finally, I said, "I better head out. It seems my father's paying attention to my curfew."

That was actually a welcome change. So Kian walked me home and then we were kissing on the stoop when my dad marched out. Never in my life had I seen him so furious. He actually hauled me away by the arm and fixed a hard look on us both.

"I asked you to come home hours ago, Edith. You didn't ask permission to go to your boyfriend's house tonight. You nagged me so much to be around more that I got groceries and I made dinner, so we could eat together like we used to. I'm making an effort here, in answer to *your* demands, and—"

"Excuse me, I had no idea we were having dinner because you didn't tell me. I haven't seen you in *days*, it seems like. How am I supposed to read your mind?"

"All you had to do was check your messages," he snapped. "And this attitude is not helping. You're grounded, two weeks, nothing but school. Give me your phone."

I shot a horrified look at Kian. Our time was limited enough already. And how was I supposed to work with Raoul? When he said I needed those skills, he wasn't screwing around.

"This is *complete* bullshit," I protested.

For the first time in my life, my father slapped me.

IT CAN ALWAYS
GET WORSE

Kian stepped between us. "Don't—"

"Stop," I said, knowing there was no way this wouldn't turn into a huge mess. "You better go home."

"Not when you're in trouble." He put a protective arm around me, which was sweet but by the way my dad's face darkened, it wasn't helping.

"While I appreciate everything you've done to help, this is a family matter. You won't be seeing Edie anytime soon."

My heart in a knot, I stepped away from Kian. "It's okay. Night."

He didn't look pleased when my dad dragged me into the house, and I got why. My cheek was still stinging. I'd never mouthed off like that to my father before, never cursed at him, that I could recall. He'd probably attribute the aberrant behavior to Kian's influence. Which meant I'd be lucky to see him ever again, let alone in two weeks.

I don't have time for this.

Inside the apartment, it was ominously quiet apart from the

ticking of the clock. I sat down on the beige couch without waiting for my dad to order me. He took a seat opposite, anger knitting his brows into a formidable line. I tried to look penitent, but deep down, a sense of injustice percolated, bubbling away along with the witch's brew of anger and outrage that came with this grounding.

So unfair. He ignores me for weeks, then expects me to read his mind.

I got a fifteen-minute lecture, followed by a five-second apology. Though I said all the right things, I was still pissed off when I retreated to my room. He had no idea what I was facing, or how much worse things could get. These days I had battle scars, wounds I'd taken trying to fight. I doubted my dad would understand that, either.

Curling onto my side, I went to sleep only after a lot of mental gymnastics. In the morning, Dad stuck around to make sure I honored his edict about staying home. It could be considered progress, I guessed, since we ate six meals together over the weekend. Monday morning, though, he seemed half crazy with the need to get back to his research.

"What about drama club?" I asked, eating a spoonful of squishy high-fiber cereal.

"Hm?" In his head, he was already at work.

"I'm not allowed to go anywhere but drama club meets three days a week after school."

"Oh. Extracurricular activities are fine. But come straight home."

I choked back a joke about him fitting me with an anklet that tracked prisoner movements. Knowing my dad, he'd find someone at the university who could jury-rig one. So it was better not to put ideas in his head.

Nodding, I scraped out my bowl and put it in the sink. "I'll be back around six."

"Have a good day."

"You too."

At school, the atmosphere was weird and hushed as I headed for my locker. Two students were whispering as I walked by, though not about me. "No, seriously, it's true. She has a picture and everything."

"Yeah, right," the guy scoffed.

"What's the deal?" Once, I would've been afraid to speak up like this, afraid of drawing negative attention.

The girl replied, "Apparently Allison Vega was working on a student council project after school Friday night and she saw something in the hall."

I raised a brow. "Like what?"

If she was responsible for this gossip, there was a 99 percent chance it was malicious, designed to foment panic and chaos. But the other two were taking it seriously, and all around me, people were checking their phones. My dad had given mine back this morning with the understanding he'd confiscate it again tonight, once I was removed from any possibility of needing emergency assistance.

"Blackbriar's haunted. Allison thinks it's Russ or Brittany."

Or Cameron, I thought. But nobody else knew he was dead, apart from Davina and Jen, who were taking *my* word for it, and there was no way they'd talk to Allison about it. Okay, maybe this wasn't bullshit. Because there was a spirit following me around, enough to seriously freak me out, if I didn't have so much other weird shit weighing me down.

"You don't believe me?" the guy said, copping some attitude. "Check this out."

He shoved his phone at my face, so it took a few seconds for my eyes to focus. I saw that the e-mail had five FWs before the subject of "Holy shit," then the pic popped up. It was a hallway in the science annex, all of the overhead fluorescents were off, but there was enough ambient light from the high windows to give the sense the picture had been taken around twilight. Near the end of the corridor, an amorphous shadow stood, freestanding, framed in the doorway. It seemed to have shape and mass, independent of any light source, yet it was also transparent. A chill rippled over me. I'd never seen Cameron, apart from flickers in my peripheral vision, but this could be him.

"Pretty crazy, right?" The girl looked like she wanted to call one of those ghost-hunting TV shows right this minute.

"Could be Photoshopped," I pointed out.

But I didn't think so. It cooled off some of their excitement, though. The guy cocked his head. "Shit, that does seem like something Allison would do. Send around a fake ghost photo, get everyone pissing scared, and then announce she was punking us."

I half smiled. "Thanks for filling me in. I have to get to class."

The rest of the morning, I played good student. Davina needed consoling because people were talking shit about Russ, calling him the strangled specter. Which was flipping macabre and, pretty soon, morons were talking about cold spots and feeling hands on their necks in the shower. While I thought Russ was an asshole when he was alive, it sucked that he was turning into an urban legend—and *oh, shit.* I needed to put this rumor to bed before enough gullible people made it come true. Sadly I had no idea of the tipping point—how *many* people needed to buy in—before Blackbriar actually had an entity created in Russ's monstrous image.

My blood ran cold. *And Allison knows that.*

During lunch, I went to the new Teflon table and tapped her shoulder. "Can we talk?"

Allison glanced up, flipping shiny dark hair. *Yeah, she's eating well.* It occurred to me that she must've found it hilarious pretending to be bulimic to pass better as a human. The scientist in me entertained fierce curiosity about her species and how she differed from other immortals; the rest of me realized that I didn't have time for distractions.

"I have better things to do and they don't include validating your existence."

Leaning in, I pitched my voice low. "I know what you're doing with this stupid Blackbriar ghost."

Her perfectly lipsticked mouth curved into a pleased smile. "Call it a social experiment."

"You don't know how many people it takes either, do you?" From the flash in her eyes, I'd struck pay dirt.

But she didn't answer. Instead she turned to the dude next to her and loudly complimented him on his stupid hair, spiked with enough product to put someone's eye out. Sighing, I went back to my own table and pondered ways I could completely discredit the story. By the time school ended, I was already exhausted. Since Kian knew I was grounded and forbidden from seeing him, he didn't pick me up. That gave me the window I needed, breathing room from both my dad and boyfriend, to make my training session with Raoul.

Who looked impatient as hell when I ran into the gym ten

minutes late. "Do you take this seriously? Do you understand what's at stake?"

Between my dad, Kian, Allison, and the Harbinger, the urge to burst into tears hit me hard but I wrestled it down. *Crying won't help. It won't save Kian or make my dad understand. It won't break the Harbinger's deal, stop Allison, or make me stronger.* So I squared my shoulders and bowed like I'd seen students do to an honored sensei.

"I'm sorry. I'll do better."

Mollified, he said, "Stretch out, run your katas, and then show me what you can do on the practice dummies. Once you're ready, we'll spar."

I did as I was told and earned the right to punch his gloved hands after an hour of brutal sweating. That actually felt really good. Raoul called a halt, let me drink some water and walk around, then we met in the center of the mat. He took up a battle stance, both of us unarmed. I was still too inexperienced to be trusted with a practice weapon.

"Come at me," he invited.

This was never going to be my first instinct. The idea that I could ever kick someone's ass seemed ludicrous, but I readied myself and went in, only to be taken down hard. All the breath rushed out of me as my back slammed into the mat. I lay there for a few seconds, wheezing and seeing stars.

Raoul made an impatient noise. "You're small. You're weak. You're tentative. Congratulations, anything in the game will eat you before you get in a single strike."

"Is this your idea of a pep talk?" Somehow I managed to roll over and wobble to my feet.

"It's your reality. I'm trying to teach you how to survive."

"And to save Kian," I said.

"That too. Again."

Raoul threw me five more times, each time harder than the last. He didn't hit me today, but I couldn't penetrate his guard enough to make it worthwhile. I was bruised all to hell by the time we called it quits. I didn't say anything as I limped toward the exit.

But he called after me, "You're stubborn. That'll help."

A faint, exhausted sigh escaped me. "I hope so. It never has before."

"And you know what it's like to be broken. You won't let it happen again, will you?" He was relentless, digging at old scars to see if there was any raw putrefaction beneath.

"No," I said softly. "I won't roll over again. I won't go quietly."

For the first time since I'd known him, Raoul gave me a warm, true smile. "I'm counting on that, *mija*."

The two weeks of my punishment went slowly. I Skyped with Kian, trained my ass off with Raoul, and ate dinner with my dad. Things were a little better at home. He was making an effort, so I tried to do the same. I couldn't say it was perfect; tiny fissures had formed in our relationship. It was hard to forget the burn in my cheek after he hit me, easy to remember all the nights I went to bed without seeing him and left in the morning the same way. Yet he was all the family I had left, so I had to patch things up.

I also had homework and friends to reassure. It seemed like there weren't enough hours in the day because I poked around online, searching obscure texts and trying to find some medieval codicil that would free Kian. So far all of my Google-fu qualified me only as a noob, not a ninja. The answer was probably in a dusty old book, hidden in a quaint corner shop somewhere in Europe written in ancient German, and I'd never in a million years find it.

So tired that even my eyeballs hurt, I put my face on my desk. I lay there for a few seconds before realizing it was late enough that my dad should be home by now. He hadn't missed dinner in weeks. Blearily I looked at the clock on my laptop. 8:59. I'd been researching Kian's problem since I got home just before six and hadn't even touched my homework yet.

Telling myself it was nothing, I got my cell phone and texted my dad. Should I make something for dinner?

No reply.

I waited for five minutes while fear beat a bass tempo in my skull. My hands shook when I called him, but it went straight to voice mail. A cold chill went down my right side and I turned, half expecting to see the shadow that Allison had allegedly photographed. I was already putting on my shoes when the weeping letters appeared on the misty windowpane.

HURRY.

That was all I needed to see. As I ran down the stairs, I texted Kian, Meet me at the station. Dad in trouble. Heading to BU. Bursting out of the building, I startled the birds nesting in the eaves. At first I was too terrified to register but they paced me, soaring in lazy circles overhead like an aerial honor guard, or maybe impartial observers.

"Harbinger," I breathed.

They stayed with me until I stumbled underground, where I lost time on the stairs. There was no way I could wait for Kian, though, when I sprinted to the platform as the next train was about to leave. I barely slid through the doors and grabbed on to a pole, breathing hard. For a few seconds, the metal supported my whole weight since my knees shook too hard to hold me. The normally brief ride seemed to take forever but it gave me a chance to catch my breath. I'd left without my coat, so it was freezing when I got off at the university stop and sprinted for the lab. There were other people around but I paid no attention to them as I dodged and wove, closer, closer. The birds found me again on campus, so the only thing I could hear was the taunting flutter of wings. They didn't caw, only circled silently, come to bear witness and report back.

I need a weapon, I thought, but there was no time.

My worst fears crystallized when I skidded up to the door of the science wing where Dad worked; the glass was smashed all over the ground and the metal frame was bent inward, partly torn from the hinges. I raced down the dark hallway, following the thumps, crashes, and cries of pain that had to belong to my father.

His lab was completely trashed, and the monsters inside it absolutely defied description, like something out of Lovecraft— grotesque and enormous, covered in eyes, mouths, and tentacles, and the smell . . . the smell was swampy, stagnant water, slimy, fetid flesh, and half-decomposed vegetation. They didn't look remotely smart enough to be doing this of their own volition, so that meant they were somebody's muscle. The fact that I wasn't peeing down my leg just looking at them was a good sign.

My dad was holed up in his office, adjacent to the lab, and they were bashing in the door, just like they had the other one. I restrained a burst of hysteria. *I'm not too late this time.* An incredulous look dawning, he spotted me and shook his head frantically, telling me to get the hell out. I shook my head. *Nope, not happening. I'm not scared of monsters. I'm not, I'm not.*

A tentacle slammed into the glass beside the door, splintering it. *Okay, maybe a little. Still not leaving.*

But this was way more than I could handle on my own. *Maybe I can lead them away so my dad can escape. I'm fast.* So I glanced around, looking for something that said diversion. Ten feet down the hall I spotted a janitor's cart and my brain lit up. *Please be a smoker. Please.* When I found the lighter, the idea solidified. I made a few more preparations, my hands shaking.

Finally, something's going my way. I put on rubber gloves, then shoved the cart toward the lab. Another crash told me they were almost through the door. This had to be Dwyer, determined to neutralize Wedderburn's advantage. *Gained by murdering my mom.* I hated them both with a ferocity that defied description. Right now, though, I didn't give two shits who had sent these mindless brutes. I had to get my dad out of there.

It was possible I'd die trying.

I pulled my shirt up over my face—crappy gas mask but it was all I could do—and got a bucket. Every chemistry teacher I ever had told me *never* to do this. First bleach, then ammonia, and I kicked the cart as hard as I could toward the beasts. *Chemical reaction: first hydrochloric acid . . . Next we get chloramine, poison gas. Do these things breathe? Guess I'll find out.* The wheels' rattling motion drew their attention away from the door and I used the seconds to light up an oily rag I'd tucked into a half-empty plastic Coke bottle.

Please let there be enough ammonia. Come on, liquid hydrazine. I need a big boom.

"Take cover," I shouted at my dad, just before I hurled the demi-Molotov.

I sprinted away from the doorway as the fumes exploded. The walls trembled and I smelled something horrible, like rotten meat on the grill. On my hands and knees, I crawled through the smoke, trying to keep low. *If we don't get out of this soon, we'll die too.* The sprinklers kicked in, dousing the corridor and laboratory. An inhuman rumble of pain and rage told me at least one survived my surprise.

As I reached the threshold, I took stock. *Holy shit. I actually killed one. Well, destroyed it. Whatever.* Chunks of rubbery, charred flesh were spattered everywhere, dripping off the walls in viscous globs. I choked down some bile and took a shallow, stinging breath. My eyes were burning like the water was full of chlorine; that had to be the remaining chloramine vapors. If the lab was bad before, it was total devastation now with small fires guttering everywhere, struggling in the deluge. I slipped toward my dad's office, frantic.

And the remaining monster charged me.

"Are you crazy? Get out of here!" My dad's voice was hoarse, probably from the smoke, but I ignored him.

It was all I could do to stumble aside and dart around an overturned lab table that the beast smashed with one lash of a tentacle. The floor trembled and I staggered backward, tripping over debris, but my training with Raoul had improved my reflexes. Instead of falling over, I righted myself and scrambled for a weapon. Not that I thought I could really kill it, but . . .

I can save my dad.

"I'll keep it busy," I yelled back. "Get moving, it's after you, not me."

He called something but I didn't hear it. I laid a hand on a broken table leg with a jagged, pointy end. Considering the monster's overwhelming size—at least twelve feet—a David and Goliath comparison seemed apt but I was fresh out of slingshots. The longer my dad lingered, the less chance either one of us had of making it out, between the fumes and the Cthulhu beast—part man, part dragon, part octopus.

He won't go. Despair cloaked me like darkest night.

Still, I raised my weapon like Raoul had taught me. I might not be very good at this, but I was a fighter now, right? The monster lashed at me and I tried to leap clear. *Not fast enough.* The blow caught me across the back and I actually felt my ribs caving in. It hurt to breathe. I tried to maneuver but the slick floor and glass fragments made it impossible. My palms sliced open as I tried to haul to my feet, red smearing the makeshift weapon I was barely hanging on to. Distantly I realized my dad was beside me, trying to drive the creature away.

Failing.

It hit me again, sweeping me like rubbish against the far wall. The impact cracked my ribs on the other side; the pain was excruciating. I couldn't move anymore, except to blink. My lashes gave a dark fringe to my last moments. I thought about my mother . . . and Kian. Vi. Ryu. Davina. Jen. *At least they'll miss me.* Blood trickled from my mouth, and I stared up at the horrid thing that would kill me.

Except it didn't.

I heard the flutter of dark wings all around me, and then *he* was here, all darkness and ominous promise. The Harbinger's voice whispered like silk across a blade. "Take only the one you came for. She belongs to me."

Save him instead, I tried to say. My lips moved. No sound came out.

The monster made an awful, gargling noise, as if in acknowledgment, and then snatched my father up, lurching away through the broken doorway. Tears trickled out the corners of my eyes but I had no strength to wipe them away.

The Harbinger knelt with dreadful tenderness and plucked the matted hair away from my cheek. "What am I to do with you?"

At his touch, the pain receded enough for me to whisper, "You could've saved him."

"He's not mine to protect," came the indifferent reply.

My throat worked. "I hate you."

"I know, dearling," he said, oddly wistful. "I know."

Then, mercifully, he brushed his hand down over my eyes; the pain went like a snuffed candle, and with it the whole world.

AN ALIEN, IMPOSSIBLE THING

I woke in someone else's bed. The mattress was softer than mine and the covers were faintly scented with lavender. Darkness cloaked the room, so I could make out only the vague shapes of furniture in the room: chest of drawers, rocking chair, steamer truck piled with books and magazines. Nothing about the space seemed particularly ominous.

The next thing I noticed was a peculiar lack of pain. With the injuries I'd suffered, it should hurt, just lying here. Breathing had felt like I had shards of glass slipping in and out of my lungs, but other than a residual soreness, I didn't feel too bad. That . . . was impossible. Unless . . . was this my coma dream awakening? I tried to decide if I felt like I'd jumped off a bridge but I came to no conclusions; on the bright side, if I'd leapt and survived, then my parents should be nearby. Afraid to let myself hope, I struggled upright and sat trembling on the edge of the bed.

The door opened, silhouetting a feminine figure in the light from the hallway beyond. "You must be confused."

The woman flipped the switch in the room and the fringed lamp on the bedside table came on. Illumination revealed a homey room, done in inviting earth tones down to the rumpled quilt I'd just crawled out from under. My feet were bare on the throw rug, which seemed to have been woven from strips of fabric. I was wearing a clean white flannel nightgown and I guessed it must belong to my hostess. Whoever she was.

"You could say that."

The last thing I remembered was—rage swept over me—the Harbinger cutting a deal with the Cthulhu beast, letting it take my dad. My hands curled into fists. Anger was a refuge because fear and sorrow lurked behind it, a river of tears in which I could drown.

"I can see certain memories are starting to return. Are you hungry?"

"First I have questions."

"So I imagine. But you can ask just as well while you eat, don't you think?" Her tone was so sweet and mild, I felt like an asshole to insist.

Getting up proved a little tougher than anticipated, but I managed on my own. Which I shouldn't be able to do, frankly. Given how pulverized I was, it should've taken weeks to get me ambulatory. Unless . . .

"What day is it?" I demanded.

Smiling, she told me. I relaxed a little, though I didn't understand how I could've healed so much in two days. My head hurt, as if I'd just shaken off the effects of some powerful narcotic. In my bare feet, I shuffled along behind her into the kitchen, all lemony cream, ruffled curtains, and kitschy-cute feminine style. It was impossible not to be charmed by the gingham-check cushions, and as I sank onto one, I couldn't decide what to ask first.

In the clear morning light, I got my first good look at her. She was brown-skinned with short, curly hair and an open, honest expression. Her features were broad but soft with faint smile lines at the corners of wide brown eyes. She offered me a cup of tea, pouring hot water into my mug from an electric kettle, and the sweet aroma of peppermint wafted up.

"I'm Rochelle," she said. "Or at least, that's the name I'm using now."

"You've been called other things over the years," I guessed.

"The Harbinger said you were clever. It's nice to know he's not always wrong."

"It doesn't sound like you're a fan."

"Of his? No. But I honor old debts."

"And that's why you healed me?" I'd already figured out she must be a defunct goddess of healing, but I was too groggy to match one of the old names to her, let alone a bunch, like I had with the Harbinger, Wedderburn, and Dwyer.

"You're not a hundred percent," she admitted. "My power's no longer sufficient for that."

"How is that you have any left at all?"

"There are still a few corners of the world where they light candles and invoke me. These days I work as a doctor . . . and live mostly as a human." Her tranquil smile made me trust her instinctively, so I fought the urge.

"You're not part of the game?"

She shook her head and got a plate from the fridge, then popped it in the microwave. This seemed so strange—so *ordinary*—for someone who used to grant prayers and heal the sick. "I don't hate humanity, so I can't get on board with creating so much misery and bodily harm for my own amusement."

I paused, struck by what she'd said. A while back, I had a conversation with Kian, where I guessed that was why they competed. "That's why? I mean, there's no endgame. The contest just goes on and on."

"Exactly. It's a way to dispel the ennui. And for some it's about petty revenges and evening the score with a rival. Humans made their gods in their own image, so all the faults are magnified on a grand scale."

How depressing.

The microwave pinged. She got a hot pad and gave me a plate covered with dishes I didn't recognize. There were eggs in sauce and some kind of oatcake, but it seemed like a bad idea to sniff suspiciously at the food. Besides, it smelled good, and if she wanted to harm me, the time to do it would've been when the Harbinger carted me in here, crushed like a bug. My stomach growled, sealing the deal.

Picking up my fork, I ate half of what she'd given me without saying a single word, while she pulled the tea bag out of my cup. The remaining liquid was golden brown and deliciously redolent of mint. Serenity stole over me; all my concerns seemed like distant memories and tension seeped out of my muscles. My parents, the Harbinger, Kian . . . they could all wait until I had a meal, right? Something about that didn't seem entirely right but I ate my breakfast anyway.

"That's good," Rochelle said, smiling. "It's important to keep up your strength even when action is critical. The Harbinger will be here shortly."

That startled me enough that I dropped my fork. Reality crashed the dome of tranquility she'd shaped around me. *Oh my God, my dad, where's my dad, and Kian must be so worried. I've been gone for forty-eight hours.*

"Where's my phone?"

She shook her head. "You didn't have it when you arrived. The clothes you had on were ruined and there was nothing in your pockets."

Shit. It must've bounced out when the monster was knocking me around. God only knew what Kian made of the trashed lab, my phone smashed amid the wreckage, and both my father and me missing. *But the Harbinger probably let him know, right?*

"Do you know if he notified anyone?"

"The Harbinger?" Rochelle laughed as if I'd proposed something preposterous. "You do realize he delights in chaos. So if he could create disorder by *not* telling someone where you are, what do you imagine he's done?"

"Not told a soul," I said glumly.

"Don't despise him too much. He's this way because of the stories. At this point he'd change if he could but we can only push our natures so far."

"Are you talking about me?"

I had a riotous impression of dark wings in the window and voice where there was no throat capable of speaking, and then the wings were a cloak or a topcoat, hard to say with the shadows looming over Rochelle's once-bright kitchen. When light and darkness came to equilibrium, the Harbinger was perched on the chair opposite me, drinking my peppermint tea. He wore the bohemian finery I'd noted the first time we met, hat neatly on the chair next to him.

"You're showing off," she observed. "Last time you called, you knocked at my door."

It seemed as if he were smiling, but I still couldn't look directly at his face because of the awful weight of his tragic beauty. His mien made me want to throw myself into his arms but I also wanted to flee, screaming. He was an alien, impossible thing, inscrutable, unknowable, and his gaze crawled over me like a thousand insects or butterfly wings, both, neither.

I hated him. *After I fought so hard, he let it take my father.*

I feared him. *When he spoke, the monster listened.*

But there was something else, deep and strange, quivering in the pit of my stomach. It wasn't longing like I felt for Kian, but I had to acknowledge the feeling. *Reluctant curiosity. Fascination, even.* If the moth was capable of reason, it might feel the same, circling a flame. *It's so very bright. What will happen if I move a little closer?* This was probably a sickness, similar to radiation poisoning.

"If I become married to the mundane, my dear Brigid, then I may as well find a job. How's *your* work with the poor and infirm?" His mordant words didn't seem to faze her as she took my teacup away from him and set down a fresh one.

"Rewarding," she said gently. "It's not the same energy I get from the odd ceremony, but it keeps me going."

"Better than eating people," I muttered, thinking of his compact with Kian.

The Harbinger said nothing. Rochelle's peaceful aura seemed to be working on him as well. The sense of constant motion and the lightning-charged air died away. For the first time I focused on his features, apart from the glamour or whatever he had. The Harbinger wasn't as handsome as I'd initially thought. In fact, his face was thin and pale, bony at brow and chin, cheekbones gaunt rather than elegant, and his eyes were gray. His brows were heavy, black slashes that gave him an angry, impatient aspect. But his hair, that was every bit as pretty as it had been, still long and black, star-kissed with silver. I didn't feel sick to my stomach when I completed the inspection, either. To my eyes, he looked tired, as if protecting me had sapped more energy than he'd anticipated. His gaze met mine, so *old* that I went breathless. It was like staring into time itself while suspended above a bottomless pit.

"It's clear you two have unfinished business, so I'll leave you to chat," she said.

When she left the room, the first prickles of lightning came back. My skin tingled, and I looked away, braced for the time when he'd hit me visually like a force of nature. *Did Kian know what it would be like under the Harbinger's protection when he made the deal?* I truly hoped the answer was no.

"You still hate me," he said unexpectedly.

I couldn't tell if it was a statement or a question. But I nodded anyway, in case he was checking. Then I demanded, "Who took my dad? I have to save him."

"What makes you think I know?"

"That thing recognized you. So it stands to reason you know what it was. And who it works for."

"You underestimate my renown. Do you think there are many immortals of my caliber who choose not to play the game?"

That was a good point, but . . . "You're jerking me around. Why?"

He let out a faint sigh. "If I tell you, you'll go after your father.

131

And I don't have the power to save you. Edie Kramer, you are exhausting."

"Sorry." The apology was instinctive and I regretted it at once. Though I had a ton of grievances against him, I hadn't meant to suck him dry like a psychic vampire, but I'd rather not admit it.

His expression shifted, the minute difference undecipherable. "But that doesn't alter your resolve . . . and that puts me in an awkward position because if I let you die, that voids my compact with your beloved."

"Really?" Wait, no, that wasn't a solution. He'd offered to eat me a while back if I wanted to die, but giving up wasn't the same as trying your best to save someone and failing.

"You've changed since we first met, grown more intractable and courageous. I understand how you became the little queen."

Those words rang a bell in my head, but I couldn't place them. When it hit me, my eyes widened. "Mr. Love . . . ?"

The Harbinger's face shifted for a few seconds, showing me the teacher who drove poor Nicole nuts. "I'm touched. I wondered if you would recognize me."

Holy shit. I remembered how afraid of him I was, the way we clashed, and how the symbol reacted to him. Weirdly, they didn't activate in my defense when I went up against the monster in the pit, when I sparred with Raoul, or while the Cthulhu beasts attacked me at the lab. *I wonder why not.* Distracted, I pondered for a few seconds. As for Raoul, my brands probably sensed he didn't mean me any harm. *Possibly the other assailants weren't smart or powerful enough to trip the alarm?* At best, I was only speculating.

"Trying to solve complex problems with insufficient data?" It was like he read my mind, and how disturbing if he *could.*

No, it's a just good guess. He already said he's tapped out.

Not letting the Harbinger intimidate me, I demanded, "Why did my mark throw you so hard? It hasn't responded to anything else."

"What makes you think I'd tell you, presuming that I know?"

Quietly I wondered if I could hurt him. At the moment, I really wanted to, especially given how he stood aside and let that thing steal my dad.

"I wouldn't," he whispered.

It sounded like he wanted me to try, as if that were the first step down a road I couldn't turn back from. So I folded my hands in my lap. "You really were draining Nicole dry."

With a languid shrug, he said, "I took what was freely offered. And . . . she'll survive."

"But she'll never be the same."

"Should that concern me?"

Clenching my teeth, I started to list all the reasons why the answer was yes, but he went on without waiting. "I regret this necessity, but I cannot permit you to return to your old life."

"Excuse me?" That shocked all thoughts of justice for Nicole out of my head.

"It's fair recompense when you consider it. You *did* steal my favorite pet, so it's only right that you should replace him. And there are perks." When he gestured, a chill rolled over me, not painful but . . . bizarre. Invasive.

"Absolutely not." I tried to get up and found that my arms and legs didn't belong to me.

"At my current strength, it's the only way for me to protect you. If I let you go out into the world and cause trouble, it'll be the end for you, dearling."

"I don't care," I gritted out.

He went on as if I hadn't spoken. "You may have already gathered that my former pet is a tad . . . strange, a by-product of such a long life. Humans don't always take to it."

That distracted me enough to do the math. *Aaron was born in 1922. He was taken when he was six, in 1928.* In that time, he'd only aged eight years or so, an average ratio of 1:11. Extrapolating a normal life span of seventy years . . . *holy shit. I could live to be 770.* If the Harbinger didn't put me in a pit for a gladiator fight. Which he'd done to Aaron after only eighty-seven years, and that didn't speak well for my chances at longevity.

"Not interested."

"Then leave," he invited.

I glared, as he knew well I couldn't budge. He specialized in illusions but he apparently had some real power too. *Or maybe he tricked my brain into thinking I was paralyzed?* As soon as I registered the thought, I stood up.

The Harbinger seemed honestly startled. "You are quite remarkable."

"Not really."

"Most people panic and their emotions override their ability to reason. The fact that it occurred to you to question how I did it . . . extraordinary."

"Stop complimenting me." I scowled, fomenting the hate I'd felt just before I passed out, the pain of watching my father being taken, and unable to stop it.

"I say this in all candor, though you've no reason to trust me. If you come to me, Edie, I shall treasure you. In time you will forget the pain of your world and relish living in mine." His tone was smooth, seductive, even.

On the pale wood of Rochelle's tabletop, shadows danced in a delicate promenade, spinning in response to a faint gesture from his wrist. I could live in that world—with him. No more fighting, no more worries about my safety. Everything that caused me grief would fade away into endless revels and laughter. But I'd be pinned to the Harbinger, dependent on his good will. The refusal started as a knot at the heart of me and pushed outward until I could picture Kian's face again, and my dad's tortured confusion as he tried to get me to leave the lab. Though he had no idea what was going on, no clue how to fight, he never ran. Never left me.

Sorry, Dad.

"No deal," I said.

"You were tempted." There was a smile on his mouth but it didn't reach the mad glitter of his eyes.

I ignored that. "I'm going, unless you plan to stop me."

"He doesn't," Rochelle answered, stepping into the doorway. "I have some clothes that will fit . . . and a day pass for the subway. That should get you home."

The Harbinger stood. I didn't expect what happened next—when he lifted my chin and made me meet his dreadful, grieving eyes, as if something truly awful had just happened. The pleasure came on, excruciating and against my will. He made me conscious of the extreme heat of his fingertips against my skin as he drew a curved line from my jaw to my cheek; I squirmed, imagining more, when I didn't really want that *at all*. Reluctant excitement warred with shame when I jerked away, breathing hard.

He smiled. "Stay out of the shadows, pretty one. They belong to me. And I don't like being denied anything I want."

It was tempting to ask why but intuition told me I needed to go. Now. While Rochelle was calming him and running interference. The room felt like lightning could strike at any moment, along with gale-force winds. I had no context for the depth of this rage. So I jerked away and ran to the bedroom, where track pants, slip-on shoes, and a sweatshirt awaited me. The clothes were a little big, but not bad. Searching around the room, I found the ticket she'd mentioned and ran for the door. From the kitchen came a great boom, followed by raised voices and shattering glass.

"What freedom?" the Harbinger roared. "You're sending her to her death."

Despite the ominous prediction, I dashed out without looking back. The soreness ripened into actual pain when I tried to run down the stairs, echoes of the severe injuries from two days ago. Breathing hard hurt too so I slowed to a walk once I reached the sidewalk. As I spun in a slow circle, taking in identical brick buildings, nothing gave me any hint where I was, so I risked asking a stranger. Luckily, the old woman I stopped was friendly and in no hurry; she gave me detailed directions on how to get to the closest station.

Ten minutes later, I stepped from the platform onto the train that would take me home. If I had a phone, I'd call Kian to let him know I was safe, but Rochelle hadn't given me any spare change either, assuming I could find a payphone. *I hope she's okay. The Harbinger seemed like he was about to go off the rails when I bolted. Wish I knew why.*

As the train sped away from the station, I had the uneasy feeling that I'd added the trickster to my growing list of enemies, a mistake I might not live to regret.

THIS PIT OF DESPAIR NEEDS CARPETING

Once I left the subway, my steps turned automatically toward Kian's apartment.

Mine was just an empty shell now, and my dad's disappearance hit me all over again. The pain nearly made me topple over on the sidewalk; I caught myself on a brownstone, leaning heavily enough to draw looks from passersby. It was late morning and cold as hell, the wind chill biting through my sweatshirt. My ribs ached from the cold, as if I breathed too hard I could crack them all over again.

The phantom taste of copper clung to the back of my throat as I went up to Kian's front door. It seemed wrong to disappear for two days and then just . . . knock, but I had no other options. I wasn't prepared for how ravaged he looked when he flung open the door, staring with absolute incredulity. For a few seconds he was just frozen, staring, then he staggered against the door frame, his knees apparently giving way. I tried to hold him up but I couldn't. My sides were still too tender to bear that much weight, so I went down too, and then he put his arms around me like I might be made of smoke and would dissipate with a touch.

"You're real. Right?" Kian moved his hands over my back, testing for himself.

"Yeah."

"Why didn't you wait for me?" His voice broke as he leaned his forehead against mine, shaking too hard to stand.

"I couldn't," I whispered.

"Your dad . . . ?"

Misery knotted my throat until I could barely answer. "They got him."

"Is he—"

"I don't know. If they wanted him dead, it would've been easier to do it there than kidnap him, wouldn't it?" That gave me hope that whoever had taken him wanted to use his research or abilities in some fashion. If that was true, I might still save him.

"Do you have any idea how scared I was when I got to the lab and found it completely trashed and on fire? When I couldn't find you anywhere . . ." Kian buried his face in the curve between my neck and shoulder, seeming on the verge of a complete breakdown.

I managed to knee-walk us into the apartment and shut the door, so we both collapsed against the other side of it, curled into each other until I couldn't tell who was supporting whom. He touched me compulsively—my shoulders, my arms, my hair—and I cried like I couldn't before. The questions had to wait until we both calmed down; he held me without asking and I wept until his trembling subsided. Then we stumbled into the living room, which looked like a tsunami had swept through. There were printouts everywhere, crumpled maps with red circles and purple Xs all over them, pillows and blankets on the floor.

"What happened?"

He threw me an incredulous look. "Are you serious? We've been searching every inch of this fucking city for you. The circled, Xed areas, we've already checked."

"Who's we?"

"Raoul, me, Aaron—who's out looking for you right now—your friends Jen and Davina."

"Seriously? You called them in on this?"

"What did you expect me to do, Edie? You're lucky I didn't lose my damn mind. Where the hell were you?"

I collapsed on the couch, wincing. There was no way he'd calm down before I filled him in, so I did—in the fewest words possible. His jaw got tighter as I spoke, until I suspected Kian was grinding his teeth, especially when I told him that the Harbinger asked me to come to him, whatever that meant. I was sure he hadn't meant it in a romantic sense, unless you were the kind of person who enjoyed leashes and cages.

When I finished, he didn't say much, just got on the phone to call Raoul, who was currently canvassing with my picture. Another few days and they'd probably have put me on a milk carton. He also texted Jen and Davina, then I borrowed his laptop to reassure Vi. She tended to worry if I didn't answer her messages quickly. So I wrote:

Sorry, I lost my phone. Haven't had a chance to replace it. Hope things are going better for you. Want to Skype tomorrow?

I wasn't in the mood but if I could keep from stressing her out too much, that would be best. Otherwise she'd steal her mom's credit card, book a flight, and show up at my doorstep. Which would be all shades of a complication I didn't need.

An hour later, Kian had brought me a backpack full of clean clothes and I was in the shower when the search party arrived. I checked my ribs in the foggy mirror, angling my body so I could see the deep, faded bruises wrapping around my torso. It was insane that I wasn't in an induced coma with bleeding organs and a ruptured lung. A shivering breath escaped me as I remembered the enormous thing that carried my dad off. With near hysteria, I wondered what the university security cameras would make of that fracas, if the monster would show up on video, or if it would look like something else.

Maybe the equipment will just seem to be malfunctioning, like it's been jammed.

When I came out of the spare bedroom, everyone was assembled in the living room. Which someone had tidied up a little. Davina ran over to me and hugged me gently; Jen was a little slower but she seemed legit glad to see me back. My gaze went to Raoul, wondering if he'd mentioned my lessons. He seemed to guess the question and shook his head slightly.

"Kian already filled us in," Davina said. "That is some crazy shit."

"I'm sorry to drag you into it."

Jen shook her head. "We were worried and went to your house, where we ran into Kian, who was just sitting on your front steps. Once we realized you were missing, we had to help. I just wish we'd actually *found* you."

"It was a catch-and-release detainment." I didn't feel like making light of my situation, but the alternative was to sit and cry.

"So sorry about your dad." Davina put her hand on my shoulder.

Aaron was sitting at the kitchen table, just watching everyone with nervous, darting eyes. He was okay with Kian and me, but I guessed adding three new people to his circle freaked him out. I could relate as it hadn't been long since I had nobody to talk to at all. And now, there were five people willing to go without sleep and wander the city asking random strangers about me. Hard not to be touched by that. Hell, Vi and Ryu would've helped too, bringing my friend-and/or-ally total to seven.

Maybe this situation isn't hopeless after all.

"Thanks. But I haven't given up, I have some ideas about how to track him down."

Davina nudged me with a conspiratorial smile. "Mind showing me your belly button?"

"Heh." I flashed it at her, loving the fact that we had an in-joke.

Once she explained the reasoning for it, everyone else did a quick shirt-flip so we could all be sure there were no immortals masquerading among us. Jen and Davina both stared a little too long at Kian's golden six-pack, seeming unwilling to swap that for Raoul's hairier belly. Aaron was very pale and thin, but he'd definitely been born to a human mother. I relaxed a little, though the need to rescue my dad pulsed like a sore tooth.

"You can't stay in that apartment on your own," Raoul said quietly.

"Why not?" The protest was instinctive, but truthfully, I didn't want to. Nor was I eager to crash on Kian's couch. I wasn't ready to flipping live with my boyfriend.

Kian sighed as if the answer should be obvious. "It's too dangerous."

My lips went flat against the urge to tell him I could probably kick his ass in stand-up fight, unless he had a secret black belt he never mentioned.

Raoul warned me with his eyes not to open that can of trouble today. Sighing, I said, "Then what do you propose?"

Jen said, "My room is huge. I'm sure you could stay with us. My mom's very cool about stuff like that. If I tell her your father is traveling on the lecture circuit, she wouldn't want you home alone."

I hesitated. This time it wasn't because I didn't think that could work or that I was worried about her safety—she was already in pretty deep—but I recalled what Allison said. Basically even if Jen was human, I wasn't fully sure where her allegiance lay. *Who do you trust more, Jen or Allison? Who would definitely lie to cause trouble?*

She saw my hesitation and her face fell. "If you don't want to, it's cool. We don't know each other that well and all of that shit went down last year . . ."

"No, I was just considering logistics, wondering if your mom would impose a curfew or hinder my search for my dad. Will she want to talk to my dad?"

Jen's widening eyes said she hadn't considered any of that. "Shit. I don't know."

"Are you sure about this? It might not be safe having me around." I felt like I had to remind her of that. Guilt about her failure to stop my humiliation last year shouldn't push her to endanger her parents.

"Uhm . . ."

I let her off the hook. "Don't worry about it. Having me around is high risk, basically an invitation to screw up your life."

Jen bit her lip, dropping her gaze to the floor. "Sorry. I really do want to help."

"It's enough that you joined the search party."

"I can stay with you," Raoul offered.

"In my dad's room?" Though misgiving flickered through me, Raoul could definitely protect himself. He was training *me*, for God's sake. And it would make me feel better if he was around. It wasn't like I was using him to replace my father, either.

"Okay," I said.

Kian was frowning. "Is that safe? There are eyes on Edie all the time and if word gets back to Wedderburn—"

"It won't end well for me, I know. But I'm already living on borrowed time, am I not?" Raoul gave a weary smile, as if he was sick of the cloak-and-dagger bullshit.

"Just be careful, okay?" Kian clapped Raoul on the shoulder, a bracing gesture when his eyes were saying all kinds of crazy worried stuff.

When an imperious knock sounded, we froze. I gauged the windows, wondering if Raoul could slip out that way if need be. Jen answered the door hesitantly and I don't think anyone was more astonished than me to find Allison Vega standing there in her cheerleading uniform. She swept past Jen and Davina in a cloud of mango-fruity-smelling perfume.

Allison seemed to take stock of our war council and sighed, tipping her head back to stare at the ceiling. "This is the lamest thing ever. How did any of you survive before I got here?"

"I don't know what you're doing here," I snapped back.

"Saving your ass apparently. Word is, you pissed off your protector and are fair game."

"He can't do that," Kian snarled.

"Calm your tits." Allison sat down without being invited and crossed her legs daintily. "I'm sure you've told them about me by now?"

"I have questions," Raoul interjected.

She gave the older man a long look, one I'd ordinarily qualify as challenging or defiant, but there was a curiosity too. I didn't know what to make of that silent exchange but she was smiling when he looked away. Raoul rubbed his fingers over his forearms; it freaked me out to see that Allison was capable of unnerving him. In the short time I'd known him, he was always so calm and purposeful.

"You're not young at all," Aaron said unexpectedly. "You . . . are a very old thing."

"Out of the mouths of babes. Shall I speak in ancient Sanskrit? Nah, no point. Nobody remembers the old tongue." Allison rapped her knuckles on the table. "I've just called this crap to order, so settle down."

I was curious enough about her intentions that I perched on the edge of the sofa and Kian joined me, quietly linking our fingers. Jen and Davina sat at the dining table with Allison and Aaron while Raoul opted to stand near the door. That was probably smart if she was setting us up; her plan might be to stall long enough for reinforcements to get here. Deep down I hoped she was on the level because I needed all the help I could get. Even from people I hated.

Fortunately Davina had no problem being attitudinal with Allison, regardless of what she was. "State your business then, bitch. You're no friend of mine."

"Don't be bitter. Aren't you more confident about your abilities because of how hard you worked trying to make the squad?"

Davina lunged at her, only to be restrained by Jen. "I thought you hated me because you're new money and I'm no money, but that's not it, is it?"

Allison grinned. "It was fun to crush your dreams, little girl. They were so fragile."

For a few seconds, the rest of us might not have even been in the room as Davina seethed. "Did you have anything to do with what happened to Russ?"

The girl-looking thing hesitated, appearing uncertain for the first time since she'd swept in here, ostensibly to do me a favor. "I knew something was feeding on him. I had no idea there was a kill order pending. I don't pay that much attention to politics."

Raoul had been listening with careful attention, likely assessing Allison as a potential asset. "Exactly where do your kind fit into the game?"

"I have no horse in this race, if that's what you're implying." Her lip pulled back in a half snarl that sent shivers over me even as her face seemed to waver for a few seconds, as if she could look like something else entirely.

"Let's hear her out," I said.

Question and answer could wait until we heard what she'd come to say. Allison nodded at me, either in thanks or agreement. Then she spoke. "You definitely shouldn't trust me. But until further notice, I'm on your side. I've always had a soft spot for the underdog and it's clear you have a hell of a fight on your hands."

"What do you bring to the table?" Kian asked.

"Contacts, mostly. I understand your dad's gone missing?" She didn't use the word *kidnapping*, which I appreciated.

I nodded, then described the thing that took him. Allison's mouth twisted as she listened. It was hard not to shake her and demand info but Kian's hand on mine kept me calm. I noticed Jen and Davina trading holy-shit looks. I appreciated them not asking if I was high when all this went down.

"Do you recognize it?" Raoul asked.

Allison shook her head. "But there are tons of awful uglies prowling the dark shadows. People are always buying into some new horror. With humanity's penchant for grimdark, it's a wonder any of you are still around." Then she stood up. "There's no need for me to hang around. I'll put the word out on your dad, and I have your number, Edie. I'll text if I hear something."

Two words I never expected to say came out then. "Thanks, Allison."

She smirked and brushed past Jen and Davina, lingering long enough to make Raoul uncomfortable. Everyone was tense until the door shut behind her.

Aaron actually shivered. "I don't like her. She smells sour."

"Try being on the same squad with her," Davina muttered.

"It's disturbing that she chooses to hang around a high school," Raoul observed.

I suspected that was because it was a great place to start drama, lots of negative energy to eat on a daily basis. But we were allies, at least for now; there was no point in speculating. I just had to believe she meant it when she said she'd help me find my dad. Of course, maybe that offered the most potential for a splatterfest and she'd be on the sidelines soaking it in.

Pushing to my feet, I said, "Let's not worry about it now. Raoul, are you ready to go?"

He picked up my backpack as I slipped into my borrowed shoes. I was about to leave Kian's place, over his vociferous protests, when someone knocked on the door. Nobody seemed to have any clue, though I guessed maybe Allison forgot to tell us something. To my astonishment, when Kian answered, Rochelle stood on the other side.

She radiated urgency when she beckoned. "There's not much time. The Harbinger's looking for you, and he's in no mood to talk. I tried my best to convince him otherwise but he's decided the only way to save you is to—"

"Make me his pet," I finished.

Rochelle inclined her head somberly. "You have other options, Edie. But there's darkness down every path. Do you trust me to teach you how to unlock the power you need to survive?"

No, I thought.

But I followed her anyway.

DEAD BOYS
DO NOT MAKE
GOOD PETS

"Are you crazy?" Jen asked, running after us.

"You just *met* this woman." Davina seemed to agree with Jen.

"I have to take help when I find it. You get how messed up everything is, right?"

They didn't respond, so I took that silence as a yes.

Raoul wore a speculative look, as we paused in the hallway outside Kian's apartment. I didn't care what anyone else thought. If she could teach me something that would give me a leg up in the game, then I was on board. I handed him my keys.

"Here. You can move your stuff in. I'll be back later." Unless this was a calamitous misjudgment. I was willing to take the risk.

Aaron stood in the doorway with a lost look. "If it's okay, I'll stay here."

"No worries," Kian said.

"Do you plan to accompany us?" Rochelle asked.

He stilled, a dangerous glint in his green eyes. "Is that a problem?"

"Not for me."

Kian relaxed and took my hand. "Then let's get going."

We went our separate ways outside with me promising to text Jen and Davina as soon as I got a new phone. Actually, money might become an issue. *No, I'll get my dad back before I have to worry about rent or the electric bill.* It was hard to stay positive, but if I let it, reality could truss me up and leave me helpless.

Rochelle took us to Jamaica Plain on the orange line, where we got off at Green Street Station. She went west from there, winding through avenues unfamiliar to me. This area was full of small, quirky shops and cafés, and the population was diverse. I followed her through multiple turns until we came to a narrow street where all the buildings were constructed using the same red brick, giving it a peculiar, uniform air. She stopped in front of what looked like a consignment shop of some kind. The dusty front window was full of interesting oddments: a mannequin half tied into an old corset, a wig of long black ringlets, two music boxes, one of which was open to show the tiny ballerina spinning in endless circles, along with a broken fan, and two dingy satin shoes. There were no store hours posted and the faded sign above the shop read FORGOTTEN TREASURES. BY APPOINTMENT ONLY.

"It looks abandoned," Kian said.

"Looks can be deceiving." Rochelle got out a heavy key ring and fiddled until she found the right one, an enormous iron thing with sharp teeth. "Here we are."

The shop sighed when she popped the door open, emitting a

gust scented with dried lilac and dust. Hesitantly I stepped over the threshold behind her, wanting to believe she hadn't lured me here to turn me over to the Harbinger or worse, Dwyer & Fell. Tinnitus flared sharply and I spun in a shaky circle, looking for the source.

"It's the artifacts," she said kindly. "Think of it as a feedback loop."

"Wait, so everything in here—"

"Is charged, so to speak. I've been collecting cursed and haunted objects for centuries. It started as a hobby, but then I realized how much harm I was preventing, just by keeping the wretched things away from people."

"Yet here we are," Kian observed.

Rochelle switched on a lamp with a fringed shade that threw rosy light over the jumbled premises. "Don't touch anything. Some of them are probably quite hungry by now."

I threaded through the narrow gap between a sheet-draped harpsichord and a grimy leather chesterfield with carved legs. On closer examination, there was a deep, dark stain on the seat. "Noted."

A shiver rolled through me. I'd just gotten used to the idea of monsters; now I had to adapt to the possibility that household items could be possessed and might try to kill me. But there was no doubt there were unfriendly forces in this room. Rochelle seemed mindful of this as she picked a path toward the back counter. I made sure to stick to her route and not brush against anything. Kian copied me, staying close, as Rochelle emptied a box atop the counter. She showed no fear in sorting the objects but she had the power to protect herself.

"This." With a flourish, she showed me a square compact, Art Nouveau style, either pewter or badly tarnished silver. Rochelle snapped it open to reveal a cloudy mirror; the other side had space to affix a photo.

Sometimes it sucked being human. "Sorry, I don't get it."

Her expression went grave, her eyes deep and somber. "Remember I mentioned your passenger?"

Cameron.

I nodded. "What about him?"

"There's a way you can use him, if he's willing. I sense no malice from the spirit and I believe he wants to serve you."

"What the hell?" Kian gritted out.

Rochelle explained better than I could about the ghost hanging around me. I couldn't remember if I'd told him about what happened in the locker room and feelings I'd had before. So much shit had happened, it wasn't like I meant to leave him out. To my surprise, he didn't lose it over my ghost infestation and seemed all right with whatever Rochelle had in mind.

But he's been in this world longer. Weird is relative.

"If it'll keep her safe, do it," he said, once she finished.

Rochelle glanced my way, but I had some questions first. "Are there any dangers?"

"Yes." Her answer came way faster than I could feel comfortable with but it was probably good she wasn't lying. "The biggest risk is you getting addicted to the power and becoming disinclined to set your spirit familiar free when the time comes."

"Seriously?"

"Where do you think stories of wizards like Merlin and Rasputin came from? They were human, once. But if you traffic too long with the dead, you *will* be forever changed."

"So I might not even be a person anymore? It could . . . turn me?"

151

I wanted so much for Rochelle to reassure me, but that wasn't her style apparently.

She paused, weighing the pewter compact in the palm of her hand. Then she whispered, "I mentioned that all your paths are dark ones, did I not? Though I'm no oracle, I believe this offers your best chance at survival."

"What do you think, Cameron?" It seemed unlikely he could answer but I hated the idea of imprisoning him without checking in.

Kian jerked his head toward me, eyes widening. *Oops. Forgot to mention that, huh?* But Rochelle glanced around as if she sensed a change in atmosphere, then I felt it too. The nape of my neck prickled with goose bumps and the air got perceptibly colder. Kian stepped closer in reflex and put an arm around me, not that the threat was anything he could see.

"You're always with her," Rochelle said softly. "I thought so. Knock once if we should proceed, twice to decline." One clear rap sounded on the wall immediately to my left. She turned to me with a satisfied expression. "Your familiar has volunteered. That will make the binding easier."

That word had all kinds of icky connotations but I didn't argue when she started setting up. First she cleared off a long table, then she unearthed long metal trenchers, which she arranged in a rectangle with the pewter compact between them and me on the other side. Candles came next and an assortment of herbs, sprinkled into the trays. Finally she went into the back and returned with a pitcher of water.

Probably seeing my confusion, she explained, "It's the perfect conductor. I'll submerge the talisman and you'll dip your hands when the time comes, forging the link."

"Okay." God, this shit was strange, especially for someone who preferred science to magic. No matter how I tried, I couldn't figure out a formula for any of this.

"Go around the table, wait for my signal."

I did as instructed; Kian stood nearby to my left, though what he planned to do if this went heinously awry, I had no idea. Still, it was pretty cool he was right here, taking the risk along with me. The chill in the air intensified as proof that Cameron was still hovering.

"Why are you helping me?" I asked her.

Probably I should've questioned sooner. This would likely piss off the Harbinger, definitely Dwyer & Fell, and I had the impression that Rochelle got along by staying neutral. At this juncture, her aid could almost be interpreted as allegiance to Wedderburn's faction. It wasn't that I hoped she'd realize this was a bad move and back out but I had to be sure I wasn't signing some kind of implicit contract, like, *by accepting my assistance now, when I knock on your door in three months, you have to help me bury this body, no questions asked.*

And how bizarre that this was how my mind worked now.

"You remind me of someone." Her expression went sweet and soft, eyes glazed by time and distance.

Even I couldn't bear to pry further. "Then . . . thank you."

"This is all I can do," she warned. "I won't answer if you knock. And I certainly won't fly to intervene as the Harbinger has done, on more than one occasion."

"He's obligated," I mumbled.

She raised her eyes, an amused light in them, and a cruel smile twisted her mouth. For the first time I saw the opposite side of the coin. Healing wasn't only kindness; there was also pain. "Is that what you think? He's enthralled, Edie Kramer, and that's dangerous. You see, the Harbinger is like a cat. Do you know anything about feline behavior?"

"They pretend to be tender and affectionate," Kian said. "They purr. They show softness. And when you least expect it, they bite."

Rochelle nodded. "They also kill their favorite toys. Repeatedly."

Fear was too weak a word for the knot in my stomach. I didn't want the Harbinger to find me fascinating. Maybe I should've displayed more awe, less speaking my mind. It had probably been a long time since anyone failed to kowtow in his presence. That was the only reason that I could imagine; otherwise his interest made no sense.

"Can we get this done? I'm feeling vulnerable."

"Remember this moment." Her eyes met mine.

"I will."

"And recall that you cannot keep the power that you're borrowing. To permanently confine a spirit for your own use, that is true evil."

Her somber mien hammered home how dangerous this must be, how much potential it had to turn me dark. I imagined myself as a witch covered in talismans and shuddered. *No, this is temporary. I'll set Cameron free as soon as I can.* Helping me would probably let him move on too, as I suspected he was stuck because he needed expiation for the dog-girl video.

"I'll treat him as a companion, not a slave," I promised.

"Then let's begin. Kian, I need you to take five steps back. Yes, by the wall is fine."

Rochelle opened the compact and set it in the tray, then she lit the candles at cardinal points. I had zero experience in rituals but I could tell this one was legit from energy sizzling against my skin. Every creepy thing in this room perked up, looking our way. She poured water from the waiting pitcher into the trays and then she signaled me.

"Hands in, up to your wrists. Don't pull back, no matter what happens. I'll let you know when it's done."

That's not ominous at all.

Nervous, I did as instructed, and the water already felt different, icy cold though it had been sitting at room temperature. The cold worked into my bones, so I felt my hands stiffening, knuckles sharp and achy with it. She whispered a word in a language I didn't speak, then another, until they blurred together in a soft susurration, whispery rasp of paper over stone, and the water on my hands became a river. Crazy, but I felt the current flooding along the trenchers, sweeping from my end to hers and back again. The candle flames flickered from nonexistent wind while the room just kept getting colder. Soon I could see Rochelle's breath when she chanted. Though the sun hadn't changed position, it was darker in here too, a cluster of shadows that belonged to something besides Cameron. It took all my self-control not to scream and run off, but I held on. The ceremony came to crescendo with the darkness in the water swimming like ethereal fish toward the compact. As the black cloud reached it, the thing snapped shut with an audible click.

Her face sweaty, Rochelle staggered backward. "It's done. Come meet your familiar."

"Did that hurt you?" She did *not* look good.

It took a few seconds before she could reply. "A little. After this, I'll go to the shelter and heal the homeless. Their appreciation will top up the tank enough to get me by."

"Thank you."

"Like I said, this is the last help I'll offer. Who knows if it'll be enough."

"It will be," Kian said firmly. "I'll make sure of it."

I picked a careful path through the forgotten treasures to the other side of the table, where the compact waited. The water was clear now, normal looking. "Is it safe for me to pick up?"

She offered a strange, half smile. "You're the only one who can."

Kian didn't like the sound of that, no surprise, so he reached for it, but the water blocked him as if it were glass, not liquid. He tapped along the surface with a deepening frown. "How is that possible?"

"The object's bound to her," she answered.

Curious, I tried and my fingers slipped right in. I picked up the compact with no problem. It felt heavier in my palm than I expected; that could be imagination since I knew intellectually that it now contained Cameron's soul. Rochelle nodded at me when I went to open it. Since this was all so new, I had no expectations. Sheer surprise rocked me back a step when I saw that the empty space across from the mirror contained an image, bizarre and three-dimensional, like one of those "magic" 3-D photos or puzzles. I stared at Cameron; he seemed to stare back. He didn't move or blink yet he gave the impression of awareness.

So. Flipping. Creepy.

"Can he see me?" I asked.

Rochelle nodded. "And hear you. I'll show you a few simple uses for him before I go. The rest you'll need to work out on your own. Each spirit has a different specialty and since yours is young, he may not know yet what he can do."

At that point, I got a lesson on how to tap my familiar's power and, right away, I understood her initial warning. The rush of energy was . . . euphoric, indescribably delicious. My whole body glowed with pleasure; it felt like basking in the sun, making out with Kian, and acing a test. *All* at the same time. In a few seconds, I was stronger. Faster. Those results could definitely eat away at the desire to work hard. Steeling myself against temptation, I followed Rochelle out of the shop.

"Is there anything else I should know?"

"As long as you can see his picture in the compact, it means he's got some power to offer. If it fades until you can barely make it out, then you need to let him rest."

"Okay. I'll remember."

"Take care, Edie. You too, Kian."

He waited until she locked the door and moved off down the sidewalk before he reached for me. Reaction was setting in, and it was kind of uncanny that he understood that about me. I could be cool while the crazy stuff was happening, but afterward, I needed a safe space to lose my mind for a few seconds. He rubbed my back as I clutched my talisman, hovering on the brink of tears. Everything was just too damn much but I couldn't curl up into a ball.

My dad's depending on me. I have to step up.

"Does this mean I'm a witch?" I mumbled.

"Does it matter? You didn't trap that asshole. He was already hanging around, Rochelle just taught you how to make him useful."

He was trying to make me feel better, but he had no idea how amazing it felt to power up on somebody else's dime. I didn't want to turn into a maniac, looking for other artifacts to infuse. It wasn't like I could do the ritual myself, so that was some comfort, but my reaction to the spirit boost had been strong enough to make me nervous. Depending on how much I had to rely on Cameron to get through this and save my dad, there was no predicting what it might do to me. Rochelle was trusting me with a bomb, basically, and I hoped I didn't detonate it.

I let Kian comfort me for a few more minutes, then I stepped back and opened the compact. Cameron stared back at me, unmoving and pale as death. "Help me get my dad back, then I'll cut you loose. Deal?"

A bang on the door behind me—I jumped, heart thumping like mad. Then I realized Rochelle had set the terms. *One knock for yes, two for no.* It wasn't an elegant means of communication but maybe we could do better down the line. Working out complex systems was kind of my forte, so the chances were good that I could create some kind of ghost-chat infrastructure, given time.

Damn. I don't have much of that. We'll make do.

"Next question," I asked. "Does it hurt, being trapped?"

There was a long silence, then eventually he knocked once, softer. That sounded more like "kind of" or "maybe." I wished I hadn't asked because now I felt bad about using him. But I didn't have a choice if I wanted to rescue my dad. *Sorry, Cameron.*

To save my father, I'd do a lot worse.

BLAMING CTHULHU
NEVER HELPS

Sunday, Kian bought me a new cell phone. The police came to see me too, which was completely horrible. I suspected the officer knew I wasn't telling the whole truth, which extended the interrogation. But was I supposed to admit that a Cthulhu monster carried my dad off? That would get me shunted off to a psych unit.

Monday afternoon a big guy was waiting for me when I left Blackbriar. Between the lessons I was taking with Raoul and my spirit mirror, I might be able to take him. I sized him up as he approached. Kian was off with Aaron, talking to some people about who might've abducted my dad. Hopefully he'd text me with information soon.

My whole body tensed as the man in the black suit and impenetrable mirror shades stepped up. "We have a mutual friend."

"Who do you work for?" This didn't seem like the Harbinger's style but then, he was known as a crazy, unpredictable bastard, and from what I could tell, he reveled in that reputation. He *had* sent men in suits to round me up before, but this guy wasn't one of them. *How many minions does he have?*

"We've met before," he said, smiling. "And I saw you recently too. Should I be hurt that you don't remember?"

I stared. Actually something about his yellow teeth *did* strike me as familiar. But I couldn't place him. His features were nondescript and his short hair offered no clues either.

"It's been a busy year. Give me a hint?" So far he wasn't showing any signs that he meant to hit me on the head.

No joke, I screamed when his face flicker-melted into that of the scary clown I'd met in Wedderburn's office and seen on New Year's Eve. Stumbling back a step, I glanced around like a tweaker making sure nobody else had seen that. *Shit*. There was a kid standing behind me, pale and trembling. His mouth opened but no sounds came out.

"Did you see . . . ?"

God, I hate to do this.

"What?"

"That dude—"

"My bodyguard?" Which made me sound pretentious but other kids at Blackbriar had them. "What about him?"

"N-never mind." The boy sprinted past me and practically dove into the waiting town car.

Well, there's a new phobia for him to talk about in therapy. I just hoped they didn't put him on psychotropic meds. Wedderburn's muscle wore a smirk when I turned back to him.

"Walk with me," he said.

"I don't think we have anything to talk about."

"You'd be wrong. Boss says I'm supposed to stick with you, take your orders, until we bring your dad back."

Surprised, I jerked a look at him and he seemed to be serious. "I figured he was behind this."

After what he did to my mom.

"Nah, this is classic opposition. From gossip around the water cooler, his game with you in play was going smooth as hell. They can't let him execute."

"I guess that doesn't mean killing people, because from what I've seen, that's fine."

The thing laughed. "Good one. And, yeah, I mean they can't let him just power through without throwing up some blocks."

Rage exploded behind my eyes. "You realize this is my *father* we're talking about. It may be a minor inconvenience to Wedderburn, but—"

"Settle down," he cut in. "I don't care about your feelings or your problems but I *am* here to help you find him. Wedderburn's got feelers out, just like you have, and when he figures out where those idiots are keeping your old man, we'll move in."

"Sounds like he's pretty sure those idiots are Dwyer & Fell."

"Who else would it be?"

That made sense. The Harbinger had no interest in my dad; he wouldn't even protect him. And while he was plenty pissed off at me, I could reasonably clear him of that kidnapping. He made a deal with the monster, which recognized him but didn't treat him like a boss or a master or whatever. *God, this shit is confusing.*

"Point. So what am I supposed to do with you?"

"Treat me like furniture. I go where you go. I'll escort you to and from school. I'm not supposed to let anyone touch you before you turn eighteen."

"Define 'touch.'" Did this mean I'd have a killer clown blocking me from spending time with Kian? Explaining that would probably give me an aneurysm.

"I'm muscle," he said on a sigh. "And protection. Get it?"

For a few seconds, I considered arguing, but I'd learned my lesson about biting off more than I could chew. "I got it. So what's your name?" Kian had already told me, but I was curious what it would say.

"Buzzkill."

Crap. A sudden problem occurred to me. If he went into the condemned school with me, he'd recognize Raoul. Likewise, the apartment. So the situation would force me to be more of an asshole than I wanted to be to someone helping me, even if it was at Wedderburn's direction. He might still consider me an asset—it didn't seem like he'd taken losing Kian badly—but I hated him with every fiber of my being. If there was a way I could save my dad, ensure he lost all his points, and free myself from the game, that was the path I'd run down. *Headlong.* By killing my mother, he'd made sure I'd never want to hurt anyone else more. I refused to let myself imagine anything irrevocable happening to my dad because of Dwyer & Fell.

I'll save him. I have more resources now. Time to act like a jerk.

"Do what you have to. But don't expect me to make it easy for you. I don't have a spare bedroom for scary assholes, and I don't want you within fifty feet."

"So standard restraining-order radius?" He was smiling, as if I'd delighted him with my reaction.

Yeah, he'd probably think it was weird if I wanted him in my house.

"That's fine."

Taking me at my word, he fell back, trailing me from the specified distance toward the station. I used the break to text Raoul quickly, warning him we might have a situation. He responded with curt questions and I told him everything I knew. Finally, he asked, Does Buzzkill seem suspicious? Glancing back, I couldn't tell.

Nothing he'd said or done made me think he knew about Raoul, so I typed back, No.

Fine. We'll have the lesson as planned. I'll use a different exit.

Raoul's risk of capture was freaking me out; my chest hurt when we got off at the stop closest to the abandoned school. The area was bad enough to unnerve a killer clown apparently because he quickened his pace, cutting the distance between us. I tried to hurry.

No luck.

Buzzkill caught up with me. "What the hell are you doing out here?"

"Training," I said.

"At what, murder school?"

"That's very judge-y coming from you, killer clown."

In response, he showed me his true face.

"Stop it. You wait here. I'll come out when I'm done."

"I'm not supposed to let you out of my sight."

"What'll you do when I go home? I already said you're not welcome."

"That's not your problem. And Wedderburn would put me down if I let you go in there on your own."

I had to admit, the place looked shady. The building had long since accepted its abandonment, settling comfortably into broken glass and creeping nature. Vines grew up one side of the building, and the parking lot looked more like the site of a meteor crash than a place where you could safely stash a car. Buzzkill set his jaw, his eyes yellow and scary. Even in a business suit and holding a briefcase—probably containing his implements of torture and death—he radiated a terrifying menace. It made people double-take at him because their intuition warned them of danger but their gullible human eyes interpreted the illusion he wore as normal. Harmless, even. I stifled a humorless laugh. Based on his implacable stance, I didn't foresee winning this argument.

Bottom line, I couldn't leave him out here and risk him trailing me. If Raoul got caught, I'd never forgive myself, to say nothing of Kian. Maybe Raoul and I could train at home, if we moved all the furniture out of the living room. Not ideal but better than the alternative.

"Fine. I'll reschedule."

Turning, I ran toward the station over uneven, broken sidewalk. When I got some distance, I sent Raoul an abort message. If I'd known Buzzkill would refuse to honor the promise he made, I would've canceled at school. Then it occurred to me how stupid it was to expect *anything* from a killer clown. His existence was so bizarre and creepy that I had no words, so I kept staring at him as he followed me from a distance.

When we stopped at the station, I had to ask, "Okay, so what's your story?"

"Look it up. You're supposed to be smart, right?"

That ended all conversation between us. Yet he was with me through the transfers, keeping watch from the other side of the train and making commuters nervous. He stalked me all the way back to my apartment, and weirdly, since I knew he had orders from Wedderburn to protect me, I felt a little safer. Buzzkill said nothing when I hurried into my apartment.

Be careful coming in, I texted to Raoul. We're under surveillance. For his sake, I hoped the artifact he'd stolen when he vanished was completely foolproof. I checked everywhere, though I couldn't have said what I was looking for. In my dad's room, I lost it for a few seconds after drawing in a deep breath scented with his shaving lotion. Tears sprang to my eyes. Usually he kept the door shut but now there was no reason not to look.

I stilled, staring at the bed. My mom's side was carefully made, pillows in place, while the covers on his side were bunched and rumpled; it was like he didn't feel comfortable sprawling because he'd been sharing a bed for so long. More than anything, it drove home how broken he was without her, how much he missed her. Even I hadn't realized how important she was until it was too late to say so.

My dad had left notes scattered on the bedside table. I sat down on the mattress to flip through them. The equations made sense but it was hard to envision how to build something like this. Beyond a theoretical sense, the biggest problem with time travel was getting humans to survive it. Subatomic particles could slip through but a whole person? Given current understanding of physics, a team of scientists in China had gone so far as to say time travel was impossible. Not that their findings impacted my mom and dad's work.

Mine now, if the fucking game has anything to say about it.

The worst part was, part of me felt like I owed it to my parents to finish what they'd started, if I could. But that move seemed too much like accepting my fate and I'd already vowed not to go gentle into that good night. It would be way better if I could find the exclusion to the rule, some way that ended with me besting these creatures.

At the moment, I wasn't hopeful.

I flipped to some of my dad's nontheoretical notes, which read like his half of a conversation he wanted to have with my mother. *About timelines? It's better to think of them as alternate worlds.*

Because I can't accept time as a straight line, simple forward and back. It's more like skipping forward to glimpse one possible future or back to what might've happened in one version of reality. And, no, I don't believe in fixed points in time, much as I love Doctor Who. I theorize it's possible to create a new wrinkle anywhere, especially when you incorporate the issue of space-time, and time as distance.

Moreover, time is relative, right? So there's no way to be sure what time stream you're in when you skip. It's more like ripples on a pond. So bearing that in mind, we were talking about temporal echoes... That was where the entry stopped, probably because my mom wasn't around to interject thoughts and kick around hypotheses like they always did. My heart hurt.

Leaving the research, I went into my room and got out my laptop. This wasn't remotely the most important thing on my to-do list, but sometimes you needed a quick sense of accomplishment in order to tackle the hard stuff. I input "Buzzkill killer clown" in the search engine and came up with a stream of results. Picking one at random brought me an urban legend site, not surprisingly, as he didn't feel like an old god. He even talked like an Internet meme.

Charles Edward Macy was born in the forties to itinerant carnival workers, exact DOB unknown. He trained under the clowns in the big-top show until he was eighteen. For unknown reasons they expelled him from the group and he struck out on his own, settling in the Miami area in the early sixties. By 1970, he was a fixture at children's parties, performing a small magic show and making balloon animals. But Macy had a secret. The clown beloved by children as Dr. Smiles had a dark side, as his community would eventually discover.

In 1978, the party stopped forever when Sheriff Will Gladstone made a grisly discovery—seventeen bodies were buried beneath Macy's garage. In the subsequent media circus, the murderer was nicknamed Buzzkill and his trial had to be moved out of county due to his notoriety. Eventually he was convicted of these heinous crimes and given the death penalty. In 1986, after numerous appeals, he went to the electric chair. According to witnesses on site, the current malfunctioned and it took three tries to kill him. After the second flip of the switch, Macy choked out, "You'll never be rid of me. Your children will never be safe."

Incredulous, I stared at the page. "Seriously? That's like three stories, merged into one. Freddy Krueger, something by Wes Craven, and John Wayne Gacy."

But apparently enough kids had read this and passed it on as gospel since the eighties for there to be a real, undying Buzzkill in the world, working for Wedderburn. Who was currently watching my house. *Holy shit. That's . . . sobering.* Pity panged through me. This creature was evil and monstrous because we made him that way; it wasn't like he got to pick his origin story. Yet he still scared the crap out of me. His bloodlust was real and so was the danger.

Half an hour later, Raoul slipped into the apartment. I studied him to make sure he was safe. "How did you get by Buzzkill?"

"It's not as much of a problem as you seem to think. But your texts sounded like you were about to have a panic attack."

"What . . . ?" I spluttered.

"The artifact prevents magical tracking, yeah. But it's also got a cloaking feature. I wouldn't have risked stealing it if it couldn't withstand scrutiny."

"Explain more."

He lifted what looked like a simple religious medallion. "How does that appear to you?"

Confused, I told him.

"That's because something like this is common and wouldn't draw your eye. The actual necklace is considerably more remarkable. The amulet does the same thing with me."

"Makes you more inconspicuous?"

"Now you're catching on."

"Wow. And that works on immortals?"

Raoul nodded. "There's an obscure myth about some god who wanted to seduce a mortal, so he needed to pass among them, otherwise his divine splendor would give the game away—"

"Let me guess, this is a Greek story."

"I think so. It's called the Amulet of Agamemnon anyway, because he allegedly stole it from the god in question for impregnating his sister."

"I'm surprised he had time—what with the Trojan War, plus all the rape, murder, and incest. He had quite a colorful family." But that made me question something else he'd said. "If the necklace makes you less noticeable, why were you were worried about the Harbinger's 'winged messengers' before? You said you needed to stay off the street."

"Because the trickery doesn't work on them. Their brains are too simple, so their eyes show him whatever they actually see."

"Like remote viewing." Though I wasn't finding much humor in anything these days, I couldn't restrain a snicker. "Dude, your weakness is . . . birds?"

"Rodents too." It seemed to pain him to admit, "Any animal familiar can trip me up."

Since his freedom and safety were at stake, I shouldn't tease him. Yet I couldn't stop myself. "I guess we're not going to the zoo. Just in case."

He shot me a dark look. "How amusing."

I was even more touched that he'd joined the search party. Just the mere act of wandering around, looking for me, had to put him at risk. While humans and immortals might not be able to ID him, there were birds and squirrels everywhere. How bizarre that such a small thing could've led to his downfall.

Glad it didn't.

Something else dawned on me just then. "Wait, immortals can *crossbreed* with us?" Okay, that was kind of a horrible revelation.

"If the story says they can." Raoul acted like this wasn't completely horrendous.

"So Zeus and a bunch of other old gods are fertile. That's a worry I did *not* need."

"It shouldn't bother you more than any of the thousand other unpleasant facts you've recently become awake to. Let's get the furniture moved."

It was a good thing we didn't have any downstairs neighbors; otherwise, they'd definitely be banging angrily over how we shoved everything out of the way, leaving only the area rug in the center of the room, almost like an arena.

"This is okay?"

Raoul offered a cautious nod. "It's not ideal, you could get hurt if you don't fall properly. On the other hand, a confined space will force you to greater bodily awareness."

"I'll do my best," I promised.

"That's what I like to hear. By now you should be doing this automatically—"

"Stretches and katas," I finished.

Since I'd already changed into my workout gear at school, I was ready to start. Raoul moved into the kitchen doorway to give me maximum space, which I appreciated. Some of the styles were complicated and my balance wasn't the best yet. If I fell over trying to get my feet in position, I'd rather not land on him. By the end of an hour I was good and loose, ready for him to kick my ass. I took up a fighting stance and Raoul strolled toward me with limber grace, despite his age. The silver hair really didn't give an accurate impression of how tough—or skilled—he was.

Which made me wonder. This definitely wasn't something the average person would know, let alone be able to teach.

As we circled, I asked, "How is that you know all this stuff anyway?"

Raoul feinted at me instead of answering. I watched him, poised on the balls of my feet and ready to block the next strike. Finally, I could counter about half his moves. The rest ended in bruises that I was currently hiding from my boyfriend.

"That's an *excellent* question," Kian said in a dangerous tone.

Sweaty and scared, I whirled to see him standing in the doorway wearing an indescribable expression.

RIGHTEOUS ANGER IS KIND OF HOT

"I knocked." He came in and shut the door too quietly. A muscle moved in his jaw, and one hand curled into a fist. *Damn*. I had *never* seen him this angry. "Nobody answered, but I heard noises. Given the situation, I came in to check it out."

"Hey." That wasn't the dumbest thing I could've said but it made the top ten.

"Funny thing, you being here when you claimed not to need a pickup because of drama practice . . . and getting a ride with Jen."

"This is my fault," Raoul murmured.

Kian's eyes were like shards of green glass as he folded his arms, leaning back against the closed door. "I have plenty of pissed off for you too."

Raoul is looking out for you, I thought. It wasn't that I didn't understand his outrage over catching me in a lie but if he gave us a chance to explain—eh, yeah, that probably wouldn't make it better. Kian wasn't a fan of schemes that risked my neck.

"I hope you'll let me clarify." Raoul took a penitent position, folding his hands as if Kian had the right to scold him.

"You disappear without a word for how long," Kian snarled, "and the next thing I know, you're playing Mr. Miyagi with my girlfriend. I'm starting to wonder if you ever gave a shit about me at all."

Since all of this was about saving Kian's life—and I, the most uncoordinated person in the world, was learning to fight for *him*—I lost my temper. "Why are you even here? Did you miss stalking me?" As soon as the angry words popped out, I regretted them but I couldn't suck the accusation back in.

Kian flinched. "You can think that if you want. But I was just checking your place to make sure it was safe when you got home. I didn't know you were with Raoul." That visibly bothered him.

"Shall I answer her question first?" Raoul seemed to realize we wouldn't be training until the shit finished splattering.

Kian's expression made me think we might need a wet vac. "Go ahead."

I sat down on the rug, beckoning for the other two to do the same. Raoul waited until we stopped rustling, his gaze fixed on his palms, but I had the feeling he saw something else entirely. The silence built until Kian cleared his throat.

Finally Raoul said, "I didn't want either of you to find out this way, but . . . I'm part of a resistance movement, dedicated to stopping the game."

"No shit." Chills prickled upward, starting at my ankles and creeping to my knees. It stood to reason there must be something like that but . . . "You're not the Illuminati, are you?"

A half smile came and went, flickering out like a candle when

Raoul registered how unamused Kian still was. "Sorry, there are no stories about us. We're careful to keep it that way or we couldn't maneuver. Amongst ourselves, however, we're dubbed the Black Watch."

"That doesn't explain anything," Kian said.

Raoul went on, "My mandate was infiltration, as I was the first catalyst born to the order in centuries."

I came to the obvious conclusion. "Damn. You went to extremis, knowing what would happen in advance?"

He shook his head. "My whole life was a misery and I never knew why. I was reared like a slave, whipped and beaten. Yet I knew nothing but the Black Watch, so I did what they told me without question and when my master said he had no further use for my life, I ended it."

Holy shit. I pictured some seriously screwed-up monastic order, all grim faced and ascetic, cranking out acolytes who would die on order without question. They'd bookmarked Machiavelli's truism about the end justifying the means and then tattooed it on each other's foreheads. *Doing terrible things is cool for the right reasons, yes?* That hit too close to home since *I'd* taken the deal out of a burning desire for revenge.

"At which point you were offered three favors," Kian guessed.

"Yes. Nobody had ever asked me what I wanted, so I had no idea how to respond. It was . . . earthshattering, truly. My liaison said I could have some time to think about my requests, as long as I accepted the bargain right then."

"What if you'd immediately wished all your tormentors dead?" I wondered aloud.

"That would have been the end of the resistance. But they had

173

done their work *very* well. With no part of my mind could I have framed such a demand. Not then."

Now? But if I kept interrupting, he'd never get this story told. I flicked a glance at Kian, but he wouldn't meet my eyes. Wincing, I contemplated all the ways I could grovel for that stalking comment. *So dumb, I didn't even mean it. That's why I thought being with me for real must be a letdown.* An ache set up shop in my throat.

"I'm starting to understand," Kian said softly. "Let's hear how it ends."

"Afterward, my old master came to me. He said I had graduated from a long and arduous period as an initiate. From this day forward, I was a knight in service to defeating an ancient evil. I started combat training then and continued to 'think' about my requests. I spent five years at a monastery in Thailand, until my liaison told me my time was up. At that point, I requested the favors my master had laid out for me and I did everything he ordered."

"To screw up your timeline." Kian shook his head, sighing. "They actually sent you undercover to work for Wedderburn. That's . . . insane."

"I served two masters—Wedderburn and the Black Watch—for many years. Then my new instructions came—to vanish and prepare for the next stage." He raised his eyes then, sharp with purpose. "Mark me, whether you will it or not, whether you're ready or not, you'll both play a role in what's to come."

Crap. Then Raoul was helping me, yeah, but he wasn't a free agent. That meant I owed these lessons to the Black Watch, another faction jockeying to control me. Regardless how much help my training was, if they expected me to follow orders with the same blind loyalty they'd brainwashed into Raoul, just no. I shook my head, unable to muster a response.

Kian was having no such trouble. "That only explains how you know how to fight, not why you're teaching Edie."

That, I could handle. Then he could get mad at *me* for agreeing to it. "Because he knows you. He didn't think you'd want me throwing down with things that could smash me, eat me, or devour my soul. Figured you'd get mad at him for enabling me to be even *more* reckless."

He dropped his eyes, sheepish, and faint color washed his high cheekbones. "Okay, maybe those are not incorrect statements. But did you ever stop to think that I'd hate you hiding shit, lying to me, more than the idea of you taking stupid risks?"

"We'll put a pin in 'stupid' for now," I said. "And, no, it didn't. Because I'm book smart, people dumb, as you already knew. So I'll probably drop a metric ton of *should know better* on you before we're done. But I'm *really* sorry. For keeping secrets and what I said before—"

"It's okay, Edie."

"It's really not. But say you forgive me anyway?" I tried a smile.

He didn't return it but the hard glass left his eyes, so they were warm and bright again. I reached for his hand and while he didn't meet me halfway, he let me take it. God, it felt good not to hide this from him anymore.

"There's very little I wouldn't forgive you for."

A frisson of fear flickered through me. It seemed downright dangerous for Kian to love me this much, especially when I screwed up so hard on a regular basis. But I couldn't obsess about my relationship right now. Not with my dad missing.

"So what's your endgame in training me?" I asked, turning to Raoul.

"The Black Watch wants to recruit you. Eventually."

"Am I supposed to ruin my timeline on purpose and go work for Wedderburn?"

Raoul's eyes said he didn't find that funny. "My master doesn't explain his strategies."

"How do you feel about him now? I mean, you've been free for a while. Sort of." Could blind loyalty exist outside of a vacuum? I wondered if the conditioning could possibly hold in the real world once someone got a taste of making their own moves.

The older man steepled his fingers, lowering his head to contemplate for a few seconds. "I think he's desperate to win a fight that cannot be won, and desperate men are dangerous."

"Will you train me too?" Kian folded onto his knees. "If I learn, I might be able to protect Edie better."

I exchanged a look with Raoul, reading his thoughts from the angle of his head and offering a faint nod in response. *He doesn't need to know why. Letting him think it's strictly self-defense is best.* Without being told, I got to my feet.

"Follow my lead," I said to Kian. "First are the stretches and katas . . ."

Two hours later, we were both sweaty, though Raoul remained irritatingly impervious. There wasn't space to spar with three of us, a problem I'd have to solve as soon as possible. I got bottles of water while I filled Kian in on the fact that Buzzkill was now ostensibly working for me. Not that I believed for a second he'd follow my orders if I asked him to do something that contravened Wedderburn's interests.

"I'll find us regular gym space somewhere," Raoul said. "Don't worry about it. The school was convenient because there's nobody around to ask questions but we can adapt."

"Keep me posted."

"Me too," Kian murmured.

Soon after, Raoul headed out, ostensibly to look for facilities capable of letting us all practice at the same time. Afterward, the apartment was too quiet. I couldn't look at the boy who loved me; I wronged him *constantly*. Maybe he'd started our relationship feeling guilty but he shouldn't anymore. In silence I checked my phone. Allison was supposed to be looking into my dad's kidnapping, and I *hated* that she had resources I didn't. Nothing so far. Wedderburn was also supposed to be digging around, but I didn't trust his good intentions. Though inaction chafed, I didn't know what else to do. It wasn't like I could run a search for properties owned by supernatural entities.

But maybe . . .

Ignoring Kian's startled exclamation, I ran to my room and brought up Dwyer & Fell. All corporations left tax records because even if the company was a smoke screen, they had to pay lip service to the mortal world. So there would be records, a revenue stream, holding companies, and probably shell corporations. It would take time to dig through all of this but it was better than doing nothing, waiting for someone else to solve my problem.

"What're you doing?" Kian asked, coming up behind me.

He probably wanted to yell at me, but he wouldn't. It might be better if he did. Clearing the air seemed like a good idea, but I'd learned he refused to argue, regardless of how much I provoked it. If I kept on, I'd just hurt him again. He was trying so hard to be my perfect hero when what I wanted was a real flesh-and-blood boyfriend who screwed up as much as I did.

Quietly I explained. "It's a needle in a stack of needles but it's probable that he's being held in a property owned by Dwyer & Fell but there are *so many* related companies."

And this wasn't even my field of expertise.

"Why don't you bring your laptop over to my place? I don't like you here without Raoul, especially with Buzzkill lurking around."

"He won't hurt me." *Right now* was the unspoken subtext.

"I wouldn't bet your life on it."

It didn't seem worth arguing about, so I dropped my computer into my backpack. "Is Aaron there?"

"Probably. He doesn't go out much unless I'm with him."

As I turned, he caught my shoulders in his hands. With his thumbs, he traced over them delicately, gazing down into my face as if he might find the answer to a riddle there. He smelled a little salty, musky, and I had the urge to put my face against his neck. Restraint seemed like the only option. I didn't deserve to be comforted. Yet Kian didn't seem to know that since he pulled me into his arms.

"It feels like you're slipping away," he whispered. "I know you're scared for your dad, but . . . I need you too. God, I'm such a selfish asshole—"

"No, it helps." I wrapped my arms around his waist and squeezed my eyes shut.

For a few minutes, we just held on to each other. I listened to his heart and marveled at the fact that he'd fallen for me. But . . . there was something I'd never asked. Maybe it was time.

"How long did you watch me?" I whispered.

"Over a year.' He hesitated. "Do you remember the day last fall when you got free food and books?"

Surprised, I tipped my head back. His cheeks were red. "I do, actually. It was weird, luck broke my way all day long."

"That was me," he said.

"Oh God, really? Then . . ." Honestly I had no idea what to say, but that day was one of the few bright spots in the gloom of my life. I finally settled on, "Thank you."

"It was all I could do, then." He threaded his hand beneath my hair, so that a shiver went through me.

I had only a few seconds to realize a kiss was imminent and then his mouth was on mine. Sweetness flooded me as I parted my lips to taste him deeper. He made a muffled sound against my lips, breath mingling with mine. Kian was a slow, deep kisser, taking his time to taste and explore, and the heady pleasure of it made me tremble. Soon I was just holding on to his shoulders while he backed me up against the wall. He felt so good, so strong, and I remembered that night weeks ago. If only I could turn my brain off, I'd forget the crap I was dealing with and just go with the endorphins.

Logic didn't drive me to pull back, though. My rational brain swam in a delicious cocktail of dopamine and serotonin, until I couldn't think at all. He was lean and hot against me, more insistent than usual with lips and hands. I ran my palms over his back, deliciously drawn by the play of his muscles.

When he finally broke away, breathing hard, my lips felt soft and swollen. I could hardly whisper, "You know this isn't the time, right?"

"I'm aware. Give me a sec and we'll go." He turned away, his eyes so hot they left pinpricks of heat on my skin.

"Sorry," I whispered.

About so many things.

By the time we left my building, he was calm. Kian joined our hands and shouldered the bag with my laptop in it. His attention sharpened as we walked, probably looking for Buzzkill or anyone who meant me harm. But the killer clown was in camo mode and he didn't make contact. I had the ugly sensation of being watched; as ever, there were huge, eerie black birds wheeling overhead.

Go on, I thought. *Report back to your master.*

• • •

"Wait here," Kian said.

"Huh?"

He went into his bedroom and I heard him rummaging. Then he came out with a plain brown bag, so small that I had no idea what it might contain. He offered it to me silently.

Puzzled, I opened it up and found a pretty handmade necklace in various shades of blue and green, like the ocean on a string. "What's this?"

"Remember when you wouldn't take anything from that lady who was selling jewelry?"

As I nodded, realization dawned. "That was the only present I didn't accept that day."

"I was hoping I'd be able to give it to you in person."

Since this was a choker and I already had on the infinity symbol necklace, I offered my wrist. Kian looped it twice around, turning it into a bracelet. I kissed him softly in thanks and we were just starting to get into it when I realized his apartment was really quiet. Usually we'd be interrupted by now.

By Aaron.

"Where's the kid?" I asked.

With a tired sigh, I pinched the bridge of my nose. Then we checked everywhere, calling for him. Ten minutes later, we paused in the hallway, Kian visibly worried. At this point he was like a little brother to him, and he'd grown on me too. The boy had zero survival skills and was timid to the point of incapacitation around strangers.

"You think someone took him?" I asked.

"I have no idea."

I did one last circuit of the apartment and when I went into Kian's room, the tinnitus struck. Clutching my head, I dropped to one knee and a pale hand stretched out toward me. My heart leapt into my throat and I scrambled back toward the dresser. *Jesus, monster under the bed?!* It took me a few seconds to register that this looked like a normal human hand, now disappearing back into the darkness. Still, I was shaking when I crawled toward the bed.

"Edie?" Kian asked.

I let out a little scream, falling on my ass just before I reached the covers to pull them back. My heart nearly exploded too. Between my hammering pulse and the ringing in my ears, I could hardly breathe. Without speaking, I pointed. He dropped to his knees next to me and raised the blankets to reveal Aaron curled up in the fetal position on the dusty floor. His eyes were huge, and he seemed to be trembling.

"Did something happen?" I reached for him and the reaction spooked him, so he scuttled back against the far wall out of reach. Perplexed, I shot a look at Kian.

"He's never done this before." He flattened himself on the floor but didn't make any sudden moves.

The rasp of Aaron's breathing was loud in the bedroom, fast and shallow, like he feared we were about to murder him. Nobody could fake the terror the kid was projecting. It crawled along my skin like a shadow, until I backed off. Kian had spent more time with him; maybe he could calm the boy down.

"Everything's okay," he said soothingly. "Just come out and we'll talk."

Aaron didn't respond, not even to blink. Dread pooled in the pit of my stomach, hot as pitch. I backed off a little more to see if the tinnitus abated but the incessant noise whined on at a level that sent sharp sparks of pain through my skull. Kian didn't seem to hear it, which made me wonder why I'd acquired this immortal sensor when he'd spent so much time with Wedderburn. Did you build up immunity over time, so you just didn't notice it? Or maybe the human brain became selectively perceptive in some kind of self-defense mechanism.

I couldn't have said how long we crouched on the floor, patient like Aaron were a wild animal. Kian never budged. Toward the end of our vigil, impatience scratched around inside me. *Dammit, I don't have time for this. I have to find my dad.*

"Who are you?" Aaron finally whispered, one fist pressed against his chest. "What is this place? And what am I doing here?"

DIMENSIONAL X-RAY SPECS ARE TOTALLY A THING

At first it was almost impossible to convince Aaron that we wouldn't hurt him. Kian coaxed him for like half an hour before he crawled out from under the bed, wide-eyed and trembling. The last thing we needed was more problems but we couldn't just say, *Okay, you have amnesia, good luck with that,* and shove him out the door. He'd always been weird but this was over that line into bizarro territory.

"What do we do?" I asked as Kian reached for the kid.

When the boy burrowed under his arm, trembling like a bird, I got the sense that he recognized Kian as a protector, even if he couldn't recall interacting with him. I stood up slowly, careful not to startle him. Kian met my gaze and lifted one shoulder in a helpless shrug. We'd gotten him medical attention and had been trying to find his family, up until we realized he was a refugee from time, but I had zero ideas how to address something like this.

"Maybe we should call Raoul?" he suggested.

That seemed like the best move. He had more experience with

this supernatural stuff. He'd been working for Wedderburn for a couple of decades when he got the order from his boss in the Black Watch. So maybe he'd heard of some freaky shit that could result in sudden amnesia? Not that Aaron had seemed completely normal when we stole him from the Harbinger. A chill shivered through me as I considered that this could be me, if I'd been dumb enough to agree to the trickster's insane proposal.

"I'll do it." He was off finding gym space where we could all train without Buzzkill deeming the place too suspicious to let me enter alone, but—"Wait, maybe Buzzkill could tell us what's going on with Aaron. He's part of their world anyway."

Kian stared at me with horrified fascination. "You want to invite that thing in?"

I shook my head quickly. "We'll take Aaron to meet him. He's lurking outside anyway, making sure Dwyer & Fell don't murder me while Wedderburn tracks my dad down."

"How can you say his name so calmly?" I heard the unspoken part of the question—*when he killed your mother.*

Letting out an unsteady breath, I held out a hand to reveal how badly I was shaking. "I'm so angry that I can't stand it. I pretty much always am. But right now I'm still positioning my pieces and building my strength. Going after Wedderburn would be the last mistake I ever made—with the Harbinger raging and the opposition coming at me. Right now I need his resources because I still have a chance to save my dad. Choosing revenge at this moment might reduce my chances of getting him back safe, which I know Wedderburn wants because of the timeline."

"Wow," Kian said. "I don't know if I could be so logical in your situation."

"It's not easy. I don't want anything to do with Wedderburn. But I'll do whatever I have to, including deal with him or Buzzkill or Allison Vega. Whoever can help me most, well, I'm not too proud to take a knee."

"Okay then." Turning to Aaron, he murmured to him, until the boy nodded.

He seemed really disoriented, having trouble focusing his eyes. Kian dressed him for the outdoors like a much younger child. Aaron stood quiescent while being bundled in coat, hat, and gloves. I put on my winter gear too and went out, waiting for Buzzkill to show himself. Pacing, I watched the quiet street; not many people were out as the day waned toward evening. Lights were on in other apartments and the weather was chill and gray, hinting at precipitation. I'd never see snowflakes as beautiful again, only evidence of Wedderburn's power.

Eventually, Buzzkill approached in bodyguard skin. He seemed more annoyed than curious. "You'll freeze out here."

"Would that be problematic for you?"

"Well, yeah. People dying on my watch, that only happens after the order comes in."

"So you'd still slice me up?"

He showed yellow teeth and lifted his briefcase. "With pleasure."

I'd known that but it was pretty unnerving to realize he could imagine turning me into meat, even as he shadowed me to keep the opposition away. I wondered if he knew about Cameron, a weight in my coat pocket that made me something more than human. Though I feared using that spirit strength because the rush hit me like a drug, it also reassured me that I wasn't completely powerless anymore.

"I need your help," I said, ignoring the fact that he was trying to freak me out. "There's a café two blocks down where we can talk."

"Are you seriously asking me for coffee?" A smirk gave him a truly disturbing air.

"Yep." Turning, I beckoned to Kian, who was standing at the top of the steps with Aaron, who looked absolutely terrified.

He hid his face in Kian's shoulder, unable to speak for a few seconds.

"Do you see it?" the boy whispered eventually.

Surprised, I took another look at Buzzkill, whose face was visibly wavering, like he was having a hard time holding his illusion in place, this close to Aaron. The result was a disturbing flicker at his head, similar to damaged old celluloid film. Nausea flooded me as his monstrous clown visage popped at random intervals, trippy as hell.

"What the hell *is* that thing?" Buzzkill demanded, backing away from the kid.

Kian and I traded looks. Then I answered, "We rescued him from the Harbinger. Isn't he a normal kid?"

"I think you already know the answer to that. Look, we can't go to a neighborhood coffee shop. I'll give everyone in there a psychotic break." He seemed to read my expression because he added, "Yeah, normally, that'd be funny as hell but I'm under orders to be inconspicuous."

"There's Cuppa Joe," Kian reminded Buzzkill.

"Good idea." That was where Kian first made me an offer I couldn't refuse, and he'd said the place was company owned. Which meant we might find other creepy things waiting for us there, but

186

they should be aligned with Wedderburn, and we weren't trying to keep Aaron a secret from him.

"I'll get the Mustang," Kian said. "Wait here."

Aaron tried to follow and I took his hand to stop him. It surprised me how cold he was; I could feel it radiating even through his gloves, an inhuman sort of burn that whispered of corpses and frozen boys crawling through the snow with burning blue eyes. When he swiveled his head to look at me, I trembled and tried not to shrink away. Buzzkill showed no such delicacy; he gave the kid a wide berth as we moved past him. White flakes spattered down, lazily guttering from the gray clouds above. Everything in the world was sepia or silent movie, except for Kian's car and his green, green eyes. I got in back with Aaron while Buzzkill rode shotgun.

"You can talk on the way," our scary driver invited.

So we told him the abridged version of events, ending with Aaron's current state. Buzzkill didn't say a word, which surprised me. He was psychotic but a surprisingly good listener, a quality you didn't expect in a killer clown. Once Kian stopped talking, Buzzkill angled in his seat to take a closer look at Aaron, who cowered against me. I didn't blame him; the evil clown face was still pulsing in subliminal strobe, whispering against his illusion of normalcy.

"He smells human underneath," Buzzkill said. "But there's something else too."

Buzzkill slipped a pair of spectacles on, stared at the kid, and then shuddered. That did *not* bode well. Quietly, so as not to alarm the kid, I took off one of his gloves and wrapped my hand around his. He thought I was trying to warm him up and gave me a grateful smile. Guilt battered my casual façade because I was actually feeling for a pulse at his wrist. For few seconds, I thought he was dead and it took all my self-control not to scream and fling myself against the opposite side of the car. But then I found it, very slow and sluggish, like I'd expect from a person with hypothermia. But he wasn't showing any of the other symptoms.

What the hell is going on?

The killer clown didn't say anything else until we got to Cuppa Joe. As before, the place was populated with elderly people yet I didn't think they were human, something about their eyes and teeth and the veins in their hands hinted at monstrous otherness. The same waitress from before greeted Kian with a warm smile, Buzzkill less so, and she was neutral when she studied Aaron and me. Going over the specials, she seated us at a back booth, away from everyone else. That was probably wise.

"What can I get you?"

"Bloody virgin," Buzzkill said.

"You think this is a bar?" Shirl demanded.

"I said virgin, didn't I?"

The woman sighed but wrote it down. I asked for hot chocolate and Aaron just nodded. I took that to mean he wanted the same. Kian got coffee. Then she went off to leave the ticket for the kitchen, spiking it onto the spinning wheel. This diner was so retro. We waited for our drinks because there was no point getting into it, only to be interrupted. Once we had our beverages, I took a sip, because while the patrons here might be creepy, they had a great kitchen. Buzzkill stirred his eerily red cocktail with a celery stalk, making me wonder if it *was* virgin's blood.

"Go on," I encouraged.

"Something's latched on to him, something old."

My thoughts sprang immediately to the Harbinger because I remembered how he'd fed on Nicole and how he planned to devour Kian's essence entirely. But, no, that didn't track. While Nicole grew pale and listless, she never forgot who she was. So it stood to reason that whatever had a hold of Aaron, it wasn't Harbinger related.

"Do you know what it is?" Kian asked.

Good question.

Buzzkill shook his head. "It'd be faster if you just put on the glasses."

Reaching across the table, I took them. They looked like plain aviator shades, but they couldn't be, if they'd help me understand the thing feeding on Aaron's memories. Taking a deep breath, I slipped them on and glanced over at the boy. I barely swallowed a scream. The rest of the world paled, became distant and two-dimensional, but at the base of his neck, something hideous perched. It was grotesque and swollen, throbbing with energy that swirled in awful violet and citrine swirls. With each pulse, it felt like I was watching it draw Aaron's soul out through his brain stem, though the answer probably wasn't that simple.

"What the hell," I breathed, yanking off the glasses with a trembling hand.

Kian took them, and to his credit, he handled the revelation better, though he paled.

Aaron glanced between us, obviously confused. "Am I sick?"

"Kind of," I said, as Kian answered, "Don't worry about it."

This time the look we swapped was loaded with contention. I could tell Kian thought we shouldn't let him know he had a huge, crazy-ass problem latched on to his skull, but I couldn't see any benefit to hiding the truth. Buzzkill clearly didn't care about the kid's feelings, and I was worried that I leaned toward agreeing with the killer clown. Feelings wouldn't save Aaron.

Shit. Maybe I'm already a monster.

"Tell me the truth," Aaron whispered.

I said, "If he's brave enough to ask, he deserves an answer."

I let Kian explain as best he could. But it didn't seem to make sense to the kid, who felt around on the back of his head. "There's nothing here."

Just because you can't see or touch it doesn't mean it can't hurt you. That was my new mantra, not that it offered *me* any comfort, either. I glanced at Buzzkill, wondering if he had any words of wisdom, but he was drinking his bloody virgin with an indifferent air.

"Wait, you can *drink?*"

"Is that important?" He wanted to know.

"No, but I'm curious."

"You heard how that worked out for the cat, right?"

"I'll risk it."

"Then, yeah, I can. Don't have to, but I can. Since I was allegedly human once, my 'afterlife' has some perks."

"Perks?" I asked, despite myself.

Buzzkill only smirked.

Oh God.

Aaron wore a blank look while Kian was quietly revolted. He got the conversation back on track. "So about the brain sucker . . ."

"You got me. I've never seen anything like it."

"It doesn't come from any of our stories?" I asked.

"None I've heard. But . . . there are things in the universe that didn't come from humans. Old things. They were around before."

"Like Allison Vega," I blurted.

Buzzkill cocked his head in inquiry. "Who?"

"That's probably not her name. She said something about speaking Sanskrit," Kian put in. He went on to tell the killer clown what we knew of her, including how she feasted on dissent and didn't have a belly button.

"Oh," he said, losing interest. "In the old days you called her kind demons. But that doesn't mean much outside of religious context. To be fair, I understand why they're pissed at humans. They had a good thing going here before you climbed out of the primordial ooze and made this world your bitch."

That was a separate problem. I sighed. "I bet they thought it was funny when we started using the collective unconscious to create our own nightmares."

"At first, probably," he agreed. "Though you realize I wasn't around, right? On the immortal longevity scale, I'm a fetus."

"A terrifying fetus," Kian muttered.

He flashed that awful grin. "Thanks, kid. Just doing my job."

The sad part, that was true. "This thing attached, it's not a monster we made?"

"No way. It only pops on the subatomic level. Which tells me it's probably some kind of dimensional beastie. I could check with Wedderburn, if you want." His scary eyes dared me to say yes.

I had a little more hot chocolate before giving him the go-ahead. Asking for information wouldn't be worse than letting him help me save my dad—after he had my mother murdered. Hatred burned like an ember in my chest, until it felt like I didn't have a human heart anymore, like I'd swapped it for a lump of coal, now kindled to a thousand degrees by white-hot loathing. I hoped Buzzkill couldn't see it, or he'd certainly warn his master.

Not that I expected Wedderburn to take the threat I posed seriously.

I hoped he wouldn't survive to regret it.

But I had other issues pressing first. Aaron. My dad.

Lately school didn't even feel like a dot on my horizon when it used to be my whole world. I could feel myself detaching from reality. It was easy to understand why Kian came across as he did when we first met, removed from humanity. Live too long in this world and the mundane one started to feel like the echo, the shadow that belonged to other people.

Buzzkill's side of the conversation didn't help too much. He just repeated what we'd told him and what we all saw through those weird-ass glasses. Then he went quiet, listening.

Aaron got up while Buzzkill was on the phone, head bowed. "Is the restroom over there?"

"Yeah, straight back that way." Kian pointed toward an arch way past the last booth.

Buzzkill put down his cell as Aaron left. "I wasn't wrong," he began. "Wedderburn says the things don't really have a name but he calls them temporal parasites because they tend to latch on to people who are somehow screwed in the time stream. From what he's seen, they're kind of a . . . cosmic cleanup crew."

"That doesn't make any sense," Kian said.

"Think about it. You told me this kid's from 1922, but he's only fourteen years old or whatever. How's that work if he remembers he should be almost a hundred? He's out of time. Not his fault, the Harbinger did something to him. But can shit like that go unchecked?"

"I have no idea," I said.

"Wedderburn says the answer is no—that the universe hates a paradox. So there are forces outside the game that exert pressure to restore equilibrium. Why do you think he's so hot to lock down his control of the time-travel technology you and your old man invent down the line?" At my expression, he made a face. "Like you don't already know."

Kian had shown me some confidential files a while back that hinted as much. This was confirmation, however.

"Why is one person so critical to the universe?" Kian asked, talking about Aaron.

"As a former catalyst, you're seriously asking me that? Hell if I know. I can't break it all down for you, I just kill things."

"So basically, Aaron has a dimensional parasite locked on to him," I cut in. "Did Wedderburn say what the endgame is?"

Buzzkill shrugged. "It's not set in stone. Sometimes the host dies or sometimes they're just wiped clean, tabula rasa."

Kian's eyes widened. "If he can't remember that he was born in 1922, it's a soft reboot. He becomes just another damaged kid."

"Give the pretty boy a prize. And thus, balance is restored," Buzzkill said.

"He was really cold." Judging by his pulse earlier, it sounded like this reset might end him. I nudged Kian across the table. "He's been gone for a while. You should check on him."

Nodding, he stood up and headed off, but he was back in thirty seconds, white faced and breathless. "Aaron's gone, I think he went out the window."

Swearing, I jumped out of my chair as Kian flung some money on the table for Shirl. I raced outside and around the building, hoping to catch sight of him. He was so young and helpless, despite his

193

chronological age, that I couldn't stop the terror rolling over me. Buzzkill caught up with us in the alley behind Cuppa Joe. He sniffed the air, twice, and froze, but I only smelled the rotten food from the Dumpster, along with a hint of urine.

"What's wrong?" Kian asked.

"Brace yourself," the killer clown said with dreadful relish. "Dwyer's coming in hot."

HEART
IN A BOX

"Pun intended?" Kian asked.

In that moment, I loved him so much that it hurt. The witty one-liners were so much a part of the action-hero role he wanted to play. I couldn't believe he had the presence of mind to snap one off, just before everything went insane. Unfortunately, he didn't have the combat prep he needed, and that scared the crap out of me. Yet at this point I was starting to get why he didn't care about his own safety. I'd lost so much that I'd rather die myself than take another emotional hit. Physical pain was finite, right? Death should be an ending; it wouldn't be a triumph, but if I could die saving my dad, my friends, or Kian, it would be worth it.

Buzzkill smirked. "Hey, I *am* a clown."

Kian reached for me, taking my hand in a gesture of solidarity. The cold air around us heated, melting the snow accumulated against the alley walls into a swath of steam. At the same time, a glowing nimbus surrounded us from all sides, so bright that it burned out my vision briefly, replacing it with the burn of staring too long into the sun. Sudden terror burst like a rotten fruit. Did this mean Dwyer was leading the strike team personally? I didn't expect that. I figured he'd send minions, like the monsters he'd used to kidnap my dad.

No time to think. I couldn't let my flight reflex kick in either. Fighting wasn't my instinctive reaction, but to survive, I had to. I'd throw down for a chance to save my dad and to defend Kian. Before the temporary blindness passed, I dug into my coat pocket. Cameron should be fully powered up since I hadn't used him since the binding and lessons at Forgotten Treasures. Sucking in a stabilizing breath, I flipped open the compact and whispered the first command Rochelle had taught me.

Strength flooded my body until the top of my head tingled. My skin also felt iced with cold, as if I had dead hands plastered all over me. I tucked the mirror away and waited for my vision to clear. I heard Buzzkill swearing and the sound of him digging into his briefcase for the tools of his trade. I was most worried about Kian, who hadn't trained with Raoul and me much. If it came down to it, I know how to strike, block, and fall, not that I was convinced I could physically stand against Dwyer and his ilk.

When I could see again, we were in a bubble of sorts, no longer part of the modern world. I'd seen something like this before when we visited the Oracle in Wedderburn's compound. Kian had called her a forfeit, caught in amber, because she couldn't exist in the real world. Was this place like her cave? Despite the dangers, I wondered about the physics involved in creating subspace like this one. I'd give anything to study the phenomenon . . . but Dwyer or his crew would soon be trying to kill us. That reality snapped me back to high alert.

The walls were pale and nondescript with pockets and shadows in the distance. That much power scared the shit out of me.

As if answering my thought, Dwyer strode toward us with minions in tow. And the sun god smiled. He wore white today, a stark contrast to the bronze and gold of the rest of his hair and skin. He took a step forward, holding up a hand to keep the monsters at his sides in check. They seemed to be feathered serpents in rainbow hues, something from the Mayan world, I thought, but their hisses and fangs and the way they bobbed and wove, staring at us, told me we were definitely prey. The movements were hypnotic, so I wrenched my gaze back to Dwyer. Ra. Apollo. Whoever the hell he was.

"I'm sure you know by now," he said.

"What?"

"That I have your father."

"We're not here to talk," Buzzkill cut in. "You invited us, so let's dance."

A quick glance showed me his true form, a terrifyingly demented clown with yellowed eyes and teeth, serrated blades in each hand. The outfit and hair should've made him hilarious, but I shivered as I looked away. *Glad he's on my side at the moment.*

"I'll get to you in a minute, freak show. This is a one-time offer for amnesty. Come with me, and I'll reunite you with your father. The two of you can work at one of *my* labs, under our protection. What's Wedderburn done to deserve your loyalty? You're a smart girl, I'm sure you already know what he did to your mother."

"I'm aware," I choked out.

The fact was, I'd be stupid not to consider it. But Buzzkill slid me a look. "Don't be dumb, kid. Wedderburn would rather see you dead than helping the opposition."

"Don't even think about it," Kian growled.

I wasn't sure who he was talking to, both of them, probably. The bravado was sweet, but he couldn't handle this for me. Not without being destroyed in this weird-ass clash of the Titans. So I opened my fingers and stepped away, drawing the enemy's gaze.

Dwyer flashed a blindingly bright smile. "But, you see, I feel exactly the same way."

Shit. I'm a wishbone. They'll pull on me until I break.

Then a faint whisper sounded in my head. *Remember how you felt when I had you on your knees?* The rage and humiliation nearly choked me, even a year later. Some memories didn't fade. *Cameron?* I whispered silently. He was part of me, wrapped around me, and the sensation was god-awful with horror.

Use that. Use it now.

"I'm not yours to take," I snarled at Dwyer.

Nobody was more startled when my fist connected with his jaw, and dark energy spilled from my fingers, blasting him back. *Cameron?* But my spirit familiar didn't reply. That wicked strength surged again, fueling my rage. For too long, I had been afraid—of the assholes at school, of monsters and immortals, of failing my family and friends, of losing the people I loved. It was time to fight back.

He didn't fall, but he did pause, rubbing his jaw with gilded fingertips. "You dare?"

But I didn't give him time to shit-talk. I went after him again, trying to remember everything Raoul had taught me. In my peripheral vision, Buzzkill rushed the feathered serpents, but the wind was rising, gusts pushing me away from my target. I stumbled as the brightness increased. Soon there was a corona in my eyes and I couldn't find Dwyer. I took his first hit squarely in my stomach; it should've scrambled my intestines but Cameron's cold seemed to absorb some of the force. I tumbled backward but, thanks to Raoul, I knew how to fall and I was on my feet in a few seconds.

Kian called, "Edie!"

I couldn't look at him.

The heat was rising, along with gale-force winds. It was all I could do to keep my feet while Buzzkill slashed at the feathered serpent I figured had to be responsible for the storm. The other one joined in, adding thunder and lightning to the melee. It snapped to the ground only inches from where I stood, raising all the hair on my head and singeing the soles of my shoes. Dancing backward, I narrowly avoided a blow from Dwyer. His expression radiated grim amusement, as if he didn't expect me to make this so interesting.

He'd hurt me badly, and it would probably get worse. The nearest snake god lashed out at me, judging me more dangerous than Kian. That made me happy even as Kian swore. I dodged the strike and wished I had a weapon. Barehanded combat sucked against such powerful opponents. A shrill cry of terror made me whirl around, just fast enough to avoid the follow-up in the form of lashing teeth.

To my horror, Aaron came flying out of the shadows, tossed like flotsam on the killing wind. *He must've been hiding nearby when Dwyer pulled us here.* The kid hit the ground hard and bounced several more feet. He wasn't moving like prey, more like a bag of clothes, but the snake god struck, sinking long fangs into him again and again. I ran at the thing but Dwyer knocked me away. *I can't believe I forgot about him.*

"Hold on," Buzzkill yelled. "Boss will send reinforcements but it'll take some time for them to pierce the bubble."

That strike nailed me squarely in the back, and I would've hit my head hard enough to knock me out if I hadn't known how to roll with it. I tumbled forward and came up on my feet, wobbling but still in the fight. Wearing an unreadable expression, Dwyer came at me again, riding the wind like a chariot. He loomed over me, trying that damn aura, but my spirit familiar kept me from feeling the worst of it. Instead of kneeling I struck at his kneecaps; that was how high he was above me. He tried to kick me in the head and I flung up my forearm in a reflexive block. The light that had rocked the Harbinger at school blew the sun god back. *Thanks, Wedderburn.* My marks were a fail-safe; now I was sure. If I'd tried to go with Dwyer, they might've burned so hot they would've killed me. Flinching, I remembered how much they hurt when I left Boston with Davina. *Damn. I basically have a bomb in each wrist.*

Dwyer swore in a language I didn't recognize, and I swung toward him, squinting. "That's not standard issue," he added in English.

My eyes focused as I caught my breath. My stomach was definitely bruised, and it slowed me down when Dwyer put out a hand. A ferocious glow kindled in his palm, the kind of brightness that said he'd burn everything down if he had to. The fire exploded like a backdraft, so it hurt to breathe. I dove but there was no shelter, and the wind caught me, buffeting me into the far wall. This was a pocket space created by the sun god; how long could he hold both our prison and keep summoning the power he needed to smite me?

When my eyes stopped stinging from the extreme heat, I stared in disbelief at the charred body nearby. I'd seen footage from bomb explosions and not been prepared for the damage. Buzzkill was still fighting. *Is that... That is...* Nearby, Kian hit the ground hard, bleeding from multiple puncture wounds. *Then it's Aaron. We saved him from the Harbinger and he died on our watch.* I didn't have the time to ponder the implications—if the life we'd pulled him out of had been better than a fiery death.

Buzzkill sliced the head off a feathered serpent, but the thing didn't stop. Instead its body simply writhed until another grew in its place. He cursed in quick succession. "I can't win here. They can't kill me. I can't kill them. But you . . ."

I'm weak. Human. And Kian's already down. The snake-thing bit him.

He wasn't moving either. My anger went ice cold, and Cameron . . . sank into me more. His despair over Brittany, being helpless and trapped, his emotions rushed through me like water across a broken dam. He didn't care who the target was; he just wanted someone to pay. It was all I could do to keep him from taking my body entirely. Through pure force of will, I choked him and took his fury as my own. I had no idea how I looked but Buzzkill actually gave way when I surged forward, both hands raised in a fighting stance.

"You can hurt me," I said coldly. "But you can't break me."

Dwyer lobbed more of that flash fire at me and I rolled *through* it. The move cost me, burning away most of my spirit strength. Cam's power was finite, and I'd nearly tapped it, but I kept running. Sheer purpose drove me forward and Cameron guided my hand with monstrous accuracy. My curled fingers sank into Dwyer's chest and I kept pushing. He didn't have the same biological consistency as a human, no flesh or bone, but I was definitely hurting him. My fingers curled around something hard and hot and when I pulled my hand out, I held a blazing stone, ugly, seething orange that contrasted sharply with the beauty of his exterior.

His expression dazed and frightened, Dwyer stumbled back as the pocket realm imploded. Shards of light rained down around me as I threw myself on top of Kian. When I opened my eyes again, I was lying in the dirty alley behind Cuppa Joe on top of Kian's still body, Aaron's unrecognizable corpse nearby. Wedderburn arrived a few seconds later in a shower of ice and hail; I hardly felt it as it sprinkled on my back.

"You angered the Harbinger only to get his poor pet killed . . . and *this* is what you saved dear Kian for?" The cold god chuckled. "Sometimes I wonder if you're as clever as academic records imply, Miss Kramer."

"Maybe not," I gritted out.

"Pity. Your plans never seem to work out as you hope. It would've been kinder to let Buzzkill execute Kian Riley. Much quicker than poison."

The ember burned my palm but I didn't open my fingers. Some quiet instinct whispered that if he saw it, he would take it by force, and I couldn't let that happen. A glance at Buzzkill told me he was weighing his options, but in the end, he kept quiet. I didn't know why. Something like hope shivered through me, delicate as cricket feet. Excruciating pain now, but I couldn't let on.

"I'll take care of him. Go." The last word came out gritted through my teeth. For a few seconds, I feared Wedderburn would linger and then I'd die of shock, but instead he swooshed away in a showy departure of winter wonders.

Moaning, I slammed my hand into the snow the cold god left behind. It cooled the stone to bearable proportions, and the throb in my palm died away to numbness, probably not a good sign. I was more worried about Kian, who still hadn't stirred. Lifting myself off him, I made sure he had a heartbeat. *Yeah, faint but there.* Panting, I rested my head against Kian's chest.

"You can't keep Dwyer's heart in a snowbank. He's weak now but he'll be back for it."

"Why didn't you tell Wedderburn? He probably could make great use of this."

"Probably," he admitted. "And . . . I'm not sure. Technically you're my boss right now, so I could say it's because I knew you wanted to keep it a secret."

"But that's really not why."

He shook his head, taking on the nondescript bodyguard role again. "Hang on a sec, I'll see what I have to help you."

"Huh?"

Rather than answer, he rummaged around in his case and produced a small square box. "This should do the trick."

Buzzkill popped it open to reveal a lead-lined container. My whole arm felt dead, and it took most of my strength to lift the stone and drop it inside. He sealed it up and handed it back to me. My head was fuzzy from exhaustion and pain as I tucked it into my jacket pocket, but I couldn't pass out.

"I'm going into Cuppa Joe for a sec. Gotta tell Shirl that we need cleanup in aisle death."

"That's not funny."

Poor Aaron.

But I couldn't even grieve because I was so damn worried about Kian. While Buzzkill went inside, I tried to bring him around, but nothing worked. His inhalations grew lighter and fainter, until I feared I could hear the death rattle in his chest. *Oh my God, no. Not like this.* Fear and rage went battle royale in my brain. Maybe it was futile to feel this way when he had an expiration date. In a few short months, he was turning twenty-one, and on his birthday, the Harbinger would drink him like a refreshing beverage.

The first tears were falling when Buzzkill stomped back toward me. "Get that meatsack on his feet, or we're leaving him. Find his keys."

His brusqueness jolted me into movement born of sheer antipathy. A glance at my compact told me Cameron had only a little juice to give; he was a faint shadow, but I showed no mercy in calling him again. The whispered word left me with an empty mirror and just enough energy to hoist Kian over my shoulder.

"Bullshit," I said. "Did *you* complete driver's ed? Because I did."

For once, Buzzkill was speechless as I stumbled past him toward the Mustang. He followed with a few choice imprecations about me not knowing when to quit, but I ignored him. I slung Kian into the passenger seat and called Raoul while waiting for Buzzkill to get in back.

My guardian/mentor picked up on the second ring. "What's up, *mija?*"

"I hope you're not far," I said shakily. "Because this is an emergency."

IN AN EMERGENCY, CALL THE KILLER CLOWN

Quietly I updated Raoul. He listened without interrupting and then to my vast relief, he took over, his voice flat with fear. "Meet me at his apartment. I have to get a couple of things, and then I'll be right there. Get rid of the clown."

"Understood." I started the car without turning around.

I didn't actually have my license, as I'd only finished taking the class at school. Which was why I didn't drive Davina back from New Hampshire, but this was life or death. I couldn't let a laminated card stop me from getting Kian some help. Hospitals would probably be a waste of time, considering the supernatural quality of the venom. When I got there—*if* I got us there—I'd confirm with Raoul. Much as I wanted to check on Kian, I didn't dare take my hands off the wheel or my eyes off the road.

City driving was terrifying. I'd done behind-the-wheel practice as part of the course, but since Blackbriar was located in the burbs, traffic was nothing like what I faced at the moment in Boston. My knuckles went white on the wheel. If I clipped somebody or took out a fire hydrant, that would delay us, and Kian couldn't afford me to screw this up. Saving him before was a choice I made, not a wild drive across town on unfamiliar roads when I'd driven a car for exactly twelve hours before, always with a professional instructor on the passenger side equipped with his own brake and steering wheel. My heart felt like it would lurch out of my throat.

Finally, I pulled up outside the apartment building and ran around to see how Kian was doing. He didn't look good. The places where the snake god had bit him were turning black with red streaks raying out from the punctures. Buzzkill didn't say anything; he just slung Kian over one shoulder, probably knowing I had nothing left. As we went toward his door, I freaked out silently. *If Raoul's there . . . but, no, he said immortals shouldn't recognize him.* But I was none too eager to test our luck. So far, it had mostly been bad and worse.

I unlocked the door with Kian's key and said, "Put him on the couch."

"If you don't do something, he's dead in under an hour." The quiet statement made me shove Buzzkill toward the door. "Ugly dying too. Want to hear how it'll go?"

"Shut *up* already!"

He paused, resting a hand on the door frame. "Wedderburn might be able to do something, but I'm sure you already know, he never works for free."

"Kian would rather die than go back in hock to Wedderburn."

Buzzkill nodded. "Try not to piss anyone else off. You have more than enough enemies."

"Very public enemies," I agreed.

How angry was the Harbinger? He'd said I had almost exhausted his powers, but maybe that was an exaggeration. Mentally I ticked off the things I'd done to agitate him: ruined his party, stole Aaron from him, refused his weird offer to make me his pet, and finally . . . got the poor kid killed. Knots formed in my stomach, Gordian whorls of grief and regret.

The clown observed Kian for a few seconds, and whatever he deduced made him shake his head. "I could kill him. Just this once, I'll make it quick and painless."

"Get out."

"That's no way to thank a comrade in arms." But he went, reducing my problems by one.

As soon as the door closed, I knelt beside Kian and took his hand. "Hey, you have some time left. You can't quit on me now." His lashes fluttered but his eyes didn't open. Tears dripped from my cheeks to his, one rolling toward his lips, where it trembled and spread. In fairy tales, the tears of your one true love would be enough to cure him.

He didn't stir.

Either I'm not his true love or happy endings are a lie. Crying quietly, I touched my brow to his, listening to the dry rattle of his breath. It sounded like he could leave me at any moment, and I *wasn't ready.* There were so many things we hadn't done together. I didn't expect forever, but I wanted more time.

A few minutes later, Raoul burst through the door with a paper sack. He barked an order as he skidded to a stop beside the couch. "Boil some water."

In seconds I had a pan on the stove while he unpacked various objects: an agate cup, amethyst pendant, a bone spoon, a rock I couldn't identify, what looked like shark teeth, and something even weirder. I paced, waiting for the water to heat, and as soon as I saw bubbles, I grabbed a pot holder with my good hand and raced into the living room. Silently Raoul poured the water into the cup, then added all the other objects. If he was making a magic potion, it didn't sizzle, steam, or turn colors. To me it just looked like he was soaking strange stuff.

"What is all that?"

"Supplies," he said tersely. "We'll talk afterward."

Chastened, I slumped to the floor, cradling my bad hand against my chest. Likely I needed medical attention. I could also use a plan, because Buzzkill was right; Dwyer wouldn't wait long before coming after the ember I'd pulled from his chest. I suspected it would probably act as a tracking device too. As long as I had it, he'd be able to home in on me like I was GPS-chipped.

Ignoring me, Raoul kept stirring while I shivered. Reaction set in, heavier and harder than shock. I remembered Rochelle's warning about getting hooked on the rush from using my spirit familiar and I bowed my head. My hair smelled of smoke, and the ragged ends I could see tumbling over my shoulder were black and charred. I didn't get up to check it out.

Finally, just as I wrestled with the urge to tell him to hurry up, Raoul cut the fabric away from Kian's bites, then he simply poured the hot water into the punctures. Where there had been no response, Kian screamed, a raw, awful sound, but he still didn't wake up. Raoul repeated this process until the water was gone, and there were only those strange objects in the bottom of the cup, damp and inexplicable.

"Did it work?" I demanded, studying Kian anxiously.

"I don't know."

"You should have all kinds of resources—Black Watch artifacts, why *aren't* you sure?"

"They have given me nothing," he said. "Would my master have asked me to steal from Wedderburn, if he had anything sufficiently powerful to conceal me?"

"Then it sounds like they're worthless," I muttered.

"Perhaps. But they're also the only ones who know about the game."

I ignored that. "Explain what you did to him before I lose my mind."

"Everything I have here is from the ancient world, items that people believed would counteract the effects of poison. A hornbill spoon, a chunk of a celadon dish, an agate cup, fossilized shark teeth, snakestone—"

"So if enough people believed in one of these objects, then it'll work. If not . . ." I couldn't complete the sentence.

Neither could Raoul. Instead he nodded quietly.

"What's snakestone?"

"Ammonite fossil, an extinct sea creature similar to the nautilus. Ancient civilizations prized them because they resembled a coiled serpent."

"Sympathetic magic?" I guessed.

"Seems likely." Raoul went quiet then, and in his expression I read infinite sorrow.

Kian wasn't wrong in thinking this guy cared about him. I bet he hated taking off.

Knee-walking closer to Kian, I cupped my hand around his. For now, he was still breathing. His wounds were still puffy and dark, but maybe the red streaks didn't look so bad? That might be wishful thinking. Raoul stayed beside me, on his knees as well. To a random observer, it would probably look like we were praying.

I held the pose until my shins ached, along with all my other damage.

"Should we take him to a hospital?"

He shook his head. "The doctors wouldn't know what to do. Antivenin treatments are primarily successful for modern medicine when they have a specific antidote on hand. Sometimes people die even after getting treatment because the doctors can't get a hold of what they need soon enough."

"That's not helping," I whispered.

Frowning, Raoul peered closer at me. "You're the one who looks like you need a doctor."

"Yeah."

My hand was definitely screwed up. I couldn't unfurl my fingers; they were curled atop the burn I'd taken stealing Dwyer's heart. My back, stomach, and sides hurt too, but it wasn't as bad as it had been in the lab. My spirit familiar shielded me to some degree.

"Let me see."

I recoiled as he took my hand, not because it hurt. Because it didn't. That seemed worse; I couldn't feel it when he forced my fingers open. From the wrist down, it was a dead zone, and when I saw the charred mess my palm had become, I almost threw up. I turned my face away, tears starting in my eyes.

"*Mierda*," he breathed. "What did you do, grab a live wire and refuse to let go?"

Right, he didn't know about the heart in a box. "Something like that."

"We have to get you to an ER right away."

"But Kian—"

"You could lose the hand if we don't act fast."

"I'll risk it," I said quietly. "Kian will either wake up from your maybe-cure . . . or he won't. Either way I won't leave him alone."

I sat beside him for an hour, longer than Buzzkill predicted he'd live. We used ice packs to keep the swelling down and Raoul got him to swallow some water. That gave me hope that he might be turning the corner. Two hours later, his fever spiked, but generally, that was a good sign, right? It meant the body was trying to fight an infection.

By this point, I was beyond shaky. "Okay, I think I better see a doctor. You stay with him, okay?"

Raoul nodded. "I'll text you if there's any change."

I stumbled out of the apartment and down the steps with a dish towel hiding the massive eyesore my right hand had become. Dwyer's stone heart was still burning a figurative hole in my coat pocket, safely inside Buzzkill's mystery box. The killer clown fell into step with me, coming out of nowhere, as I wobbled toward the station. It wasn't far to the hospital where Brittany died. For obvious reasons I didn't want to go there, but in my current state, I couldn't find my way anywhere else.

"You have absolutely no plan, do you?" Buzzkill sighed.

"Did you work that out all by yourself?"

"Don't be an asshole to someone offering you a freebie. Come on."

"Huh?"

Instead of the hospital, Buzzkill took me to headquarters. When I realized we were outside WM&G, I nearly broke my ankle trying to run away. But the clown collared me and dragged me in through the lobby, where I found the receptionist done in ominous shades of orange to match the scary new décor. Iris looked like something

211

out of a weird fashion magazine with a towering updo, the kind that required wire and scaffolding during the French Revolution. The rest of her was straight out of the sixties, polyester skirt and jacket with tall boots and insanely long fake eyelashes.

She reached for the security button until she registered Buzzkill behind me. "Are you taking responsibility for her?"

"Don't sweat it, doll."

I raised incredulous brows, but Buzzkill had a hold of my elbow, drawing me toward the elevator bank. He pushed the call button and scanned his card when we got into the first one that opened. He took me to the thirty-sixth floor, a part of the complex I'd never seen. As we rose, a bizarre canned version of "Don't Worry, Be Happy" came on. Like things weren't weird enough, Buzzkill whistled along.

"What are we doing here?"

Before he could answer, the doors slid open, revealing a sign on that wall that read MEDICAL and RESEARCH with arrows pointing either way. We swung right, following the scent of antiseptic, like a hundred times stronger than you'd find in a hospital. There was also an odd unidentifiable odor, similar to hot metal.

"Patching you up," Buzzkill answered eventually. "I know you'd rather see Boss's head on a stick than ask for help, but there are certain perks available."

"You said it would cost me to get him to save Kian," I protested.

"He's out of the game, remember? Whereas *you*, chickadee, are still Boss's favorite little play-pretty. How's that stupid saying go, don't bite off your nose, and all that. Unless you're actually biting off someone's nose. In which case go ahead. But remember, there's a surprising amount of gristle."

"You are everything that's wrong in the world."

"If you knew how much self-control I'm exerting to keep from fileting you, kid, you'd pin a medal on me."

"Let go!" I struggled, convinced he was taking me to be dissected. Wait, no, he had all the knives, and now we were headed to the perfect setting. There was probably a drain in the floor to hose off the blood afterward.

In answer he shook me like I'd seen mama cats do to fractious kittens. When he dropped me, I stumbled through the doorway to Medical, drawing the attention of two things working inside. They weren't human but they didn't seem like monsters either. Actually they looked like medical droids from various SF films: shiny, cylindrical, balanced on two wheels, with multiple appendages, though *attachments* might be the better word. The closest one enveloped me in a blue beam, then an image of me popped on holo along with a list of my physical issues: slight anemia, various contusions, a tiny gastrointestinal perforation likely caused by blunt force trauma, and a third-degree burn on my right palm. On closer inspection, the room seemed to be a clinic of sorts. I recognized the names on some of the bottles on the shelves from my chemistry classes. My breathing dropped away from the risk of hyperventilation.

"Just let the thing work on you," Buzzkill said with visible impatience. "You think you're the first idiotic catalyst to run afoul of the opposition? That's what this is for. It's not like *I* need a healthcare plan, genius."

"Oh." Now I *did* feel pretty stupid. If I'd known, I could've come here after the Harbinger's party, but nobody had given me a membership packet.

Sheepish, I climbed onto the exam chair and stayed quiet while the medical robot did things to me. This was way better than the hospital because the bot had no questions about how I'd come to be so injured. Which made sense. The fewer facts on file, the better it had to be for those involved in the immortal game. *In fact . . .*

"Is that why Dwyer pulled us into that pocket space?"

Buzzkill gave me a half-frown, half-puzzled look. "What are you yammering about now? Never had *any*body talk to me this much before."

"Pocket space, I'm trying to figure out why Dwyer fought there. It cost him in terms of energy expenditure, which meant he didn't have as much to hit us with. So I need to know why."

"Oh." Realization gave the clown a puckish air. "What makes you think I know?"

"Well, you can guess better than I can."

"Fine, since you're buttering me up. Two reasons. One, he doesn't want human interference. If fireballs and lightning storms explode in the middle of Boston, people will notice and try to help. Two, if he's already got you isolated, all he has to do is incapacitate you."

"We made that tougher than he expected."

Buzzkill smirked. "That we did. Not bad for a little girl and Internet meme."

"Come over here and say that." The bot shot something into my arm that made me feel more than a little loopy.

It had been giving me shots and then it whipped out what looked like a laser but I was too happy to care. I didn't feel whatever it did to my stomach but the meds were wearing off a little when it fastened my right hand to the chair. A sharp pinch stung my arm; Edward Needlehands was drawing blood, but I had no idea why. Dazed, I watched the red flow up a tube and into the machine, and it made centrifugal noises.

"What the hell," I mumbled.

The droid spoke for the first time. "Procedure about to begin. Please do not move."

My hand pinned in place, the med-bot shot my palm with a fleshy wad that crawled into the wound. I screamed, thinking I had to be tripping from the pain meds, but Buzzkill came over to watch with a fascinated expression. That told me this horrible treatment was happening.

"Is this where I grow a chest burster five days later?" The words came out more like a whimper instead of the bravado I wanted.

"You're funny, kid. No, it's a more advanced version of the skin gun. Combination of stem cells, sea squirt DNA, and keratinocyte cell-spray."

That sounded like actual science, but . . . "It *moved*."

"Yeah, that's the sea squirt DNA. It's engineered to feed on your dead cells while your own stem cells heal the burn."

Less risk, using the patient's own tissue. "Will the feeling come back?"

He shrugged. "They only *called* me Doctor Smiles."

"Okay. How long before we can go?"

"Please rest for twelve minutes and allow the bonding process to complete." That came from the bot, politer than most ER doctors.

Later, as I climbed out of the chair, my phone buzzed. I nearly dropped it trying to read the message from Raoul.

Get back here. Kian needs you.

CUE THE
ROAD TRIP MUSIC

Right about now, I wished I had one of those fancy watches that let me port around. Of course that would also mean that I was working for Wedderburn so maybe it was better to take the subway with a killer clown. My hand still didn't have any sensation in it, and the bot had wrapped it in a bandage before I took off.

It was late enough that we'd missed the commuter rush; my knee jogged up and down on the way back to Kian's place. I hoped like hell that Raoul's message meant he was awake and asking for me, but the knot in my stomach hinted otherwise. Guilt chained itself to my ankles. *I shouldn't have left him.* But the wound on my hand and the damage to my stomach was serious, so it wasn't like I went out for ice cream. I studied the blue bead necklace he'd wrapped around my wrist not long ago. The azure and aquamarine stones contrasted beautifully against my skin, but they also shadowed it, echoing the blood showing in my veins.

Buzzkill sat across from me, looking like a businessman on the way home from the office. He waited a few seconds after I got up to disembark, and as soon as I could, I was running. My heart thundered in my ears, and I sprinted like I could outpace the fear and grief. A few minutes later, I burst into Kian's apartment without a word to the clown. He knew not to come in, which solved any question about what to do with him.

Raoul glanced up. From what I could tell, he hadn't moved much. He was still on the floor beside Kian, though he also had a bowl of ice water and various other remedies scattered around. The apartment smelled of herbal infusion and Kian seemed to be breathing better, but he was sweaty as hell and thrashing around. After taking my jacket off, I tossed it over the nearby armchair, then I paused by the sofa.

"Did he wake up?"

"Sort of. He's delirious and he thought he was supposed to be watching you. I had to hold him to keep him from leaving. I was hoping if he heard your voice, he'd settle down."

Bending down, I kissed Kian's hot cheek. "Are you causing trouble? Well, you can relax, I'm here now." To Raoul, I added, "I'll take over, if you want to get some rest."

He hesitated. "Are you sure?"

"Yeah. Use Kian's room."

The older man didn't argue with me, which meant he must be pretty tired. Once Raoul went to bed, I tidied up the living room and then I settled with Kian on the couch, substituting myself for the sweat-drenched pillow. I checked his temperature, which was 101. High, but not scary enough to rush him to the hospital. With some coaxing, I got him to drink a glass of water and take a little pain medicine. The bites were definitely looking better, though I had no idea which of the artifacts had soaked up enough human belief to be efficacious. I tried picking each of them up, but nothing set off the tinnitus.

"You have to get better," I told Kian softly.

I whispered to him until my throat went hoarse, brushing damp, silky hair away from his brow. Tending Kian, I tried to plan my next move. There *had* to be a way to capitalize on stealing Dwyer's heart. If I didn't act fast, the sun god would strike again, and this time, he'd be really pissed, plus there'd be no offer of amnesty. Wedderburn would know how to best make use of it, but he'd also take it from me and use it against his old enemy.

No way. I stole the damn thing. It's mine.

Sleep claimed me before I had an answer. When I woke up, it was dawn and Kian was staring up at me, dazed but lucid. Relief shot through me as I touched his cheek.

"How you feeling?"

"Like I got run over by a feathered serpent. How am I still alive?"

"Raoul," I said, showing him the arcane supplies.

"Wow. I kind of thought this was it. I had the *weirdest* dreams. But waking up with you makes it all worth it."

I smiled down at him and leaned close to kiss his nose. "He saved you, not me. I just kept watch on the night shift."

"You've been saving me for years," he whispered. "Before you even knew I existed."

"Saying stuff like that when you're too weak to make out with me is just cruel."

"Who said I can't?" He tried to lever up, but I had to help him sit. When I raised my brows in quiet challenge, Kian sighed. "Okay, maybe not right this minute. It's going on my to-do list."

"Kissing me?"

"You, period."

"*I'm your to-do list?*" I grinned, wondering if he meant it to sound so dirty.

Color washed his cheeks but his grin widened, and then it hit me like an ocean wave, knocking me down hard, water in my lungs until my eyes stung. *Aaron. I have to tell Kian and Raoul. They're going to be so mad . . . I let Wedderburn's people deal with him like he was a bag of garbage to be hauled away.* Maybe there hadn't been a better option at the time but I didn't like myself much for making the expedient choice. Each time I opted to save my own ass, it felt like I lost part of myself.

But the alternative is dying.

"Edie? What's wrong?"

"We lost Aaron."

He frowned at me in obvious confusion. "Yeah, I remember that much. He ran away from the diner."

"He was hiding in the alley somewhere. Dwyer pulled him in with us and he . . . Aaron got caught in the crossfire. He didn't make it. I'm so sorry."

His lashes fluttered, then his gaze dropped away from mine, like he didn't want to show me what he was feeling. "Damn. I really wanted to save him. I'm a shitty hero, huh?"

"Most heroes are idiots," I said. "Pretty much every move they make is devoid of all common sense, and it only works out because they have stunt doubles."

"You really don't mind that I'm useless?" The softness of his tone hid nothing of the sorrow over Aaron's loss.

"How can you say that? Without you, I'd probably give up. I'd decide there's no way for me to save my dad or to get out of the game. But you've been telling me I'm something special since the first day we met. You're the reason I keep on, even when things seem hopeless. I was afraid you'd be furious. Aaron died because of me."

Collateral damage.

"*Dwyer* killed him, not you. It's not your fault, Edie."

Kian wrapped his arms around me, leaning against me more than he usually did. The fever had sapped his strength, but his head felt good on my shoulder. I didn't even know I was crying until he touched my wet cheeks. Opening my eyes, I saw that his eyes were bright with tears too. We wept together for Aaron, the poor, helpless kid we couldn't save.

Raoul came out as I got up to wash my face. The mirror told me I looked every bit as hideous as I felt, now that the pain meds were wearing off. My hair was burned in a bizarre pattern, so I got the nail scissors from beneath the sink and cut it as best I could. That left me decidedly ragged, especially on the left side. With a faint shrug, I hacked that hank all the way off, close to my scalp. Punk rock chic was the best I could do, so I brushed my teeth with my fingers and yielded the facilities.

After I came out, Raoul helped Kian to the bathroom. When we'd all cleaned up a little, we had breakfast. It was a weird-ass morning, but I didn't have the leisure to grieve. Once all this was over, I'd try to find Aaron's original family, though I doubted I knew enough about him to track people down from 1922. Still, I owed him something. If we couldn't locate his descendants, then we'd put up a memorial at a columbarium.

"You decided to stay with us, huh?" Though his tone was offhand, I could tell by the shadows beneath Raoul's eyes that things had been scarier than he let on while I was out.

"I've got a little time yet. I intend to make the most of it." Kian's hands were still shaky, however, when he spooned up his cereal.

"Speaking of . . . I have something special here." I went to my jacket and pulled out the box, cracking it open just enough to show them the glowing ember inside.

The heat was staggering, enough to singe my fingertips before I snapped the box shut. Weirdly Buzzkill's impenetrable container gave no sign of the fire contained within. *Why the hell was he carrying this around?* Then again, he usually had surgical tools on him so maybe Wedderburn often ordered him to cut something out of another immortal and the desired body part might be the supernatural equivalent to radioactive. Assignments like that would be right up the clown's alley.

Raoul dropped his coffee cup with a clatter, slopping amber liquid all over the counter. "Is that what I think it is?"

"If you think it's a sun god's heart, then yes."

"Edie, we can't sit around the apartment. We have to move."

Talk about stating the obvious. "I *know* that. I've been thinking all night, and the only solution is to turn this into a weapon. Unfortunately, I don't know any legendary blacksmiths."

The older man smiled. "Fortunately, I do. Time for a road trip."

• • •

Three hours later, we were in Vermont, and my marks didn't seem to mind. Unlike the trip I'd taken to New Hampshire, which was unrelated to the game, my brands seemed to realize that this jaunt was game related. Which made me wonder how in the hell *that* worked, but I was way past admitting that science couldn't explain all things. Certain aspects of this bizarre competition definitely qualified as magic, reluctant as I was to use that word.

St. Albans Town was a picturesque village on the edges of Lake Champlain. Normally I'd hesitate to call an American town that but the term applied. Charming Cape-style houses mingled with cute bungalows and the faded elegance of ramshackle Victorians. Even in winter, it was pretty here, though it was a black-and-white Ansel Adams beauty. Raoul drove down VT 36 to Samson Road, which seemed a little on the nose. Maybe that was why the god of the forge was living here.

God, I hope I'm right about him having a sense of humor. But stories never mentioned that trait. Usually he was characterized as grumpy with a giant chip on his shoulder. *No, that's mostly Greek and Roman. You don't know anything about Norse or Celtic smith stories.* But I knew there were Javanese and Hindu legends as well. *How does that work anyway? Do they swell to incorporate all versions of similar gods?* That sounded . . . uncomfortable, to say the least.

Raoul bore left, driving with confidence onto a dirt road, though it was marked Private. Worried, I leaned forward. Kian was asleep; good, he needed the rest. The older man met my eyes in the rear-view mirror.

"I can make the introductions. Govannon is no friend to Wedderburn, even if he realized I'd escaped his service. But he knows me by another name . . . from another life."

"Literally?" Maybe that was a stupid question, but I'd learned to discount no possibility, no matter how improbable it sounded.

Raoul laughed softly. "No. I think I told you that I studied in the east for five years? My master there still honors the great smith.

In ages past, Govannon supplied weapons to the monastery, though he's mostly retired these days."

"He is?" My tone must've given away my disappointment.

"We can always ask," he said. "'A decent boldness ever meets with friends.'"

Raising my brows, I said, "You're quoting the *Odyssey* right now? Seriously? It took that guy forty years to get home."

"We'll try to be more efficient," he said, parking the car in front of the clapboard house painted lemon yellow, a bright contrast to the dark boughs of the barren trees around it.

The house backed up to the water with a stony path leading down to the gray and rippling lake. Something about the setting felt familiar, as if I'd dreamed this, but to my chagrin I couldn't remember how it went . . . or more important, the ending. There was space beside the house for several cars, but I was most impressed by the workshop behind. Smoke was coming out the chimney of the outbuilding, so at least we wouldn't be turning Govannon out of a warm bed.

"Looks like he's awake."

Kian stirred at that, rubbing his eyes. "I'm up. Are we there?"

In reply Raoul opened the door. "Let's go say hello."

"Uhm. You said he's no friend to Wedderburn. How about you know who?" I lofted the box containing the sun god's heart. "Will this piss him off?"

"Just the opposite. I'm sure it's been eons since he had a chance to work with anything so powerful. That's part of why he's retired, the challenge is lost in churning out simple tools. And without extraordinary materials, there can be no new legendary weapons."

Raoul paused as we all climbed out and then he said, "You, Edith Kramer, are writing your own story. One day they may talk of the girl who stole the sun god's heart."

"Literally." Kian said it this time, not a question, and I managed to smile.

It took all my self-control not to let my teeth chatter—and not from the cold—as I followed Raoul toward the workshop. He didn't seem worried, but given that all of the immortals except Rochelle had hurt me in some way, I didn't have high hopes for this encounter. Even the Harbinger, who was supposed to protect me, sent his death birds after me, and there was no *telling* what he'd do if he got a hold of me now.

Kian fell in step, wrapping my hand in his. His fingers were long and warm, and it nearly killed me to realize all over again that we had so little time. *But all the more reason I should prize each moment, right?* I gazed up at him, trying to picture how he'd look if nature had taken its course on that awkward freshman. *I wish I could see his face, the real one, just once.* The strength of that longing surprised me.

Before Raoul knocked, a mountain of a man flung the door open. He loomed in the doorway, nearly seven feet tall with enormous shoulders wrapped in yards of faded flannel. Bulging biceps strained the fabric and I'd never seen a chest like that outside of an action movie. His skin was weathered like old leather but I couldn't see much of it for the luxurious copper beard and long hair, loosely caught in a leather tie. With eyes like embers, he studied us. Scarred hands as big as frying pans made me think he definitely could forge a weapon out of Dwyer's heart. The only question was if he *would*.

But he was already frowning. "Yes?"

"I'm sorry to bother you, maestro."

Unexpectedly, Govannon's expression cleared, as he seemed to recognize Raoul. "Li Jun, what are you doing here? Did Master Wu send you?"

Raoul bowed low and kept his head down until Govannon said, "None of that, come in, old friend."

Could immortals and humans ever call themselves that? Nevertheless, I went in, still holding Kian's hand. Inside was an old-fashioned forge, complete with anvil, hammer, tongs, and tools whose names I didn't know. I'd never seen anything like it outside of a historical village. The temperature within immediately made me want to take off my jacket; it looked like he had been stoking the fire when we arrived.

"Master Wu has passed on," Raoul said. "His successor may contact you at some point, but I'm not with the monastery anymore. My duty lies elsewhere."

Govannon seemed to feel . . . something at the elderly monk's passing. I couldn't tell what it was. "Has it been so long? I . . . have no sense of time."

"It's been fifteen years since we spoke last," Raoul told him.

"Hm. And what young sparks have you brought?" When his shining gaze fell on me, I braced myself against the urge to step back.

There was an earthy, iron weight to his regard, one that whispered I wasn't worthy to be in his presence, different from the Harbinger's glamour, the cold god's dread, or Dwyer's bright arrogance. Govannon was all the quiet majesty of a primeval forest. He didn't need to threaten me or posture for me to sense his permanence. Everything about him was massive and solid, like a boulder set by glaciers a million years ago.

"I'm Edie." That wasn't nearly enough, but all I could manage for the moment. Following Raoul's lead, I bowed to him until he gestured for me to stand up.

"Kian." He did the same, prompting a half smile from the smith.

"Your reverence is noted. But . . . I sense you have business with me, lady. Am I wrong?"

Raoul didn't answer; neither did Kian. I'd taken Dwyer's heart. Now it was up to *me* to push the advantage.

"You're not." This time I spoke more firmly. "I have some ore that could be turned into a devastating weapon, and you're the only one who can work it."

A minute pause. Then Govannon said, "Color me . . . intrigued."

When I gave him a glimpse of the ember in a box, his bushy bronze brows shot up nearly to his hairline. "I took this yesterday. If I don't acquire a better way to defend myself, he'll repo it and burn me to the ground."

"The strength you used yesterday was fleeting?" the smith asked.

"It's finite." I didn't show him my compact, but I didn't need to look at it to know my spirit familiar was still weak as hell.

"I'd love to do this for you." Govannon's eyes shone like copper coins.

"I sense a but."

"Astute of you, lady. Before I agree to this commission, I must be sure you're *worthy* of wielding one of my weapons."

A GEM CANNOT BE POLISHED WITHOUT FRICTION

"How do I prove I am?"

Govannon smiled, sharp like one of his famed blades. "You must pass a test, of course."

Kian tightened his grip on my hand, but I didn't let him protest. "Okay. I'm sure I don't need to tell you how important this is."

"For me as well," the smith replied.

I remembered what Raoul said about how long it had been since Govannon worked with anything but regular metals. "Just tell me what to do."

In answer, he gestured, and the workshop disappeared. Suddenly I was alone on a rocky precipice, but I'd had this happen often enough now that I barely paused. There was no wind, no sensation of cold. Which meant this was an illusion. When Kian actually ported us to a mountainside in Tibet, I felt the difference. So whatever this was, it was happening in my head while my body hung out in the smithy.

Govannon hadn't explained anything about the test or what my ultimate goal was; fine, I'd wing it. I followed the rocky trail around until I came to a clearing. Two trees grew side by side, and they were in full blossom, contrary to the season in the real world. The tree on the left had one enormous white fruit unlike anything I'd ever seen. The closest comparison would be an oversized squash, but the texture was more like cantaloupe with a snow-white peel. On the right, the boughs groaned with a plethora of tiny red berries; they grew in clusters of five, rough like raspberries, but the color was similar to holly.

Let's see, most red berries are poisonous. But I'm probably not here to decide what to eat. Maybe I'm not supposed to do anything *with the fruit. Could be a distraction.* So I tried to pass between, but the branches slammed down, blocking my path. *Okay, obviously I have to make a choice, here.* But there was no additional information forthcoming.

Hoping I wasn't making a rash decision, I turned to the berries and carefully plucked one sprig, then took a step forward. The branches didn't slam down this time. *I made the right call?* Unsure, I continued until I came to a brazier at the head of the path with forks heading right and left down either side of the mountain. Govannon's face appeared in the flames and he spoke in a booming voice.

"Prove to me this wasn't chance. Explain your choice."

God, this sounded dumb. "Well, there were plenty of red berries. It seemed better to take some of those than to pull down the big melon thing. I mean, there's only one, and that means it must be special, right?"

"That is the selfless choice," he agreed. "Proceed, lady."

Then the fire went inert, simple flickering light that gave off no heat. I studied the paths but neither had distinguishing characteristics; it wasn't like one was tough and the other easy. They seemed to have the same grade incline and more or less the same amount of stones. This might not be a test, though. So I took the closer one and climbed down. Along the way, I came across a wolf with its foot caught in a snare, but when I tried to help it, the animal snarled at me. Even in a dreamscape, I wasn't eager to have my arm ripped open, and Govannon might be powerful enough that any damage I took here would transfer to my physical body.

Hm. I wonder if feeding it would calm it down. But I don't want to hurt it. Since I had no way to be sure if these berries were good to eat, I plucked one off the stem, broke it open, and tasted the juice. It was sweetish, and even if it was poison, a taste wouldn't be enough to kill me, right? I waited for a while to see how I felt. The wolf settled down, glaring at me out of amber eyes. Every now and then, it snarled, but at least it was no longer gnawing at its own foot.

Eventually I decided the berries were harmless and I plucked another one, leaving me with three. I rolled it toward the wolf, who devoured it hungrily. To my astonishment, it fell over a few seconds later. *Oh, crap, was that wolfsbane? Is that even a thing?* I ran toward it to make sure I hadn't killed it, but it seemed to be asleep. *Hm, maybe the berry has a sedative effect on canines?* When I pulled its hurt paw out of the trap, I wasn't even thinking about tests. After ripping my shirt in strips, I fashioned a bandage for its foreleg and wrapped it up tight. Then I backed off because I didn't want to be too close when it woke up.

I sat down some distance away and just waited. The wolf was out for what seemed like a long time for one berry, and when it stirred, it stretched and looked around, no longer mindless with pain and terror. It sniffed and nuzzled the wrapping on its paw, but didn't try to chew it off. Then it glanced over at me, all keen attention.

"You're okay now," I said softly.

The wolf responded by bounding toward me and I jerked back, but instead of attacking, it jumped on me with friendly intentions, licking my face like a dog. Trembling, I ran my hand across its back. Cautiously, I stood up and it fell into step a few paces behind me, tail up as if ready for adventure. It limped a little but not enough to slow us down.

"So you're Team Edie now? Awesome."

A quiet chuff came in response, and I glanced over my shoulder to find the wolf giving me a look that seemed a little too wise. When the ground leveled out, there was another brazier. I stopped short, then took a second look at the wolf.

"Huh. You were the next test?"

"Indeed." The fire came to life once more with Govannon's face. "The cleverness in how you instinctively sought to help a hostile creature, how you risked yourself to do so, and the compassion you showed in tending its wounds . . . you've more than passed the test of cunning and kindness, lady."

"Wow." I wondered what was on the path I hadn't chosen.

"As your reward, the wolf will accompany you through the last trial."

"Thanks," I said, but the god of the forge was already gone.

The wolf yipped, nudging my leg. I rubbed its head and continued on the path. Level ground now, we'd reached a plateau and there was no choice but to go straight. In the distance I glimpsed wooden stakes in the ground, arranged in a circle as if marking out a primitive arena, not a pit like I'd fought in for the Harbinger, but something more like a Native American proving grounds. The ground was dry and dusty beneath my feet and strewn with stones.

A large humanoid paced in the center, a giant club dragging the ground behind it. The creature was clad in roughly tanned skins and it had a misshapen skull. When it turned, I saw it had only one big eye in the middle of its forehead. *Cyclops? Seriously?* Somehow I doubted I'd be able to tame it with berries. It roared when it spotted me, but it drew up short when it reached the stakes. Apparently I had to step into the ring willingly before it could attack.

"Face me," the monster bellowed.

"Combat trial, huh?"

A growl sounded low in the wolf's throat and it crouched to attack. I wasn't ready to fight; I had no weapons, but that didn't stop me when I went up against Dwyer. So when the wolf charged I raced after it. The animal was too quick at first for the Cyclops with its ponderous club. When it slammed the spiked weapon into the ground, the earth trembled, and I tumbled backward before getting close to it. In the movies, the heroine would do a wildly improbable aerial flip and land on its back, smash berry juice into its eyes to blind it long enough for her to tear its throat open with her bare hands. *I* had a hard time rolling fast enough not to get stomped in two. Without my spirit familiar, my fighting prowess was just a hair above rudimentary. While I knew how to strike, fall, and block in theory, reality was a lot more chaotic, plus Raoul was never actively trying to crush my skull when we sparred.

The wolf wasn't faring any better now, especially with its hurt paw. When it nipped at the Cyclops, the creature knocked it five feet back with the club. I reacted instinctively, diving forward to take the killing blow. I only knew that I'd saved the wolf and its blind loyalty would be its doom. Agony exploded in my spine, and the world went dark.

When I woke, I was on the sooty stone floor in Govannon's workshop, cradled in Kian's lap. Tentatively I moved, checking for permanent paralysis. But there was only phantom pain, so I sat up, feeling nauseated and shaky. Raoul gave me a hand when Kian tried to hold me longer, and Govannon watched us, his weathered features impassive.

"I'm sorry," I said, unable to hold his gaze. "I couldn't defeat the enemy. So I botched the last challenge."

"Who said you failed, lady?"

"Huh?" Startled, I glanced up to find the god of the forge smiling.

"Your first instinct was to protect the weak. The point of these challenges was not to test your combat prowess but your *worthiness* to wield one of my weapons. Training will make a warrior queen of you, but I needed to learn of your heart."

"So you'll forge this for me?" Hesitantly, I proffered the box, unable to believe that failure was what the god wanted.

"It will be my pleasure. I'll be some while in the shaping of it, so if you've any special requests, you'd best make them now."

Since I was still processing, I glanced at Raoul and Kian. "What do you think?"

"Are you offering an enhancement?" Raoul asked.

"Indeed. This *will* be a special weapon, but I can't make the wielder immortal or anything so extravagant."

"Can you protect me from other immortals?"

Govannon paused, thoughtful. "Make it more difficult for them to harm you? Yes."

"That might give me the edge I need, along with my spirit familiar. I'm not sure if this counts, but it would also be helpful if it didn't always look like a weapon. Because if I can't carry it, the most powerful blade won't do me any good."

"Noted," Govannon said. "And, no, that's a feature."

Like Raoul did in the beginning, I bowed low, waiting for the smith to dismiss us.

He didn't waste much time in doing so. "The three of you should wait in the house. Feel free to eat or sleep, as the need strikes. Oh, and if you could feed my pets, that would be good."

Unexpectedly I found myself standing outside the workshop with Kian and Raoul. Who looked slightly worried. ". . . Pets?"

I was wondering what kind of animals the god of the forge might keep too, but when we went in through the back door, I was surprised by the homey feel. He had lace curtains in a delightfully old-fashioned kitchen, complete with fluffy white cat sunning itself on a pale latticed chair. When it spotted us, it meowed indignantly and pawed its empty dish. Glad to have something to do, I rummaged in the cupboards until I found a few cans of cat food. When I turned on the electric opener, four more cats came running from elsewhere. It was the cat-pocalypse for a while until we found dishes for everyone and gave them breakfast, lunch, or whatever this was. I'd completely lost track of time and the pallid winter sky gave little sign. Checking my phone told me this was actually dinner; I was apparently out for a while.

"Are we vulnerable here?" Kian asked, after the cats settled down.

Raoul considered for a few seconds, then replied, "Less than we were in Boston. If Edie pressed Dwyer hard enough to take his heart, then he's licking his wounds and recouping his strength. But there's no doubt he'll strike as soon as he's confident of victory."

"He won't underestimate you again," Kian warned.

"That's fine. While he's recharging, my spirit familiar is too."

That prompted me to check the compact. *Shit. I can barely see the faint outline for Cameron's face.* It would likely be a week or longer before I could count on the kind of strength and protection he'd offered during the fight. Belatedly it occurred to me to wonder if he was okay. Apart from being dead, that was.

"Cameron?" I whispered.

At first no reply came.

But Rochelle said he's always with me.

"Did I push you too far?"

Two very faint raps.

"Sorry. I got carried away." I stared at his faint outline in the compact for a few more seconds before closing it and putting it away.

Kian was watching me, his expression dark. "You . . . talk to it?"

"He's a person." Or he was.

"Someone who hurt and humiliated you, Edie."

And the dog-girl video was the last straw, the thing so bad that I couldn't move on from it. Back then I had no idea what pain was. I didn't think my life could get worse—I thought if I could make the people who hurt me suffer a little—it would all go away. But that didn't change anything, and their pain only made me feel horrible. Then my mom died . . . and now my dad was gone. Taking a deep breath, I forced away the ache of guilt and sadness.

Once I have a weapon from Govannon, I'll be better prepared to face Dwyer. And get my dad back. Wedderburn and Allison were trying to locate him for me, but I couldn't just sit and do nothing in the meantime. There was no telling what Dwyer would do, if my dad refused his offer of employment. And I couldn't imagine him quietly accepting the job from someone who'd kidnapped and terrorized him.

Assuming he's not already dead. Assuming Dwyer didn't cut out his heart in retaliation for what I did.

Cold sweat broke out all over my body. *No, I can't think that way. I can't panic. I need more information. I need to be logical.*

With the cats fed, I needed to keep my hands busy, so I put the kettle on to boil. In Govannon's fridge, I found lots of cheese. Since he presumably didn't *need* to eat, he must love the taste. Fortunately for us, there was also bread, so I made toasted sandwiches to go along with the tea. By the time I got the food on the table, the rising hysteria was coiled into a tight knot in the bottom of my stomach.

Trying to stay calm, I said to Raoul, "What about Fell? I don't know anything about Dwyer's partner. Same with Mawer and Graf, actually."

"Fell . . . in the simplest terms, is a god of death. But that's deceptive. Across cultures, he's been male and female, king and/or queen of the underworld, so he's both. And neither. It depends on his mood how he or she presents."

"And Death is aligned with the sun god? Huh."

Kian sat down beside me, adding milk and sugar to his tea cup. "You think that's weird?"

"I guess I associate Wedderburn more with death, though he's technically on my side."

It occurred to me to wonder why Buzzkill wasn't here . . . if he'd missed me running out with Kian and Raoul. *Or maybe he is . . . and he's spying silently.* I risked a paranoid look around. *The cats would probably react to an invisible killer clown, right?* But they were all sprawled on the floor around the table in various no-dignity poses. A large Maine Coon was licking its belly.

Raoul said, "From what I've been able to figure out, agreements don't always occur as you'd expect from the stories. The rivalries, however, sometimes do."

"Like the gods of winter and sun going head to head?" I guessed.

"Exactly. Fell is running his own game against the goddess of fertility, counting on Dwyer for backup."

"Oh, so the fact that Fell didn't help Dwyer during *our* fight might cause conflict?" That was an interesting insight.

Raoul shrugged. "It's possible, but I suspect Dwyer's shamed by taking such a loss."

Propping his chin in hand, Kian frowned, but it was a contemplative expression. Fortunately he seemed to have gotten over me talking to Cameron. "So there are multiple games going on, even amid tangled alliances."

"There are hundreds."

That made more sense to me than there being some organized mass competition with one single judge ranking a final winner. But the sheer scale was insane and overwhelming. All of my misery came about because I'd gotten between Dwyer and Wedderburn. Period. They were determined to use me, move me like a pawn on a board.

"Okay, so what about Mawer and Graf?"

Raoul ate half his sandwich before he spoke again. "Mawer was a catalyst who struck a deal with Wedderburn and he asked for immortality as his first favor."

"How did that work out?" I could imagine.

"Wedderburn flash-froze him and put his name on the sign." The somber light in Raoul's dark eyes told me he wasn't kidding.

"Damn. I'm glad I didn't ask for that."

"No shit," Kian muttered.

Remembering, I said, "But Mawer witnessed my mom's death contract."

Raoul nodded. "Mawer witnesses *everything*. But he can't do anything. Wedderburn has a twisted sense of humor."

"Yikes." Kian shuddered.

Raoul went on, "Graf was the god of war. I only met him once." A wholly involuntary shiver worked through him. "That was enough. You might not believe it, but of that duo, Wedderburn is the nice one."

Considering my mom's grim fate, I feared to contemplate what War might do for the sake of the game.

THE AGE OF
CATS & HEROES

We didn't see Govannon again for two days.

Before my phone died, I sent messages to Davina, Jen, Vi, and Ryu. I let the first two know I'd be out of school for a while, and Davina called me right back.

"Are you okay?" was her first question.

I glanced around the forge god's living room, which was oddly decorated with tons of commemorative plates. "I'm intact, working on getting my dad back."

"All right. I just had to hear your voice and make sure something terrible wasn't using your phone or wearing you as a skin suit."

Shivering, I said, "You are seriously disturbed."

"Do you blame me? Darkness is stalking you, girl."

She wasn't wrong. "For now I'm among friends."

"Let me know if there's anything I can do."

While I said I would before we hung up, basically I was lying. It was time for me to admit the truth; my involvement in the immortal game meant I had to cut ties with most of my normal life. Kian was the exception since he knew as much as about it as I did. As for Jen and Davina, I had to find a way to let them go without hurting them.

Turning to Raoul, I handed him my phone. "I need you to pretend to be my dad. Tell them you're pulling me out of school for emotional reasons—that I'm having trouble dealing with my mother's death." That was certainly true.

Nodding, he made the call. Kian wore a heavy look as he realized what I was doing. *Yeah, I'm moving into this world. I can't straddle the line anymore.* My marks didn't respond, so apparently my education didn't play a huge role in my invention. Blackbriar would be crushed to realize that without their prestigious diploma, I could still create some pivotal technology. Working with my dad was supposed to be key, so Wedderburn better get his ass in gear and figure out where Dwyer was holding him.

"Yes, this is Alan Kramer, calling in regard to Edith's education." Surprised, I glanced over at Raoul, who had completely lost even the faintest hint of an accent. He didn't sound much like my dad but the office staff wouldn't know that. "Yes, I'll hold."

They apparently connected him to the headmaster, and he relayed my version of events. Raoul listened to whatever they had to say on the other end of the line with a grave, suitably parental expression, as if the director could see him. That was kind of funny. It didn't take long to wrap things up.

"They've agreed to accept your assignments online and to set up remote testing for you."

"Wow," I said, surprised.

"You can return whenever you feel ready."

I gave a tired smile. "Why not? I'll put it on the to-do list."

"He said as long as you turn in work and take the tests, he doesn't see why you can't receive your diploma in May since you've been such an exemplary student and there are extenuating circumstances."

That was nicer than the headmaster had ever been to me in person. But maybe he looked up my academic record . . . which *was* impressive. Before I could respond, the back door banged open and Govannon strode inside, filling the whole house with the scent of hot metal. It came from his very pores, not from the weapon he was holding.

"I haven't made anything so fine in a thousand years. Thank you, lady, for the chance to serve my life's purpose once more." His humble tone made me feel weird.

"Uhm. You're welcome. Thanks for helping me."

"My pleasure. They say we have passed beyond the age of heroes, but I hope time is a wheel and that I shall yet live to see the cycle start again. Perhaps with you, lady."

With a flourish, he pulled off the linen cloth, and the pommel caught the sunshine from the window, nearly blinding me. I flung up a hand and took a closer look at the slim elegance he was holding. The blade had a graceful arch, and it didn't look so long or heavy that it would exhaust me to use it. I'd seen weapons like it before. A few seconds later, I remembered it was called a wakizashi. The blade itself was an exquisitely worked silver edged in gold, though I knew the base material came from the sun god's heart.

When I took it from him, a shimmer of heat went up my arm, and I immediately felt safer, more centered. *That must be the protection I asked for.* I didn't kid myself that it made me invincible, however.

I wouldn't let this sword turn into a crutch. Yet I definitely enjoyed flourishing it, sheer joy in the lightness of it and the whistle as it cut the air.

"It suits you," Govannon said with obvious pleasure.

He closed the distance between us and pressed my thumb into a faint depression in the hilt. The wakizashi responded with a shiver, flowing around my arm in a glimmer of molten gold. Now it was a rather ornate bracelet. I stared at him, stunned.

"That's amazing."

"A little," he acknowledged. "It's yours now. You should name it."

"Right now?" Alarmed, I couldn't imagine coming up with the perfect idea for a legendary weapon off the top of my head.

"When the time is right, you'll know," Govannon said.

"We fed your cats, as requested." Raoul took some of the pressure off by bringing up the animals.

"What about the dragon out back?" Govannon was so deadpan, I couldn't tell if he was serious. "You've been starving him for days?"

"Uh." Kian got up to peer out the back window with a harried expression.

The break had been good for him, allowing him to recover fully from the lingering weakness resulting from the snake god bites. I had a feeling most people never woke up.

"Joking. You're very serious people, aren't you?" The smith grinned, showing white teeth, and joy lent him a stunning beauty. Unlike the clown, his smile was warm and sincere.

"It's been that kind of year," I said quietly.

"Well, I hope your quest is successful."

Raoul bowed, and I followed suit. Ten minutes later, we were in the Mustang heading back to Boston. I only hoped it wasn't too late.

I slept most of the way back. On waking, I saw the city lights were twinkling in the distance, but it was my arm that freaked me out—and not because my marks were burning. Instead my sword arm felt magnetized. The bracelet kept swinging my arm to point due west. Raoul glanced over his shoulder; he looked tired from the drive, but he wouldn't let Kian spell him. After our last stop, he'd chosen to ride in back with me, though I protested it might make Raoul feel like a chauffeur. Kian wrapped an arm around my shoulder, leaning close to examine the way the armlet worked me like a lever.

"What's going on?" Raoul asked.

"I'm not sure. The weapon seems to be telling me something."

"Any idea what?" Kian studied the graceful gold curve wrapping my arm, but other than making me point, it was uncommunicative.

"Nope. Govannon didn't say the weapon had a mind of its own, right?"

Raoul shook his head. "No, he definitely would've warned us."

"Great, so that's not out of the question." I made a snap decision. "This might sound nuts but I feel like we should check it out. If it tries to take us out of Boston, we'll turn back."

"I've done stranger things," Kian said.

Instead of heading back to the apartment, we turned as indicated, heading farther west. Eventually we parked in front of a ramshackle apartment building. It should've been condemned years ago, but from the wraithlike figure of the old woman gazing down from a dirty window, it obviously hadn't been. I expected her to recoil when she noticed us looking up at her, but her blank stare never wavered. She wore an old-fashioned high-collar nightgown and her lank gray hair flowed past her bony shoulders. Then, to my bewilderment, she began to dance.

"What the hell."

I didn't understand what we were doing here, what the wakizashi was trying to tell me, until I caught sight of the thin man across the street, watching her divine madness. The creature stood as if transfixed, captive to her awkward, ungainly turns. It hadn't noticed us yet, but I'd touched it. Therefore, there might be some kind of connection between the thin man and me since the thin man worked for Dwyer and the blade was forged from the sun god's essence. So in the most scientific terms I could manage, we were a sort of limited feedback loop. That meant, if I could capture the thin man, it could lead me to its master.

And hopefully, my father.

"I know why we're here," I whispered.

Without explaining, I banged on the back of the seat. Raoul got out even as Kian grabbed my arm, trying to get me to slow down. But I couldn't, not now. Not when I was so close.

When my feet hit the pavement, Buzzkill was there. I didn't have time to spaz out over him seeing Raoul. He didn't seem to recognize him, which meant the amulet was working. Instead the clown was focused on me.

"Where the hell did you go, kid? You know how worried I've been?"

"Worried?" I laughed.

"That I'd have to admit to the boss that I lost you, yeah."

"Not important. If you're coming, let's do this. Stay here," I added to Kian and Raoul.

Kian tried to push past, but Raoul caught his arm. I didn't look back as I strode toward the thin man. It didn't seem to notice me until I was right on top of it. *Part of the shielding effect of the wakizashi?* At that moment, the perfect name popped into my head.

Aegis.

As I thought that, the weapon flowed from my wrist to my hand. Buzzkill actually looked stunned, eyes wide. "Holy shit. That's—"

"Mine. Eyes on the enemy, all right?"

Disgruntled, he said, "Yeah," as the thin man snapped alert.

It tried to vanish on me, but I pinned it between the brick and my blade. The creature seemed to recognize Dwyer's essence, so it quieted. The cemetery reek of it washed over me, along with an echo of the horrors it had shown me. But I knew the truth of it; this monster was born of madness and disorder, so no wonder it was drawn to the old woman still capering in her window. Her psychosis was complete, impressive in its disregard for the rest of the world.

"Take me to him," I whispered.

"You cannot compel me, living dead girl." But the paper-tiger tone had no teeth, all empty rustling, and it didn't move.

It couldn't.

"I think you know what I'm holding. Go on, refuse me again."

The thin man flinched, just a hint of recoil, but that sent a delicious, luxurious chill through me. That fast, the tables turned, and *I* had some power in this world. Standing a little straighter, I added pressure. I had no idea what would happen if I ran it through, but the thin man didn't want to find out. It tried to grab the blade and black smoke poured from its fingertips. I recalled Govannon saying that he needed to learn of my heart.

Does that mean the sword will reject anyone who isn't worthy? Damn.

"I'll take you to him," the thin man wheezed. "But there will be no profit for you in it. The son of the morning star will burn you down to ash and bone."

Then it grabbed me and pulled me into a crack in the wall. Its touch was still pure madness, boiling into my mind like molten sewage. Dead dogs, rotting logs teeming with larvae, an empty house with tumbledown walls, half etched with arcane symbols. I shoved the images away and refused to let them in. When it let go, I was somewhere else.

Buzzkill slid in behind me. I didn't know how we'd gotten wherever we were, but it was obviously the entryway to a mansion. The floor was inlaid with a stylized sun, done in gold and ivory marble. Overhead, a huge chandelier dangled with hundreds of crystals, all glimmering and reflecting the light. The place was warmer than I expected for its size, a definite sign Dwyer was here.

In a voice laced with rust and rage, the thin man rasped, "My father's house has many rooms; if that were not so, would I have told you that I am going there to prepare a place for you?" Creepy as hell for this thing to quote the Christian Bible.

A shiver I didn't entirely understand worked through me. "Find Dwyer, or my father. Either one will spare your wretched life."

"No need to threaten the help," came a deep voice from the top of the stairs. "I didn't expect you would be polite enough to return my property."

"Think again. I'm here to kill you."

"You and that clown?" A laugh escaped the sun god as he strode lightly down the steps toward us.

When he hit the ground floor, he stumbled a bit because Aegis

245

came to attention in my hand, angled in the perfect battle stance. *I* didn't do it but it recognized him, just as it had the thin man, and I suspected it knew we were enemies. *He must be so pissed.*

"What have you done?" he roared. "I will take your heart and *eat* it for this. This . . . this is grotesque." His throat worked with visible rage.

I smirked. "Govannon sends his regards."

"I'll deal with him next."

There was no point in delaying this further. I might die here, but at least I wouldn't take Kian or Raoul with me. Beside me Buzzkill's knives were in his hands and together, we flanked Dwyer. If he called for reinforcements, we were completely screwed. So I ran at him, feinting left and slashing right. He dodged and I twirled, marveling at how light Aegis was in my hands. It also seemed . . . hungry, which struck me as faintly cannibalistic.

The blade clanged against the wrought-iron stair railing, throwing sparks. Vibrations traveled up my arms to my elbows and my bones ached. I expected the same fireballs he'd mustered the last time we fought, but it hadn't been that long and I was using part of his own power against him. *Maybe . . . he can't?* Relief flooded me, quickening my steps. Dwyer gave way beneath my onslaught, but as he yielded ground, he whispered and then he had a spear and shield in hand. Before my eyes, he went from a pale linen suit to full golden armor, and it didn't seem to slow him.

"Afraid?" Buzzkill taunted.

Focused on me, Dwyer didn't respond. When he attacked, it was all I could do to parry as I wasn't experienced with weapons, and he had better reach. His ferocious attacks left me regretting my cockiness. His spear tangled with my wakizashi, but he failed at disarming me. Aegis clung to my fingers like a lover. Though I was hopelessly outmatched, I didn't give up.

This isn't a test of your combat prowess. I had no idea why I heard Govannon's voice at that moment but it heartened me. Somehow I fought on, and Aegis was where it needed to be. I couldn't break Dwyer's guard without my spirit familiar but I wasn't dead yet. Buzzkill skated in behind him smoothly. With an awful grin at me, he sank one of his serrated knives into the seam of the sun god's chest plate. He twisted.

For a split second, the sun god dropped his guard. That was all Aegis needed.

It didn't even feel like me wielding the blade, more the other way around. My arm swept up and around, a clean sweep through his neck. Dwyer's face went white; there was no blood when his head toppled forward, eyes still staring in shock, as if this could not possibly happen. And then, he was just . . . gone, twinkled out of existence.

Not even a stain on the floor.

Buzzkill growled ten completely filthy words. "You know what you have there, kid?"

"A miracle?" I whispered.

"That thing has the power of unmaking. You must've impressed the *hell* out of the forge god. It means he trusts you to decide what monsters need killing."

My knees went weak. "So . . . Dwyer—"

"He's passed on. Ceased to be. Joined the choir invisible and whatever else you can add, euphemistically speaking. Though really, I think . . ." Buzzkill stopped, quietly sober for once. "He's just gone. For our kind, there's nothing else."

"Is there for us?"

With a flicker of annoyance, he shrugged. "Do I *look* like a frigging meatsack to you? Let's find your dad before Fell senses a disturbance in the Force."

SAVING THE DAY
ISN'T ENOUGH

t took an hour to search the property completely.

Buzzkill broke down a door in the basement, and we found my dad in a well-equipped lab, not working, just sitting. It didn't look like he'd done anything, which didn't surprise me. I was glad Dwyer didn't have him tortured for refusing to comply, but it hadn't been that long by immortal standards, so he probably hadn't given up on wearing him down. Dad blinked slowly when I came through the door.

His voice was rusty with disuse and disbelief. "Edith . . . ?"

"Dad!" I ran to him and wrapped my arms around him.

His thinness horrified me. It was bad before he was taken, but now, I'd be surprised if he'd eaten since the day he disappeared. The bones of his back were all too prominent, and he smelled indescribable. But he hugged me with all of his waning strength and buried his head in my shoulder. For a few startled seconds, I felt like the parent welcoming home a lost child. But then, Dad hadn't exactly been taking care of me—more the reverse—when the monsters carried him off.

"How did you find me?"

Yeah, I had no comprehensible answer for that. "Let's talk later."

"Did the police bring you here?"

That . . . required more explanation. "He's federal," I lied, tilting my head at Buzzkill.

"I suppose they'll want to interview me," he said tiredly.

He was weaker than I expected; I had to help him out of the chair. *Maybe he was on a hunger strike?* Since he wasn't eating regularly before they took him, that worried me. Dad put his arm around my shoulder.

"I haven't touched anything but water since I've been here," he informed me. "They got to me somehow before the kidnapping. Made me *see* things, Edith. You can't imagine the horror. I think it may have been a hallucinogen in my clothes or lab equipment."

It was probably better if he was looking for a rational explanation for seeing Cthulhu monsters. I didn't want him living in my world; we'd have to visit where the roads intersected. So I offered an encouraging "yeah?"

"If they used the ventilation system, the evidence would have long since dispersed. I suppose there's no way to check?"

"I'm not sure. The place was pretty wrecked when they took you." *Thanks to me.*

"So I didn't imagine the explosion. You were there too. Weren't you?" His uncertainty made him seem . . . vulnerable, a word I'd never applied to my dad before.

"Yeah. I couldn't stop them, though."

"Did they hurt you?"

"Not really." Okay, that was a huge lie.

When I was a little kid, I thought my dad knew everything. He could *always* tell when I fibbed to him. It usually ended in a lecture about the importance of honesty and then I'd get a peppermint. To this day, I associated the rustle of the cellophane with telling the truth.

This time, however, he only gave a weary nod. "That's good."

While I was grateful to avoid questions I couldn't answer, grief weighed me down. This really was the end of an era. Now I could deceive my father with impunity and I missed the days when he seemed omniscient, omnipotent, even. Even if I understood that was childish perception, there was solace in it. Because now that I knew the truth, I had to take up the slack.

Taking a deep breath, I supported my dad up all of the stairs and outside. The thin man was nowhere to be found, but he wouldn't waste time in telling the supernatural world what I'd done to Dwyer. More scary things would probably come to get revenge and test my blade. I didn't kid myself that possessing Aegis made my life less dangerous, though it did prepare me better to defend myself and the people I cared about.

The drive was a beautifully manicured semicircle before the mansion with a fountain in the center. At the moment, the water was turned off. Shadows stirred in the depths, as it had at the mall before Christmas. I wasn't alone in noticing.

Buzzkill swore. "Wedderburn's watching us. Damn. I thought he trusted me more."

"Are you upset by that?"

"Wary. Disappointing Boss tends to be the last move you make."

With admirable aplomb, the clown stole a luxury car parked

outside. He met my gaze with a silent half shrug as I helped my dad into the passenger seat. Then I got in back, unable to believe I was trusting him with our getaway. Dad buckled in with trembling hands and tilted his head back against the seat in exhaustion.

"I don't know what agency you work for, sir, but you have my eternal gratitude."

"That's a first," Buzzkill mumbled.

"What?" Dad asked.

"Uh, it's just unusual to be appreciated. In my line of work." That was beyond awkward, but fortunately my dad was too tired to pick up on the nuances.

"Yes, people do tend to blame the government," he said. "Even for things you couldn't reasonably be expected to prevent."

The clown cast a look over his shoulder, as if to say, *Making small talk with your dad was not part of the deal, kid.*

Before he could dump a bunch of crazy reality on my poor father's head, I cut in, "Could you stop at the store? I have to charge my phone."

"Seriously? I'm not your driver."

"Please?"

Buzzkill grumbled but he actually did it. I was gone two minutes and came out with a basic convertible charger kit. I passed it forward to be plugged into the car lighter and my dad took care of it. Seeing how shaky his hands were put a knot in my throat.

To the clown, I added, "Why don't you drop us off at the hospital? He needs to be checked out."

"I'm fine," my dad protested weakly.

I ignored him. "Thanks. We'll handle your follow-up questions later."

"Whatever," Buzzkill muttered, pulling up outside the ER.

"I thought you couldn't drive," I whispered.

"I never said that. You assumed."

God, how embarrassing. I hopped out with a faint sigh. Buzz-kill grabbed my arm. "You know this is it, right, kid? We're done now."

I pitched my voice low so my dad couldn't overhear. "And you're back to being Wedderburn's number one, no ally of mine. Got it."

"Which means I have to tell him about that thing now." He cut a look at the bracelet wrapped around my forearm.

"Won't he be pissed you didn't tell him before, about when I took Dwyer's heart?"

Buzzkill summoned an impressively impassive look. "I don't know anything about that. You went off my radar for a while and came back with that weapon."

"He'll still kick your ass."

"Worth it to be there when you ended Dwyer. But I suspect he'll be preoccupied. You didn't just whack the sun god, you also ended his game with Wedderburn. I'm not sure how he'll react to that. You handed him a win, sure, but now what's his goal? Plus, it has to make him wary. If you could do that to the opposition, what's to stop you from coming at him?"

"I have reason," I muttered. "But I don't have a weapon made out of Wedderburn and his fortress is more impregnable than Dwyer's. Touching the thin man and stealing that heart gave me an opportunity. Headquarters strikes me as a lot more difficult to storm."

"It is," Buzzkill warned softly. "If you carry that god-killer onto the premises, I'll put you down, no hesitation."

"Noted. Thanks for your help."

Rounding the car, I opened the door for my dad, who was still sitting there in a daze. He stumbled, climbing out. His brain definitely wasn't firing with all synapses or he'd have a ton more questions. His ribs felt way too prominent when I wrapped my arms around him, helping him into the ER. Then there was a scramble of questions and I fudged the answers, more interested in getting him some care than anything else.

"They were agents of a foreign government," he was telling the ER nurse.

Over his head, she gave me a look that asked, *Is he crazy?* With a pang of remorse, I offered a helpless shrug in response that also contained a kernel of maybe.

Aloud I said, "He hasn't been eating or sleeping. Since my mom was murdered a few months ago, he's just . . . well, I'm really worried about him."

All of that was true. Hopefully they could treat him physically and mentally.

The nurse's expression cleared. "Sleep deprivation coupled with emotional trauma can cause delusions and hallucinations. Try not to worry, I'm sure we can help your dad."

God, I hope so.

We had good insurance through the university, so I spent the first half hour filling out forms. In two weeks I'd be old enough to take legal responsibility. *Scary thought.*

Once they had my dad checked in, protesting the whole time that he was fine, I plugged my phone in and called Kian to let him know where I was. To my astonishment, he yelled at me for five minutes, hardly taking a breath. I'd rarely witnessed him pissed off, and never at me, at least not where he'd shown me how he felt, and the outpouring was awesome, in a loud I-love-you-I-was-worried kind of way.

"Come to the hospital," I said when he paused for breath.

"On my way." He actually hung up on me.

My dad's room was dark and quiet, now that they had him in bed and medicated. They'd taken blood samples and were running tests to figure out what his medical problems were. Though I didn't want to, I found the cop's number who had investigated the destruction of the lab. If I didn't contact them, it would look worse later on, a complication I didn't need.

The call rang twice before Detective Lutz picked up. "Yeah?"

"This is Edie Kramer, I'm at the hospital with my dad."

He didn't ask anything else. "Mass Gen? I'll be there in fifteen minutes."

It was more like half an hour, and he was arriving at the same time as Kian and Raoul, which saved me a little. Tension drained visibly out of Kian's shoulders as he processed the fact that I was alive and whole. But he couldn't scream at me about supernatural dangers with a policeman in the room. He tried to question my dad, but they'd given him something to help him sleep, so he was out like a log.

Detective Lutz turned his laser-beam eyes on me, then. "Talk to me about finding your dad. Did he come home on his own? Was there a ransom demand call?"

"She's only seventeen," Raoul said softly. "Don't you need her father's permission to talk to her?"

Thank you, late February birthday.

"And who're you?" Lutz demanded.

"I'm a friend of the family, looking out for Edie while her father's under the weather." While his tone was polite, Raoul's firmness made it clear he wouldn't let anyone mess with me.

"I'll be back when Dr. Kramer's awake," the detective said finally.

As soon as the door closed behind him, Kian raced across the room and wrapped his arms around me. "Tell me you didn't plan that. When you disappeared on us, I died a thousand times."

"No, I had no idea it would go down like that. I honestly didn't mean to leave you both behind." It wasn't a plan, but I *was* relieved.

"What happened?" Raoul asked.

There were a couple of chairs, one for the other side of the room, which Raoul quietly pulled over. Right now there was nobody sharing with my dad, better for us. I curled up with Kian while Raoul sat down in the other one. In a whisper, I explained everything they'd missed, and when I finished, the older man was staring at me with an expression of wonder tempered with awe. It made me wildly uncomfortable.

"It has begun," he finally breathed.

"What has?" Like me, Kian radiated wariness.

"My master in the Black Watch will want to meet you. You *are* the weapon we were promised in the battle against the dark."

"She's a person," Kian snapped.

Peacemaker wasn't a role I expected to play between Kian and Raoul. "We don't have to settle it tonight."

I curled deeper into Kian's arms, like he could protect me from the immortals who wanted me dead and the humans who wanted to use me to kill their enemies. My future was shaping up like rock and hard place. Though I'd won the game for Wedderburn, that was never his intention for me. Now I'd shown I wouldn't be manipulated, that I wasn't a game piece. I had no idea how he'd respond. But it probably wouldn't be good.

Eventually Raoul left, probably to report in to his superiors. Alone in the hospital room with my sleeping father, Kian pulled me fully onto his lap and wrapped his arms tightly around me. Listening to his heart was the most peaceful I'd felt in weeks. *Please, let me have this now. Don't let anything else go wrong for a little while.*

"What have the doctors said?" he asked softly.

"He's malnourished and dehydrated. More complex test results won't be available until morning, probably. I hope there's nothing serious."

"Me too. He's already been through a lot."

"Because of me."

"Hey." He tilted my face up so I had to meet his gaze. "Don't say that."

"Why not? It's true. If I hadn't let the Teflon assholes push me to extremis, none of this would've happened. If I hadn't taken the deal, he and Mom would be together and grieving, but . . . together. That probably—"

"If I hadn't taken the deal, Tanya would be alive and I wouldn't. You never would've met me. And even if you went to extremis, maybe the person Wedderburn sent wouldn't have talked you into it."

I frowned at him. "Don't do that. It's not your fault."

"Or yours. There's no point in looking backward, Edie. We can't change anything. So regret is pointless. All we can do is move forward."

"I guess. I just . . . I hate what my life's become." Saying it made me feel so shitty, but it was liberating too.

"You have a chance to be more," Kian whispered. "Before, I only hoped you'd survive to repay your favors. But now, with Aegis, you're powerful enough to carve your own path. Kill Wedderburn like you did Dwyer, and that's the end of it."

"What about Fell and Graf?"

He hesitated, stroking long fingers through my hair. "I don't know. Alliances are odd things. They've agreed to provide support for someone else's game but I don't know how they'd feel about a partner's death. It could be a purely business agreement or there might be emotional bonds after centuries of association."

"Yeah, it's not something I can imagine either. It's hard to picture Wedderburn inspiring warm feelings in anyone, especially the god of war."

"If they're smart, Fell and Graf will cut their losses and let you go."

"They might also think I'm a threat and that I can't be allowed to keep Aegis."

Kian nodded. "In that scenario, they come at you and take it by force."

"Then it's not about timelines or games anymore. It's just life or death."

"You're better prepared to fight, but you're also a danger to them, one they haven't experienced in a long time. I suspect apex predators won't rest easy knowing you're out there."

"That's what I think too."

In that case, killing Wedderburn wouldn't end the danger. I'd wind up on the path the Black Watch wanted me to travel, devoting my life to hunting and killing dangerous immortals. If I stayed on course to repay the favors, I'd be helping Wedderburn, the asshole that had my mother murdered as part of a *game*. And none of that remotely took into account anything I might want for myself.

As if I know.

"Can we turn it off for a while?" I buried my head in his chest, listening to his heart's steady rhythm along with the beeping from the equipment that guaranteed my dad was alive and well, currently in no danger.

"Okay. What do you want to do instead?"

"Let's pretend we're normal. What would we do for Valentine's Day?"

"Oh, good question." Kian set his chin atop my head, still playing with my hair. He hadn't mentioned my not-awesome haircut; to be honest, I wasn't sure he'd noticed. He really didn't seem to register if I was pretty, which made me believe he'd wanted me when nobody else did. The pleasure of that was . . . indescribable.

"Dinner and movie's not enough," I said. "It's our first commercial romance holiday."

"I'm sensing scorn. Don't mock true love."

"Boston makes it challenging. Most outdoor activities won't work unless we bundle up."

"Hard to look sexy in a parka," he agreed.

Though the conversation was making me smile, it was also bittersweet. I tried not to let on. "Could we do the planetarium show you promised me?"

"Absolutely." He seemed delighted that I remembered. "How do you feel about roses?"

"My mom always said they were a waste, but . . . I love them. I mean, they're already cut, so it's not like people are murdering flowers just for me."

"So you're good with *some* traditional romance trappings." His green eyes sparkled, making me glad I'd started this stupid conversation.

"Definitely. But not chocolate. I'd rather have gummies. Or jelly beans. The good gourmet kind, not the gross sugary ones."

"Are you serious? Okay. Making a mental note."

We were still whispering silliness when the nurse came in to shoo us out. She was polite but firm. "Visiting hours are over. You can see your dad in the morning."

In your world I can. She obviously didn't know what I did—that nothing was certain—and tomorrow never came.

SOMETHING
SO AMAZING

Kian drew me out of the room, somewhat against my will. But since I had two choices: leave or be evicted, I decided against throwing down with the nurse. My dad was zonked out anyway. I resolved to be here first thing in the morning.

I still hadn't processed everything; the reality was just too big. The credit belonged to Govannon, but still—I'd killed a god. Well, *destroyed* might be a better word. So was *immortal*. But still. While I was reeling, Kian took my hand and steered me out to the Mustang. The ride home was quiet. Without asking, he took me to his place. Somehow he knew I'd rather stay there than go back to my place, where Raoul might be waiting to pitch his order.

It was strange heading into the apartment without Aaron. Though I hadn't realized it, I'd gotten used to having the kid as Kian's shadow. Grief trickled in. He'd deserved better than to be left behind, even in death. Sometimes I didn't like how logical I could be, how capable of making awful choices for the sake of my own survival.

"It wasn't your fault," Kian whispered, opening my door.

I didn't even realize he'd gotten out of the car. That showed how out of it I was. Hardly surprising, the last few days had been . . . eventful, to say the least. Somehow I managed a smile as I hopped out and followed him into the apartment. Arm around my shoulder, he nudged me down the hall toward the bathroom.

"I'll get you a shirt to sleep in."

That sounded awesome. It felt like forever since I'd slept well. And maybe I shouldn't tonight, either. But from what I knew about the immortals, their perception of time was much different. So I doubted Fell would come at me immediately for retribution. Death would probably ponder the implications before taking action, and by human terms, I could be fifty before it decided what to do. On the other hand, it could also decide I was too great a threat to their way of life, so maybe I'd have executioners at the door in the morning.

Mortal danger, deadly enemies, and complete uncertainty. Business as usual.

I spent twenty minutes in the shower and when I stumbled out, hair still wet, Kian had cup ramen waiting. Since that was his best dish, I tried so hard not to laugh.

He made a face at me, pretending to be offended. "What? At least I'm consistent."

"That's true."

Once I ate, I was so ready for bed, but there was a new layer. Right now, there was no pressing crisis. Nothing to keep me from thinking about sleeping with Kian. We'd crashed out together before, but it had been a while since we did more than curl up like tired puppies. But the relief of finding my dad unharmed left me too exhausted to get into the "anything more" right now. Without waiting for Kian to finish in the bathroom, I crawled into his bed. Two minutes later, I was asleep.

Though I didn't know when he came to bed, I woke up in the middle of the night feeling really warm. A few seconds later I understood why. Kian was spooned up against me from behind, as if he couldn't stand being away from me even in his sleep. The sweetness of it tightened my throat. Deep down I still didn't understand what was so special about me or how he could've fallen in love with me from watching me go about my sad daily life. But maybe that was the key. He saw me as somebody who would understand what he went through because we were basically on the same path, just a few years apart.

Slowly, so as not to wake him, I turned in his arms and realized I was touching skin. I'd known his arms were bare, but not chest and back too. *Hello, hot shirtless boy.* Which was admittedly shallow but there was no denying his beauty. He'd suffered for that choice.

My arm rested across his waist and I was absurdly conscious of how good he smelled. I'd used the same body wash but the coconut-lime mix mingled with his pH and . . . left him, well, the scientific term would be *lickable.* I closed my eyes and tried to go back to sleep, but when his fingers sifted into my hair, that definitely wasn't happening. It felt so good that I shivered.

"You're awake?" he whispered.

"Yeah. What time is it?"

"Late or early, depending on your definition."

"Did I wake you?"

"Kinda. You've been stroking my back for five minutes." I heard the smile in his voice.

Oh God. How embarrassing.

After he pointed it out, my hand stilled. But I could still feel the firm, smooth muscles beneath my fingers. "Sorry."

"You think I mind being woken up that way? The only way it could be better is if you were kissing me instead."

"Uh, that's above my pay grade. I'm not sure about the etiquette of doing stuff to sleeping people. I mean, am I even *allowed* to—"

"If it's me, you are." Kian cut into my nervous babbling with an amusement that I regretted providing.

Be cool.

"Maybe I should get up." I shifted, hot from having all of him wrapped around me.

My cheek rested against his bare chest now, and it was all I could do not to start pressing kisses into his skin. But I had no idea what I was doing or if he wanted to. Kian knew I'd never had a boyfriend, and so he was letting me set the pace. I appreciated it, but I had no idea how to tell him I was ready to level up, sex-wise. *Why am I so awkward?* I'd never wanted anything so much, but I might screw everything up, do it wrong or—

"We have four hours before we're allowed to visit your dad," he said gently. "And I feel like I should warn you, the way you're squirming is turning me on."

Whoa, that's honest.

"Me too," I whispered.

He took that as an invitation, thank God, and kissed me. His mouth on mine was pure fireworks. I had a few confused seconds to enjoy the heat and then he deepened it. His tongue . . . shorted out my brain. These blissful moments, there was only longing. He tasted faintly of cinnamon toothpaste, and I couldn't get enough.

When we broke apart, I was panting and he immediately set his lips on my neck. Tingles shot through me when he tugged the loose fabric off my shoulder, nuzzling. He slid his palm up over my ribs, smooth and hot. Silently I answered his unspoken question when I pulled my shirt off to let him touch me more.

"Is this okay?" His voice came out hoarse.

There were no words for how good it was. He touched my breasts until I pulled him down on top of me. Last time we had all our clothes on, and it still felt amazing. But now I was ready for everything. Kian went for my collarbone and kissed downward until I was really squirming. His hands were everywhere, and sometimes I felt like stopping him because it was weird and brand-new but it was too good to keep him from touching. And I was exploring too. When I moved my hands, he let out a low groan.

Yeah, now. Right now.

I kissed his shoulder, touching him for the first time. "Tell me this has a happy ending."

He moaned softly, then pulled my hand away. "Do you want to . . . ?"

"If you do." That might be a dumb thing to say when I could tell the answer. Of course, that was just his body talking. Maybe he wasn't ready emotionally.

"God, yes. Be right back." He set land speed records for getting to the bathroom and back. In his boxers, he was insanely hot in the half-light and I tried not to act both excited and freaked out, because I was totally both. In theory, the idea of sex was gross, messy, and hugely impractical. In reality, I couldn't wait to find out for myself.

"When did you get those?" I asked as he opened the box.

His smile flashed as he ducked his head. "After Wedderburn didn't execute me. I figured I should be ready when you were."

"I like that about you. No, scratch that. I *love* it."

"And I love you." Kian said it with such matter-of-fact tenderness that my heart felt like it would explode.

"Me too."

The foil packet crackled. *Oh my God, this is actually happening.* I tried to help out with the condom but he wouldn't let me.

"What's wrong?"

"Seriously, you can't do *that* for me. Or we won't get any further."

"What—*oh*." Hopefully it was too dark for him to see me blushing. Since this was my first time, not his, it made me feel good to know he was so worked up. "So . . . how do we . . ."

Yeah, I can't ask that. Dammit, pausing for protection has me thinking again.

"Don't worry so much," he whispered.

He seemed to understand I wasn't quite there due to the intermission so we went back to kissing. Stroking and caressing him felt almost as good as his hands on me, and eventually, I was moving with him, mindless. He surprised me by rolling us.

"It's all up to you."

I didn't think, I just did what felt right. There was some resistance but not enough to make me stop. Once I had him, we both went a little crazy.

Afterward, he disposed of the condom and came back to cuddle me. I was still light-headed, baffled. I never dreamed I could make sounds like that. But the best part, I wasn't alone. He was just as mindless, as lost in me. Phantom pleasure shivered through me.

We snuggled for quite a while before I spoke. "On a scale of one to ten, I'm going with damn."

"Damn's not a number," he pointed out.

"Huh. But I've heard it's always awkward and bad. Does that mean we're outliers?"

"'Always' is an empirical impossibility. Even among control groups, there are always statistical exceptions."

"You know you're hot when you science at me, right?"

"Please. I'm always hot." Kian kissed my temple.

"True. Can I have another poem now?"

"You want me to be a romantic cliché, don't you?"

"Hey, I let you off with the rose petals on the bed, didn't I?"

Grinning, he admitted, "Original or someone famous?"

"Psht to famous poets. Weren't they all on opium or dying of a depressing disease?"

"Most of them, probably. That or clinically depressed. So you want me to get out of bed, rummage for my notebook, and read you something. Is that right?"

"Please?"

"For the record, I'm not doing this just because you sexed me into submission," he grumbled as he went into the living room.

Nice butt.

I felt a little weird ogling him but since he was my boyfriend, consent was probably implicit. He'd said I could feel him up in bed and looking was definitely less invasive. I propped myself up and turned on the bedside lamp, then pulled the sheet up to my chest. That might be goofy, but I wasn't as confident as Kian. Half the time I still didn't look at myself naked, even now that I looked good. Years of avoiding mirrors and dodging photos had a choke hold on my psyche and I wouldn't change inside that fast. So I'd go on faking it until the shift became real.

When he got back in bed, I was a little alarmed at how natural it felt, how *fast* I could get used to something so amazing. He opened his arms, journal in one hand, and I went into them. His heartbeat thumping beneath my ear sounded like home. The rhythm had a tiny skip or hesitation, a difference I cherished. Around me, Kian flipped the pages, sounded like a lot of them. I closed my eyes to focus on his voice.

"You know how you told me to start writing again?"

"Mmhm."

"Well, this is a new poem, the first one I've written in years. It's called 'For Edie.'"

Then I did kiss his chest. "I already adore it."

He cleared his throat a few times, his heart beating faster. It seemed incredible to me that I could make him nervous. "Write down my soul again / Inky dark, paper heart / Alone I only knew to burn / Yearn / Outside, looking in / Dying spark, where to start / Wondering where you end and I begin / To make sense of love / You are love / I am yours / We are infinite." He paused, waiting for my reaction. "Sorry, it's a little beat-poetish. I haven't written in form in a long time, used to be pretty good at the sonnet. God, I should have written you something else. Something less—Edie, would you rather have a sonnet? I can—"

"No thanks." I had no yardstick for knowing if it was a *good* poem but the way he stressed *you*, *I*, and *we* put a lump in my throat. "This means a lot to me."

He'd spent time with a pen, thinking of me and staring off into space. The idea of Kian daydreaming about me while searching for the perfect words? *I love that.* Curious, I opened my eyes and pulled the notebook down for a look. Yeah, sure enough there were false starts and scratched-out lines, words replaced with others. It looked like a poetry ransom note and took some doing to pick out the final lines amid all the edited wreckage.

"Don't judge the process." He pulled the journal away and closed it.

"I'm not. I'm admiring. In English classes I have the worst time coming up with original material. Even my essays are too heavily bolstered with quotes from other people and indisputable facts."

"I like that about you," he said.

"The fact that I have no imagination?"

"That's not true. If it was, you wouldn't be so into science fiction and fantasy. And it's a pretty big leap from enjoying someone else's world to being able to create your own."

"Hm. Well, I have too many questions about the way our world works to focus on inventing something else. Plus, some of it seems incredibly contradictory."

"You're talking about the immortals now."

I nodded. "It drives me crazy that I can't quantify everything."

"Welcome to my world."

"I've been here for a while."

"Thank God," he murmured, kissing the top of my head.

"Okay, so according to the clock, it's almost six. Do we go back to sleep or . . . ?"

"I'm open to suggestions."

"I'll probably be busy with my dad for a while."

"Is that a warning?" He clicked off the lamp and set his poetry notebook next to it. "Don't worry, I know you'll have a lot on your plate."

Getting my dad home, dealing with the authorities, possible vendetta with Death. To say that almost sounded like sarcasm. But Kian meant it.

"Just a statement. I'm thinking."

"About what?"

"Our options."

He pulled me down so I was cuddled with my head on his chest. It took me some maneuvering to work out what to do with my arm, but once I got that, it became really comfortable. I could get used to this. Then the realist asshole part of my brain—stupid frontal lobe—whispered, *No. You can't. He's still terminal.* While I might have gotten my dad back, I'd also gotten Aaron killed, along with how many of the Teflon crew? I immediately felt horrible for being in bed with Kian—for being happy and forgetting about my mom, even for a second. If I let them, these thoughts would pull me down to a dark, dark place.

"What are they?" Thankfully his voice broke the awful spiral before it could become a shame-phoon.

"Well, we could sleep."

"Or . . . ?"

"We could do it again. At least, *I* could. What about you?"

"Seriously? If you had any idea how much I want you . . . or for how long, you'd cut the question from your vocabulary."

"Less talk, more kissing."

The second time was slower and less frantic, but just as good, maybe better because I wasn't nervous. It was all sweetness and heat as Kian tried to control himself. Near the end, instead of kissing me, he pressed his face into the curve of my shoulder, so I could *feel* it happening to him, crazy-wonderful when he panted and shivered.

I was in the neighborhood but not . . . done, but I guessed he knew that. Quietly he touched me.

"You want me to . . . like this?"

"Here."

It turned me on that we were both learning. Ironically his uncertainty relaxed me, so I could let go. He watched my face, killing me with the intimacy of his eyes, but I didn't look away. People had said it to me before, and I always thought they were exaggerating—that it was abstinence propaganda—but sex *did* change everything. We were more now.

"Are you okay?" he asked.

"More than." I was actually weak in the knees and my thighs were wobbly when I went to the bathroom.

Dad's waiting. Though I wasn't ready to start the day, like Charon the Boatman, life didn't wait. It went on, always.

So would I.

NEVERMORE
THAT MELANCHOLY
BURDEN

The hospital had no reason to keep my dad, thankfully.

But once I got him home, it was tough because his behavior bordered on paranoid, not that I could blame him. I had no idea what he'd gone through while Dwyer held him hostage. The second day after he came home, he tried to go straight to the lab to check on things, and I straight up lied.

"They're still repairing," I said, though for all I knew the university had everything fixed already. "You can't do anything there, and the doctor said you need to rest and eat well for at least a week."

Though he grumbled, Dad sat back down on the couch. "You're making me feel like a feeble old man."

"Anybody would need to take it easy after . . ." What did I even say?

He was convinced that they'd gassed us with some experimental hallucinogen and that was definitely a more logical explanation than reality offered. The fact that he was confused, afterward, made me wonder what Dwyer had done to him. At the hospital, the doctors told Detective Lutz that my father had certainly experienced a traumatic event and that some of his responses made them think someone had attempted to brainwash him. Lutz grilled us for two hours on the day Dad was discharged. I understood his frustration; there was major property damage to the university science building and he needed to know who to blame.

I had no easy answers.

That night, I made vegetable beef soup for dinner and turned on the news to watch with my dad. We both needed normal right now, as much as he needed good food and sleep. He frowned but put down the science journal he was reading. They opened wide with conflicts in various parts of the world, narrowed focus to other parts of America, and then for the last story of the night, the pretty anchorwoman said brightly, "Breaking news, extreme animal-rights group FAAN, which stands for Free All Animals Now, has claimed responsibility for the recent explosion . . ." She went on to explain how they'd posted some video on the Internet with their faces blurred out and voice modulators on, threatening to strike a university in New York, if all science programs didn't immediately cease and desist with all animal-related experiments.

My dad was transfixed by the broadcast clip. "But . . . my department doesn't do that. I'm working with lasers and mirrors, not chimpanzees."

Since I knew damn well it was a PR grab, I could only joke, "Maybe they heard about Schrödinger's cat and made a bad logical leap."

"Do you think so?" My dad seemed to be taking me seriously.

"Who knows? People who blow things up to make a point about

being more compassionate . . . do you figure they're firing on all cylinders?"

"Probably not," he conceded. "But . . . it doesn't explain why I was taken. The men who held me never said anything about animal rights."

Damn. Dad's too smart for fall for that.

"Maybe someone approached them."

"To blow up the lab to cover my kidnapping?" He paused, turning that over in his head.

Please decide it makes sense.

"Could be," he admitted eventually. "I'm not sure why these men were so fixated on me, though, if they paid a fringe group to ensure the focus was elsewhere."

For the timing of this to be perfect, FAAN would've needed to announce their responsibility sooner but my dad didn't seem as bothered anymore. "Your work is pretty famous. How many magazines have you been featured in now?"

"I don't even remember." That wasn't surprising. "I suppose they might've been in cahoots. I've heard FAAN is international . . . and I'm sure my captors were foreign nationals."

"Why?" I asked.

"They kept asking me to work for them. One of them said they'd make much better use of my research and that they'd pay me handsomely to switch allegiance."

I bet they were talking about Wedderburn, not America. But under no circumstances could my father find out about any of that. "What was it like?"

"Tiring," he said softly. "At first it was just endless talking. I tried to explain that I don't work for the government . . . that I'm not in the private sector and I'm not interested in their consortium but they didn't take no for an answer."

"They wouldn't." He couldn't know how true that was. Immortals weren't used to being gainsaid, which was how I'd pissed the Harbinger off.

"I wouldn't eat anything they gave me because I was afraid I'd start hallucinating again. For a while I was alone in a room, nothing but a chair and white walls. Then they took me to an incredibly well-equipped lab, I guess to show me how much money was on offer. And I tried to explain that my work is still largely theoretical—that I'm decades away from a prototype or a trial. But none of them paid any attention. From there, it got . . . rougher."

That would be the brainwashing that they mentioned at the hospital. "Ice water, bright lights, message on repeat, no sleep?"

Averting his eyes, he nodded as the news shifted to a sitcom. "If you don't mind, I'd rather not talk about it anymore."

"Sorry."

"Don't be. It's natural that you're trying to make sense of it all. I've been doing exactly the same thing."

"Making progress?"

Eyes closing, he nodded. "If you want to turn on a movie, something funny maybe, I'd like that a lot."

"Okay." I found an old comedy on Netflix and sat with him while he slept.

At half past nine, I persuaded him to go to bed and I made sure he actually turned off the lights. Before he was taken, I'd had the unsettling thought that I was becoming the parent and now having him back only underscored that reality. I never thought I would but I missed the days when he lectured me about weird stuff and took up hours of my time with strange, random fascinations I didn't share. My dad used to lean more than a little toward the Asperger's side of social interaction, but now he was just a shadow.

Around ten, Kian texted me. Everything okay?

Yeah, I sent back. You?

Like I'd suspected, I hadn't seen him much in the last few days. I didn't like leaving my dad alone. He still wasn't himself or he'd be asking why the heck I wasn't in school. For some reason he hadn't connected the fact that it was early February, yet I wandered around our beige apartment free as a bird. Doing my homework felt like a waste of time when I might buy it any day now, thanks to my potential feud with Death.

God, my life is weird.

Missing you, he replied.

It hasn't been that long.

Eventually I caved and did some homework then e-mailed it to my teachers, and I was happy to hear from Vi as I hit send on the last assignment. It seemed like a long time since I'd talked to her back when things were at their worst; I did my best to dodge and talk to her only enough to keep her from hopping on a plane for an emergency intervention. I put her on video and saw she'd gotten some cute pink tips, all very ragged-punk, and it suited her. She was also wearing lipstick, something I'd never seen on Vi before.

"You Skyped with Seth first," I said, smirking.

She blushed. "Duh. I'm glad you finally answered. What's been going on?"

Shit. She didn't know *anything* about my dad's disappearance. So I downplayed it as much as I could and stressed the fact that my dad was home and safe. I also left out my own role in bringing him back. At this point, I suspected I knew how it felt to be Batman, always weighing what I could share, how much, and with whom.

This sucks. I should totally have gotten a cape and a utility belt.

"Oh my God," Vi said when I finished. Her eyes were huge. "Do you think the people who kidnapped your dad had something to do with . . ." She trailed off, unable to complete the thought or even say "your mom" in that context.

I didn't blame her. Skirting Mom's death had become a habit for me. Since I'd wept at her grave, I didn't like thinking about her, especially now that I had the wakizashi. Part of me wanted nothing more than to forget *everything* and hunt down the bag man along with those creepy kids. It would be different now that I had a spirit familiar and Aegis. Unlike last time when they'd lured me out, taunting me, I wouldn't need the Harbinger to intervene.

You're powerful, Cameron whispered. His voice in my head felt like a vein of black ice, chilling me to the core. But he also made all the pain stop. No more conflict. No more doubt. Just a dark, delicious promise. *You wanted revenge on us . . . and you got it. Just imagine what you could do now.*

"Edie?" Vi seemed to have been repeating my name for a while. "Are you okay?"

"With everything going on, I'm pretty tired. What were we talking about?"

"I just asked—or didn't actually—but I wondered . . ."

"If the same people who killed my mom also took my dad?" There, I said it, my tone sharp and glacial.

"Yeah." She couldn't meet my gaze, playing with some pens lined up on her desk.

"Probably. It seems to be connected to their work."

"Are you safe?" she asked.

God, she was a good friend. No matter how much I avoided or ignored her, she didn't stop caring. The cold kernel burning like dry ice at the heart of me thawed a little. I stopped thinking about the bag man.

"I think so."

"Listen, I'm not telling my parents any of this, and I'm not taking no for an answer from you. In a month, I get time off for spring break, and I am definitely coming to see you."

"Okay," I said.

"When's your break?"

"Always. I'm finishing school on independent study. With all of the crises lately, I can't make myself sit in a classroom when I'm worried about my dad."

"I get that." Vi's tone was gentle. "But it means we can hang out the whole time I'm there. Seth said he'll try to come for the weekend, at least."

"Wow, really? So it'll be like a reunion."

"Minus Ryu."

"Heh, well. We can't expect him to come from Japan. Have you talked to him lately?"

She shook her head. "Not since Christmas. He was in the States for a while visiting his grandparents, but he was too busy to Skype."

"That doesn't surprise me. He was the most popular guy in the SSP."

"He's kind of a flower boy," she agreed.

It was time to change the subject; Ryu felt like he belonged to another lifetime, back when everything was simple. "E-mail me when you know when you're arriving. I'll pick you up at the airport."

"You have a car now?"

"My boyfriend does."

"Kian, right? I saw you kissing on campus. He went all the way to California for you, and you guys weren't even *dating* . . . he must've been so into you."

Weirdly, she wasn't entirely wrong. Back then I didn't realize how long he'd been watching or how much I meant to him. I had no idea he'd quietly given me the best day of my life. With a half smile I twisted the blue beads on my wrist.

"Maybe," I said. "But we couldn't get together. Things were complicated."

"Yeah, starting a new relationship when someone's going away for the summer doesn't make sense. It was smarter to stay single until you got back."

"Exactly." Though not for the usual reasons.

We talked a little longer, mostly about the robotics project she was working on, and then her brother, Kenny, came banging on her door demanding that she do the dishes like their mom had asked four times already. Vi sighed and said, "Sorry. Apparently I'm not allowed to have a social life or go to sleep if there's a single dirty cup in the house."

Kenny yelled, "The kitchen's gross, Vi! I used the last clean glass this morning. We haven't seen the sink in two days. It's *your turn*."

"Oh my God, will you shut up already? Tell her I'll be right down."

Their exchange made me smile; I'd always wanted an annoying younger sibling. "Talk to you later, 'kay?"

"Yep. I'll check in with you soon. Be careful. It sounds scary there."

"It is," I admitted.

After hanging up, I remembered that she was an hour behind me, so it was only ten thirty there. Here, it was ticking away toward the witching hour, and I was so freaking tired just from hovering over my dad all day. Worry was weirdly exhausting. Quietly I washed my face and brushed my teeth, not lingering in front of the mirror. Since that terrifying day that my reflection confessed to wanting to kill me and/or steal my life, I was afraid to spend much time primping.

I turned off the lights and got in bed. The curtains were open, showing a thin gold sliver from the streetlight nearby. It angled across my floor and I stared at it, willing my brain to shut up about disaster scenarios. Sleep had nearly claimed me when the *tap, tap, tap* came at my window. Jolting up, I half expected to see the creepy black-eyed little girl in her bloody pinafore.

But no. Instead it was a large black bird, rapping against the glass with its beak.

Peck, peck, peck.

"It can't be," I said.

Peck, peck, peck, peck.

Muttering, I went over to the window and raised the sash, so icy wind washed over me. The screen was still between us, though the bird could probably tear through it. For a few seconds we just stared at one another. I hadn't seen the Harbinger since he went nuts in Rochelle's kitchen. The bird didn't speak—and I started doubting my own certainty. To test my theory, I came a little closer. A normal crow would startle and fly away. This one waited.

Wondering if this was the dumbest idea ever, I slid back the screen. "Did you want to come in?"

Then in a dark flutter of smoke and feathers, *he* was perched with inhuman grace and balance on a ledge far too small to hold him. "Are you inviting me? Rituals and niceties matter, especially to someone like me."

"I guess I am."

"Yes or no, dearling."

"Then . . . yes." I stood back so he could leap lightly inside, and I closed everything after him to banish the chill.

Retreating to my bed seemed like the warm, safe option, so I scooted back under my covers. I also needed to get away from his aura, washing over me like a noxious sweetness. He was a gloriously red poison apple, tart juice to tingle my tongue even as the slice lodged in my throat. The Harbinger paced, his great coat flapping about his ankles with each stride.

"What have you done, you wicked thing?"

"You're talking about Dwyer?"

"Indeed. You cut the sun from the sky. Aren't you worried that glaciers will envelop the world again with no counter for our Wedderburn?"

My eyes widened. "Not until now. Is that possible?"

"Who knows? There's always been a sun god for as long as there was a winter king. But you've changed the game board, you adorable idiot. I'm quite jealous, you know. Your ability to create chaos rivals my own."

"Is that why you came? To warn me I might've caused the next ice age?"

Ignoring the question, he perched at the foot of my bed and wrapped his arms about his knees. "No. It's simply an interesting diversion. Like you."

"You don't seem so mad anymore." It was a cautious observation, one I wasn't 100 percent sure of, since he might be hiding it and would soon make my room explode into wood chips.

"Crafty little cat. With Govannon's gift, you have *so* much potential. Are you *truly* not afraid of me?"

I thought about that. "Not really. I've seen so many scary things that I have to draw the line somewhere. You're mercurial but you've helped me. And you've never hurt me, though I was pretty pissed off when you let those Cthulhu assholes take my dad."

"I am not your knight," he said silkily. "Don't mistake the compact with your beloved for something more. Under the right circumstances, I would, indeed, hurt you, dearling. Maybe . . . until you liked it."

His tone struck me as off. Desperate even. It was strange that I'd come to know him well enough to realize it, but beneath that glossy menace, he was a ragged thing, raw and wounded. Wondering if I was crazy, I still whispered, "What's wrong?"

"Why are you asking?"

"I don't know. Why are you in my room at midnight?"

"Because you invited me."

I saw we'd get nowhere this way, so I let it go. "Then what did you want to talk about? Let me guess, you have a warning or punishment for me."

For the first time since his arrival, the Harbinger smiled. "No. Quite the opposite, in fact. I'm a gambler, you see, and I must have my curiosity sated."

"About what?"

He leaned forward and let his hand hover over the golden wristlet wrapped about my forearm, but he didn't touch. His gray eyes went dark as old pewter, with a glimmer like distant lightning in their depths. "There's a way you can save him, dearling."

I stilled. "Kian?"

"This is the *only* way." The Harbinger took my hand and flattened it against his chest; it was like touching marble or alabaster, hard and unyielding, no life within. "End me, as you did the sun god. And your beloved will live."

THE GIRL WHO HUNTED DEATH

Frozen, I whispered, "This is a trick. That's what you do."

"Do you think so?" The Harbinger tilted his head back, offering his neck. "If you're so sure, put the blade to my throat. Take my head and let there be an end to all this. You hate me, yes? Consider what I did to Nicole . . . and Aaron too. Imagine the crimes against humanity you'll prevent with one swing, and as an added bonus, your darling boy, well, he lives. Huzzah, no? Of course I'll no longer be around to shield you from immortal wrath, but that hardly matters. You've no need of my protection any longer."

"I can't just execute you." The words came out before I thought them through, but they were true. "It was different with Dwyer. He attacked me on multiple occasions."

"But you hunted him to his stronghold with a blade to cull him from existence. You didn't wait for him to strike again. That shows a certain martial predilection, dearling, and shouldn't you save your boy at all costs?"

I remembered what Rochelle said—keeping a spirit familiar

enchained forever being true evil. But I thought it also applied to doing whatever it took to achieve your desires, regardless of the cost. Yeah, I wanted to save Kian, but . . . I couldn't just behead the Harbinger while he was sitting on my bed for no better reason than to get my boyfriend out of trouble. While he might be scary and destructive, he'd also helped me a lot, and I couldn't get past the idea that he was in terrible pain beneath all the spectacle and buffoonery.

"You should go," I said quietly. "I'm not doing this. I can't."

From a flicker in his shadowed gaze, I guessed that I'd surprised him. "Why not? I won't fight. That would be ridiculous. Rather I submit and await judgment for my sins."

"No way. You know I'm only seventeen, right? Plus . . . it's not your fault. That doesn't help the people you've hurt, but I know we did it to you." As Buzzkill said, *we* wrote the stories. These creatures were humanity's darkness, given strange and terrible form.

"How astonishing," the Harbinger breathed.

"What?"

"You *care* for me. I'm no longer purely a monster in your eyes."

"Don't be stupid."

"If that wasn't true, you wouldn't hesitate to strike," he said gently. "You have ample reason, as my demise represents the only sure way to save your Kian."

"But it would be wrong."

"Only if I'm not a monster, Edie Kramer. Is killing a demon ever wrong?"

His words made sense, but I still couldn't bring myself to press the side of my wrist and activate Aegis. The idea of executing the Harbinger made me feel sick inside. My hands curled into fists. He wore a silly, charming smile, and I didn't trust the playful side of him. As Rochelle had said, in many ways, he was like a cat. Instead of doing anything dangerous, he fell back onto the lower half of my bed, not something I ever thought I'd see. His aura dimmed to low buzz, an intentional downshift that let me observe his true features.

"You're most unusual, you know. When I wore the false face that attracted everyone else, you found me creepy and unsettling. And when I show you everything, you offer kindness."

"I'd always rather have the truth," I said.

"Perhaps I'm meant to be *your* pet," he mused, folding his arms beneath his head. "Will you care for me and keep me out of trouble?"

I hoped he was joking. "That sounds like a lot of work."

"Sadly, yes. Right now I'm on my best behavior, but it won't last. It can't." His voice dropped on the last two words, went soft and sorrowful.

"I know."

I hesitated for a few seconds because I had no idea what my role was here, but with any other friend, I'd offer comfort. So I rested my hand gently on his head. His hair felt soft and cool beneath my palm, and he angled his face to stare at me. But he didn't move, and I didn't either, except to pet him as if he really *were* my cat. His eyes closed.

"You remind me of Sigyn."

Since the name sounded familiar but I couldn't recall who that was, I said, "I'm sorry if you wanted me to kill you. I can't. Not without a reason. That would make *me* the monster."

"Maybe I did, a little, because you can end the infinite. But I was more curious. Govannon gave you that blade for a reason. Now I begin to see why."

"Huh?"

To my surprise, he remained quiescent beneath my stroking fingers. "Never mind. Just . . . do this a bit longer. And then, I'll fly away. The next time we meet, Edie Kramer, I will most likely break your heart . . . and I find myself unexpectedly regretful about that."

"There's some time yet," I said. "I haven't given up on that loophole. Now that my dad's safe, I'll focus all my energy on finding it."

"Good luck," the Harbinger said.

I thought he truly meant it. True to his word, he let me pet him for about five minutes, and then he bounded off my bed in a crackle of dark energy. There was a fresh wickedness about him, and I wondered if I was crazy for not taking the deal. Considering how he'd treated Aaron—*oh, shit. I have to apologize.*

"I'm so sorry. I thought I was saving Aaron but, in the end, I got him killed."

His tone was gentle. "I'm aware, Dwyer burned him up. Did you think I wouldn't know what became of my favorite pet? I always love what I hurt most, at least a little. And that's why you should fear me to your bones, pretty one. Because I rather adore you, and that ends badly for both of us." He paused, gazing at me, until I shivered from the intensity of it. But he didn't try to make me come to him with that awful compulsion. "Right now I wish I had a name to give you. I'd like to hear you say it, just once."

"You have like forty names."

"Exactly," he said with a melancholy smile. "And none of them are mine."

With that, he opened the window and vanished in a flutter of dark wings. Icy wind rushed over me before I shut the window after him. I had no idea how I'd explain this conversation to Kian, but maybe it was better if I didn't. He might see this as a betrayal, but surely he'd understand that I couldn't go around killing immortals because it would be easy or convenient. It took me forever to fall asleep that night.

Over the next few days, I tried to put the Harbinger out of my mind. My dad argued with me about going back for a follow-up, but after some resistance, I got him to the doctor, who pronounced him as recovering nicely. He frowned at my father, who was mumbling about work.

"That doesn't mean you're cleared to return to the lab, sir. After your ordeal, you need at least another week of quiet."

Thank God. Since my dad was hearing this himself, he couldn't quarrel with me later. He was cranky as we went home, but relief sparked through me to see that he was capable of being annoyed. At least he wasn't moping like a zombie anymore. We both missed my mom more than words could express but we had to find a way to keep moving; she wouldn't want us to give up.

Though it took a lot of persuading, I made my dad *do* stuff with me. I wouldn't let him sit around the apartment. Over the next few weeks, we went to museums and movies, spending more time together than since I was really little. There was a bittersweet edge to these moments because I knew that Fell could come at me anytime. So I had to store up the memories while I had the chance.

Raoul came by once and tried to talk to me about the Black Watch, but I was having none of it. Weirdly, he didn't mention resuming my lessons, maybe because between my spirit familiar and

Aegis, I had enough skill to get by. Which wasn't much, admittedly, but now I had power. Otherwise, it would've taken years before I had the training to face off with an immortal.

So use me, Cameron whispered. *Don't wait for Fell to come for you. Don't you want to be known as the girl who hunted Death?*

No. Definitely not. Right now, I could accept my status as a killer because Dwyer had established himself as the enemy. Until Fell took hostile action, I was in a holding pattern. Other people might be fine with unprovoked aggression. I wasn't.

Before I knew it, it was the last week of February, my birthday was coming up, and I had no good reason to keep my dad home anymore. He'd called when I went out for groceries and learned that the lab *was* repaired, so basically, he was going back to work, no matter how I felt about it. Since I had no favors left to protect him with, the prospect terrified me. This morning, he finally realized I should be in school, another sign he was coming back to his former sharpness.

"Why are you still hanging around the house?" he demanded. "Your attendance record must be in shambles, you'll be lucky if they don't hold you back."

"When you went missing, I got permission to finish up on my own."

That actually seemed to impress him. His eyes went misty and he hugged me, kind of a big deal since he wasn't physically affectionate in general. "Thank you for being so strong, Edith. I know I let you down, but I promise things will be different. We'll be all right."

"It's okay," I whispered, hugging him back.

"Do your homework first. And don't sneak off to see your boyfriend while I'm gone."

Nodding, I walked him to the door. After breakfast, I *did* finish my assignments and send them off, mostly because I didn't really want to end up with a GED after so many years of being an academic overachiever. I had no doubt I could pass the test right now but some quiet part of me wanted to graduate from Blackbriar; it had become an endurance challenge at this point.

Around noon Kian called me. "Are you busy tomorrow?"

"What did you have in mind?"

"Well, we missed Valentine's Day. So I wanted to do the planetarium show for your birthday, if you can go out."

"Holy shit. That's tomorrow?"

"You seriously forgot your own eighteenth birthday?"

"I've been pretty focused on my dad."

"Makes sense you would be. Is he doing okay?"

"Yeah, he's at work now. I still can't believe we saved him fast enough to keep Dwyer from messing him up permanently. It's like the one thing I've done right in the last year."

"Huh."

After I said that, I realized how it must sound to him. The hurt was muted in that single syllable, but . . . *dammit.* "Apart from being with you, of course."

"Is this where I say 'nice save'?"

"It's my birthday tomorrow, be generous. What time are you picking me up?" If my dad was well enough to go to work, surely I could take the night off from guarding him and go out with Kian. I hadn't been on a date in weeks. And while I'd been sticking so close to home mostly to offer physical protection if Fell came at us, I was starting to think Death was taking the slow, contemplative route toward conflict resolution.

"Six. We'll have dinner and then do our stargazing."

"Sounds amazing. And, Kian . . ."

"Yeah?"

"Thanks for remembering my birthday, even when I didn't."

He laughed, obviously pleased. *Good, glad he's not holding the tactless crap from before against me.* "It's all part of the platinum-tier boyfriend service."

"Awesome. See you tomorrow."

That night, my dad kept his promise and came home early enough to cook dinner with me. We ate healthy for the first time in what seemed like forever: baked fish, brown rice, and steamed vegetables. I'd missed his obsession with providing us the best possible nutrition, sometimes at the expense of taste. Tonight I ate every bite with gusto.

"Is it okay if I go out with Kian tomorrow night?" I suspected Dad had forgotten my birthday, but I was so glad to have him back that I didn't even mind.

"Sure. You can open your present from me first thing in the morning. But if you're going out, do you mind if I work late? I have a lot to catch up on."

Oh my God, he actually asked permission, like I'm a person whose opinion matters. "That's totally cool by me. Just make sure you eat, okay?"

"I will, Edith." Behind his glasses, his eyes smiled at me and I almost cried. It had been so long since I saw him acting normal.

For the first time in forever, I went to bed happy and woke up feeling the same way. But I'd learned to be wary of that emotion. Even now I feared this must be the calm before the storm, and I had *so much* to lose. While I'd gotten stronger, less like flotsam on the immortal tide, I couldn't be everywhere at once. Vi should be all right, but there was still my dad and Ryu, Jen, Davina, and Raoul. Caring meant vulnerability.

God, don't be such a downer on your birthday, dummy.

Making an effort to brighten up, I went to the kitchen, where my dad had breakfast waiting. "Happy birthday, Edith. This is quite an exciting day . . . you can vote now."

I had to laugh. Only my dad would consider this a thrilling milestone. "I can't wait to participate in the electoral process."

Since he thought I was serious, he beamed. "That's my girl."

We ate smiley-face pancakes, just like the ones he'd made for me as a little kid, and unlike his stuffed artichokes and poached fish, they were delicious. I also got scrambled eggs, fresh-squeezed OJ, and crispy bacon. He must've gone out first thing because I knew the fridge didn't have all of that in it last night.

"Thanks, Dad."

"I promised you a present." He slid me a flat, brightly wrapped package across the table.

Opening it, I found a book about Nikola Tesla and two gift cards, one for a local bookstore and the other for a popular clothing store. "Wow, this is awesome. Thank you!"

When I got up, he hugged me. *Two, in as many days. That's incredible.*

"Feel free to take the day off. If your teachers complain, tell them to talk to *me*." He produced a stern look.

"That's sweet, Dad, but since everyone I know is in class, I might as well keep up with my assignments. Have a good day."

"You too. Enjoy yourself with Kian tonight. I won't wait up."

Once he left, I spent the day on homework, plus texting friends who somehow knew to send good wishes. My money was on Kian for quietly spreading the word. Around three, I hopped in the shower. It didn't take long to get ready but I stared at my jeans and sweater with a wicked frown. Tonight Kian had something special planned, so I should wear a dress, right? But I didn't have anything nice.

You have a gift card.

And if I hurried, I could buy something cute and get back here before six. Making the decision fast, I grabbed my bag and phone, then bolted from the apartment. I almost ran into Raoul, probably back to talk about my destiny again. I liked the guy but he was really single-minded. Mustering a smile, I waved as I tried to move past on the steps but he grabbed my arm.

"Just listen to me for a moment," he begged.

God, that tone makes me uncomfortable.

"It's my birthday," I told him. "And I really need something new to wear before Kian comes over. I'm sure that sounds incredibly shallow but no matter what else is going on, I am only eighteen and I deserve a *new freaking dress.*"

He took a step back. "You do. I'm sorry. I didn't know. Many happy returns, Edie. Would you like some company for your shopping expedition?"

"As long as you don't try to persuade me of anything."

"I'll consider the matter tabled for today."

So strange as it felt, I went off to the mall with Raoul in tow. He sat in the man chair outside the fitting room while I tried on dresses but, unlike most dudes, he actually had opinions. Soon I was glad he'd come along because together, we managed to pick out a really cute dress. It fit my chest and shoulders, then flowed loose, so it didn't look like I was trying too hard to be sexy, and I loved the splashes of pink and purple on the white background.

We got back to the apartment with just under an hour to spare. Since I'd already showered, I just needed to do hair and makeup— and I was ready for Raoul to go, not that I meant to be rude. He seemed to get that, thankfully, because he dropped me off at the door, freeing me to get ready. Which wasn't easy, knowing Kian had this amazing night planned. My hands actually shook as I tried to put on some lipstick.

You're such a dork. This isn't your first date.

But it *was* special. I was eighteen and my dad had very pointedly made sure I knew I didn't have a curfew, his way of saying *I trust you*, and it made up for most of the shit he'd put me through in the past few months. I felt good about where we were together.

Just before six, a knock sounded at the door. I opened it.

"Holy shit," Ryu said. "I don't know how it's possible but you've actually gotten hotter."

DESTINED
TO BE BROKEN

"What are you *doing* here? Aren't you supposed to be in Japan?" That probably wasn't the politest way to greet a guy I hadn't seen in seven months, but Kian would be here any minute, and I had no idea how to explain this to him.

Ryu looked good. The blond tips were long gone, but now he had blue, along with a brow piercing. He ignored my astonishment and strode past me into the apartment. At least that told me he wasn't an immortal doppelgänger sent by Death, because supernatural creatures tended to wait for an invitation. I wondered if that was how the vampire stories got started. Then again, if enough people believed something, it became true.

"Vi set it up. She told me how rough it's been on you, and I convinced my parents to let me take some time off. My dad wasn't keen, but my mom talked him into it. She's good at that."

"Holy crap."

While I was still processing, he came over and hugged me. He held me hard against him, very Western, so I was sure it came from his American, raised-in-California mom. For a few seconds, I remembered the SSP and breathed him in. He hadn't changed his cologne, still a familiar blend of lemon, citron, and cedar. "She's waiting for Seth at the airport. I came ahead because I was worried about you."

"I'm fine." I put my hands on his shoulders to get some space between us.

He grabbed my wrist before I could stop him and slid my bracelet aside. "I knew it. Dammit, Edie, I've been freaking out ever since you sent me that photo."

Yanking my hand away, I stumbled back two steps. "I've got everything under control. Since you're here for my birthday, we'll definitely hang out but . . . don't ask questions, okay?"

"That's reassuring."

Before I could respond, someone knocked. *That must be Kian.* Tense as a coiled spring, I pinned on a smile and opened the door. Sure enough, my current boyfriend was standing there with a huge bouquet of flowers: red roses mixed with pink lilies, purple liatris, and sweet William, absolutely gorgeous. God knew how he'd respond; I knew Kian was jealous that I'd gotten together with Ryu over the summer, but he never mentioned what happened. So I was prepared for the worst possible scenario when Kian came in. With trepidation I took the flowers and kissed him.

Stepping back, Kian floored me by smiling at Ryu. "Glad to see you made it."

Wait, what?

"Did you know about this?" I demanded.

"Yeah. Those two days you went missing, I was here when Vi tried to Skype you. I answered, so she wouldn't worry, though we were all scared to death. We traded contact info so I could update her. It seems like you're not big on communicating with your friends."

"And afterward, you planned an SSP reunion for me? As a birthday surprise."

Kian smiled. "We fooled you, right?"

"I had *no* idea. Vi straight up lied to me, she said she hadn't talked to Ryu in months."

Ryu ran a sheepish hand through his hair, making it stick up even more. "Don't be too hard on her. She wanted to make you happy."

Since these two weren't snarling at each other, I was incredibly touched. I'd known Kian had something special planned for my birthday, but I thought it would be something more romantic, just the two of us. This wasn't worse. In fact, it was really sweet that he wanted me to be surrounded by my friends.

"I owe her big for this. I cannot believe you guys pulled this off. So what now?"

Kian set his hand in the small of my back. "We're meeting for dinner at the Italian place. Remember the first place we ate in together?"

"Technically that would be the diner in California."

With a sigh, Kian said, "Why must you nitpick? We weren't dating then."

"True," I admitted. "Then let's go."

As he'd said, Seth and Vi were waiting for us at the restaurant. I grabbed her and hugged her so hard, but I whispered, "You are so sneaky. Do you know how scared I was when Ryu showed up out of the blue? I thought Kian would go ballistic."

She put her mouth to my ear. "He was so cool about you being friends with your ex. I mean, maybe a little *sad*, but not alpha jealous like some guys get. You've definitely got a keeper. He cares way more about your happiness than his own pride or whatever."

Her words froze me. *Oh God. This is . . . he's giving me his blessing. He knows we only have two more months together.* It was hard to breathe for the tears choking me. The reason Kian threw this party was to show me I wouldn't be alone, even after he was gone.

The table wasn't full yet, so it startled me when Jen showed up with a guy from the lacrosse team; I thought his name was Phillip. There was one seat still open and Davina claimed it five minutes later. It was so good to see them; until now I didn't realize I missed them or Blackbriar. Once I thought that place was hell. But with everything I'd been through, I could view it differently now. We had even numbers, even though Davina and Ryu weren't a couple. I noticed him scoping out Jen more than once; but she was occupied with her date and didn't notice his subtle interest.

Since he was sitting on my other side, I nudged him. "Don't you have a girlfriend?"

He shrugged. "I'm not *doing* anything, am I? But can I just say, you have some seriously gorgeous friends, Edie."

As luck would have it, the conversation lulled just as he said it, so everyone at the table heard. Davina raised her glass in a mock toast while Jen smirked. Phillip didn't seem sure if he should take offense, so he glanced at Jen for guidance. She shook her head slightly, and Seth wrapped an arm around Vi's shoulders.

He pretended to scowl at Ryu. "Stay *away* from my girlfriend, perv."

That set the tone for the night. The food was delicious and I shared with Kian like we had that first time. Though I loved every minute of it, I had never been more conscious of the fact that our time was winding down. He touched me constantly, not in overt possessive ways but a hand on mine under the table, his fingers firm and warm. Once we finished, Kian paid the bill and we continued to the planetarium. He hadn't rented out the whole place, but he had tickets for everyone, and the show was wonderful.

Afterward, we went to Kian's place. It was a little weird for Jen and Davina to mingle with my SSP friends, but they mixed well enough. Phillip wasn't as much of an asshole as he'd seemed roaming around with Russ; he *couldn't* be, or Jen wouldn't be dating him. From what I'd seen, she was really picky about her boyfriends, though I couldn't be sure if they were together or she was just trying him out for a night.

I opened presents there, more than I'd ever gotten in my life. From Davina I had a pretty red sweater and Jen got me the cutest shoes ever. They actually fit too; I had no inkling how she knew my size. I hugged them both and then opened a fancy journal set from Vi. Seth got me a music gift card, while Ryu offered me a delicate silver chain adorned with various charms. When I looked closer, I could see they represented things I loved. I was surprised he'd re-membered, but we did talk a lot last summer, more than I'd chatted with anyone except Vi.

"Here," he said, fastening it about my left wrist without looking at the mark.

There was enough space for it right beside the blue beads Kian had given me. I stared at the two pieces of jewelry wondering if this was symbolic. Kian's quiet, resigned expression seemed to indicate that it was. But Ryu had a girlfriend, and I wasn't a mug that could be passed from one owner to the next. Quiet anger sparked to life.

The birthday part of the night done, the guys settled with the

Xbox, leaving us to retreat to the kitchen table to talk about them. "So . . . Phillip?" I prompted Jen.

"He's been persistent. So far he hasn't done anything to make him an auto-reject but I don't know if I'm feeling it."

"Cut him loose," Davina advised.

"Easy for you to say. Like four guys have already asked you to prom."

Vi sighed. "Don't mention prom, we've been arguing. Seth wants to pick one. He doesn't want to spend all the money twice."

I had no idea when the Blackbriar event would be. Not that it mattered. Kian and I wouldn't be going. Though I wasn't sure when the prom was, it seemed probable that it was after Kian's birthday. I needed to circle that date on my calendar because that was when our time ran out.

Listening to them talk, I marveled over the fact that this was my first birthday party, hosted by the first boy I ever loved.

"You're really quiet," Jen finally said.

"I'm just happy." *And heartbroken.*

At midnight, Jen headed out with Phillip and Davina followed soon after. After our New Hampshire debacle, her mom still didn't trust her completely, so Mrs. Knightly texted when she was downstairs. That left the five of us, but I could tell Seth and Vi were quietly dying for some alone time. When they met up halfway, it wasn't like they could rent a room.

So I said, "I'm sure you guys are tired. It's not my birthday anymore, so it's fine if you want to get some sleep."

Vi beamed at me. "Awesome. We'll hang out more tomorrow."

"Definitely."

I glanced at Ryu, who was still playing Xbox. "Don't mind me. I'm fine on the couch. I want to finish this level, then I'll crash."

Kian got him a sheet, blanket, and pillow. *Holy shit, he's letting Ryu sleep on his couch?* Maybe I was wrong, but that just seemed . . . too nice. I mean, he had to consider the guy competition or at least a nominal threat. Kian was the first person I kissed, but Ryu was the second, and we were together for six weeks. *Don't you mind at all, Kian?* But he showed no sign of being bothered as we went to the bedroom. Thanks to no curfew, I planned to stay the night.

As soon as the door shut behind us, I whispered, "What the hell are you doing?"

"Making sure you're all right. You'll need someone, after."

I swallowed hard. "Dammit, Kian, this is not okay. You might as well make up a will and leave me to him like an antique clock."

"I'm sorry that's how you see it."

"What other way is there? I can feel you letting go of me, and it's *not fair*. I promised to be with you until the end, no matter how hard it is, but you're not doing the same."

He turned away from me then, hands clenched into fists. "It's the only way I can cope. I'm sorry for hurting you, Edie. It's the last thing I want to do. But this is just *so* hard."

"Did you think I'd be impressed that you're so selfless? It drives me nuts actually."

"I'm not," he bit out. "I hate knowing that he's touched you, kissed you. I hate the fact that he still wants you, even while pretending he's fine."

"Huh?" That honestly floored me. "That's not . . . no. You're wrong. He was never crazy in love with me, Kian."

The laugh he produced had no humor in it. "For a smart girl, you're so stupid sometimes. You think I can't recognize someone doing what I do?"

"What are you *talking* about?"

"He might be dating someone in Japan, but he's still in love with you. You convinced yourself he wasn't because it made it easier to move on. For you, it was summer fun. For him, it was something else. His eyes are hungry when he watches you. And I know that feeling."

"So you thought you'd give me a guy for my birthday, is that it?" It was so hard to keep my voice down. I heard the Xbox, so Ryu was definitely still awake.

Kian sighed. "I don't want to fight. It's not like you have to get together with him. He's your friend, I thought you'd be glad to see him. It's why I cooperated when Vi wanted to do the reunion. I offered my apartment because—"

"Wait, so this was Vi's idea first?"

"What did you think?"

Now I felt horrible. I'd made all kinds of assumptions based on his overly altruistic personality. But before I could apologize, because he was smart, he connected the dots based on the crazy shit I already said. His expression deepened into a scowl.

"Did you *seriously* think I was stepping aside? 'Here, have my girlfriend. Since I can't keep her, you go on and get started with her.'"

"It sounds like something you'd do," I mumbled.

"Like hell," he growled.

Okay, so that made me incredibly happy. But he was too pissed to care.

"I might not have much time, but for now, you are *mine*. Tonight sucked, not least because I want you all to myself, but I'm trying my hardest not to be a selfish asshole. I could happily steal you and not let you to talk to anyone else until after I'm gone."

"Sorry."

"You have to make this up to me. Somehow."

"I have a few ideas."

It was almost three in the morning when I stopped making it up to him. We were both sweaty and exhausted. From the sounds coming from next door, Vi and Seth had more energy. Deprivation was making them enthusiastic. I laughed softly. Kian's mouth was slightly swollen and his hair was gorgeously mussed. The five o'clock shadow grown in on his jaw begged me to scrape my palm over it. His green eyes closed, a dark tangle of lashes on his cheeks.

"Have you seen your mother lately?" That might seem like a weird question but I knew how fragile she was.

He nodded. "I'm visiting every chance I get. She'll be released from the program soon."

"Where will she go from there?"

"I found her a halfway house that keeps you on track for sobriety and surrounds you with people who understand the struggle. They'll also help her find work." He didn't sound hopeful, but maybe not quite as despairing as he always had. The idea of leaving her completely alone must be chewing him up inside.

But I didn't say any of that. My sympathy wouldn't make his situation easier to bear. "Are you still in school?"

Kian shook his head. "What's the point? I won't graduate."

I really wish you hadn't done this for me.

But maybe, if he hadn't, I wouldn't have survived long enough to acquire the tools to destroy Dwyer. I would never have saved my dad. It seemed all kinds of awful that my father's salvation would result in his mother's pain.

"I'm sorry," I whispered.

"About what?" But he knew. He was just pretending.

So I took the hint and didn't pursue it. "Let's get some sleep."

In the morning, we went sightseeing with Seth, Vi, and Ryu. It was weird playing host in Boston but between Kian and me, we found places the other three would enjoy. Overhead, a large black bird kept an eye on our tour, but I didn't acknowledge it. Nobody else seemed to notice it wheeling above us, perching on electrical wires outside when we dodged into a café to warm up with pastries and hot chocolate.

"We should see a movie tonight," Vi said. "I'm tired from all the walking."

Seth poked her. "You should work out more."

"Sure, I'll add it to the to-do list, along with hanging on to my spot as valedictorian and finishing my robotics project."

Their bickering made me smile. Turning my head, I caught Ryu watching me. For an instant—just as Kian had said—his expression was open and naked, a raw sort of longing that I didn't even know Ryu *could* feel. He'd always radiated a cool and casual vibe, but what he chose to show the world and what was true? Two different things. This is why we hadn't talked much, not because he was so busy and popular—though he was probably those things also—but because he didn't want me to know.

Kian's right. He's hurting.

Apparently not realizing he'd shown me something else, Ryu gave me an easy smile. "Are you gonna eat the rest of that?"

Wordless, I slid him half of my cinnamon roll. Kian wrapped his hand around mine and I glanced at him. His brows went up, as if to say, *See?* I gave a little nod.

Yeah, I got it.

Yet there was no change I could make, nothing I'd do differently. Before the SSP, I was already half in love with Kian, even if he was unattainable. Back then I thought I understood how impossible we were together but really I had no clue. From day one, our happiness was an eggshell china cup, loosely clutched in a drunkard's hand.

No matter how hard I wished otherwise, we were destined to be broken.

AN OFFER SHE
CAN'T REFUSE

went home at six the next morning, sneaking out before Kian woke up. Though my dad had said he wouldn't wait up and I'd texted him that I was okay, it seemed wrong to roll in on day two after he left for work. By the time his alarm went off, I had breakfast on the table. He came out of his room with his hair standing in wispy tufts.

Dad adjusted his glasses as he sat down. "Did you have a good birthday?"

"Yeah, they had a surprise party for me. My friends from the SSP flew in and we all hung out the next day."

He nodded. "Still on track with your homework?"

"Yep." Without time spent sitting in class, I now had plenty of time for assignments. That approach wouldn't work for everyone but I'd always learned more from reading anyway. I used to daydream more than listen during lectures.

Once he went to work, I cleaned up the kitchen and got ready to meet everyone else. Ryu, Seth, Vi, and Kian were waiting outside his building when I ran up. Davina and Jen had school again since Blackbriar had a different holiday schedule.

"Are you guys ready for more excitement?" I asked, breathless.

"Sure. I was hoping . . ." Then Vi listed four places she wanted to go before they took off later tonight.

"Sounds doable," Kian said.

Ryu didn't seem enamored with the first stop, an art museum. He spent most of his time on benches while Vi and Seth wandered around. I'd been in here before, but not for a long time, probably on a middle-school trip. Kian held my hand as we wandered around, admiring famous paintings. I stopped in front of one that depicted the Oracle, thinking about the creature forever caught in Wedderburn's snare.

"It's not a good likeness," Kian said softly.

I shook my head. "And it's *so* weird to say that."

"Definitely," Ryu agreed.

Oh shit.

Slowly I shifted so I could see him; he'd approached quietly and I had no idea what to say. Kian's fingers tightened on mine but he didn't give me any sign how I should respond. There was no way I could fill him in, but I didn't want to lie either.

"Just kidding," I tried.

"Don't," Ryu said. "I can tell from the matching marks that there's something weird going on between the two of you. I'm not trying to learn your secrets or anything, but just know that I'm worried about you. I have the feeling you're into some bad shit."

"Sorry. I really can't talk to you about it."

"Or you'll have to kill me?" He attempted a joke, but I couldn't muster a laugh.

No, something else will.

To my surprise, he turned to Kian. "Take care of her, okay?"

"It's my prime directive," Kian answered, flying nerd colors.

Ryu smiled a bit. "That makes me feel a little better."

The rest of the day, I was conscious of his speculative observation. It seemed like he thought Kian had pulled me into some dangerous stuff, which wasn't entirely wrong. But Ryu had it wrong if he thought Kian wouldn't protect me; I was still fighting to reverse the last deal he made to do exactly that.

"This was so fun," Vi said later, over burgers.

We just had time to swing by Kian's place and take them to the airport. We'd all fit if we squished into the Mustang. Thankfully Seth and Vi didn't notice how quiet Ryu had gotten, and they talked enough to cover the awkwardness. I made sure to keep my wrists covered. I'd gotten careless lately, no wonder Ryu noticed.

As we left the diner, I spotted Buzzkill across the street. Ignoring traffic, he cut across so like five cars honked at him. Thankfully he looked like a bodyguard; I didn't want to traumatize my friends. I waited for him at the curb.

"Boss wants to see you." His gaze went to the gold armlet.

"I have people visiting. This isn't a good time."

"You think he gives a shit about that?"

Ryu and Kian stepped up on either side of me, making Buzzkill grin. I hurriedly shook my head. "No, it's fine. I have to take care of something. I know it's rude, but I'll say bye here. Kian, do you mind driving them to the airport?"

"Not at all." His tone was quiet and unconcerned, probably so the other three didn't clue in as to how bad this was.

Wedderburn must've decided I can't be allowed to keep Aegis. And I'm not letting him take it. He's the asshole who had my mother killed.

So I hugged Vi, Seth, and finally, Ryu, who held on a little longer than the rest. "Would you tell me if you were in serious trouble?"

No, I thought.

"Absolutely. He's just a friend of my father's. My dad must be upset about how much time I've spent slacking off. My birthday was two days ago."

Ryu stared at me hard but eventually he seemed to accept it. Or maybe he just pretended to—apparently I wasn't that good at reading people. I'd never guessed he saw me as anything but a summer fling. I pushed back gently, prompting him to let go. Kian was watching in silence, but I saw that it bothered him to see me in someone else's arms, probably not least because we didn't have that much longer.

And I still haven't found that loophole.

"Thanks so much for coming, guys. I'll message later."

I got more hugs and they waved for like half a block before Kian turned the corner toward the station, so they all vanished from sight. Exhaling slowly, I turned to Buzzkill. He looked completely unconcerned by how much he'd interrupted my life.

"Did you tell him?" I asked.

"You think I'd be standing here if he knew I let you keep you-know-who's heart? Just so you know, I pled ignorance. It was all I could do for you."

"Why?"

"Because it's so funny to see these assholes running scared. First time in centuries, they got something to fear. And it's some stupid kid. You can't *buy* entertainment like that."

"Thanks, I think. Should I be ready for a fight?"

"Guess that depends on you. If you go in hostile, pretty much everything in his tower will try to kill you. And while you've got that shiny on your wrist, you're not *that* good at wielding it. Of course you've got spirit power fully charged up, so maybe you feel like taking a chance."

"I'm not stupid. I know my odds of beating him on his home ground are slim to none."

"Then you should go prepared to surrender your weapon and accept his thanks for dispatching his nemesis."

"Yeah, I don't want to do that, either."

"Give me an answer, kid. Are you coming with me peacefully or do we throw down? Mind you, I don't have Dwyer's power, so it'll happen right here in front of all these nice, easily traumatized pedestrians. And I'm good with that. Are you?"

Dammit.

"Fine, let's go." I'd think about how to handle Wedderburn on the way.

"Your conscience is weighing you down," Buzzkill said.

"It's also what makes me human."

"Yeah, I don't want none of that action. You made *me*, remember?"

"Not personally," I muttered.

"You think I don't know you're stalling? Let's go."

But before I could follow him, a man on a motorcycle swooped past and swept me onto the back of the bike. I couldn't see who it was under the helmet, but anyone who wanted to keep me away from Wedderburn had to be an ally, right? I barely managed to hang on as he accelerated with Buzzkill shouting something

310

incomprehensible. We raced away from the diner with me knowing this wouldn't solve the problem, only postpone the reckoning.

Maybe that's the best I can hope for.

"Put your hand here." I recognized Raoul's voice and I relaxed a little.

He flattened my palm over the medallion that kept him hidden. If we were both touching it, would it work the same or would the effectiveness be halved? As we roared through Boston, the science geek in me tried to figure that out. The bike didn't stop for miles and miles. While Buzzkill had a preternatural predatory sense, he couldn't overcome this artifact or Wedderburn would've already found Raoul. That made me feel a little better, but I couldn't spend the rest of my life hanging on to Raoul's chest. This was a stopgap measure at best.

When the bike stopped, Raoul was careful to keep us in contact. A little dizzy from the motorcycle, I stumbled forward but he stayed with me. Taking stock, I saw we'd come to an old monastery outside the city. Given the fact that we'd met for the first time in a church, this tracked with what I knew of his organization.

"Why are we here?" I asked.

"You haven't wanted to hear what I had to say," he said quietly. "And I understand why. You feel betrayed, as if I've only helped you because I was under orders."

There was no point in denying it. "Pretty much."

"Are things ever so simple, *mija?* The human heart is complex, as you well know."

I sighed. "Fine, let's hear your spiel."

"Today I've brought you to meet my master."

Wow, unexpected.

He went on, "The time is drawing near when you must choose."

"Choose what?"

"Your path."

"You make it sound like once I make a decision, there's no way to change course."

Raoul didn't reply, and his silence troubled me. It wasn't easy moving in tandem with my hand on his chest, but the alternative ended with Buzzkill dragging me to Wedderburn by my hair. For the moment, I was safe, though I couldn't go back to my apartment . . . or Kian's. That was the first place they'd look.

Shit. My dad.

Since I'd killed Dwyer, their private game was basically over. I figured Wedderburn still wanted the technology, but I couldn't be sure how safe my dad was. If there was any chance of me completing the work alone, he might use my father as a bargaining chip to get me to surrender, both my free will and Aegis. At least he couldn't strike at Kian.

Why do you hesitate? Cameron whispered. *You're strong now. Take the fight to them.*

It would get me killed to overestimate my own abilities. While I'd bested Dwyer when I had the element of surprise on my side, other immortals wouldn't be dumb enough to give me a fair fight. No, they'd send their muscle after me until I exhausted my energies on minions, leaving me nothing for a final confrontation. Wedderburn especially was infamous for never leaving his stronghold.

Whoever Raoul's boss was, he wasn't immortal, at least. He had been quite clear about the Black Watch being the only human organization that knew about the game. Which made their resources more limited than mine, frankly. But I went with Raoul quietly, one

312

hand on the medallion, as we rounded the building. It was an old structure, covered in ivy and moss. I could tell it had been beautifully kept at one time, but now time had worked its wiles.

"This is your headquarters?" I whispered.

Raoul shook his head. "They blindfolded me when I left, so I cannot betray them. This is a meeting point, just as the church was for us."

"Cagey. So you know essentially nothing about the Black Watch, other than the fact that they abused you for eighteen years."

"It is no different from other trials our initiates have undergone to cement their bonds to the order and create strong warriors out of malleable clay." An old man stepped out from behind the dead and spindly branches of a tree that grew in the once lovely garden.

I'd expected someone more impressive, a long beard or wispy mustache, a tonsure, even some orange robes, but this gentleman was depressingly ordinary. He had on a Russian hat with fur earflaps, a plaid overcoat, and tall winter boots. His face was lined but not in a way that made me think he had special power or wisdom. If I passed him on the street, I wouldn't give him a second look.

And maybe that's his superpower?

"Children aren't clay," I said.

"You disapprove of our methods." He came toward us with a walking stick that reminded me a little of the Harbinger's, only this one had a simple brass knob on top, not a dog's head.

"It seems like you're trying to play a long game, only you don't have the right pieces."

"Are you sure of that? I trust Raoul has told you he knows less than nothing."

"Point taken."

"Miss Kramer, I have been waiting a very long time to meet you. I am Tiberius Smith, the one whom you may blame for all of Raoul's misfortunes. But whatever you may think of our training regime, he has served willingly since he graduated as an initiate. If you could see our archives, you would be horrified at the senseless suffering and carnage these immortals have wrought. Together, they have killed more of us than all our wars combined."

That gave me pause. "Seriously? But there are so many people. It doesn't seem like the human race is in danger of dying out."

"It is a complicated problem," he admitted. "But you see, as the population grows, and as our dreams flutter to life, the Internet feeds them. In ages past, there was a limit to how quickly stories could spread, how fast people could believe in them."

"So basically the World Wide Web is acting on the immortals like a virus." God, could anything be scarier? Buzzkill was a prime example of this, modern evil sworn to the service of an old and merciless god.

"A most apt analogy. I would love to tell you more of the role you'll play in years to come, but I cannot take you into confidence unless you become our champion."

"That sounds familiar," I muttered. "That's exactly what they said before I made the first deal. I hope you understand that I'm wary of people who won't give me information up front."

His warmth chilled when I didn't immediately leap at the chance to sign. "This is for our protection. Secrecy is our mandate, Miss Kramer. It's how we have survived through ages of being hunted. The immortals suspect—and correctly—that they have mortal enemies. Right now, there is a shadow on your loyalty. You think of small matters like your sweetheart and your father when the stakes are so much higher than you know."

I took a step back, closer to Raoul. This geezer's eyes bothered me. Not because they were black and diabolical, like the bag man and his awful children, but at first glance, they appeared perfectly pleasant, human, pale blue with normal irises and pupils. But the longer I looked, the more convinced I became that he had long ago lost any compassion or empathy. He cared only for his cause, and he no longer saw the value of individual human lives. Which meant I wasn't a person to him, only a tool to be used.

Just like Dwyer. Just like Wedderburn.

And that made him every bit as bad as the monsters he fought.

"My boyfriend and my dad may be 'small matters' to you, but they're pretty much *my* whole world. If you think I'll abandon them for some great cause, then you've got me pegged all wrong. I *never* wanted to be the person who saves the day."

"That is a great pity."

Something in his expression worried me, so I decided it would be smarter to hedge my bets. This was the face of a man who would shoot me to keep the immortals from gaining any advantage, and I had no idea how effective Aegis would be against people. To make matters worse, Raoul would certainly kick my ass, and I had *no idea* whether I could actually hurt enemies that bled.

"Can I think about it? This is huge commitment. I'm sure you didn't expect me to just run off and join you right this second."

Smith nodded. "I would've questioned your sanity had you been so impulsive. When you realize how imperative it is to take action, you'll need to say farewell and tie up the loose ends of your old life. For when you come to the Black Watch, you cannot go home again."

At least he's honest about that. It didn't do much to sway me to his cause, but I preferred the truth to bullshit any day.

The old man turned to Raoul. "Return her to the city. She must rely on her own wits and abilities to keep safe from the winter king until she's ready to swear her life to the cause."

Not just the cold god. Death is also gunning for me.

To me, Smith added, "Keep safe, Miss Kramer. Your course of action here will create more ripples than you realize."

"Does everyone have a secret window that lets them glimpse the future?"

But Smith didn't reply. He only turned and went down the path, disappearing between the dead winter trees. Soon it was only Raoul and me, my hand still on the pendant.

"I'm sorry, *mija*. This is meant to show you how much you need to join the Black Watch, both to fight for us and for your own survival."

"There's always another path. You just have to be smart enough to find it."

THE BOY WHO LOVED TOO MUCH

Before we left, I sent a message to Kian telling him where to meet. It would be the last time for a while, as I figured out how to handle all the heat now that I'd gone renegade from Wedderburn. Hopefully he'd stand in for me and explain things to my dad. I didn't like the thought of leaving him alone so soon, but it was the safest option for everyone; I had to keep moving, stay away from the people I loved.

Until I figure out what to do.

By the time Raoul stopped the bike, my arm was aching from holding it in the same position. He shifted as I slid off the bike, taking off his helmet to regard me. "As soon as I leave, you're fair game. You know this, yes?"

"I'm aware. I won't stay long."

Just long enough to say good-bye to Kian. After everything we'd gone through together, I owed him that much before I disappeared. Though it was bad to go on the run without a plan, I didn't have time to sit around reflecting. Wedderburn and Fell were my Scylla and Charybdis and if I didn't move fast enough, they'd crush me between them.

It was probably just nerves, but the air chilled as I pulled my hand away from Raoul's medallion. Contrarily, my marks caught fire, a warning from Wedderburn. The pain nearly drove me to my knees, and I stared at my wrists incredulously because for anything to hurt this much, there *must* be physical damage. But, no, the sigils didn't seem to be burning my flesh, just lighting up my nerves with the worst pain I'd ever felt.

I stumbled toward the fountain at the center of the park. My feet slipped on the icy sidewalk. All around the world was black and white while I felt as if I had a red target painted on my back. A fine dusting of snow covered the benches I sprinted past; there were few people out, just a handful of dedicated joggers. Tears trickled from my eyes, but nobody gave me a second glance. I could no longer move my hands; from the elbows down, I throbbed with white-hot fire.

The distance seemed insurmountable. Toppling over, I couldn't even put out my hands to catch myself. My face took most of the damage, and I tasted copper, trickling down over my mouth to pool beneath my chin. As I lay there, I heard footsteps. The marks reminded me I'd signed a deal with Wedderburn. And now, they served as a choke chain to bring me to heel. In a few more minutes, the agony might actually kill me. My eyes couldn't focus but someone picked me up, hauling me to my feet with gentle hands.

Probably not Buzzkill, I thought blearily.

Kian pulled me to him, but my knees would barely hold me. "What the hell happened? Who hurt you?"

Unable to speak, I showed him my arms. The skin was irritated now, like it had been on the trip to New Hampshire. Wedderburn's way of proving he could hurt me remotely, not just phantom pain but actual injury.

For a few seconds, he seemed like he was struggling to find words. "You . . . this is worse than I expected. *Why* did Raoul keep you from seeing Wedderburn?"

"Your time is up," a quiet voice said.

Though the tone was unfamiliar and somehow androgynous, it still sent a chill through me. Turning my head, I found a shadowy figure darkening the snow. It was impossible to make out features in the shifting haze about him or her, but more telling, a pigeon flew through that smoky veil and dropped stone dead at our feet. *This had to be Fell. Death.*

"Do you know, Edith Kramer, that a bounty has been placed on you? Wedderburn has rescinded all protections, deeming you too dangerous to exist."

"That's . . . extreme." The cold in the air was nothing compared to the asphyxiation tightening my throat. It was nearly impossible to speak in Death's presence. Add that to the pain and I couldn't believe I'd ever faced down an immortal.

You can do it again, Cameron said. *Get the compact. Call on me.*

"You owe me a debt, human child. Due to your violence, I am robbed of a partner and companion. My flank has been weakened."

"I wouldn't think Death had time for games," Kian said.

"Quite the contrary. What is life except for one long contest?" Fell took a step toward me.

I still couldn't tell anything about its appearance but that hardly mattered. The air grew thick with the stench of corpses and rotten vegetation. At this proximity, I could feel it draining the life out of me. It wouldn't take long before both Kian and I died, together, like Romeo and Juliet. And screw that, what a terrible ending.

"What should I do with you?" Fell mused.

I tried to activate Aegis but my hands were shaking too hard. There was no strength in my fingers anymore. My knees gave way, dropping me hard onto the sidewalk, and there wasn't enough snow to break my fall. Kian tried to reach for me, but he was in no better shape. I couldn't think of *any* stories where mankind fought death and emerged victorious. Somehow I slammed my wrist on the ground just right and triggered the sword, but I couldn't lift it.

"You cannot win," Fell said gently. "Even if you could wield that blade against me, the stories tell it thus: The one who defeats death must then take up his mantle and become the new shepherd to the dead. Dare you risk it?"

Hell no.

"There will be no battle here. Give me the god-slayer and I will let your partner go. There can be no mercy for one who has transgressed so against us."

"I know how the story of Icarus ends," I whispered.

But Govannon said Aegis wouldn't permit anyone else to take it.

The pain at my wrists was ebbing. Probably, Wedderburn was scrying in his weird machine, watching me grovel before Death. The winter king had complete confidence that things would work out exactly as he'd ordered. Though I'd only given up once in my life, it occurred to me now, awfully, that no matter how hard you fought, sometimes there was no way to win.

I'm just one girl.

I was never going to get vengeance for my mother, or figure out how to save Kian from the deal he made with the Harbinger. That was the clarity Death brought. My will was finite, and I couldn't protect everyone. The world might even be better off without me in it. *What did I ever accomplish anyway?* Slowly I closed my eyes and bowed my head.

Don't listen, Cameron whispered. *That's how Death seduces you.*

A tiny spark blazed to life inside me. *No, I promised I will not go easy. I promised I wouldn't quit.* My eyes snapped open. At my side, Kian was pale as ice, his lips tinged blue, and not just from the weather.

"Wedderburn," I shouted. "You're breaking your promise. He's supposed to be untouchable by any immortal in the game. *That* was my last favor."

A wall of ice formed between us and Death, just a temporary respite. "Get out of here," I snarled at Kian.

But he wore a stern, resolute expression, one I'd never seen before. Instead of listening to me, he gathered the last of his strength and ran at the ice wall, just as Death was passing through. His flesh withered and I saw the truth of it—Fell hadn't been lying when he said one touch would be fatal. My heart died over and over as I crawled toward him, watching him struggle to breathe. It wasn't like before, with the poison. This time I had no hope. Drawing his body up into my arms, I held him with all my strength. The tears froze halfway down my cheeks, the first sign that we had the winter king's full attention.

Death hovered at my shoulder, close enough that I could see the beckoning darkness behind the sharp heat of my tears. "You idiot. Why?"

"Alive, I'm a liability. Dead, I'm your reason to fight." Kian stared up at me, but he didn't see me. There was a faraway light in his eyes. "I love you."

His body went limp in my arms while Death circled us. The pain from my wrists felt nothing like this. My heart roared in endless rage, and I didn't much care if Fell tapped my shoulder while I rocked the boy I loved. Back and forth, his dark hair tumbled against my shoulder. Nothing I did could rouse him.

"That was . . . most impolitic," Fell said.

"That depends on your point of view." The Harbinger strode across the snow, leaving no tracks. His eyes were red as blood, and he wore a mantle of black feathers as if dressed for war.

"It was not my intent to harm that one."

"What does that matter when you've robbed me of a much-anticipated feast? Kian Riley was *mine*, and you stole him. I also think you've violated her agreement with Wedderburn, and that has its penalties, does it not?"

The Harbinger knelt beside me and pried my fingers away from Kian. Whatever he saw seemed to amuse him. "Look, the silly little knight's saved you at last."

My eyes stung so bad it took some time to focus. The marks were gone, though I still had Aegis and the blue beads. I stared up at them both, bewildered. "What—"

Resting a hand on my head, the Harbinger said silkily, "Simply this: If the winter king could not keep his end of the bargain, then *you* are no longer bound to the agreement."

In the mist above my head I watched an illusionary contract go up in smoke and then trickle away to ash. Death stayed silent, which I took for assent. The Harbinger wrapped one side of his feathered cloak around me. Dimly I noticed the snow soaking through my pants, but it didn't matter if I was cold. More tears trickled down my cheeks, but they didn't freeze, a subtle sign that Wedderburn had withdrawn.

"True," Fell admitted eventually.

"Does this mean I'm no longer a catalyst?"

For me to survive and be free of the game, that was all Kian ever wanted. I wished I had understood how fiercely he felt about it or how far he'd go to achieve that aim. In this moment I wanted to die too, more than I had the day I stood on the bridge. It would be so easy, just pull away from the Harbinger and—

"To steal a soul pledged to me . . . that's quite a crime." The casual tone didn't fool anyone into thinking the trickster was harmless. Rage crackled from his every pore.

"She still owes me a debt," Fell began.

"And you owe *me* an enormous one. You cannot harm the girl our young sacrifice placed under my protection."

Before I could take any destructive action, Death simply . . . vanished, leaving me with Kian's body and the Harbinger's unlikely tenderness. "Why did you step in? You said you'd break my heart the next time we met."

"Look at your face," he said softly. "It seems more likely that you'll break mine. And yes . . . I underestimated how much he loved you. Try to smile over that, dearling, if nothing else. He worked out what he had to do to secure your freedom . . . and did it."

I fought when he tried to pull me away. My arms wouldn't release from their lock around Kian's shoulders, and I buried my face in his hair. Impossible to believe that yesterday, he held me. Kissed me. *I'll never hear his voice again. Never touch him. Never—anything.* While the Harbinger watched, I wept for my lost love. He wet a handkerchief in the melting snow and washed my face, but it didn't help. I had to be a tear-streaked mess and I *did not* care.

"I was supposed to figure it out," I whispered.

"There was no loophole. Even if you searched for two human lifetimes, there was no escape clause. But he found his own way out."

"That doesn't help."

The Harbinger chuckled faintly. "Me either. You've *no* idea how hungry I am."

Eventually, the real world snapped back into focus. There were people all around us, talking in frightened tones. Someone called an ambulance, and at some point, the Harbinger had donned his handsome teacher skin. This time I appreciated the calm, respectable façade. I had no answers for their questions, only a black hole and endless grief.

"She looks like she's in shock," an older woman said.

"Probably," someone else agreed. "He's so young, you just don't expect it . . ."

"An aneurysm, you think?"

I ignored all of them. When the city came to take his body, I cried until I threw up. The Harbinger shielded me from curious looks, strangely protective, even now that he had no reward coming for helping me. Lacking the energy to protest, I let him put us in a cab to follow the vehicle to the morgue. They needed me to fill out forms, and though it nearly killed me, I did everything required of me. Afterward, the morgue tech wanted us to get out, I could tell, but the idea of leaving Kian in this place made me burst into tears again.

"He's gone, dearling. It's awful for you, but he's not here."

"How do you know?" With a glare I produced my compact. "This proves there's life after death. How do you know he's not standing right there, watching us?"

A flicker of a smile curved his mouth but didn't reach his eyes. "For one thing, I'd see him. But apart from that, only souls with regret and unfinished business hang around."

Kian finally got what he wanted; he's the big hero. Now I have to live with how awful it feels? This sucks.

"Then, what, it's all over, so I just go home?"

For some reason, my rage amused him. "If you wish. I could make you forget, just as Aaron did. You'd remember nothing about Kian or the game."

"Without a temporal parasite?"

"That was a side effect. Since you're firmly rooted in this time, no fresh nightmares will be drawn to you."

The possibility spun out before me, endlessly tempting. My mom would still be dead, along with all of my classmates, but I wouldn't remember that so much of it was my fault. For that alone, I couldn't take the easy route. So I shook my head. "I can't run from this. It would be chicken shit to forget him and everything he did for me."

"A brave choice."

"Maybe. I may wish I'd taken you up on it when I tell his mother."

"Did you want to go now?" Without waiting for my answer, the Harbinger led the way out of the hospital.

On the street, it was well past dark. My dad would be wondering where I was, and I couldn't face the thought of telling him Kian was dead. It still didn't seem real, as if this were a nightmare from which I couldn't awaken. Pinching myself hard, I *hoped*, but nothing changed. Instead of Kian beside me, I had a mad trickster god with eyes like the abyss.

325

Finally I replied, "I probably should."

The job wouldn't get easier or more pleasant from putting it off. But I'd forgotten about her release from the program and moving into a halfway house. Kian had told me, but I couldn't remember the name of the new place, and the nurse at the front desk wouldn't give me any information since I wasn't a relative. I didn't like the idea of asking them to pass along such an awful message, either.

She's finally on the road to recovery. This will break her.

"That's enough for today," the Harbinger said as I stumbled out of Sherbrook House.

"Okay."

Listless, I collapsed on the first bench I saw. My jeans were wet front and back, and I had nothing more to give. Freedom was just a word; it didn't love me, couldn't hold me, laugh at my stupid jokes, or forgive me when I was an idiot. I'd never in my life done anything to deserve how much he loved me, but that was the magic of it. *We don't have to be worthy of it . . . sometimes beautiful things just happen.*

"Passersby think I've broken your heart," the Harbinger said.

I hadn't even noticed, but I had been crying for like ten minutes, not loud sobs, but more of a quiet trickle that I couldn't stop. He rested his hand on my head, and I saw now that people were staring at us. *A grown man, a teenage girl, late at night, and she's weeping on a bench?* Yeah, it definitely looked shady. The last thing I needed was some meddler deciding the Harbinger was a creeper.

It bothered me to see him pretending to be human when so clearly he was *not*. Colin Love might've been a real person, someone he'd broken, but I didn't want to be alone, either. At this moment, it seemed like *only* the Harbinger could understand how

I felt, the ache in my sternum until there was only blood and rage, covering an endless tide of loss.

"What happened to Mr. Love?" I asked.

"This is not a happy story, dearling. Now isn't the time."

Probably not.

So I made another request, disregarding all prudence and normalcy. "I can't stand it, I *can't*. So please. Take me away from this, just for a little while."

In a whisper of black feathers, he did.

A STATE OF
IMAGINARY GRACE

n the morning, I had to locate Kian's mother and tell her the truth. Then, most likely, I'd help her make arrangements. I'd done the same for my dad. It was all kinds of wrong for someone my age to know so much about the business of death—about booking a funeral parlor and picking out a casket, choosing music and flowers—so many damn questions that dead people probably didn't care about anyway.

Kian's gone, he's really gone.

For now, I couldn't deal with any of it. I needed a place to hide. And who'd ever guess that the Harbinger would offer me shelter?

He took me to the crumbling manor where we'd attended the Feast of Fools, what seemed like forever ago. There were no monsters today, apart from him and me. Devoid of illusion, the house looked different, mostly abandoned and gone to ruin. We ended up in a well-preserved study at the center of the residence, protected from the wind and rain that had damaged other parts of the house. Here, the stained-glass windows were intact, and the room was crammed to the walls with interesting objects, though they didn't raise the hair on my neck like the ones at Forgotten Treasures. The floor was covered with an old purple-and-red tapestry while the furniture was an odd mix of old and new, antiques mingled with Ikea. Books were piled everywhere, first-edition leather hardcovers alongside pulp paperbacks from the thirties with yellow, dog-eared pages.

I had the sense he was showing me his heart.

Collapsing on the nearest chair, I ran my fingers over the red velvet pile, opulent as a throne. The legs were gilt and the back was carved in intricate, baroque style. The Harbinger gestured and a fire flared in the dead hearth. At first I thought it was just a light show, but then the room warmed slowly, by degrees. This wasn't for his benefit, so he must care that I was soaked and freezing, plus too sad to care.

"Here," he said, draping me with a knitted shawl that looked like he might've stolen it from an old gypsy woman.

"Why are you looking after me?" I asked.

"I could give any number of answers and they'd all be true."

"Pick one."

"You were given to me to protect, and it's been a *very* long time since I played that role. I'm also extremely unwilling to let the others gobble you up. Nobody breaks my toys but me."

"I'm already there," I whispered.

He offered a puckish smile. "That's part of the problem. There's no pleasure in smashing what the world has already damaged so grievously."

That didn't explain his intervention. "But Kian's gone, he didn't keep his part of the bargain. Doesn't that absolve you of responsibility toward me?"

He crouched beside me, all awkward angles and ungainly grace. Somehow he was paradox incarnate, beauty and anguish entwined. "Now, *that* is disingenuous, dearling. Do you truly reckon that there's nothing between us but your boy's sacrifice?"

"I don't know what you're getting at." But that wasn't completely true.

While it wasn't a connection like I had with Kian, there *was* something here, pain calling to pain, possibly. He spoke so easily of destruction, but each time he repeated the cycle, like Kian's mom, the one the Harbinger hurt the most was himself. Because it wasn't like he truly enjoyed the pain he caused, more that he was addicted to it. And each time, he deepened the self-loathing because he couldn't resist the compulsion we'd given him. I didn't fool myself that I was safe with him. There would come a point when his kindness lost to the desire to wound.

I didn't care if it was today.

"Liar," he chided.

I couldn't meet his gaze, burrowing deeper into the black shawl. It was still incredibly cold in here, though that might be my wet clothes talking. The shivers surprised me and I couldn't stop my teeth from chattering. The Harbinger folded to his feet and went over to a chest to rummage. I didn't like to contemplate what grisly mementos he might have stored away.

But he only pulled out an old-fashioned nightgown sewn in thick muslin with a high neck and a ruffle around the bottom. There were no bloodstains, either. I took it when he handed it to me, and from the way he didn't meet my gaze, I could see he wouldn't be answering any questions about why he had it so carefully preserved. I sensed that the owner of the gown had been important to him.

"Thanks."

"You can change over there." He indicated a fancy lacquered screen.

There was a small space behind it, also piled high with books and boxes. I managed to squirm around enough to get the job done, and when I came out, he'd taken my clothes from the top of the screen and hung them up by the fire to dry. Reclaiming my spot on the red throne, I wrapped myself up in the gypsy shawl. I thought I would feel better once I was dry but it didn't impact the misery in my head. Right now I was ten seconds away from a complete breakdown. After the way I cried in the park, I didn't think I had any tears left. As it turned out, I had underestimated myself.

"Would you like me to leave you alone?" he asked then.

It was a tactful question, and I thought hard before shaking my head. "This place might freak me out if you weren't here."

"So I'm the nightmare that keeps worse monsters at bay?" His tone was all tender amusement, laced with wonder.

"Something like that."

"You asked why I'm looking after you . . ."

"Yeah."

"My answer was not as complete as it might've been. Quite simply, it has been time out of mind since anyone chose my company of her own free will."

"Without being your pet, your prisoner, or wildly deluded about your nature?" Like Nicole, when she was pretending to be our teacher.

"Precisely. There is a certain savor in being . . . known."

"Yeah, I suppose so."

The warmer I got, the harder it became to hold my tears; it was like an emotional thaw accompanying the physical one. Burying my face in my arms, I let them come. I didn't expect the hand on my hair. A few seconds later, I realized he was petting my head as I had his. It wasn't enough to make me feel better, but for those moments, I felt less alone. He didn't speak or try to comfort me. There were no words to make it better anyway. Because in this moment, I realized that Kian *always* planned to die for me, one way or another. In his mind, there was only one way to set me free.

I remembered how he'd written a poem just for me. Would I find more of them in his journal when I went to his apartment? The tears became the noisy, choking sobs I'd withheld in the park, until I couldn't see or breathe. Eventually the storm passed because I couldn't go on like that forever, much as I wanted to. It didn't expiate the feelings, either, but crying left me momentarily hollow. When I finally raised my face, I found the Harbinger quiet and still beside me, eyes closed. His hand was still gentle atop my head, then he pulled away and retreated to another chair across the room.

"I usually take pleasure in that sound," he said.

"Then I hope it was good for you."

When he opened his eyes, I was surprised at how sad they looked. "Not today. Your tears are not nectar to me, dearling. I think . . . I'm afraid of you."

Though I still had Aegis, I'd already refused to end him, and now I had even less reason since he'd helped me so often, and he no longer posed any threat to Kian. In fact, if it wasn't so strange to contemplate, I might even call him a friend. So I shook my head.

"Don't be."

"Some things," he said, "are immutable."

"Do you really believe that? I want to believe what I do

matters—that my choices can change things. Otherwise what's the point of anything?"

"Remember, my course was set by your stories, so I've never had free will."

"Sorry. I forgot."

He laughed quietly. "It means you think of me as a person. I won't take offense."

"Am I safe?"

"With me?"

I was actually referring to the other immortals, but now that he'd brought it up . . . I waited to see what he would say. Before, he was all veiled threats and Dread Pirate Roberts's I'll-most-likely-kill-you-in-the-morning attitude. The Harbinger paused to consider. In response to a careless gesture, two headless dolls that had been discarded on a table began to dance.

Then he said, "For now. I'm sure that's not what you wish to hear, and there is a corner of me that would like to be your knight. But I am not selfless, nor am I kind. There will come a point when I must ask for something back, and you will not want to give it."

Those words chilled me a little, for I'd put myself completely in his power. Yet I wasn't without the ability to defend myself. "Thanks for telling me the truth. But actually, I didn't mean you. I was talking about the others."

"Fell and Wedderburn?"

I nodded.

"You're out of the game, but you know a great deal about us. And you have the means to do us harm. Though I can't say for certain, I imagine you will be hunted."

That was pretty much what I expected. "Okay. I'll watch my back."

"I could watch it. You know my price."

"I'm *never* becoming your pet. I like personal agency too much to live in your cage, however gilded."

"It wouldn't be," he said, making me shiver.

"So tonight is basically it for us, then. You're not getting paid for protecting me after all, so there's no reason for you to intervene again."

The Harbinger looked away, as if he didn't enjoy hearing it stated. "Indeed, dearling. This is a farewell party, however melancholy that may seem. I shall take pride in the fact that I did you no harm."

"I wouldn't let you," I reminded him.

"I appreciate that too. Occasionally it is a welcome change to be saved from yourself."

One thing had become crystal clear to me, however. I would never have a normal life. Most likely I wouldn't last long with various immortals gunning for me. There was always the Black Watch, but despite my respect for Raoul, his mentor worried me. Plus, I didn't want to spend my life fighting, though it didn't look like I had much choice.

My dad will never be safe, as long as I'm nearby.

Wedderburn probably wouldn't strike at him, even now, because he might still hope to control whatever tech my father eventually invented. But without my mom and me, it would take longer, if it came to fruition at all. Which left my dad's primary value as collateral. They would target him repeatedly, until I gave in and handed Aegis over, but I had no illusions that we'd be set free to live in peace. At that point, we'd be executed and probably not quickly or painlessly.

I have to go.

Making up my mind, I asked, "Could you do something for me?"

"The answer to *could* is probably yes, depending on your request." The dolls stopped dancing and toppled over, telling me I had his complete attention. "Will I? That's an entirely different matter. However fond I may be, I'm still a mercenary at heart."

"I want you to make another me. To keep my dad company."

"A doppelgänger, you mean?"

"I thought those were always evil, though."

"Only sometimes. They're also known as changelings. Tricking your father, this is certainly my wheelhouse. Will you tell me why?"

"It's not a secret. Since I won't be around and I don't want him to worry, I need somebody there, someone to be me, so he's not alone."

"She won't be real," he warned. "Not much personality. And she won't last forever. My power has limits."

"That's fine. If she could just stay for a while, until I'd be going off to college, that would help. It'll give him time to get used to the idea."

"Of losing you?" The Harbinger's mouth tightened. "I was a father once, and trust me when I say, there is no time sufficient for that."

"Do I remind you of your daughter?" I asked.

That might explain his unwilling interest.

He shook his head. "I had two sons, strong, beautiful boys. They took after their mother."

Wow. That's the most personal thing he's ever said. I was tempted to follow that line of questioning but I had limited time to make this deal. The night was ticking away, and when the morning came, I had to move quickly. It seemed unspeakably wrong to mourn for Kian in a single night, but he'd said it with his dying breath. *He wants me to fight.* I never promised I'd live to a ripe old age or settle down with someone else.

"So we've established this is something you can do. Now here's what I'm offering—you can feed on me like you did Nicole, so take as much as you deem fair for this service."

He stared at me. "You have alarming confidence in my decency. I could steal anything from you and call it just. You *do* know I'm the trickster, yes?"

"But *not* when it comes to your bargains. The only rule you respect comes from such agreements." I quoted him directly, reminding the Harbinger what he'd said at our first meeting.

His gaze intensified, his aura kicking in. Somewhere along the line, he'd stopped using it with me, and its return was overwhelming. "And what is the first rule? The trickster lies."

"I think you mean the doctor, and I don't believe you were, not about this."

Finally, he glanced away, his gray eyes on the fireplace. "I'm only agreeing to this because I want to keep a little of you with me. Do you understand that?"

"It's a little gross and parasitic, but yes. Did you want to keep Nicole too?"

"No. I don't keep everything I take. Sometimes people are just fuel, like wood for a fire, and there's only ashes left."

"Even ashes carry traces of what they used to be," I murmured.

"That's how they can tell certain buildings in Scotland have been patched up with mortar made from the dead."

"You know the oddest things." But he was smiling.

"Then we have a deal?"

"Indeed. When do you wish your replica to appear?"

Much as I wanted to say good-bye to my dad, it would rouse his suspicion and might endanger him. Squeezing my eyes shut, I spoke the most difficult word of my life. "Now."

"Then first you must pay," he whispered.

"Okay." I stood up, unsure what he wanted me to do. The black gypsy shawl trailed down my back, and the woven rug felt soft beneath my feet.

"Come here."

Weirdly I felt like some gothic bride, going to her doom, after having married the scarred, demonic lord of the castle, despite numerous warnings that he was no good. The Harbinger held up a hand when I got within arm's reach. If he didn't look so serious, I might be worried that this was an elaborate joke, wherein he'd chortle and turn me down. If that happened, I didn't know what I'd do because I couldn't *stand* to think of leaving my dad alone.

"Did I do something wrong? Oh, did you want me to call some power from my spirit familiar? That might make me . . . spicier or something." God, it was weird talking about myself like I was a plate of Buffalo hot wings.

"No, I only want you. I'll try not to hurt you." With that alarming statement, he pulled me against him, and it was like being embraced by cold light and marble.

I knew he didn't have to touch to feed, but maybe this was his way of communicating that I was different from Nicole. A pang of pity went through me, and I wondered where she was, if she was in a mental facility for loving him too much, giving him everything; to him, she was disposable, a brown-bag fast-food meal. That should make me hate him, but I couldn't quite get there. He'd shown me too much of his heart.

The Harbinger touched his brow to mine, and the first sharp pull felt like a pinch inside my brain, not quite a headache, but pressure. I went light-headed. It was invasive and awful, and I could *feel* him practically inside of me, learning my secrets and hidden longings. Every fear and insecurity, it felt like he fondled them before moving on. When he pulled away, I felt nauseated and a little dirty.

"Is that enough?" My voice came out hoarse.

"Yes." To my surprise he didn't sound any better, rough and shaken, though his face had more color. But when he stumbled back to his chair, his hands were trembling.

"What . . . are you all right?"

"Don't ask me that," he bit out.

"Why not?"

"Because you have too much of me already. You won't know this, Edie Kramer. I won't give you that answer."

"Sorry. Can you send the other me home now?"

"In due time." He got a bit of clay and worked it into a rough replica, then he whispered to it, and it shimmered before my eyes, evolving into . . . me. Without another word, it vanished, I assumed to my apartment.

"Thank you."

"The business between us is concluded, dearling. You cannot stay the night, for my impulse now is not to comfort or be kind."

I nodded. "Take me back. *My* work's just getting started."

338

NOTHING ELSE MATTERS

I spent the night in a twenty-four-hour diner, nursing my coffee and watching my phone. I'd sent several texts and now I was waiting to hear back. The waitress was tired of topping me off by the time I left, but this was better than roaming around in the dark. Better than anyone, I knew the monsters lurking in the shadows. At daybreak I paid my ridiculously small check and went out into the cold.

I'm never going home again.

From the diner, I headed toward the subway station, but halfway there, I heard the unmistakable ring of hobnail boots. The bag man had chased me once before and then I'd run after him, before I came into power. *The Harbinger saved me from myself.* But now there would be an end to this. I didn't know if Wedderburn had sent him after me, but I wasn't afraid of the bogeyman that murdered my mother.

There's nothing you can take from me.

Whirling, I pressed to activate Aegis and braced in battle stance. I heard his boots but I didn't *see* him. *More immortal glamour.* So before he could blindside me, I got out my compact and opened it. Cameron's face greeted me in full reflection; I hadn't used him since I took Dwyer's heart. I whispered the word Rochelle had taught me, and then that dark strength surged over me, enveloping me. She'd said I would learn about Cameron's abilities as I used him, but each time I did, it felt like I lost a little of myself.

Who cares? he whispered. *Together, we're stronger. Now we make this thing pay for what he did to us.*

Hazily I questioned that pronoun but then my eyes shifted focus, nothing I could quantify but suddenly I was seeing across multiple spectrums, incredibly distracting but also wonderful, and it showed me in purple inverse glow how the bag man was sneaking up on my left. I spun with my blade up and laughed quietly.

"Did you think that would work? I'm not the same frightened little girl anymore."

"No," the monster said, smiling. "You're practically one of us."

That horrified me, but not enough to make me drop my weapon. His jagged blade flashed, then the dead-eyed children appeared on either side of him. *Three against one.* I didn't know if the kids would actually fight. The girl-thing had given me the impression that she'd feed on me, though, if I had been dumb enough to let her in.

"Let's do this."

"Do you think I've come to do battle, you who slew a god?" The bag man shook his head. "I'm here to deliver a message."

Say it. And then I'll kill you.

"From Wedderburn?"

"He says he's waiting . . . and that he knows you'll come." He'd hardly finished speaking when I rushed him.

The bag man threw up his blade to block but he was too slow.

Through the icy spirit armor, I hardly felt the slice on my forearm. Aegis sailed past and through his neck, severing his head. He vanished in a shimmer of smoke. Maybe I should've hesitated but as the children lunged at me with claws and fangs bared, I struck them too. The girl-thing died first, followed by the boy, and then I was alone on the sidewalk in a shimmer of black particles. The bag dissipated too, so I couldn't retrieve my mother's head, assuming he still carried it. I should've felt some satisfaction at making them pay for what they did for my mom, but the pit in my stomach grew. Not hunger but something like it.

See how weak they are, compared to you? Cameron hummed with pleasure in my head, and when I checked my compact, we'd hardly expended any power. I nodded absently as I returned Aegis to its position on my wrist, then I continued toward the subway. Though I felt like absolute shit, I made the decision not to look for Kian's mom. The state would find her and give her the news. When I had the Harbinger send the replacement to my house, I'd abdicated from normal life.

As I went down the steps, my phone vibrated. I skimmed the message and then adjusted my destination. On public transport, it took longer for me to get to the church where I'd first met Raoul than when Kian drove me. *Will his mom sell the Mustang? No. I can't think like that.* Dwelling on the past would make it harder to do what I had to.

Until people started stepping away from me on the morning commute, I didn't realize I still had Cameron powered up. But evidently they could feel the cold or something off about me because there was a huge gap between me and everyone else. Smirking, I left it alone. I might be attacked anytime, and what did I care if I creeped some random strangers out?

Raoul was waiting in the confessional, as before. "Have you thought about our offer? This is faster than I expected."

"Kian's dead," I said flatly. "And that changes everything."

He swore in Spanish. "You promised—"

"It was *his* choice. I hate it and I wish I'd died instead, but . . . I didn't. He made sure."

"Stupid boy." Raoul's voice sounded thick, and I could tell he was fighting tears. "This was never part of the plan."

I didn't let his grief jump-start my own. It was locked away inside my heart. Maybe one day, when this was over, I'd let myself feel it again. Until then, the moments of heartbreak I'd shared with the Harbinger had to suffice.

"It was Kian's plan," I said softly. "Not ours. So now I play the hand I'm holding."

Raoul took a couple of steadying breaths and his tone became brusque. Like me, he understood there was a time and place. "What do you have in mind?"

I told him.

"That's suicide, *mija*."

"Maybe. But those are my conditions. If you want me to fight for the Black Watch, then you come with me. Afterward, if we both survive, I'll train with you for however long you want and follow that Smith guy's orders. But before any of that, I see the end of winter."

"I don't have a sword that lets me kill immortals," he reminded me.

"The building will be full of human minions. Can you take care of them?"

Before, I hadn't known if I could cut people down, those who lived, breathed, and bled. Now the answer was yes. Anybody who stood between Wedderburn and me had it coming.

342

"I have those skills, yes. But why is it so imperative for me to accompany you?" Raoul asked.

"Because you know the building layout. You know Wedderburn's weaknesses. Basically, you're my ringer, and I have to use you."

He hesitated for only a few seconds before saying, "Very well. I accept your terms. When do you want to go?"

"The sooner the better. I'm waiting to hear from one more person. Once I find out what she says, I'll text you." With that, I opened the confessional door.

"I won't tell Master Smith. He would not approve."

"Since I'm not on his clock yet, I don't give a shit." Feeling mildly guilty, I added, "But I'm sorry if this gets you in trouble."

"In this case, I think he'd say the end justifies the means."

"Doesn't he always feel that way?"

Raoul didn't respond, so I headed down the aisle, conscious of the shadows on either side. Sunrise caught the stained-glass panels as I passed, infusing everything with jewel tones. Outside, it was a warmer day than we'd seen recently, proving that we didn't need Dwyer for the sun to rise or for the seasons to change. I pulled up the hood on my jacket to avoid scrutiny from passersby. Cameron wrapped around me a little tighter.

You're not one of them anymore. You're special.

And maybe some part of me had always wanted that. I'd told Raoul's mentor that I never wanted to be the one who saved the day. That was . . . misleading. Because while I didn't want that, there had always been a darkness that yearned for revenge. It was what drew me down this road in the first place. Someone with a better, purer heart would've refused the deal.

Maybe it wasn't goodness that drew the Harbinger to me. It could've been the call of like to like.

I met Allison Vega at a coffee shop not far from Blackbriar. As usual, she was flawless, curvaceous, and beautiful. Her green eyes were especially vibrant, and they reminded me of Kian's. Somehow I managed not to flinch.

"You're looking worse for the wear," she said as I sat down.

"It's been a shitty few days."

"I hear you've been busy." She examined her cuticles, pretending disinterest, but I could tell she was dying for details. Even in the supernatural world, she thrived on gossip.

"More than. I'm up to four dead immortals, at last tally."

"Four," she breathed. "I only heard about Dwyer."

"Yeah, I added some to the tally this morning. And if you want to stay on my good side, you'll hear me out."

"First tell me who you killed."

Shrugging, I did. "He was the asshole that beheaded my mom. I'd like to say she's at peace now, but I doubt she knows the difference."

"You're glum and nihilistic today."

"You would be too," I said quietly. "If you watched your boyfriend die the day before."

"Holy shit."

It took a little longer to get her up to speed, but since she'd offered to help me with my dad, she might be interested in some real action. For a creature like her, it must be boring to spend her time in high school, even if that was the best place to feed. I sensed that she missed real mayhem, and I could offer that in volume.

"So basically, I'm inviting you to participate in the raid," I finished. "Lots of carnage, lots of killing. There's bound to be great stuff locked up in there too. I know for a fact that Wedderburn has a vault full of artifacts and future-tech."

"Are you offering me loot privileges?" she asked, amused.

"Does it sweeten the pot?"

She ran a red lacquered nail around the rim of the cup. "Somewhat. But honestly, you had me at 'carnage.' Things have gotten so civilized. I was just having dinner with Graf the other night, and he's so bored, you wouldn't believe it. Sure, there are a few countries where the fighting never stops but so many humans are all about giving peace a chance."

"But . . . Graf is allied with Wedderburn. If you're on dinner terms . . ." And I shuddered over what they had probably eaten. "How can you think about—"

Her smile was awful, hinting at the real face hidden beneath her candy-box beauty. "There's social, and then there's *pleasure*. Graf will absolutely understand. In fact, if we create a big enough boom, he may wade in. He loves a party."

"But against who?"

Allison shrugged. "He might flip a coin. You can never tell how War will turn."

That didn't sound like a very safe alliance for Wedderburn, but it wasn't my problem, unless Graf unloaded on us. "So I can pencil you in as 'yes'?"

"Write it in waterproof ink. Just tell me when. And since you sweetly included me in this festival of death, I'm going to clear something up for you." Her voice dropped to a conspiratorial whisper. "They once called me Lilith. And, yes, I existed before you monkeys."

Okay, even though mythology wasn't my thing, I recalled the bones of her story, which she apparently wrote, *not* us. Buzzkill had said something about demons being here first, but I didn't remember what, exactly. It wasn't likely I'd be able to ask him, either. As of now, we were mortal enemies.

"Tonight, just before midnight. We'll meet in the underground parking lot. I should be able to get us into the building proper from there."

"If you can't, *I* can." From her toothy smile, her way involved blood, guts, explosions, entrails, and evisceration.

Fine by me.

Fell wouldn't know that the Harbinger had said good-bye and cut me loose, so I should be safe from Death. That was the only immortal I truly feared since I couldn't wield Aegis when it got close. The rest of them, I thought Cameron could protect me from, as long as I didn't drain him too much. Speaking of which, I checked the compact, but his reflection was still clear and strong, and his gaze met mine in the mirror.

I'm the one who will never leave you. The promise filled me with dark satisfaction, though something niggled at me about that. Rochelle said—

What does she know? She doesn't have what it takes to fight—to make them pay for their crimes.

That much was true. I pulled the spirit armor even closer. Oddly it even numbed the pain and grief I'd felt so strongly the night before. But such things were for the living, not for the spirit of vengeance I'd become. No matter what it cost, I'd yank Wedderburn's heart out of his chest. For my mother, for Kian, for Raoul, and for *all* the people in the world he'd hurt whose names I didn't even know.

In time, we will punish them all. The voice in my head could've been Cameron, or it might've been me. How much did that distinction matter anyway?

I texted Raoul the time and place, just in time too. My phone was almost out of juice. With a quiet shrug, I chucked it into a waste can. *It's strange how easy it is to leave a life.* Hopefully the replica the Harbinger had crafted would reply to e-mail messages. If not, there was nothing I could do. My course was set.

Before tonight, I needed to visit one more place.

I went out to Jamaica Plain and with a few wrong turns located the store Rochelle had taken us to. Like before, it was locked tight and looked deserted. I whispered to Cameron, and the lock froze over, then I broke it with a decisive blow. The door creaked open. Inside, all the cursed objects perked up, practically vibrating with excitement.

"Find something that will help us," I whispered to my familiar.

My head turned, and then he used my hands to prowl through the stacks. He came up with an ornate ring coiled like a snake with small rubies for eyes. It stung a little when I slipped it on, but I also felt icy calm, completely in control. I needed that for what was to come. But before I could pick anything else, a shadow fell across the open doorway.

"After I helped you, little one, you'd *steal* from me?" Rochelle wore an expression of quiet fury; there was no kindness or compassion in her now.

"You said not to call," I said.

"Do you think the boy you lost would want this for you?" She dragged me by my shoulders to a looking glass on the opposite wall.

The mirror was unspeakably ancient, polished silver instead of glass, and in its wavering reflection, I saw a hollow-eyed thing, pale and hooded, with spectral shadows flickering all around. In this light, I was a witch or a demon, not a human girl at all. This wasn't an ordinary mirror, for it showed what was truly there.

I glanced away. "You said all my paths are dark, right? This is the one I chose."

"I won't stop you." She took a step back. "Not because I shouldn't . . . but because I *can't*. Think on that. Your blade has a taste for killing now . . . and so do you."

"Bullshit."

"Do you think it'll be over once you fight this battle? I think you've felt the hunger already. Blood always wants more."

Cold prickled where Aegis wrapped around my wrist. I barely managed *not* to say, *I can stop whenever I want.* Instead I muttered, "Govannon didn't give me some cursed sword."

"Did he not? Have you tried to put it down?"

That silenced me for a moment. But in the end, it didn't matter. Nothing did, except making Wedderburn pay. "Sorry about your lock. I'll take the ring and go."

"It's not too late," Rochelle whispered. "It's *never* too late. I've turned aside and I write my own stories now. I heal the sick. I live on their gratitude. In the old days, they sacrificed to me, one child for the sake of another, daughters for sons. But you have to want it, and you have to be stronger than you've ever been."

I remembered Raoul saying that about my training, how I needed to learn to fight to defend Kian. But in the end, Death still took him from me. *They took everything from us, everyone we love. We must make them pay. Revenge is all that's left.* Some part of me wrestled with that leaden certainty. *My dad, Jen, Davina, Vi, Seth, Ryu—*

Wait.

My mind went red with rage, blotting everything out. Rage, red as blood. Cameron spoke with my mouth, but it was all right, because they were my words too. "I'm already stronger than I've ever been. Soon enough I'll prove it."

Whatever she might've said, I didn't hear. I ran from the oppressive energy of those haunted objects, focused only on the goal.

Tonight, I kill the winter king.

NO ONE LEFT
TO TORTURE

was the first to arrive. If Wedderburn was watching, he knew that
already. I half expected there to be a wrecking crew in the underground parking lot, as I waited for Raoul and Allison in the shadow
of a stanchion. Allison came first, dressed practically in black from
head to toe. She'd even donned steel-toed ass-kicking boots in honor
of the occasion. She glanced around and I stepped into view.

"I'm here. The cameras don't show this corner from what I can
tell. Otherwise security would already be after me."

"Good thinking."

Raoul slipped in a few minutes later. In fact he crept right up on
us. Whatever he'd studied in the east, he hadn't lost a step working
for Wedderburn all those years. I didn't bother giving a mission brief;
they knew we were here to wreck up the place and ultimately ice
the winter king. Pun intended. Anybody who got in our way was
collateral damage.

I gestured toward the elevator and Raoul nodded. This was most
of the reason I'd insisted he had to come along. He knew secret

routes and access inside. No high-rise was impregnable. He led us the long way around, skirting camera angles until we arrived at the service elevator. It required a code to open, and Raoul tried one, but it didn't take.

"I expected as much," he murmured.

"Will that set off alarms?" I asked.

"It shouldn't. Sometimes people mis-key their pass codes. It used to take three failed attempts to lock the system down."

"What now?" Allison wanted to know.

"The late-shift cleaning crew will be out soon," Raoul said. "So we wait."

True to his word, five minutes passed as we watched the lights on the elevator tick downward, then the doors opened. Only one man got off, so maybe the rest of them were taking their time, cleaning out lockers or whatever? Raoul grabbed him and slammed him into the lift before the doors could close. From what I could tell, he was a normal middle-aged dude; there was no tinnitus. With his arm levered behind his back, he moaned as his face hit the metal wall.

"I don't have any cash on me," he babbled.

Allison laughed. "Do we look like muggers?"

I pressed the open button on the doors. "We'll take your pass card. And if you want to live, you'll run when he lets go. You won't call anyone. You won't report to work tomorrow night. There might not even be a building here when we're done."

"God, I wish I could quit." The man raised miserable eyes to meet mine. "You want to kill me? Go ahead. I used to be a catalyst. I was supposed to *be* somebody."

"And now you're Wedderburn's janitor?" Allison sounded scornful.

"We don't all become liaisons," the guy whispered.

"Holy shit." I had no idea that the building was staffed by slaves. But it made sense. It wasn't like WM&G could trust contractors. So the people in the building were either owned by Wedderburn and Graf or they were immortals.

"Then today is your independence day," Raoul said smoothly.

Maybe we should've killed him, but he seemed *happy* to hand over his key card. It wasn't top clearance coded but Raoul said he could work with that. I shoved the janitor out of the elevator as Allison slid the card into the slot above the floor numbers, then red ringed the floors the guy was permitted to access. Instinct guided me then. I pressed the one Kian had selected when he took me to see the Oracle.

"Do you have some kind of plan you're not sharing?" Allison asked.

"Maybe." Mostly I wanted to free a prisoner.

The doors opened and everything was as I remembered it. From the high polish on the preternaturally long corridor, it seemed the janitor took good care of this floor. I imagined him using the power buffer, right up to where Wedderburn kept the Oracle locked up. She wanted nothing more than to cease to be, after all these years alone. I'd probably try to kill anyone who came to ask me for a favor too, even if they brought offerings, as Kian had.

Kian.

The ice Cameron had wrapped around me kept me from feeling much of anything. Gratitude bled through as I led the way toward the vault. Raoul kept close to my shoulder, eyeing the cameras we passed. It wouldn't take long for security to come at us, but if he thought this was a stupid move, he didn't say so.

"Can you get in?" Allison moved quieter than I expected, and there was a predatory grace about her. I could tell she was hungry for battle.

"I hope so."

When we got to the enormous doors, I activated Aegis and sank it into the keypad with all my strength. The resultant shock jolted me, but I didn't feel the pain. My spirit armor took it, and I held on until the short opened the doors. Alarms went off all through the building, the loud, emergency kind. Allison stared at me with some expression I couldn't read, then she stepped into the smoky beyond. It would take a little while for them to get here, so I followed, knowing we'd have a battle on our hands when we left. Raoul came last, eyes narrowed at the mist.

I paused, raising my voice to call out, "We're not here to ask you to look at our futures. I came back to get you out, if that's still what you want. But you have to hurry."

The Oracle slithered into view, all supple elegance. Her hair was a thousand snakes and her eyes were entirely mad. But she didn't attack. She flicked a look at the broken door, barely visible from the wavering on this side of the threshold.

"Hurry? There is no time here, child. That is how he keeps me."

"Oh. Well, still. I didn't come to ask for anything, I don't have the paints and charms. So you know, go now. You're free."

"This is a noble gesture? Then you must be rewarded. I will offer one last vision before I go to my much deserved rest."

Before I could say I didn't care, the smoke deepened around us, isolating me. I couldn't see my hand before my face, let alone Raoul and Allison. Then the first image appeared. It was me . . . but not me. It looked as if I hadn't eaten in weeks, like I lived on misery and woe, and Aegis was upraised in my hand. Beside me stood the Harbinger and he was smiling. We stood at the head of a great army, monsters slavering to attack at our call, and the city before us burned, buildings bombed to rubble, people stumbling in bloody rags. The gaunt-faced me seemed impassive. Shivering, I took a step back.

"You don't like the path of the Dark Queen? It's one you have chosen. What you do here, today, will set your course, no longer written in water. He will fight by your side until the time is right for him to become the Breaker of Worlds. Together, you can bring an end to all things."

What? No. We already said good-bye. I don't want this future. How do I avoid it?

But the picture was already changing. I looked a little better in this version, still human at least, but I had the same zealous glow in my eyes that I'd noticed in Tiberius Smith. I stood at a podium, speaking to a faceless crowd, then the scene shifted, and I was leading a small group against the Cthulhu monsters. Men died, but I fought on; Aegis made me a formidable foe.

"Ah, here you become humanity's hope. There will be war against the immortals with you leading the charge. They call you the Ice Maiden, she who stole the sun god's heart and slew the winter king. She cannot love; she only lives for the next battle."

This is what happens if I execute Wedderburn and join the Black Watch. Rochelle's words came back to me. *I mentioned that all your paths are dark ones, did I not?* But there had to be a way to fix things. Surely I didn't turn into a heartless slayer or monster in every timeline.

As I thought that, the smoke swirled and shaped anew. In some ways, this was the most puzzling prediction yet. I sat alone in a small, dark room, stooped over a potter's wheel, painstakingly mending a broken cup. Once I finished that, I took up another fractured ceramic piece. The cycle seemed endless, as there was an incredible pile of shattered things in need of repair. I didn't look up or speak; I only labored on and on.

What the hell?

"That's enough," I said.

"But there's more to see. You have *so many* futures fighting for ascendance. In truth, it is fascinating, even to me."

"I'll find out when the time comes. You should go."

The Oracle bent double in a bow that bordered on obsequious and then she raced past us, as if she expected we might stop her. As her body hit the doorway, she melted into sparks of light, inchoate ideas losing form as the real world reasserted its pull. Taking a breath, I dove for the exit, and I hit the ground right in front of the security team arrayed against us. Raoul and Allison were at my back as they opened fire. Allison's whole body shifted then, elongating, jaws becoming more prominent. In this form I could definitely see why people had called her a demon back in the day.

Since I came out low, I avoided the first volley and then I was in melee range. These guys weren't trained for up-close tactical combat. They knew one thing: point and shoot. I sliced through a man's arm and was mildly surprised at how easy it was, like a knife through soft butter. Blood geysered from the wound and he went down screaming.

Yes. The exultant thought was Cameron's or mine, and then I swung at the next man trying to level an AR at me. Bad move in close space, so while he scrambled for his pistol, I ran him through. Kicking his body backward, I whirled at the next, only to find Raoul snapping his neck while Allison drained the life out of the final guard.

I could *see* her getting rosier and more beautiful, gross but also seductive, like the black widow that fed on its mate.

"I don't think we'll have any trouble storming this bastion," she said, practically licking her fingers.

"Resistance will be higher as we climb," Raoul pointed out. "And they will have locked the elevators down."

"Stairs it is."

He led the way to the stairwell. As Allison kicked open the door, another squad hit us. Their radios crackled, demanding an update, but they were busy emptying their magazines at the wall. That wasn't the most effective strategy and had no impact at all on Allison. Her body bulged and reshaped, spat the bullets onto the floor. One guy actually pissed himself when she unhinged her jaw. It felt like overkill for Raoul and me to wade in, so we let her have this team, and she devoured *all* of them.

"It's been ages since I fed this well," she purred.

"How many human guards do they have?"

Who cares? Cameron seemed impatient, but that . . . tone bothered me. I *should* care that ten men were dead, and that I was responsible. Right? But instead my nerves were tick-tick-ticking, jonesing for the next fight. It even seemed like Aegis was straining in my hands, pulling me up toward the higher levels where the killing would be sweeter. Blood had splattered all over me, but I didn't mind.

Wait. Sweeter? No. It shouldn't *be. I'm determined to do this, but—*

Raoul cut into my confused, muzzy thoughts. "I'm not sure, but it was at least a hundred before I escaped. He may have beefed up in preparation for our strike."

"How delicious," Allison said. "How far up are we going?"

I told her what floor Wedderburn was on, which left us

twenty-odd to climb. There would be no other pit stops, however. We made it two more floors before the next team found us. They'd sent more men in full riot gear, but it didn't help. With some dispassionate part of me, I noticed that modern weapons weren't designed to defend against blitz attacks. Allison went up the walls with her claws and dropped on them from above. The man she hit sprayed upward in an out-of-control arc and his comrades screamed as they were hit. Aegis cut cleanly through their shields and padded armor. With one neat twist, I killed my opponent and moved to the next.

Raoul was breathing hard when the last guard hit the ground. Blood from my blade flecked his cheeks, and his eyes were incredibly sad. A twinge went through me over the way I'd basically blackmailed him to get him here, but it soon faded. Above, there were more enemies to vanquish, and if Raoul had chosen *not* to help me, then he was one of them.

Allison was moving toward the next level when she called, "Can't keep up, old man?"

His reply was quiet. "I will fight as long as I must."

On the fifteenth floor, we hit immortal resistance. Instead of another squad, a blue-skinned crone waited for us. Her ragged gown seemed to have been crafted from strips of human skin and she flourished iron claws on each hand. A crackle of dark energy about her told me this wouldn't be a simple fight. The fact that she was alone meant she was tough.

But everything dies.

"Why are you fighting with this human rabble, Lil?"

"Don't call me that," Allison snapped back. "I've been updating my image, something you might work on, you disgusting hag."

"When I find something that works, I stick with it." As she

357

finished speaking, she launched lightning from those iron claws, and I dove beneath the stairs for cover.

Not fast enough.

Voltage slammed into me, and it was like being hit by a truck. Apparently spirit armor couldn't protect me from everything. I heard Raoul groaning, but Allison snarled something in a language that might've been Sanskrit, and charged. To get back on my feet, I whispered to Cameron, and raw power surged. If my body was weak, I could compensate. It gave me the push I needed to rush the stairs, using Allison's broad back as cover.

When I hit the landing, the hag and demon seemed locked in equal combat. Since Allison had a hold of her arms, the witch-thing couldn't seem to use any of her powers.

"You asked why?" Allison jerked her horned head at the blade in my hands. "*This* is why. Take a good look at that blade and tell me you don't know who forged it."

"Govannon," the witch breathed.

"Exactly. So I ally myself with this monkey or I get mowed down. As an independent, I've always known when to shift my loyalties."

I ran at them. The witch tried to do something to me with her eyes, but I focused on her arm instead. With one clean slice, I took her hand off at the claws, and to my horror, it skittered across the floor, talons scrambling for my legs. Allison growled in frustration.

"Heart or head, you dumb ape. Preferably both. I can hold her but I can't finish her. That's *your* job, Lady Demise."

"Don't call me that." I echoed her words as the hag pleaded for her life.

Allison twisted her arm behind her while the other one trailed dark smoke and her clawed hand scrabbled at our feet like a blind crab. I should have felt something—glee, pleasure, triumph, remorse—but there was nothing as I took the witch's head. Instead of light, she went back to murky fog like the bag man.

"Another dead legend," said Raoul.

Allison muttered, "Took you long enough."

I peered at him. He didn't look good. The lightning had hurt him more than me since he had no insulating spirit armor. Tremors rocked his frame and his left arm showed black and red where the bolt hit him. In long, painful-looking strips, his skin was flaking away to show raw meat beneath.

"We should get you to Medical," I said.

Raoul shook his head. "We're too far in. The time it would take to backtrack, it's not worth it, *mija*. I'll just have to bear it. But . . . thank you."

The next five floors were dead empty. And it worried me. I tried to be quiet, but of all of us, only Raoul knew how to do that. *He didn't have a chance to teach me.* Part of me wanted to join the Black Watch, once I slaughtered Wedderburn. There were so many monsters in the world and I was damn good at hunting them. With additional training, I'd only get better.

That's the Ice Maiden future. No warmth or love, only battle and death.

The emergency lights kicked in, and the alarms went silent. There might be local police in the building by now. Allison wouldn't care if she ate them, but I didn't want to become a cop killer. *Why not?* Cameron whispered. *If they oppose us, they're in the wrong. And we exist to punish the guilty.*

"No," I said aloud. "That's not true."

"What isn't?" Allison shot me an impatient look. "Did you forget to take a pill?" It was so weird to hear her familiar snark coming from a demon face.

"Quiet," Raoul ordered.

I glanced up as we reached the landing. A neatly posted sign told me we were getting close to Wedderburn, and I actually shivered. The pleasure of killing him would be beyond anything I'd ever known. I turned to acknowledge Raoul's warning, just in time to witness two serrated blades popping out of his chest from behind.

Buzzkill.

THIS IS WHERE
I LEAVE YOU

"Sorry, kid. This is where the buck stops." The killer clown stepped into view, and from the ambient red glow of the emergency lights, he looked even more demonic and terrifying than usual. His knives were wet and hungry looking.

Blood trickled from Raoul's mouth and he dropped to his knees. His breath came as a wet rattle in his chest as he tried to speak. "Not . . . Wedderburn. Right upstairs. Future-tech. You can . . . change . . ." But whatever he was trying to say, he didn't finish. He slumped forward, forever silent.

I felt . . . nothing. No anger. No sadness. And that was *completely* wrong.

Cameron buzzed in my head, trying to block the realization, but it was too late. I finally heard what Rochelle had been telling me. In conjunction with my spirit familiar, the ring I'd put on had gradually been shearing away my humanity. I didn't know what I was turning into, but it couldn't go on. *This is how I end up as the Dark Queen. If I leave the ring on and kill Wedderburn, I end up with the Harbinger.*

Buzzkill was still ten feet away but I knew how fast he moved. Quickly I wrenched at the ring—but it wouldn't budge. When I tried to pull it off, it felt like metal teeth bit into my finger, sinking in almost to the bone. *Shit. Now that it's got a hold of me, it won't let go.*

The clown laughed. "Welcome to the dark side. I wish I didn't have to kill you, but if you hand over the weapon, I'll make it quick, best offer. Otherwise I have orders to make you suffer. Boss doesn't want other serfs getting ideas."

"You seem pretty convinced you can win," Allison said lazily. "In case you didn't notice, it's two against one, and we just took out your last enforcer."

In a move so fast I could hardly track it, he sprayed something at her. She didn't dodge in time and the silver gel solidified into crystal. The demon was now a fossil, unable to move, though her eyes were alive and furious. Buzzkill showed me yellow teeth.

"That's fair, huh, *mano a mano*. Well, sort of. Considering you're a little girl and I'm a soulless monster. But let's not split hairs."

"Except when you cut off my head and eat my brain?" I was still tugging at the ring, but it *really* wouldn't come off, and this probably wasn't the time. The icy calm kept my emotions from overwhelming me. If not for the dark artifact, I'd probably be a weeping mess, considering I was now essentially alone.

I can't believe I have to fight Buzzkill.

But I should've seen this coming.

"I'll make a nice polished ivory bowl," he said, as if that would be comforting.

From his expression, he was dead serious about killing me. Judging from the weapon he'd deployed on Allison, he likely had tons of gadgets from Wedderburn that would help; he wasn't chief muscle for nothing. I only had Aegis, my mind, my lackluster fighting ability, and what was left of my spirit strength. No chance to check but I could feel it waning. I'd used a lot in pushing here. This fight would probably burn the rest, leaving me nothing for the final battle.

So be it. If this is my time, I'm ready. I had promised I wouldn't go out easy, would never give up. And storming the enemy's stronghold definitely qualified as giving them hell.

"You know," I said softly, "I saw the Oracle today, before I set her free."

"I'm aware. Boss is full-on pissed."

"And she showed me a lot of potential futures."

"So?" He shifted into shadows and I did the same, edging toward the door. I didn't stop until I felt the cool metal at my back.

"So, none of them showed you killing me."

Buzzkill laughed. "I bet she didn't show me dying either. You can't psych me out, kid. Why don't we get this over with?"

In response I whispered to Cameron and pure heat flooded my nerves. It sparked instant speed, barely enough to let me twirl aside when the knife slammed into the wall beside my head. Buzzkill flung another at the emergency light, bathing the stairwell in darkness. *Can he find me?* The answer was probably. That stupid Internet article didn't specify what abilities the deathless Charles Edward Macy possessed, but if he couldn't see in the dark, then I was sure he'd outfitted himself with night-vision goggles. *Just like that scene from* Silence of the Lambs. Only instead of a human lunatic who wanted to make a lady suit out of my skin, I had an immortal killer clown, who planned to make a fruit bowl out of my skull. *This sucks, Clarice.*

"Smart," came the disembodied whisper. "Or I'd have already eviscerated you."

Yeah, he specializes in from-behind, silent murder. He's the shadow behind you in the dark, the blade across your throat. I didn't see or hear him coming but Buzzkill was on me before I could do more than block. His knives threw sparks off Aegis, and he struck twice as fast with two hands, but the reflexes I'd pulled from my spirit familiar let me keep up. The speed hurt me, though. My wrists and fingers burned with a dim, unnatural ache.

You're hurting yourself. Humans don't fight like this, Cameron whispered.

"Huh. Between that blade and the old magic, you're not as much of a pushover as I expected." Buzzkill didn't sound tired. Or worried. I'd seen his stamina when we'd fought the feathered serpents together; he could do this forever.

I couldn't.

Already my strength was waning. I hadn't studied Buzzkill, didn't know his weaknesses, if he had any. Allison was rocking her prison, but even if it shattered when she toppled over, it wouldn't be soon enough to help me because, despite her struggles, the heavy crystal casement only wobbled slightly. *What do I do? How do I kill him?* I wasn't skilled enough with my blade to pierce his defenses, so—and then I knew.

Going boneless, I dropped and rolled, side to side to avoid his lightning strikes. When he pulled back to finish me, I used the first throw Raoul taught me. I did it wrong and Buzzkill tumbled forward instead of back, but it was enough. Just in time I brought my blade up for him to impale himself on it. Sometimes, the unexpected was enough.

He wasn't dead, though, and I was pinned. It took all my strength to twist the sword inside him, widening it until the darkness started to swirl. Like the hag, Buzzkill was a creature of darkness . . . and modern evil. Powder puffed out of his chest, smelling of cordite.

For the last time he flashed yellow teeth at me. "You got it in you to finish me, kid?"

His knives scraped up the floor toward my neck, no sparks, just the awful *scratch, scratch*, like the girl-thing at my window, back when I didn't have the power to make the monsters pay. I let out a shuddering breath and shoved him away. Then I cut off his head in a spiral of black dust.

Allison was rocking furiously by now, and I stumbled to my feet. His bag was still there, probably because it was full of real-world toys, courtesy of Wedderburn. Sure enough, I found a pocket laser that shone fierce enough for me to cut her loose. I picked up the briefcase because I might need this gear later.

"Only Wedderburn's left," Allison said, as she kicked the rest of the way out, like a baby dragon emerging from an egg. That analogy was even more apropos, considering how she looked at the moment. "I can't believe that asshole. He didn't even leave a corpse for me to kick."

"They never do," I murmured.

Her look sharpened. "You sound too . . . *knowing*. Freaks me out. Remember, I'm on your side. Sure, I gave you shit in high school, but you get it, right? That's kind of my deal. Pain, chaos, discord, and so on."

"Relax, you're not on my list. But you might be if you don't put a stop to that Russ-ghost bullshit over at Blackbriar."

"You already did that when you mentioned Photoshop. Nobody's freaked anymore since you took Cameron with you."

"That's a relief."

"*You'd* think so."

I knelt beside Raoul for a few moments and bowed my head. *Sorry.* Then I lifted the medallion, dropping it around my neck. *He wouldn't want Wedderburn to have it back.*

After my silent good-bye, Allison led the way up the stairs. "Sorry about Raoul. He seemed all right, as far as monkeys go. So, we've got, what, ten floors to go?"

"Something like that." My tone was distracted because I couldn't stop thinking about the message my mentor died trying to convey.

The fact that I'd made it this far increased the likelihood of either the Dark Queen or the Ice Maiden futures coming to pass. *But I don't want either of them. I* don't. Revenge hadn't made me happy when it was on a much smaller scale, just focused on my school. So there was no way it would help on a global level. Vengeance wouldn't bring my mom back or Kian. Or Russ, Brittany, Cameron . . . so many casualties in a war I never intended to fight.

Making a sudden decision, I switched on the pocket laser and before I could think better of it, I turned it on my left ring finger. It hurt only for a white-hot second, then the nerves died, and the finger plopped to the floor. The wound was cauterized so I wouldn't bleed out; a metallic tinkle sounded as the snake ring rolled toward the wall.

"I choose not to be cold-blooded," I said. "I choose to be human."

"What are you *talking* about? Did you cut off your own finger? You really are insane. News flash, you're not a lizard, it won't grow back."

I already felt better. *Warmer.* More myself. Cameron buzzed in the back of my head. *We were changing,* he snarled silently. *Becoming. We could've been a Fury, as from the old stories.* But he was too weak to apply the same persuasion he'd used before. Maybe this was suicide. Maybe I wouldn't make it to my new goal with only Aegis and Allison supporting me. Hell, she might even change her mind, once she realized I'd altered the game plan.

After I pulled out my mirror, I saw that the spirit's reflection was nearly gone. Rochelle hadn't told me how to release him, but I knew. It was part of our agreement, burned into the back of my mind: *This is all I need to do.*

"I forgive you," I said. "Your service to me is done, your debt paid. Go in peace."

Then I smashed the mirror on the ground. *Thank you,* the real Cameron whispered. What I had been hearing—that wasn't him. I understood that now. It was an unnatural fusion of a dead boy's rage and my own internal darkness, morphing into some monstrous thing. Rochelle tried to warn me, but I didn't listen to her. Not until it was nearly too late.

I almost turned into one of them.

So many people died today. Now, I cared. I turned away, trying not to hurl. The smell of blood rushed into my nostrils. *I'm covered in it.* When shards of glass crunched beneath my feet, I stumbled. Exhaustion hit me like a hammer and I tumbled forward, grabbing on to Allison's shoulder. She held me up with a bewildered look.

"Explain to me what the hell's going on, or I'm out."

"New plan. I'm not killing Wedderburn. I'm going to fix things."

"What the hell? How?"

As I limped up the stairs toward the next level, I clarified Raoul's last words and told her what Kian had said about the people in acquisitions. *I can go back. I can change everything.* Allison listened without interrupting.

When I finished, she shrugged. "I'm not the one dead set on ending the cold one. You promised me carnage and loot. That hasn't changed. Sounds like we might get more cool stuff by hitting future-tech anyway."

"Thanks." Grateful, I smiled at her.

She shoved me away. "Get off me, monkey. If you don't have the strength to finish this on your own two feet, then you can die here, because I'm leaving your ass."

I shouldered Buzzkill's case, eager to see if my plan was remotely feasible. When Raoul said "upstairs," I thought he meant one flight up, so we stopped at twenty-eight, and Allison broke down the door. The metal flew toward the guards that were rushing toward us, twice as many as we'd seen before. My hands shook but I raised Aegis.

"Take cover," she said. "And let me have some fun."

Though I hated letting her do this, I didn't think I could attack a bunch of humans. Not again. Not without the ring. Which I'd left lying on the floor downstairs, along with my finger. *Shit. God knows what they'll do with that.* But it had been dark, and retrieving body parts wasn't something I usually had to worry about. Plugging my ears kept me from hearing the guards scream as Allison fed. *They work for Wedderburn. They have to know this place is way messed up.* But that rationale didn't help as much as it had when I was wearing the ring.

Finally she came around the corner, fangs glinting in the red light. "Floor's clear. Future-tech is this way. They have signs posted, like they were expecting to be raided. Convenient!"

I remembered that from visiting Medical with Buzzkill. A being as powerful as Wedderburn couldn't conceive of a mortal daring to strike back. But extremis was only the beginning. I took the deal for revenge, but now it had evolved into something else. *I'm out of the game, but I can still make a move. Does that mean I'm a player now, not a pawn or even a queen?* Glad to shed that unwanted title, I dismissed the darker implications of being a competitor in this malevolent contest.

We ran down the dark hallway, though I had to cover my mouth when I saw what she'd done to the guards. The rest of the troops must be deployed in a cluster close to the winter king's office. That was exactly what I'd do during an incursion. Except that wasn't my plan anymore, so he'd left a critical area with inadequate defenses. The door to future-tech was similar in weight and construction to the one that protected the Oracle. Since they'd shut down the power, locking the elevators, I couldn't short out the panel as I had before. Plus, without protection, that move would certainly fry me like an egg.

"Can you take it down?" I asked.

She nodded. "It'll take time, though. Watch my back and kill anything that comes at us."

"I'm on it. We probably have whatever time was left between check-ins. When that squad goes dark, they'll know where we are."

In reply her body swelled. *Damn, that's freaking cool.* Allison barely fit beneath the ceiling and she slammed a giant shoulder against the doors. It only took five strikes before the doors buckled enough for us to slip between them. She downshifted to human form and came in after me. The room was completely dark, so I fished around in Buzzkill's bag until I found a light. *This is basically the best go-bag ever.*

I already knew where I wanted to go. Allison was prowling on her own, looting as I'd promised she could. Five minutes later, I laid hands on a watch that looked like Kian's, only more complicated. As I recalled, it only worked while it was on your body, and once you put it on, there was no taking it off, except after death.

Are you sure about this? Doubts seemed logical because I had no idea how this functioned, even though I apparently invented it, along with my dad, in some optimum bullshit timeline. Wedderburn might send agents after me, and I'd be more defenseless without the mirror. *But, yeah, I'm positive. This is the right move.*

Without further hesitation, I slapped it around my wrist, and the thing came to life. My arm pinched, tiny wires invading my nervous system. The screen flashed to life and I tapped it, skimming past various icons until I found the theta symbol. Since some physicists used that to represent time in equations, I activated it.

Input date and coordinates.

"Do you have a phone?" I asked.

"Are you kidding me? You want to call someone? *Now?*"

"No, I need to find out latitude and longitude. Can you help or not?"

"I'm a gazillion years old and I'm the only one in the room with a smartphone. What kind of teenager are you anyway?"

"A really weird one, I thought we established that. Get a move on. Somebody's probably tracking this watch." If I was lucky, the medallion would cancel that out. If not . . .

"Which means we'll have incoming soon. I'm on it. What do you need?" A light flared from her screen, as she brought up her browser.

"Cross Point, Pennsylvania. I'm sorry, but this is where I leave you. Will you be able to get out on your own?"

Allison laughed. "Please, I could hop out a window at twenty stories. Plus I think we killed everything on the lower levels." Her tone turned serious. "Okay, here we go. Ready?"

I added the numbers as she read them off, and then I added the date. *Now I just have to hit* GO, a crazy-simple interface for the amazing thing this device did. My father was probably responsible for that because he hated complicated systems. Ironic, given his field of study.

Sorry, Dad. I hope other-me is good to you.

Booted feet stomped down the hall, and men were shouting over the carnage in the corridor. They spoke in military jargon, which made me think they might not be run-of-the-mill guards. Allison whipped her head around, *all* the way around, and went for the door.

"Vanish," she commanded.

I deactivated Aegis and tapped the watch panel. The world whooshed away in a blaze of light. My whole body melted and reassembled; it was disgusting, nauseating, and painful as I dropped onto the pavement. Dry heaves wracked me for endless moments.

Where the hell am I? Or maybe 'when' is the better question. Did I do that right?

Gradually I realized it was daytime, a good sign. I seemed to be in an alley behind a shop, crouched near a Dumpster. The smell was gross, and an old man stared at me and then the bottle in his hand. He apparently decided it was the liquor and chucked it away.

I need to know what day it is.

One look at my own hands convinced me I had to find a public bathroom fast. If I didn't clean up, I'd be locked up on criminal charges even without a body. Without ID, my life would be impossible. Pulling up my hood, I hurried through backstreets with my

371

head down. The downtown wasn't large, and I found a convenience store pretty fast. That allowed me to wash up and check out what Buzzkill's magic bag had to offer.

Credit card. Wonder if it works now. Various containers that I feared to open. Weapons. Rope. Pretty much, it had everything you'd expect from a killer clown. *Thanks. You may have saved me.* That would probably make him laugh.

After exiting the filthy washroom, I went to the mini-newsstand in front of the register and picked up the local paper. The date matched the one I'd entered. In Boston, I was only twelve . . . and fairly happy. Kian was about to hit extremis. Since he hadn't told me exactly when, I'd chosen a random date in January to make sure I didn't miss it.

Now I understood the potter future, and *that* was the one I'd chosen. I decided to be *me*: a smart, weird but fully human, nine-fingered girl with a pretty face and a fledgling idea of how to win a game I never wanted to play. Silently I said to Wedderburn, *Come at me, bro. If you dare.*

Time to fix everything I've broken.

AUTHOR'S NOTE

This is where I confess that I'm obsessed with the Harbinger. I love him so much that he's already gotten his own short story. No question that he exudes a Loki-ish charm, but I also love exploring how wounded he is. There are *forty-two* trickster gods, and he's lived all their stories. That rather boggles the mind. See, our divine myths are rarely kind and gentle; most are chock full of rape and incest, kin-slaying, theft, and betrayal. Now imagine you have no choice but to act out these fantasies, a dark, irresistible compulsion. Now you know how the Harbinger feels. Uncomfortable, yet . . . compelling, am I right?

But as humans, haven't we always been fascinated with monsters? I mean, when you read *Frankenstein*, are you rooting for the mad scientist? I never was. We empathize with his poor, misunderstood creation instead, and we try to make sense of the darkness the monster is driven to by the lack of compassion he encounters in a strange and foreign world.

Likewise, in the Immortal Game, if I seem to sympathize with devils and dark spirits, that's not far off the mark. I'm having a fantastic time adding personality to our oldest stories, imagining what cultural icons might be like in the modern world. One of my beta readers commented that she couldn't believe I made her like a sadistic killer clown, even for a moment. To be honest, I didn't mean for that to happen. He's a monster, right? But every villain is the hero of his own story, and it's impossible not to take that into account.

In some ways, this story was easier to write because Edie is in a different place emotionally. She's no longer at the end of her rope, and she's realized it's better to fight. Yet there's danger in that path as well. Sometimes we get so caught up in resistance that we lose sight of other important aspects of our life, and we don't realize how vital balance is until it's too late. Does that sound ominous? Well, you're reading the author's note, so I presume you finished the book. I need say no more on this topic, I suspect.

Moving on, then. Before I commenced writing, I researched more old gods and more Internet memes. I'm curious if you can figure out what monster Edie fights in the pit, and no, I'm not telling. I suspect the answer will surprise you. The fun of this project is, if Edie doesn't recognize the beastie, you don't find out its name, and that adds another layer of mystery. In *Public Enemies*, you encounter lots of beasts from legend and lore, and part of your fun may come from identifying as many as you can. One or two probably won't be recognizable, unless you read the same weird books as the author. But don't let that stop you from trying!

Along the way, I spent a fair amount of time learning about gods of the forge, and I didn't like what I saw from the Greco-Romans. Vulcan / Hephaestus was always the butt of the joke, never getting a fair shake in love or war. So, I gave him a more Celtic flavor instead, and thus Govannon was born. I tweaked his name, which is properly represented as Gofannon. He was an ancient deity in Wales,

renowned as a metal worker and whose beer could make you immortal. And I thought it was hilarious to plop him in Vermont with
a bunch of cats.

Readers, I hope you enjoyed the second installment of the Immortal Game and are ready for the finale. I know I am!

ACKNOWLEDGMENTS

Thanks to Laura Bradford, who always supports my ideas. Not sure if that's because she trusts me or if we're always on the same page. Humblebrag: Since 2007, she's never failed to sell anything I wrote. Not once. That's over thirty novels, and I'm so thrilled to work with her.

Right after my agent, I always think of my brilliant editor, Liz Szabla. Partnering with her, I have learned a great deal, as she's a pro at polishing my work without changing the heart of it. I've been so excited about bringing the Immortal Game to life with her, and I send heartfelt thanks that she didn't even blink at a certain risky plot choice. (It'll be okay, I promise.)

Much appreciation to the talented folks at Feiwel and Friends who do a phenomenal job: Jon, Jean, Rich, Elizabeth, Anna, Lauren, Zoey, Ksenia, Molly, Mary, Allison, Kathryn . . . well, I'm sure I've forgotten someone, so please forgive me and understand how much I value your contributions. No man is an island, so they say, and no book is created in a vacuum. Ergo, I humbly thank you all for your time and talent.

My fantastic copyeditor, Anne Heausler, is one of my favorite people. Thank you for the wonderful comments that make editing a task I truly enjoy. I'm also indebted to my meticulous proofreader, Fedora Chen. You ladies labor behind the scenes so I can shine, and I appreciate you both more than I can say.

Time for the honorable mentions! *Public Enemies* would not exist without those who supported me: Bree Bridges, Chadwick Ginther, Donna J. Herren, Marie Rutkoski, Caragh O'Brien, HelenKay Dimon, Yasmine Galenorn, Stephanie Bodeen, Lauren Dane, Mindy McGinnis, Megan Hart, and Vivian Arend. I'm thrilled to add Rae Carson, Veronica Rossi, and Beth Revis to this list. And you, of course. Yes, *you*. (Because you're reading the acknowledgments, obviously. That's hardcore support right there.)

To my beta readers, the incomparable Majda Čolak and Karen Alderman, I would gladly buy you ponies for the amazing loyalty you've shown over the years. Sometimes other writers ask the secret to my productivity and I will never, ever tell them that it's all due to you two. Because then they might try to take you away from me.

We're nearly to the end now. Thank you, my darling family. Whenever I tell you I have an insane deadline, you never complain. My kids say, "Then we won't bother you," and my husband asks, "What can I do to make your life easier?" Yeah, I won the close-relatives lottery. You're all incredible. Thank you for loving me, for understanding, for being the best of all possible kinsfolk. I adore you all.

Finally, readers . . . really, you thought I'd forget? *No way*. Without you, I'm the crazy lady with voices in her head. But when you come along for the ride, you're paying me the highest compliment of all and giving me your time. I cherish each and every one of you for that. Thank you for reading my books; thank you for believing in my dreams.